LATROBE BARNITZ

Soul Crystals ARC of the Amuli

PRIVATE DRAGON
Publishing

Contents

Prologue

24 Years Ago

Cold. Everything was cold. It was cold despite the warm blood that ran out upon the ground. It was cold despite the warm mists moaned by dying breaths. Frost covered rocky craters that had taken the place of trees and grass.

A lone figure reached the peak of a newly formed hill of ash and debris. The figure took shape as it pulled its hands out of the pockets of its white jacket and leaned its head back to allow its hood to fall back. The young man who emerged had his eyes closed. He breathed deeply. Jets of white steam came from his nose. His face had just begun to show the wisps of scraggly brown hair. The hair on top of his head was cut short, apart from a few strands of uneven bangs that bounced on his forehead as he walked. A corpse's glassy eyes stared up at him as he started his descent down the hill.

Groups of men in military camouflage pointed and shouted at the recent arrival as he came into view. Despite their clothes, none of their weapons came from the current century. A few of them raised bows with gleaming arrows of red, green, blue, orange, or purple. They raised swords and spears, each glowing one of these colors. Their leader lifted his hand and shouted threats to the newcomer.

The young man opened his eyes to reveal two white-gold orbs, glowing like headlights in the night. An ocean of golden light rose around him. The soldiers turned their backs and sprinted for cover that wasn't there. The golden flood wiped them away, screaming and begging.

The young man now stood alone amidst the ruined earth all around him.

Chapter 1: Innocence

November 1

Paul felt as if his head was being crushed by something pushing against his face. Strange splotches of yellow, white, and light brown chased the blackness to the corners of his vision. He could feel his nose pushed to the side.

Where am I again? he thought groggily. He pulled up his head as he peeled off whatever it was that was stuck to his face. It was a book.

A cold stab of worry hit him in the stomach. *Oh right, the presentation.*

He wiped foul-smelling salvia of the book, "Go Rin No Sho, The Book of Five Rings," written by the legendary seventeenth-century samurai Miyamoto Musashi. This study of swordsmanship and philosophy was one of Paul's favorites. That was why he had chosen to do an oral report on the great samurai. Unfortunately for Paul, his admiration for samurai was outweighed by his anxiety for his upcoming history presentation, which had led to many sleepless hours the night before.

Reluctantly, he checked his appearance on his cell phone screen. He grimaced as he saw his haggard face and sleepy brown eyes. One of his stubborn cowlicks of medium brown hair was sticking upwards, so he tried smoothing it with his hand. It was no use, however. He even tried straightening his school blazer, which was now slouching down over his bony shoulders.

Suddenly, he felt the world tip sideways. He fell out of his chair, landing on his back.

"You deserved that, man!"

Paul looked up to see another student with greasy brown hair and, since no teachers were around, holding a soda bottle filled with chunky gobs of tobacco juice the same color as the boy's hair.

What was his name? thought Paul. *John or maybe Jack? He's on the football team. Or is it the baseball team? Maybe it's both?*

"I've been trying to get your attention all week," John or Jack continued. "Didn't you notice me throwing pencils at you in English on Tuesday? You've always got your head down, ignoring everyone. Then, I catch you in study hall, and you're passed out. Tell me, what kind of straight-A student sleeps through school?"

So, that's why I was getting hit by pencils. I thought it was best just to run away.

Jack/John spat more brown sludge into his bottle through his yellow-tinted teeth.

"Is sleeping through school really worse than chewing tobacco in school?" Paul regretted the words as soon as they left his mouth.

He normally would not have said something so confrontational. It was not like him to instigate someone whose arms looked to be as thick as his own legs. However, this situation just seemed too perfect to let pass.

Instantly, Paul was grabbed by the collar of his navy-blue school blazer. He glanced around the library in search of any teachers. He saw only a half dozen wide-eyed students who were avoiding his hopeful glances. Paul closed his eyes and clenched his teeth. This moment seemed so surreal. *Never in my sheltered life did I ever imagine being beaten up in a library It's my favorite room in the school. That has to be more than a little ironic.*

"I know your type," said the boy. Paul could smell his every word. "You're the kind of guy who thinks he's better than everyone else 'cuz you're smart. That's why you're quiet and rude."

Paul shook his head, his eyes still closed. "No... no, you've got it all wrong," any air of smugness was now gone. "I just... just..."

"You 'just' what?"

"Hold up a minute, Jack!" The voice didn't sound like it came from a teacher. "I'm ready to tap-in for him."

Paul finally opened his eyes when he felt an exaggerated high-five on his dangling hand. Standing there was another student who only came up to Jack's shoulder. Robby Swanson looked more like a middle school student than a high school student.

Jack let go of Paul and looked down in the newcomer's direction. "What are you even doing, Swanson? You little freak."

"Oh, come on, you will need better insults than that if you're ever going to get into the WWE."

Jack now looked more confused than angry. "Who the hell said anything about fake wrestling?"

"Well, did you honestly expect me to think you guys were doing real wrestling? Where's the mat? Or maybe you guys were doing UFC stuff? Anyway, I was about ready to give you the chair." Robby lifted a wooden chair and swung it around playfully.

Just as Robby finished his rambling, Mr. Eaves finally entered the room.

Jack turned his back to Paul and Robby as he made his way

back to his table. "You're a nutcase, Swanson. You're just not worth it."

Robby turned to Paul. "Stalling. It always works."

"Yeah, except when it doesn't."

"C'mon, believe me. I've ticked off a lot more people than you have over the years."

Mr. Eaves cast a slightly amused gaze in the boys' direction.

"Mr. Swanson," he called from behind his twitching, gray mustache. "I don't recall you being in this study hall."

"No," Robby quickly agreed. "Mrs. Rockway wanted me to make some copies on the library copier while I was in detention."

"Detention isn't until after school, Mr. Swanson," reminded Mr. Eaves. "I also don't see any papers in your hands."

"Oh, you know what?" Robby exclaimed. "I completely forgot them."

"And detention?" wondered Mr. Eaves with a twitching eyebrow.

"Well," Robby answered, "what I did was so bad that they gave me detention during school hours. I think I... uh... crashed the school server by downloading a game."

"That would be an in-school suspension which I know, for a fact, was not in the morning teachers' memo," Mr. Eaves sighed. "Just leave and stop roaming the hallways. There's nothing exciting going on in them, anyway. Better yet, go use those computer skills for something constructive. The lab is open."

"Right away!"

It should scare me how fast he can make up lies. No, wait, it shouldn't. He's an awful liar.

* * *

"And so, Musashi arrived at his duel with Sasaki Kojiro late and with his appearance being a mess," Paul thrust his thumbs into his pockets, running them along the velvet inner pockets of his blazer. He had been speaking for five minutes already. His mouth was now running without his brain's instruction. He hated doing presentations like this one. He could feel the eyes of everyone in the room on him, judging every stutter and mistake.

"Musashi utilized strategy rather than the aesthetics of swordsmanship in the duel. One could say that his strategy only used cheap tricks. However, he believed in the practicality of fighting and swordsmanship, not the aesthetics of it."

Paul glanced around the room as his mouth continued to

move. Robby was sitting backward at his desk, talking to some girl. She was now scribbling something on his hand. For a moment, she stopped writing and peered up at Paul. He dropped his eyes to the floor. Words poured out of his mouth even faster now. He clicked the button of the computer mouse. Then his shaking finger hit the button again. An uncomfortably warm redness spread along his face as he apologized before returning to the correct slide.

"And... um... itissaid... I mean... um it is said that Musashi waited for the sun to shine directly into the place of the duel in order to inhibit Sasaki Kojiro."

Paul looked sideways at the teacher who was flashing him a sign with a number "five" on it. *Five minutes. God! I'm not going to have time for everything!*

Paul sighed and continued. "In the duel, Musashi used a *bokken* or wooden sword..."

Four minutes later, Paul finished. He took a deep breath and staggered to the teacher's desk. Mrs. Jones handed him a slip of paper. It read, "47/50."

The teacher leaned over and whispered, "Great content as always, Paul. It's a good thing that was mostly what I was grading on. Your speaking skills could use some work. Try not to be so nervous next time. You always do so well that I'm never sure why you worry so much."

Paul nodded and went back to his desk. *Asking me not to be nervous is like asking not to breathe. I just do it. I probably shouldn't have even gotten an A. Mrs. Jones probably just feels bad for me. I can't speak two words without stuttering.*

"Mr. Swanson," Mrs. Jones called out. "You're up next."

Robby reluctantly ended his conversation with the girl sitting in front of him and strolled to the front of the room. He pulled out a mess of notecards out of his pocket before beginning his presentation in the booming voice of a used car salesman.

"Before I show my slides," he began, "I'll start by saying that my presentation contains a lot of exciting news. As some of you guys might have heard, there was a discovery last week off the coast of Spain in the Atlantic Ocean. At the bottom of the ocean, they discovered an entire underwater island. I think we all know what that means. Atlantis has been found!"

Paul pressed his forehead into his desk. *I knew that helping him with this project was a terrible idea. The project called for a presentation of the historical roots of a legend or legendary figure. It wasn't supposed to be about conspiracy theories.*

Seven minutes of conjecture later, Robby returned to his seat with a grin that showed that he was quite proud of himself.

"What grade did you get?" he asked as he peered over Paul's shoulder as he studied the rubric that Mrs. Jones had given him for the tenth time. "An A? Dang. I got a C. You're a genius, kid. I keep telling you."

"Yeah, yeah."

Robby slid down the sleeve of his blazer, exposing ink-smeared digits on his wrist and hand. He grinned proudly. "Allie Boucher's number."

Paul studied his friend's hand for a moment. "I hate to tell you this, but you're missing a few digits."

The sound of the bell covered up Robby's cursing.

"Hey, maybe you can sit by her at the assembly and get the rest of the number," suggested Paul sarcastically.

Robby kept his head pointed to the ground in disappointment as the two made their way to the auditorium. The room was large but filled with a musky smell that came from old velvet seat cushions. For a moment, Paul had to force down the rusted hinge on his seat before he could squeeze into it.

Aren't private schools supposed to be rich enough to afford minor things like seats that were made before nineteen fifty? Paul thought wryly.

A few rows away, Paul could hear a couple of boys from his last class talking about their grades on their presentations.

"Did ya hear what she gave that one kid?" one asked before answering his own questions. "Forty-seven out of fifty when he could barely talk up there. What's his name again?"

"I think it's Pete," the other answered.

"Yeah, P-P-Pete," the first one exclaimed in a mix of fake stammer and unmuffled laughter.

"I know, right? He's like all s-s-samurai and mushi-mushi-ishi. It's more like n-nerdy A-A-Asian fetish, I swear."

Do they seriously not know I'm right here? At least make fun of me when I'm out of earshot. What are their names again? Paul pondered. *Austin and Dallas? No, wait... there's no way that's right. Why am I so bad with names?*

Paul's right hand started shaking as he sat down. He closed his eyes. *I should just go hide in the bathroom until with is over.*

Memories he had long tried burying tore their way back to the surface of his mind like a drowning man reaching for the surface. He could see his Aunt Morgan with her eyes rimmed with red struggling to complete the sentence, "*Paul...your dad...he...passed away when...*"

"What's this assembly for again?" asked Robby who had gained back some of his composure after his recent rejection.

His words were enough to draw Paul back from the confines of his mind.

"It's the Amulus presentation. The same as every year," explained Paul, trying to sound casual. "Someone from A.R.C. or A.I.M. will talk about Amulus, and they'll see if we react to any crystals."

"I know everyone thinks these things are boring now, but I've always wanted to be an Amulus," Robby said with enthusiasm. "I mean, who doesn't want superpowers?"

"I'm sure your family and their company would love that," retorted Paul with mock sharpness. "I've read in the news that they have been trying really hard to shut down A.R.C. and A.I.M."

Robby shrugged. "They don't really like superhumans policing themselves. I think my dad called it 'letting the inmates run the asylum. Me on the other hand, I've read enough comic books to like superheroes. I don't really care what my family thinks as long as I get superpowers. I mean... like, don't you want superpowers?"

"I guess," answered Paul, "but it doesn't seem very... enjoy-able this way. The way things stand, Amulus are either taken and held by A.R.C. or tested for medical research by A.I.M. Either way, you can't really live a normal life. Think about it this way, the law basically protects people from Amuli. That's because people are afraid of them. On the other hand, the Amuli get stripped of their rights for life. Plus, there is always the chance you could..." Paul took a pause and mumbled. "You know, whatever."

"Or," started Robby raising a fist into the air, "you can become a superhero and fight against "evil" organizations like A.R.C. and A.I.M."

Paul smiled. It felt as if Robby had been cheering him up all his life. They had known each other since they were six, after all.

"If it comes to that, I'll be your sidekick."

The arrival of a group of people on the stage of the auditorium interrupted their conversation. The school principal, Mr. Lance, eagerly strode across the stage, leading a group of five men and five women dressed in black suits with blank expressions. Mr. Lance's maroon jacket made him look like a cardinal amid crows. The suits carried large black cases to a table where they carefully laid out several metal objects. The more eager of the students craned their necks to get a glimpse of the strange items.

Displayed on the cloth-covered table was a variety of weapons and jewelry. None of the weapons displayed were modern but instead came from a variety of time periods. On the left side of the table was a collection of swords including several medieval, arming swords from Europe, Renaissance-era rapiers and longswords, and even a late Roman spatha. Also on the table was a collection of bows, including two English longbows. The last category of weapons consisted of guns, including a blunderbuss and a Revolutionary War-era rifle. Embedded in the handles and hilts of each weapon were crystals that were mostly clear except for faint hints of color. The jewelry comprised of bracelets, necklaces, and rings, each containing the same type of crystal as the ones found in the antique weapons. The old lights of the auditorium reflected onto the metal and wood of the items, giving them a yellowish hue.

"I'm thinking the musket," whispered Robby as he attempted to peer over the basketball player sitting in front of him. "My grandpa used to tell me my great-great-great- whatever fought in the Civil War."

"That's actually a Kentucky long rifle," corrected Paul softly. "It was actually much more accurate than a musket, and it's probably from the American Revolution or War of eighteen twelve. They're called 'Kentucky' long rifles, but they were actually first made in Pennsylvania. Back then-"

"Hey," interrupted Robby, "history class ended already, and now, the world's greatest showman is about to take the stage."

"Settle down, everyone," began Mr. Lance in a vain attempt to quiet the drone of conversation in the room. "I know everyone is excited for this year's presentation from Amulus Regional Containment. I know that I sure am! I'm sure each of you is familiar with the valuable, valuable work they do in the world. Nevertheless, Mr. Luper will explain the work he does to help keep to the world safe for all of us. Now I give you, Mr. Gregory Luper!"

One of the men who had been carrying the cases took the principal's place at the podium. He had a short, dark beard that could have used a trimming and hair that much needed combing, both were flecked grey. Despite his unkempt appearance, he had a powerful presence in the room. As he moved to the podium, the steady curves of well-built muscles could be seen under the covering of his sleeves and pant legs.

His expression was that of boredom and his eyes were like two hazel, black, and white marbles.

"Right then," he said after clearing his throat. "I'm sure everyone here is used to this system by now. If we have any volunteers, please come to the stage and walk by these items. If any crystals start to glow, then please speak up. Remember, government law states that it is your right to choose whether to take part in this process."

Mr. Lance came speed-walking back to the podium after the agent vacated it.

"While each of you decides on whether or not to come up to the stage since," interrupted the principal in an attempt to save the formalness of the presentation, "I will recount the history of the Amulus and also that of A.R.C. and A.I.M."

"Here we go," whispered Robby to Paul. "I saw his file when I was doing filing in detention one time. He got his master's in theater before going back to school for teaching. It explains so much. Like Arthur Miller said, 'All the world's a stage.'"

"That was Shakespeare," corrected Paul. "Come on, that's an easy one. Everyone knows that."

Robby shook his head. "That was the first play-writing-guy on my mind. I fell asleep when we read *Death of a Salesman* in English yesterday. When I woke up, the salesman was dead, so I figured that I didn't miss anything."

Paul chuckled as Mr. Lance began his speech to a chorus of groans.

"It was only a few decades ago that the idea of superhumans was only seen as material for movies and comic books," the principal began in a voice resembling that of a movie trailer narrator. "However, in the nineteen-eighties, it was discovered that supermen really could exist."

A voice in the crowd briefly interrupted Mr. Lance, shouting, "Oh God, this again?" This was accompanied by ensuing bouts of laughter.

Mr. Lance cleared his throat and continued undeterred by the now-muffled laughter. "Logic-defying treasures were found after being hidden deep underground in regions around the world. These treasure troves were made up of antique weapons and jewelry dating from ancient times all the way to the late eighteen hundreds. Set into each of the items were curious crystals, resembling gemstones. When one particular researcher touched a crystal, something truly astounding happened."

The principal paused and held up an array of wiggling fingers as if he were trying to hold the attention of a group of small children. A flurry of teenagers rolling their eyes greeted him.

"The crystal glowed and, upon further inspection, the scholar realized he had been gifted with enhanced strength. Not only that, but he had a shining aura that he could cast around him in bursts. It was discovered that the constant aura could disintegrate high-speed projectiles, making the holder of the crystal effectively bullet-proof. Naturally, militaries around the world raced to get their hands on these crystals and people who could use them. Further research showed that every crystal had only one user who became known as Amuli. A crystal is bonded to an Amulus for life, they are inseparable. Equally inseparable are the crystals from the weapons or jewelry to which they are fused. Inseparable and unbreakable."

There were more groans from the crowd as Mr. Lance reached the crescendo of his performance.

"The time of these discoveries occurred at the tail end of the Cold War. Both the United States and the Soviet Union saw Amuli soldiers as an outlet to their hostilities that was not as drastic as the mutually assured destruction of a nuclear war. However, they were wrong. When the two forces met in western Alaska, the world saw annihilation not seen since Hiroshima and Nagasaki. Within hours of the commencement of the battle, huge swaths of land were wiped off the planet, including most of Alaska's western islands.

"The worldwide community was outraged and horrified by the actions of the two world superpowers. Desperate, the United Nations took steps to put the power of anima out of the hands of nations for fear that worse conflicts would follow. The organization created two companies in order to police and contain Amuli around the world. They were created by Amuli for Amuli. Amulus Regional Containment was made to house Amuli as well as to protect

Amuli around the globe from the world and from themselves. A.R.C. ushered in a new era of cooperation between the nations of the world. Even developing counties with less than effective governments and totalitarian states became subject to A.R.C.'s guidance. Its sister company, Amulus International Medicine, specializes in studying the amazing healing properties exhibited by Amuli and applying them for scientific and medicinal purposes.

"Here today, each of you will have the opportunity to walk past these anima items and to see if you may become an Amulus. As always, this is completely voluntary, and if you volunteer and do not emerge as an Amulus, do not be heartbroken. Amuli only make up only a small fraction of the world's population, numbering less than a hundred thousand people total. Above all else, this experience is simply a way to involve you young people with this important process, while, possibly, making your dreams come true. Without further ado, volunteers may now proceed forward and pass by the anima items. Come on now don't be shy."

The A.R.C. representative rocked back on his heels and blinked his eyes as if he were waking up from a nap on his feet. "Right. The volunteers can come forward now."

In the front row, a few giggling girls formed an impromptu conga line as they paraded to the stage. Two rows in front of Paul, a group of boys joking around shoved their friend out into the aisle. Red-faced and laughing, he scrambled back to his seat.

It's a joke to them, Paul observed. *A generation ago, things like Amuli were new and frightening. Now, everyone is desensitized to something as crazy as this. There hasn't been a major incident involving a rogue Amulus in years... in the United States at least. It's all become so normal.*

"Let's go, sidekick," Robby muttered as he slid out of his seat.

Paul begrudgingly stood up and carefully shuffled past a student who fallen asleep leaning forward into the seat in front of him. Paul could not see the student's face but the stench mixture of weed, alcohol, and sweat singed the hair inside his nostrils.

"Seems like Dane's been pre-gaming before school again," whispered Robby.

Paul shook his head. "I don't understand why..."

"Now's my turn to teach you something. Pre-gaming is..."

"I know what 'pre-gaming' is, Robby."

Robby shrugged and left it at that.

No matter how much his legs protested, Paul couldn't let Robby see how much he didn't want to participate. He just wanted to fit in and treat this event as a joke like everyone else.

Paul's heart pounded as he joined a short line of students at the side stairs of the stage. He was sure some blood vessel in his neck would burst as he could feel it beating in time with his heart.

As he passed one row, Paul heard a chorus of spitting as Jack and his friends sent brown goo into empty water and Gatorade bottles.

"Ya, know," muttered Jack as he wiped his mouth on his sleeve, "I can see where some of the Hunters are coming from. Not like killin' all the Amuli, but that they're not natural. I mean, why do they get to be more powerful than everyone else? They're so strong that they could take over the government if they haven't already. And, all this parading their guys around schools to make more of 'em? It's weird, man. Only the Hunters are just sayin' what everyone else is thinkin'."

The other boys in the row nodded and grunted in approval.

This was the last speech Paul wanted to hear. *I wonder what he would do to me if he ever found out that my dad was an Amulus. Not that I've ever told anyone.*

When the procession reached the anima items, he shivered. Suddenly, he was five years old again.

~ ~ ~

Aunt Morgan held up a shimmering gold chain. "This was your dad's."

Paul reached out a hand, feeling the bumps of cool metal.

"It used to be a necklace. There was a blue crystal that went in the center, but it's gone now."

She took a deep breath and a thick film of tears swelled in her eyes. Paul stared deeply into the blue eyes. He had never seen her cry before. He'd seen her laugh a thousand times before that. She was always happy and strong. The only mother he had ever known.

"The people you see on the news... and the ones you learn about in school... the ones with those powers. You see, your dad was one of them, an Amulus. He found this necklace when I was young, about ten." Her voice wavered again. "Oh, Paul, I wasn't sure when I was supposed to tell you all this. I was going to wait until you were older, but you're so smart for your age. You're so smart, and you deserve to know. You have to keep this a secret though. Your dad wanted this all to be a secret."

~ ~ ~

Every one of Paul's steps on the stage made him feel like he had lead weights in his shoes. He was sure that he was about to fall through the floor. It occurred to him that this entire event was ridiculous.

In what world are high school students offered weapons and superpowers? On the other hand, being an Amulus is so rare that one is seldom found in one of these events. This is all a formality.

A way to make ordinary people think that they in control. In reality, they are the ones controlling us. This is all in their best interest since it increases their numbers.

Paul stared down at the gleaming blades. They were as haunting as if they would have been stained with blood. According to A.I.M.'s reports, anima items never showed tarnish or damage no matter how long ago they had been created. The exact reason for this was still not known to the public. That was another reason for Paul to dread the low possibility of becoming an Amulus. Both A.R.C. and A.I.M. were very restrictive about the information they released. All the public had been told about the two groups were their chief purposes as Mr. Lance had described. There was only an occasional press release about A.I.M.'s research and A.R.C.'s missions in securing for rogue Amuli. The inner workings of the organizations remained complete mysteries. Conspiracy theories ranging from alien invasions to human sacrifices were abundant on the internet. Massive multinational organizations like A.R.C. and A.I.M. naturally attracted bizarre theories about possible clandestine activities. It had become something of a hobby for Paul to research these theories, partly for curiosity's sake and partly for a good laugh.

Paul took in a deep breath as he reached the end of the weapons section of the table.

Maybe it was a mistake to be so worried about this. Paul thought to himself, allowing a slight ripple of relief to wash over him.

His eyes caught a soft blue glinting in the corner of his

vision. He felt as if something was squeezing his stomach and pushing its contents up to his throat. He turned to see the last item on the table, a golden necklace with an iridescent blue crystal. The color of the chain was different, but the crystal was just as he imagined it, slim and as bright as a sapphire in the sun.

The memories of his childhood came rushing back again.

~ ~ ~

"It was hard for him at first," Aunt Morgan continued with her eyes gazing past the present and back to old memories. "He was always being pursued by Hunters, the evil guys who want to kill all the Amuli. Our parents, your grandparents didn't know what to do. A.R.C. and A.I.M. had just been created and had only taken in a few Amuli at that point. We moved around a lot back then, but it didn't help in the end. The Hunters caught him when he was walking home from school. We were so scared. I was young that I didn't understand everything, but I knew that I missed my brother. Weeks went by before we heard that A.R.C. had rescued him. After that, he went to work for them, and I could only see him once every few months.

"He met your mother there. She was a researcher for A.R.C. It's not fair that you can't see how much you are like her. She was the smartest person I've ever met and extremely kind too. She was the sister I always wanted. Then it all went wrong. You were only a few months old when more and more Hunter groups started to form. Paul... your dad... he... died

24

when... the Hunters got to him. They tracked your mother down too..."

~ ~ ~

"What's up?" asked Robby curiously from behind Paul.

Paul shook his head, trying to shake the spider-web of memories from his head. "I... uh..."

He followed a ray that extended from the auditorium lights onto the crystal.

So that's what was causing it to glow. Paul realized as he felt a weight being lifted from his body.

One of the representatives who were surrounding the table gave Paul a stern look that meant it was time to get moving. Paul's face reddened when he noticed that all the suits and most of the students were staring at him for holding up the line. Now, he really did wish that stage floor would swallow him whole.

Paul slumped back into his seat and leaned into the collar of his blazer in an attempt to conceal his reddened face. He felt a slight tap on his shoulder, which was followed by a heavy-handed thump. Peering over the fabric of the blazer, he saw a pair of broad shoulders.

"Hey, I'm... uh... sorry about earlier," Jack mumbled his apology.

Paul gave a surprised, slow nod.

"I was ticked off 'cuz I got a poor grade on a test in my computer science class," Jack murmured while rubbing his index finger under his nose. "It just sucks, ya know? My dad wants me to major in computer science in college, so I've gotta figure this stuff out."

Paul continued to nod. He was still half-expecting Jack's mood to snap from apologetic to accusatory. It wasn't like Jack to claim to be completely at fault about anything.

"Then, I saw you sleeping in the library," Jack continued, "and I was like, 'who's this guy who always gets A's but never seems to work hard at all.' No offense, but you always seem bored as hell and never want to do anything with anyone."

Paul winced. As with most sentences that he had heard begin with "no offense," there was some offense given.

"Anyway, I was pissed because my dad always tells me I'm going to major in computer science in college because it's the future or whatever. I was wondering if you could look over some of my homework to see if I'm on the right track. I can't keep C and C# or C-flat or whatever straight. They all just seem like random numbers and letters."

"Sure," Paul answered shakily.

He was completely thrown off by this display of regret by Jack. He still expecting another backhanded comment, or worse, an actual backhand. Either he had turned over a new leaf or had really done poorly on that STEM test.

"Actually, Robby is even better at coding than I am. You might want to ask him."

Jack shook his head. "Nah. Swanson would probably play some kinda prank on me and give me the wrong answers."

Jack's stony face made Paul unsure if he was joking. Paul gave an uneasy smile, just in case.

"So," Jack closed his eyes as if he were about to do something painful. His speech became unsure and awkward, which was a far cry from his usual smugness. "I was wondering if you wanted to stop by my family's cottage on the river this weekend and help me. Afterward, some of the guys and I are having a party, and my parents don't care what we do. They're chill like that. If you helped me... then you would like... be able to come."

The color drained from Paul's face. *Oh, great. The last place I want to be is in a small cabin filled with giant, drunk teenagers. But if I say no, Jack is going to freak out on me again and may never forgive me for it.*

"Well, I..." Paul began speaking as his brain thought up a solution. "I'm actually going to be busy this weekend... but... email me a copy of your homework, and I'll look it over."

Jack was clearly holding back a smile of relief. "Oh, okay.

That works for me."

"My email is just my name with the school email address at the end."

"Alright, thanks. So, we're cool now, right?" Jack punched Paul in the shoulder that was meant to be playful but instead spread a painful, icy numbness down the scrawny boy's arm.

"Yeah," Paul agreed before waiting for Jack to walk away so he could massage his arm without embarrassment.

Chapter 2: The Gift

The air was cold, biting even. Old leaves crunched underfoot. Newly fallen leaves stuck to shoe soles.

"We should have brought coats," Robby announced not for the first time as he hopped over a pile of leaves.

Paul trudged on beside him, head down against the wind. There was a prickling in the outer parts of his ears, like a hundred frozen needles were digging into them.

"You okay?" asked Robby, who had produced a knitted hat out of the inside pocket of his school blazer and placed it over his close-cropped hair, "You've been kind of distant all day."

"I just didn't sleep well last night."

"Oh, aren't your aunt and uncle going away this weekend? Your uncle's software company is merging with Baka Corp. in Japan, isn't it?"

Paul let out a slight chuckle. "It's actually called Taka Corp, and it's funny that you said 'baka.' You know in Japanese 'taka' means hawk and 'baka' means idiot."

"Paul, I've watched enough anime to know what 'baka' means," Robby responded with a mock sigh. "And, if you have to explain the joke, it makes it less funny."

"Hey, maybe I'll have to learn Japanese now, too. This whole thing is actually a big deal. Not only did they buy Uncle Nick's startup, but they're throwing him a party."

They passed a block of houses still decorated from Halloween the day before. Fake cobwebs and pumpkins covered every porch. Black and green mold had appeared on some of the pumpkins. Paul wrinkled his nose as the decaying smell drifted toward him.

"I guess it kind of sucks they're leaving you at home while they go to a party when it's your birthday," Robby commented. "I would come over to hang out, but I've got some college track coach coming by for dinner. It's the whole recruitment thing."

"Which college?" asked Paul curiously.

"Um..." Robby grimaced. "I can't remember. It's some small place. Did you know that there are like a million colleges in Pennsylvania?"

"I'm pretty sure Pennsylvania only has the third most colleges in the U.S. after California and... uh... New York," responded Paul with his sometimes-annoying habit of answering rhetorical questions.

Robby always seemed to be busy. He was a track star who had scholarship offers even when he was a freshman. Last year, he had finished second in the state in the one-hundred-meter sprint and third in the two hundred meters. When he wasn't training, his parents would put him into some "junior assistant" position in their company. Robby insisted that this position usually consisted of sitting on a computer for hours while he downloaded and played gaming emulators. He had already put viruses on ten computers in an attempt to get fired. However, his family seemed to be more concerned with putting him to work than his ruining of expensive computers.

Paul sighed. "Right now, I just feel like going to bed, anyway."

Robby made the turn down the road to his house. "We'll do something tomorrow. I'll text you. I can always kick your ass in Nova League III again. I have a new strategy for taking down Ken the Blade with Montgomery the Legendary Gunslinger. It's a sword versus a gun. I mean, who fights against a gun with a sword, especially with the short, skinny sword that Ken has on him?"

Paul snorted a laugh. Robby's trash-talking about their favorite fighting-game series was usually more comedic than spiteful.

"Swords are cooler. Anyone can point a gun and shoot it. To use a sword, you need strength and a fighting-style."

"No way," Robby argued, shaking his head. "Function over form. You have to think practically."

"The saying is, 'form over function.'"

"I know what I said," Robby breathed through his ever-present smile. "Anyway, I'll see ya around, man."

"See ya."

Paul walked on, taking a second to view the houses of Robby's neighborhood. Most were the size of mansions and filled with rich rednecks. No one ever suspected Robby of being wealthy. Even to Paul, he had always been just Robby, not Robby Swanson, the richest kid in town. Everyone at Schwert Academy was there because their family had money or because they received a scholarship. Most of the rich kids thought themselves better than the students there on scholarship. After all, their parents paid full price to send them to school. That wasn't Robby's opinion at all. He would be friends with anybody, provided they put up with his antics.

"Hey, Robby?" Paul called after him.

"Yeah?"

Paul took a deep breath. "Do you ever... ever think people get the feeling that I think I'm better than them?"

Robby shook his head. "Man, you care too much about what people think. You're just a normal guy, just a little shy, I guess. Just come out of your shell a little. You think too much."

"Thanks, Robby. See you around."

Paul found his street. It was a newer development. All the houses were a similar, dark red brick. There were no mansions in this neighborhood. Whoever had designed these houses seemed to have fallen in love with squat houses and pyramid-shaped roofs, so much so they had built thirty of them. It occurred to Paul that there was a possibility that he might move into a neighborhood more like Robby's development with the influx of money from the merger.

Paul wrestled his key out of his backpack and into the lock. He froze when he noticed a dark blur in the corner of his vision. In his peripheral vision, the swirl of movement was the size of a fly, but his brain told him it was much larger. Startled, he turned around. There was nothing. He also smelled something sweet in contrast to the fragrance of decaying leaves. It was floral and so sweet that it was almost unnatural.

Paul looked around for a second, expecting some post-Halloween prank from Robby. There was still nothing aside from the swaying of naked tree branches. Paul shook his head and chalked it up to a rogue squirrel.

I could have sworn that I saw someone. I guess that I really do need some sleep.

He opened the door and stepped into a wall of warmth and almost crashed straight into his aunt.

"Oh, Paul, I'm sorry," Morgan apologized to her nephew. She was dressed casually in jeans and a pink hoodie, pulling a bouncing suitcase behind her. She was only in her mid-thirties and appeared even younger. There was always a childlike playfulness in her eyes.

She hurried to her car.

"You guys are leaving already?"

Morgan swung her suitcase into the car's open trunk. "Yes, Paul, for some reason the merger party has been moved up a few hours. With the time difference between here and Tokyo being what it is, I can't keep all the time zones straight. I just know that I will be jet-lagged past the point of exhaustion. We weren't told about this until an hour ago because someone forgot to send an email or something. Luckily, our gracious hosts, the Taka Corp., have bought us new plane tickets. And right now, we have to get to the airport to catch our flight."

"We'll make it," said Paul's Uncle Nick as he followed Morgan and stashed his suitcase in the trunk. Nick wore one of his many striped, button-down shirts which hung loosely on his tall but skinny frame. His eyes were perpetually sleepy from entering computer code and were covered by a pair of wire-frame glasses. It was common for people to mistake Nick for being Paul's blood relative instead of Morgan.

He put a hand on his nephew's shoulder. "I know that you would like to come with us, but you'll be able to see Japan a lot more in the future after this merger. I'll take you along when I'm there over the summer. We can see all the sites, Mount Fuji, the Imperial Palace, and all the shrines and temples, but believe me, we may be going to a party, but it's just a formality. Most of this trip is going to be signing papers."

Uncle Nick's blue eyes, magnified by his glasses, were filled with genuine regret at disappointing his nephew.

Paul nodded, but disappointment dripped into his voice. "Yeah, that will be fun."

"And here," his uncle handed him a small, narrow, gift-wrapped box, "happy birthday."

"Ta-da!" exclaimed Morgan, temporarily forgetting about her rush to pack the car. "C'mon, I want to see you opened it before we leave."

Paul glanced down at the wrapping paper before tearing it open. Rows of smiling teddy bear heads stared back at him. His aunt had been using the same wrapping paper since he was five years old when she had bought a lifetime supply from a warehouse store on an impulse. The bears always brought back memories of birthdays and Christmases long past.

The wrapping paper gave way to a plastic box covered with more plastic.

"Nova League IV!" shouted Morgan, giddily. "Your uncle got an advanced copy from Taka as a present. I hear that Nyma the Warrior-Queen's moves have been updated in this one. Ken the Blade better watch out."

"And how many times have you beaten Paul in Nova League?" asked Nick as he attempted to stack the last of his luggage in the truck. The suitcase immediately slid off the pile and onto the driveway, spilling several pairs of black dress pants.

"Only three times," she responded as she refolded a pair of pants, "but I've beaten Robby in at least half our matches. Not to mention how much better I am at you in these games."

"It's all about the matchups, you know."

"Yeah, yeah. Maybe you should work on your coordination. It would serve you in video games and real life."

Paul let a smirk creep onto his face. *They always sound younger than me when they argue about video games. Maybe growing up in a house like this is why people tell me I'm mature. It's because I had to be... Nah, I guess it's not really true. Teachers always called me mature because I was too scared to speak out of turn or get in trouble.*

Morgan looked at the time on her phone. "We seriously have to go."

"I think we have everything," assumed Nick. "If we don't, we'll be stumbling through Tokyo convenience stores looking for toothbrushes or whatnot."

Morgan shook her head. "C'mon, you're Mr. Important, now. You can order people to do that for you."

She stuck her head out the window right after climbing into the car. "Ok, Paul, just two rules. Don't get hurt and don't destroy the house. Oh, and one more, if Robby comes over, don't let him destroy the house. That's probably the bigger threat."

Paul nodded. "Okay, good luck."

"See you Tuesday, Paul!" Morgan called back as they pulled away.

"... Tuesday..." Nick's soft voice was drowned out by the noisy muffler of his car.

Paul had only just placed Nova League IV in its correct place after the previous entries in the series amongst his alphabetized collection next to his Taka Nova System when he heard a knock on the door.

"Did you forget something?" Paul asked as he opened the door, expecting his aunt to come rushing through the door. "Oh!"

Instead of his cheerful Aunt Morgan, a blank-faced mailman stood on the doorstep. Paul recoiled, red-faced, and berating himself for speaking before opening the door.

"Uh... sorry. Thought you were someone else."

"Just need you to sign," the mailman responded flatly as he handed Paul a tablet.

Paul quickly scribbled his signature before he was handed a package. *What his name? He's been our mailman for like ten years. Is it Mel? No... that sounds too much like mail. I'm making that up.*

He had seen the mailman joking and laughing with the other residents of the neighborhood and occasionally with his aunt or uncle. *I wish I were better at dealing with people. It's like everyone in the world was born a conversationalist except for me.*

After awkwardly thanking the mailman, Paul examined the package on the kitchen table. It was addressed to his uncle with a large sticker labeled, "TAKA CORP." The stamp showed Taka Corp's hawk logo. *This might be important.*

Paul quickly called his aunt. "Hey, a package from Taka Corp came in the mail. Were you guys expecting something?"

"Were we? I don't..." Morgan's voiced was drowned out by the static and rushing wind. "Sorry. I had the window down... and you know driving on these backroads... can't get signal worth..."

"So, what should I do with it?

"You know what, just open it. Call back if... better signal at the airport."

"Okay, I'll just open it and call you back later."

Paul looked down at the brown, narrow rectangle on the table. He tore open a cardboard panel and let the box's contents slide out. The object that emerged was covered in dark, lacquered wood with a metal ring part way up from its bottom. Covered as it was, it gave off a sinister, deadly aura. It was an object meant to kill. A sword.

Paul turned his attention to the weapon itself. He marveled in its slightly curved shape in its black wooden sheath and its black hilt with white diamond designs down the center. It was not just any sword. It was a *katana*, the sword of the samurai. It was alone without its *wakizashi* or *tanto* mate in the traditional two sword pairing or *daisho*. He unsheathed it slowly out of the lacquered wood. It gleamed silver and black in the light. Along its middle ridge, he could make out the black, zigzagging line which showed the integrity of blade, folding over and over by a master smith. Engraved into the black-metal guard, was a dragon circling the blade with its gaping mouth reaching for its tail.

This must have been really expensive if it really is from feudal Japan, Paul realized. *Taka Corp. must see a lot in my uncle if he gave him a gift like this. At least, I'm assuming it's a gift. That's the only explanation for receiving it like this. I didn't think anyone in Japan would part with one of these so easily. They're more pieces of art than weapons, a Japanese national treasure.*

Wait a second... is it legal to ship weapons like this through the mail?

As Paul ran a finger along the metallic smoothness of the dull edge of the back of the blade, he noticed a strange, buzzing sensation starting in his arm with more vibrations strumming in his chest. His initial reaction was to attribute this to his excitement, but something deep inside of him told him that something was wrong. He could feel this something churning inside him like a river rushing through his veins and arteries inside of blood. It was exhilarating and frightening at the same time. Paul sat down, trying to catch his breath.

What's going on? I'm practically hyperventilating. Is something wrong with me or am I just this excited about the gift? Is it my heart?

That was when Paul noticed the glow. It was a dull, medium green light reflecting against the table of the unlit room, hampered by the grey clouds of autumn outside the window.

No. It can't be. There's no way.

The light was wriggling through the threads of the wrappings of the sword hilt. Paul touched the silk diamond that seemed to be at the light's origin. He pushed the diamond inward. To his surprise, it gave way, and he could feel a hard, smooth object behind it. When he removed his finger, the silk diamond came with it. It came off the hilt easily, like a silk sticker.

The glow was now blinding. Despite the intensity of the green brightness, Paul stared right into it like a child trying to look straight at the sun.

No. No. No! The singular word kept repeating itself over and over again in his mind like a prayer.

I'm going to die like my dad.

Darker thoughts were now pouring their way through his mind, black as tar. *Wait. Did they know? Did my aunt and uncle know there was an anima weapon being sent to them? No way. They couldn't have known. They would never do this to me. Even if they did, the odds of having two Amuli in one family are astronomical. What about Taka Corp? Did they...*

Suddenly, it felt like the weight of the world was pushing against him, crushing him with weariness. He could feel darkness forming in the corners of his vision, and he was now looking down a bright, blurry tunnel.

As the darkness took him, he remembered a comment that he once read on a message board. It had said that Amuli would often blackout when first discovering their powers as the result of some sort of eternal energy being depleted. Despite his unknown power, he felt weaker than had ever before in his life.

He didn't even feel himself slump forward and slam his forehead into the table.

Chapter 3: Awakening

A lone girl was walking down the street. No one saw her in the autumn night as most had taken shelter from the cold. If there had been a passerby, they would have noticed that she was not dressed for the weather. Her white-blonde hair hung down around her in slight waves. She wore a white dress covered by prints of red and pink flowers. Her only protection against the cold was a small, white overcoat.

She moved quickly from shadow to shadow, taking a wide berth around streetlights. Somewhere between walking and running, each footstep was lighter than the drop of a pin. She stepped off the road and onto the muddy grass of autumn without the sound of muck making the sound of a suction cup around her shoes. Her slim figure disappeared into a bush as her shadow mixed with its shade.

The girl turned around just in time to see another group of shadows emerge from the night. Her deft eyes counted ten of them. Most of them wore blank expressions with their eyes looking almost translucent in the semidarkness. They formed a semicircle around the girl who was still almost kneeling in the bush which was now clearly not hiding her.

The man at the center of the crescent moon shape was the only one who displayed any sort of expression. He had a smirk curling upward on the side of his mouth. While the other men held a variety of weapons from swords to bows to one man with a cudgel. Each man wore a simple mask with dots for eyeholes and several around the mouth. The masks were all a different color. From left to right, they were blue, purple, green, orange, white, and violet, respectively.

"Looks like we have the same target," the orange mask in the center remarked in a gravelly voice. "It's a pity that we had to come to this little backwater stink hole to have a showdown like this."

The girl simply stood up, saying nothing. Her expression was as blank, showing no fear in front of this danger.

"You know that you can always surrender," the man continued, gently rubbing the flat of a plain sword on his shoulder. "A.I.M. always welcomes new recruits, especially those crossing over from the other side. I imagine that you have some nice intel that you could give us. Better yet, you look like a psychic, unless you're hiding a weapon on you. A.I.M. likes psychics, they're pretty rare, you know? I mean, even if they're not as strong as warriors."

While he was still speaking, the girl leaped from her position. She moved so fast that the man's eyes had not comprehended her movement. In an instant, the man on the farthest edge of the semicircle went to the ground. After a blinding, golden flash illuminated the area for an instant, a hole appeared in the man's chest. As he fell, the pavement was visible through the wound. He did not make a sound.

The leader gave a cry of surprise as he finally realized what was happening.

* * *

Paul opened his eyes and put a hand to his pounding head. It took a second for him to remember what had happened before the blackout. For a second, he thought that he was still passed out in the school library. A fresh surge of anxiety sprang through him when his mind finally caught up to speed.

He then realized that his life was over.

It was dark outside. Paul wondered how much time had passed while he was unconscious. Had he not been so tired and confused, he would have had the presence of mind to look at a clock.

The exhaustion was still crushing him. The internet post he had read actually seemed to be accurate. He was so tired that he couldn't think straight. Questions about his future were swirling in the corners of his mind, but the fatigue drowned them out. The numbness was both a blessing and a curse in that way.

The one thing Paul knew was that he needed sleep. He would

worry about his life later.

As he rose from the chair, the world started spinning. He put a hand down to steady himself. Slowly taking his hand from the chair to the wall, he made his way from the kitchen to his room, feeling his way through the dark like a blind man. As he collapsed onto his bed, he noticed a pressure between his fingers.

It was the sword. He had thought he had left it in the kitchen, but it was still in his hand. He had to remove every finger one by one from the hilt before letting it fall to the floor. It had been stuck to his hand like Velcro.

He collapsed again, this time into his pillow.

There was a difference between waking from after a night's sleep and waking after suddenly losing consciousness, as Paul discovered. When his eyes flicked open, he was peering through a haze of confusion. Somewhere underneath the fog, his heart was pounding in his throat, telling him that something was wrong.

Paul reached for the battery-powered light on his bedside tabled and turned it on. Soft, yellow light bathed one half of the room. The other half was a giant shadow. Leaning against the wall underneath the window on the threshold of light and dark was a figure, another partially illuminated shadow. Startled, Paul slipped and fell on to his back with a shout.

It was a girl. The first thing he saw was her eyes. They were large and sad looking, like two blue and white marbles covered by shining tears. She wore a white dress with prints of red and pink flowers. White straps went over her pale, slender shoulders. She had on a necklace. In its center was a mesmerizing gold stone shimmering in the half-light.

Paul scrambled, crawling backward. One hand swiped his cell phone from his dresser. The other reached desperately for the doorknob, but he never took his eyes off the girl. A red blotch caught his attention.

She was bleeding. Her hand was trying to cover an ever-growing red spot on her side, another red flower joining the others on her dress. In her other hand was the *katana*.

"Wh-what are you doing?!" Paul's voice broke on every word.

The thief stayed silent aside from her breathing, which was deep and shaking. Paul could hear it from where he stood. She closed her eyes and slid down the wall, smearing crimson onto it. The sword rolled from her grasp.

What do I do? Paul's thoughts were racing. His heart had been pounding in his ears since he saw the girl. *What is she doing here?*

He pressed the power button on the phone. It stayed dark. *Did I forget to charge it? No, I could have sworn that I did.* He half-stumbled downstairs to the landline. There was no tone when he picked it up. Paul swore as he slammed it down.

What now? What's going on?

Paul ran to the bathroom, grabbing the first-aid kit before coming back to his room. The thief was in the same place, sitting against the wall, her eyes staring at the ground. The splotch had grown to cover the entire area from her hip to her chest. Her eyes were unfocused, fluttering. Paul fished the hydrogen peroxide and gauze out of the first-aid kit. His hands shook as he moved closer to the injured girl.

"I-I'm sorry. I don't... know how to do... this," he stammered.

Her blue eyes look into his for a second. There was something strange about her expression. She didn't look to be in pain but instead appeared tired, as if she were about to drop into a peaceful sleep.

She quickly grabbed the medical supplies from his hands. Paul fell back, startled yet again. He was even more startled as she pulled up her dress to access the gash. He turned around, his face turning bright red.

This situation is getting more ridiculous by the second, he observed. *Where did she even get that cut? Is it from the sword? She will need a hospital. I really need to call an ambulance... and the police.*

He noticed a faint, green light in front of him.

The sword lay where the intruder had dropped it. The crystal was not as bright as it had been when he first picked it up, but still lit the floor with an eerie glow.

He stretched his hand toward the *katana*. *As he grabbed* hold of it, he noticed the heat again, it was hot but it didn't burn. The warmth ran through his body like a river and the glow grew again. It covered his arm and spread over his body until a green aura covered him. The darkness took him again.

* * *

He was in bed again. Paul shot up, his breath escaping through his mouth in one enormous gasp. His head swiveled as he searched the room.

There was no glowing Japanese sword on the floor and no bloodied girl leaning against the wall. There was a voice deep inside Paul that was telling him to close his eyes and go back to sleep. Despite this, he rose from the bed, slowly making his way to the window.

It was open. When Paul's hand touched the windowsill, his fingertips came back stained with red. More red flecks dotted the glass.

Paul stood frozen in place for over a minute, feeling the sticky blood clinging to his fingers.

What am I supposed to do? Run to the police station? Would they even believe me if I told them a teenage girl tried to steal a magic

48

sword from me? Even an ambulance would take a few minutes to arrive. There's no way she would have been able to stop that bleeding with just gauze. She might be bleeding out on the street or in the woods right now. I just can't let her die out there!

In order to aid the person who had stolen from him, he ran downstairs and into the night.

I just don't want her to die! I just don't want her to die! Paul chanted in his head as he pumped his legs. *If she dies without me doing anything, what does that make me?*

In the orange glow of the towering streetlights, Paul could see steam rising from his mouth and nostrils. He blew some steam into his fingers and continued his search, berating himself for not wearing something more substantial than his school blazer.

I have to get her to a hospital or something. That's just within walking distance. On top of the blood loss, that girl is going to get hypothermia. Wait a minute, why would a thief wear a dress? A dress in Pennsylvania in November? Do Amuli feel the cold like other people? At least, I think she was an Amulus. That gold stone on her necklace was probably an anima crystal.

Paul continued to glance from the street to the yards of the houses he passed. A darker part of him wanted to abandon the search or to fail in finding the girl. It told him that maybe he would cease to be an Amulus if the sword was lost. Nevertheless, he kept walking as the wind swept relentlessly through his messy, nut-shell brown hair.

49

It took only a few minutes to reach the downtown of Pallisville. Paul had expected the thief to take this route. The other way would have led her to more housing developments while going through downtown would eventually take her out of town and into the wooded back roads.

The entire area was empty this time of night, not that it was completely crowded during the day either. Most of the buildings towered over three floors, built in the oil boom days alternating between red brick and tan stone. For all of Paul's memory, these buildings were cracked and bare. There were some businesses and knickknack shops scattered along the ground levels, but the upper floor windows were dark and empty.

Paul was about to give up the search when he reached the last row of buildings. He finally noticed moisture on the sidewalk. At first, Paul mistook it as dew that had fallen from the blades of grass, growing in the cracks of the disheveled pavement, but then he saw that the dark drops were growing larger and closer together. Closer inspection revealed that the droplets were actually a dreary crimson color, turned black under the obscuring of nighttime darkness.

There were voices. He instinctively hid behind a nearby building, nervously strumming his fingers on the sandy, old brick. His heart pounded again.

Why I am doing this?

"Where is it? We know you hid it. I'm not going easy on the

one who wiped out the entire advanced force!"

Paul leaned out, his eyes just peering past the wall. There were three people, lit up by strange colors. Two held weapons and not modern ones at that. One was a spear and the other a medieval Morningstar. Both were glowing. The spiked club oozed a color that was a strange mixture of black like that of pure darkness and silver-rimmed on the edges. The strange, black cloud could only be seen in the light of the nearby streetlamp. The man holding the spear was cloaked in a green light similar to that of the katana.

There was a third light. It was gold. It radiated from the hand of the thief.

"Make it easier on yourself," said the same voice, "I asked 'Where?'"

The man with the spear shot a blast of light at the girl. She fell to her knees and her head tilted to the side. Paul swore that her eyes were on him, looking past the brick wall. He had been sure that he was out of sight, over a block away from the thief and the armed men, yet she was staring right at him.

Paul slid down the brick wall, shaking as dust rubbed onto the back of his blazer.

What is this? Why is this happening?

"Can't speak?" the spearman's question roared through the air. "Did A.R.C. cut out your tongue? I know you're not dumb.

That was smart work, taking out the Psychic like that. If we didn't have another, I would probably have been screwed fighting you alone."

She's from A.R.C.? Paul was taken aback. *Then why was she trying to steal from me if she's from an official organization? I would have given her the sword. I don't want it. I don't want any of this. If she's from A.R.C., then who are these guys? Terrorists?*

The spearman obviously wasn't getting want he wanted. The girl still said nothing. Her eyes gave nothing away. There was no fear or anger in them. They were as lifeless as blue and white marbles. The man's spear was now poised to strike the area in-between those eyes.

She's going to die, Paul felt helpless. *He's going to kill her. I'm about to witness a murder... and I can't do anything about it. If I had just found her before she ran into these guys, maybe this wouldn't be happening. Is this all my fault?*

He could imagine the spear striking like a snake through her forehead and the last of her life trickling through a stream of blood down her face.

Snap out of it! Paul's thoughts screamed out in his brain. *Don't be such a coward for once in your life! Do something that's not like you for once. If she dies without you doing anything, you will hate yourself forever.*

The grass behind the building was glowing. For a moment, Paul thought the emerald glow was being caused by the streetlights shining on the grass. As his eyes focused on the light, he noticed an outline of a familiar object underneath the overgrown weeds.

The katana was calling to him. He felt some inescapable desire to hold it. In his hands, it felt like an extension of the body. It was a natural part of him now.

He felt hot again. His body contained a churning ocean of heat and strength. Then his legs were moving. It was as if there were strings on his limbs, pulling him towards the sword like a marionette. Before he knew what was happening, he was gripping it with two hands.

Paul was only dimly aware of the reflection in the window. His normally brown eyes were now glowing the same color as the sword. A green outline surrounded his entire body. His legs kept moving, no matter how much he wanted them to stop. With the building obstructing their line of vision and their focus distracted by their stubbornly silent captive, neither of the girl's captors saw the small-scale light show just a few hundred yards away.

"Do you understand we can blast you, cut you to an inch of your life? Give up, you scum!" the man with the spear spat each word at the young burglar.

He was ready to kill the girl. He couldn't care less about orders now. They could simply kill her and search the area.

Then he noticed something moving behind him.

A single figure stood there cloaked in blinding green. The girl stared at the newcomer, just as surprised.

"Reinforcements," observed the man with the spear. "Take him. He's just a kid, like her."

The man with the Morningstar flew towards Paul. His speed was incredible, inhuman.

The club came down before he could blink. He raised the sword to block it. He braced the dull backside of the katana with his hand, praying the thinner sword would hold together.

The club was stopped in mid-strike. Paul peered into the man's eyes. They were black on white with no iris in-between.

The weapons pushed hard against each other. Even with his newfound strength, Paul felt the strain. He grunted, searching himself for more of this power. The more he dipped himself into the pool of pure power, the more he felt his consciousness slipping under the river of energy. His arms screamed that they were about to give out. Paul let his head go under.

The area around Paul exploded in green light. A pillar of fire shot up to the sky. The fire surrounded his opponent, engulfing him. He only stared at Paul with blank eyes as he began to wither in the flames. There was no screaming or crying as his body crumbled, beginning with his hands and spreading as his entire body turned to dust.

"I've never seen energy like this!" the man with the spear yelled.

He sprinted towards Paul, even faster than the other assailant. He came with the spear, then feigned. His shoulder slammed into Paul's chest, propelling him like a rocket and smashing him through the nearest building.

The spearman remained on his feet, peering into the rumble. "I guess you weren't so tough. You had me going for a second."

He spat on the ground as he turned away.

He thinks I'm dead. I should just stay here. That explosion should have alerted the whole town. Paul's mind came back to the surface as the gravity of the situation hit home. *What am I doing here, saving a girl who tried to steal from me? No, I can't think like that. It isn't fair. She's a human being, too. She doesn't deserve to be executed in the middle of the street.*

Paul didn't feel any pain, which would have been strange if fear weren't clogging the flow of all the other emotions in his mind. Through the dust, he saw the man moving toward the thief. He raised the spear, ready for the kill.

Paul felt something in his hand. The sword had never left him. Light flooded outward from his body as his mind was once again swept under the current. He rose from the rumble.

His clothes were torn and bloody, caked with dust. His arms hung loosely, but the green fire lifted him to his feet.

His head was cloudy. *Attack. Attack. Attack.* The words repeated over and over in his mind. At this moment, he was not Paul Engel anymore. His body had become a weapon made of anger and fear. Blank eyes were locked on his next opponent.

He swung the *katana*, and a fiery shock wave flew through the air, striking the armed man in the back. It sent him flying eventually crash landing on the ground, then skidded down the street for several feet before coming to stop. He laid still on the road.

Paul caught his breath as the world came back into focus, leaning on his sword. He was in control again. His right mind slipped back on his head like a shoe, but then his vision narrowed. The world shook. He stumbled onto where the girl was lying on the pavement. She was now unconscious, maybe dead.

She's pretty. It felt like a strange time for such thoughts to be floating around his clouded mind.

Paul fell headfirst into the street beside her.

Chapter 4: Fugitive

Paul was floating. That was what his brain was telling him. Reaching for a coherent thought was like grasping for a cloud. Then, he felt a rhythmic drumming beneath him. He eventually realized that he wasn't just floating but moving at the pace of the drums.

He opened his eyes to see the ground passing quickly beneath him. He saw flashes of grass dyed gray by the night and spots of yellow gold like headlights. The motion made his head swim and his stomach lurch. His arms and legs flailed in reflex, the ground rushed up to meet him.

Paul rolled on the ground, choking before regaining his breath. He could feel saliva mixed with dirt spilling over his lips. His head swung around wildly as he attempted to get his bearings.

It was still dark, but the sky was a dark gray, just a shade away from black. The next thing Paul saw was a solemn, bruised, and bloodied face. A pair of eyes, an almost unnatural shade of dark blue, stared back at him. The rest of the face was bathed in a golden light coming from an upward raised hand.

Paul gasped as he recognized the girl who had attempted to steal from him. He still didn't know what to make of her. Judging by what their attackers had said, she was from A.R.C., an organization charged with gathering and protecting Amuli while apprehending rogue Amuli like the men who had attacked them. The glowing energy in her hand and the necklace around her neck marked her as an Amuli as well.

There is something weird about her and this whole screwed up situation. Oh, God! What did I do? Did I just kill someone... or two people? But I didn't know what I was doing. My body was moving all on its own. Who is this girl?

He did not hear any sirens or commotion, which meant that they had quickly traveled deep into the woods. It was not difficult to go off the grid in this rural part of Pennsylvania. Paul was long gone from any police officers or fire-fighters responding to the damaged building he had crashed through.

Paul tried to back away from the girl, first doing a pitiful crab walk before rising to his feet. His head felt like a balloon, bobbing up and down, and his neck felt like the string. His legs buckled as he felt the world tilting. He hit the ground again.

She was carrying me... like a fireman's carry. Paul realized that his flailing had sent both of them to the ground. *But, what about all her injuries? And she can't weigh over a hundred pounds. How was she able to do that while holding her side together?*

Paul looked to the gash running up the girl's side. The color of the wound had changed from crimson to brown. At first, Paul thought this was the result of the blood drying, but then a burnt aroma found his nose.

She cauterized it! Paul realized. *She must have used the heat from the anima crystal. How do you do that without passing out from the pain?*

"*We must keep moving.*"

The words rang around inside Paul's head. They didn't feel like any of his thoughts. It was an alien, artificial sentence implanted in his brain. Not only that, but he could almost hear them resounding in a brusque, robotic voice. A female voice.

Paul stared straight at the girl, gaping.

"*Psychic Amuli are able to transmit thoughts to one person at a time,*" the strange thoughts continued to pour through his mind. "*Psychic communication is advantageous at this moment, as enemies may still be in the area who would hear any verbal commination.*"

The girl climbed back to her feet. Her hand instinctively pressed against her injured side. The other clutched a familiar, sleek object. The *katana* was inescapable for Paul. No matter where he went, somehow it was always near him. *If only it didn't even exist.*

Paul attempted to reach his feet as well. As soon as his legs straightened, his body felt like a marionette without a puppeteer. The joints in his knees and ankles wouldn't lock in place. He groaned softly as his body swayed before collapsing again. On the ground, his hand traced the frayed strands of fabric that had once been his school blazer. His shoulder was a giant scab made of crusty, sticky scales.

The thief offered him a bloodstained arm. Paul hesitated for a moment before grasping her forearm with a weak, unsteady hand. He could feel the power in her smaller body as she pulled him to his feet with ease. He came to rest awkwardly against her side with an arm around her shoulder. Her skin felt as smooth as silk but littered by rocky scabs and swollen bruises. Normally, the experience of resting on a girl's shoulder would have made Paul's heart flutter and his stomach queasy. However, the bizarreness of the current situation had mostly numbed his senses to all feeling except fear. Ironically, he felt incredibly weak in the knees.

Underneath the sweat and dirt, Paul could just make out a hint of perfume. He figured that it had once been floral scent—maybe roses—before it mixed with the more unpleasant ones. It smelled oddly familiar to him. *Where did I smell something like that before?*

"*If you wish to communicate,*" the voice in his head started again, "*you must form your thoughts into concrete words and imagine that you are sending them to me. Abstract thoughts and memories are too difficult to discern for Psychics.*"

"*Okay,*" Paul responded internally. "*This is so freaking weird... oh, wait... no, you weren't supposed to hear that part. I'm sorry... I...*"

If the girl had read his rambling thoughts, then she had chosen to ignore them. For the first time, Paul remarked on how unsettling this mystery girl was to him. This time his thoughts took the form of images and feelings which was a slight comfort to know that she might not be able to read them. Something was frightening by her demeanor and the icy cold thoughts she pushed into her head. Even her movements were robotic, without a hint of human fluidity. She was completely focused on the situation. When she looked at Paul, he felt like a lab rat with all of his emotions and feelings being judged by an uncaring scientist. He didn't even know her name. A glance at her stony face made him apprehensive about asking for it.

The two lumbered on with their way lit by golden light. To Paul, it felt like the mystery girl was supporting both of their weight.

She probably is.

Despite her petite appearance, he felt like he was being supported by a block of iron. Her only sign of weakness was the hand pressed into her injured side.

It took Paul several stumbling steps to work up the courage to ask one of the many questions on his mind. "*Um... I'm sorry. Can you hear me?*"

"*Yes,*" a single, cool word was the only reply.

"*Where are we?*" The question seemed logical, but for some reason, Paul felt like a complete idiot for asking it. He half expected a cold reply that would hit like a slap in the face.

There was a short silence in his thoughts before the answer came. "*I am currently unsure. My best estimation is that we are five to seven miles from Palisville.*"

She had carried him for over five miles while dealing with a wound that went almost the entire way up her side, burned shut. At this point, this fact shouldn't have surprised him, but it did.

His next question was one that he had been dreading. "*Where are we going?*"

"*An A.R.C. extraction team should be somewhere in this direction,*" the internal voice came back matter-of-factly. "*If we are able to find the nearest roadway, we may be able to track down the van.*"

Not for the first time, Paul realized how much he did not want to go to A.R.C. Being taken in by them would mean his life was over. He would live on, yes, but it was not much of a life by anyone's imagination. He may have only had one friend and two family members in his life now, but he did not care. It was what he knew, and the life that he was comfortable living. The realization made him want to throw himself to the ground and crawl back home. His body even spasmed absent mindedly, causing the girl to readjust her grip on him.

"I... think we should go to the hospital," his thoughts came out before he had come up with a better explanation for not going to A.R.C. Every thought he sent to this girl seemed completely idiotic to him. She had probably been through this type of situation dozens of times. She was the expert, and he was the rambling, scared-to-death civilian. *"I mean... we're both hurt, right?"*

It was all so stupid. A.R.C. would find them at the hospital and if they did not, could the police protect him from the men who had attacked them? Paul doubted it. Amuli were said to secrete an aura that disintegrated projectiles like bullets before they reached their bodies. Only an Amuli could really fight an Amuli, it seemed.

"That would be unwise," the girl answered. *"Returning to Palisville would likely mean danger for us. Sufficient medical care will be provided for us at the A.R.C. base."*

The awkward silence returned after that exchange. Paul fell into the rhythm of right foot forward, left foot forward, and then berated himself for asking stupid questions. *Or maybe it was really asking pertinent questions in a stupid way.*

On the twentieth instance of this routine, he began to hear movement in the trees. Sticks crunched and leaves rustled. At first, Paul chalked this up to squirrels and chipmunks scurrying about. That was until he caught a glimpse at his crutch's face. Her eyes had snapped to attention, analyzing every branch and every trunk in the forest. It made Paul feel like he was in one of the horror movies Robby had forced him to watch. After all, there they were, a pair of teenagers lost in the wood and possibly being pursued by men who wanted to kill them.

When the voice started, he was sure that he was in a slasher film. Either that or he had gone insane. He couldn't make out the words. In the shock of the moment, his brain couldn't comprehend him. All that he knew of them was that they were loud as if they were coming from a loudspeaker, filling his ears and the vibrations shaking his body into shivers. The sounds echoed through the spider-web of branches and the gray slits of sky between them.

"And now was acknowledged the presence of the Red Death," the voice said as it crept into Paul's ears slowly and deliberately. "He had come like a thief in the night. And one by one dropped the revelers in the blood-bedewed halls of their revel and died each in the despairing posture of his fall. And the life of the ebony clock went out with that of the last of the gay. And the flames of the tripods expired. And Darkness and Decay and the Red Death held illimitable dominion over all."

Chapter 5: Red Masque

This is absurd, Paul remarked for not the first time that night. *Someone is quoting...Poe?*

He and his companion frantically searched for the source of the voice. It was not for several moments until a dark, gray shadow stepped out onto a light gray tree branch. In the dark and from the distance they were standing, it was impossible to make out the shadow's size and the actual color.

"I apologize for the theatrics," the shadow said. "It's actually something that is expected of me, believe it or not. It may help to think of all this as a theater audition. You have already outperformed the other participants tonight. The girl has certainly left them bleeding as if from the plague. Now, I have to find new revelers for the masque."

Then Paul was falling again. The ground hit him in the side again. The girl had let him fall without a word or thought pushed into his mind. At first, he thought she would run off and leave him. He could imagine seeing her back turned to him, growing small and less visible in the night as he waited in silence for the man on the branch to take him. Instead of running away, she rushed toward the shadow man. Without warning, two glowing gold orbs appeared on both of the girl's hands. She whipped the orbs forward in two sideways curling arcs. The orbs came close enough to the figure to remove the shadow from around him. He was wearing a slim-fitting black coat with its hood pulled over his head. All of Paul's attention was focused on the man's face. It was covered with a mask, a hideous skull with its mouth twisted into a snarl. The mask was a deep crimson as if covered with blood.

Then, the masked man was gone. The two orbs slammed together, making a soundless explosion. Sticks and branches rained from the trees. Paul covered his head, pressing his face into his forearms.

"I see that you get right down to business," came the disembodied voice again. "That's not a surprise considering what I read in your file, but I see that you've lost your mask, too. It was a frilly white thing, wasn't it? Something you would wear to a masquerade ball. Very fitting for the two of us."

Paul took his head out of his own trembling arms. The masked man was on the ground now, his hands dripping red aura like fire from a torch. Two more golden orbs flew towards him. This time, he ducked before springing forward at the A.R.C. agent. She turned to the side, letting him fly passed her. A glowing, gold fist slammed into the masked man's forearms, raised upwards in a well-placed block. The girl's leg shot out, sweeping those of the man before he could regain his composure. He was on his back but only for a second before rolling sideways and back onto his feet. The thief's fist struck the ground this time.

"Excellent fighting skills," murmured the masked man as he circled his opponent. "You're even better than in the reports. I–"

The girl rushed him again before he was done speaking. The man stepped backward, dodging one fist and then the other. His foot flashed forward, slamming into the place between the girl's knee and her thigh. Her legs buckled for a moment, but she stayed on her feet.

"Not one for conservation, I see," the man continued.

The rest of the fight was too fast for Paul's eyes. He caught only glimpses of fists, feet, and forearms. Some strikes hit empty air while others created the crunching sound of bone to bone with the cushion of skin and flesh in between. Occasionally, there was a flash of red or gold. His mind went over the scenarios of the fight.

If the girl wins, she'll take me to A.R.C. If the masked man wins, I don't know what will happen. He may even want me dead for what I did to his friends. If they kill each other, then I'm on my own trying to find a way out of the woods. That would be easier said than done since it involves trying to find the nearest road on legs that don't want to work. Considering the wooded hills of Western Pennsylvania make up most of this side of the state, getting lost will probably mean that I'll die out here. Like it or not, I have to pray that the thief takes down the man in the mask. I don't think it matters that she broke into my house and tried to steal from me at this point.

Breaking down the situation had a strange, calming effect on him. He could think clearly for the first time in hours, despite the fear peaking inside him.

The masked man was gone once again. The girl's fist struck empty air. Her head moved from side-to-side, trying to catch a glimpse of the dark red mask. No matter where she or Paul looked, the man wasn't there. He had faded like mist into the night.

"That's enough for now," said the invisible man's voice. "You've met my expectations. I'm sure we'll be in touch again."

Satisfied that the mask was gone, the girl offered an arm to Paul again. His body felt heavy. It was as though he was a rock, sinking into a pool. Any previous adrenaline had worn off, and he even found it difficult to keep his head up and his eyes open. Despite all the energy she had exerted, the girl was still able to support his weight and trudge along through the trees. They continued on for several minutes as Paul desperately tried to hang onto consciousness.

His eyes stayed locked on the ground as if there were some force pulling them down there. When the girl stopped, he raised finally raised them. He gulped when he saw three more masked figures. Two in the branches of the nearest tree and one on the ground before him. Unlike in the previous encounter, these people had given no sign of their approach.

No twigs had been snapped, and no words had been spoken. Paul was close enough to view each of them in detail as they stood before him.

The one on the ground was taller than the others and broader in the shoulders. He wore a completely black suit, black coat, pants, shirt, and tie all covered by a black trench coat. As he moved, his jacket and tie swirled about him like a shadow. A simple, smooth gray mask with no features concealed his face, save the eyeholes. In his hands was a staff of dark wood with a pale blue light being emitted from near its top.

The figure on Paul's right was slimmer, with a dark hair tied back and flowing down its back. A thin, purple mask hung over this person's eyes and down just beyond the cheekbones. He only caught a glimpse of a second person in the branches before inhuman groan came from behind him.

Paul, the girl, and the three figures all focused on the man emerging from the mass of trees and bushes behind him. He was half-slumped over, dragging one of his legs behind him. One arm hung loosely over his chest. Much of his clothing was caked in shades of black and brown. The orange mask he wore was cracked in several places. A tuft of greasy red hair emerged from one of the upper cracks. His working arm was dragging a short sword along the ground.

"F-found you," the staggering man breathed as red spittle ran along the exposed part of his chin. "The advanced force... except for me... the backup...you little... you little..."

"I see that you were followed," an icy cold voice interrupted the injured man's insult.

Then there was blood. Paul could still make out the splash of crimson color in the night's grayness. The red-haired man crumpled to the ground with a diagonal, dark swath cutting him from shoulder to hip. When the man was facedown, Paul saw that the wound was so deep that it extended out the victim's back.

Paul heard a *clink* originating from a few feet beside him. He shuddered as he realized the figure who had been hidden by the branches was unsheathing a curved blade. This sword was like his own, only slightly shorter and lighter. Its handle had a curve, crafted to be swung with one hand, with a heavy metal guard to protect that hand.

A saber, Paul noted with his vision aided by the weapon's glow.

A better look at the figure revealed that this person was only slightly taller than Paul but with larger shoulders and well-muscled arms. A mask made of interlocked metal wires completely concealed the face. Painted on these wires was a red spiral, a ranging whirlpool that better obscured the wearer's face. Amidst the wires, Paul swore that he saw two eyes, glowing an angry red before flickering out.

It took Paul a moment to place where he had seen such a mask before. *It's a fencing mask. I didn't expect to see that, but I guess nothing should surprise me right now. I suppose that it does go with the saber.*

The world started to sway again. At first, he thought it was the girl supporting who was moving unsteadily, but then Paul looked down to see that it was his legs that were struggling to stay upright. It was like trying to gain traction on the deck of a capsized ship. His head swam as his body slumped onto his human crutch.

"He's been burning through his anima way too fast," the voice came from the figure in the small purple mask who had suddenly appeared in front of him. As the world tilted, Paul saw a silver shaped in a holster bouncing against the figure's hip as it approached.

They have a gun? No, she *has a gun,* Paul corrected himself, judging by the sound of the voice.

"It appears so," the man in the black suit agreed calmly. "It is rather amazing that he is still conscious."

Paul could see darkness in the corners of his vision, tightening his view of the world to a tunnel. *No... not again. I don't want to pass out again.*

"Perhaps I spoke too soon," the man corrected himself. "Very well, I will take him."

Take me where? Paul was only dimly aware of being lifted onto a pair of strong shoulders. The man's back was like steel covered by fabric.

Take me where?

Chapter 6: Sunrise

~ ~ ~

Streetlights zoomed along through the window like shooting stars. Late evening snapshots of the neighborhood came into view through the side windows. Teenagers finished a two-on-two basketball game by porchlight. An old man walked his white-nosed retriever around his yard by flashlight. Half-stumbling out of his car, a businessman tugged on his sweaty collar to remove his tie.

The nondescript sedan continued its way down the street before making a turn into a nearby driveway. A youthful man emerged and made his way to the door with long, sure strides. With his fresh, clean-shaven face, he could have been any age from his late teens to mid-twenties. He had sky-blue eyes with a hint of laughter behind them. His mouth, however, was a sober, thin line.

He knocked on the door a couple of times, and then a couple of more times when there was no answer. Finally, he gave one last heavy, ringing knock.

At last, the door slid out to a crack. There appeared a pair of eyes with their whites crisscrossed by red blood vessels.

"You shouldn't be here, Engel," the door slammed shut.

"I just want to talk," insisted the man at the door. "I know that you don't want to see me, but this is important. Please! I just want to help if I can. Just give me a few minutes."

There was the sound of muffled conversation from behind the door. Michael couldn't make out the words but could make out the raised voices of a heated argument.

Finally, he heard a loudly muttered, "Fine," before the door opened again.

"Please, just five minutes," Michael insisted. "It's urgent. You have to know what's coming. You must know."

"Yeah, we know."

A man emerged from behind the door. His shoulders were slumped and uneven in his standing posture. The look in his eyes was one of disdain for the visitor at his door.

"We know that errand boys like you are coming after us. We know that you can't leave us alone."

"I'm not here to take you in, Aiden," Michael stressed with tension rising in his voice. "This situation isn't you versus me. It's not that simple, and it's never been that way."

74

Aiden shook his head. "It's always simple. Guys like you are the ones who want to make things complicated. You just can't leave well enough alone."

"Aiden," Michael said softly, trying to diffuse things. "I'm not here for a philosophical debate. I can make you an offer. You know the pull I have with the research division. I promise you I will do what I can to protect you if you submit to my division."

Aiden gave a sarcastic chuckle. "Protect us? When we're the most powerful people in the world?"

"Power takes many forms," warned Michael. "You can't be vigilant at all times. Especially when it's just the two of you. I can give you protection around the clock."

Aiden shook his head. "Right. So, you want us to be your lab rats now instead of the other higher-ups."

"I promise that I will give you as much of the normal life as I can," assured Michael. "You won't have to run anymore. I will give you both positions in the research division. That way, you will have total control over any tests you do or any missions you will go on."

"I don't think you understand," Aiden replied.

His face was slowly turning red, which brought out the patch-like quality of the stumble on his cheeks.

"I don't think you understand what it's like. I don't think anyone in this world understands what it is like for me...I mean for the two of us. We've been experiments since the day we were born. Something for people like your research division to poke and prod and test. No way are we going back to that!"

"I'm trying to tell you that it will be different," the heat was starting to creep into his voice as well.

A woman appeared behind Aiden. Her eyes were as red as his and her golden blonde hair was just as disheveled. Unlike Aiden, she stood tall and straight despite the tired lines on her face. Aside from her regal appearance. What stood out about her was her belly, swollen and sticking out from the rest of her figure.

"Abby!" Aiden cried angrily. "I told you to stay back!"

"And, I told you I'm not hiding," she replied coolly, "especially from a friend."

Michael let out a sigh. It was long, heavy, and low. "I think I understand now. I guess I should have expected something like this."

The color drained from Aiden's face, changing it from an angry reddish pink to pale, milky white. "You've seen too much."

A fist swung out, glowing as if it had been dipped in molten gold. Michael was ready and the blow barely whizzed by his nose as he turned his head sideways.

Then it was Michael's turn. His blue covered fist slammed into Aiden's ribcage, sliding upward in a devastating upper-cut. Michael's free hand gripped the man's forehead as he doubled over. A shot of blue light ensured that Aiden was now sprawled out on the ground.

"He'll be out for a few hours," explained Michael to Abigail who had remained standing in the doorway, seemingly indifferent to the scuffle. "We should probably drag him inside in case someone sees."

"I can do that," Abigail responded as she slid the much larger man inside the threshold. "His temper and lack of control have always been his weaknesses in fights."

"Right," nodded Michael as he caught his breath. "If you had come at me, then I would have been in trouble."

Abigail shook her head. "No point. It would have been a meaningless fight that would have endangered the baby. It's just like you said, I know what is coming next. I appreciate the warning. Aiden will, too, when he wakes up."

"And, my offer?" questioned Michael.

"As you just heard," answered Abigail solemnly, "things have become complicated over the last few months."

"I see." Michael began to turn away, disappointed. "I wish the situation were different. I hope that everything works out for you three."

"Have hope for us all, Michael," insisted Abigail, "and if there is no hope for us, have hope that our children will be able to live in peace."

"How did you... I never..." Michael paused as he was climbing into his car. "Nothing escapes you, does it?"

~ ~ ~

Dad?

A dozen thoughts ran through Paul's head in the between the moment he regained consciousness and the moment he opened his eyes.

A dream, Paul realized. *It was extremely vivid and lifelike but only a dream.*

He was in a white room. At least, he could tell that much before his eyes completely focused. The walls were white. The line of beds beside him were white. The sheets of his own bed were white. The overhead lights reflected on the sheets and the walls, adding to the mental fog blocking his vision for a moment.

Is this a hospital? Paul did not know how to feel about that. Doing something as relatively normal as being in a hospital would almost be a welcome change compared to all the insanity that he had experienced over the past few hours. Still, hospitals meant pain, fear, disease, injury, and death. It wasn't necessarily the place where he wanted to be. *I wish I were in bed... my own bed... away from all this craziness.*

There was some movement in the corner of his vision. The thief was there again as he woke up, sitting in a chair next to his bed. She had bandages racing up her side, but the swelling in her face had gone down. After a quick survey of his own body, Paul found similar bandages around his arms and forehead. As he turned toward her again, the girl made a move to leave the room.

"I appreciate your aid in helping me to complete my mission to bring you here," she thanked him curtly as she exited. "I made an error in judgment in attempting to separate you from your anima weapon. I had thought that it would have made you more difficult for our enemies to detect. I apologize for not respecting your innate fighting ability."

Just then, a second figure entered the room. This time, it was the man in the pristine, all-black suit without his mask. The face he revealed was one partially covered by a scruffy, black beard partly mottled by gray. He seemed oddly familiar to Paul. It took several moments for him to place the face.

He's the man from the A.R.C. presentation, Paul didn't know how long it had been since he heard had heard Robby light-heartedly mock the presentation. *It feels like years ago. Was it just hours, or maybe a day ago? How long have I been*

79

unconscious?

"I see that you've become acquainted with Alice," the man began in a positive-sounding voice. "You seem to have made quite an impression on her. That 'thank you' was as about as friendly as I've seen her."

Paul stayed silent, having no idea of what to say in this bizarre situation.

"I'm Luper, by the way," he continued, "Greg Luper. I happen to run this little outpost."

As soon as he opened his mouth, nervousness seeped into his voice.

"P-Paul," he gave his name in a stammer.

"Paul Engel," Luper nodded. "It may be uncomfortable for you to realize this, but I already knew your name. A.R.C. has that type of resource. Facial recognition, access to different databases, the entire thing."

"A.R.C.?" Paul's one-word question came out as a whisper.

"Right," Luper nodded. "You're in an underground A.R.C. outpost about an hour from Palisville. Specifically, you're in our medical wing where you've been asleep for almost a day. Thanks to A.R.C.'s budgeting, we're without a doctor or even a nurse here, but I happen to know my way around a ring of gauze. I hope that I did not mess you up too badly."

I was asleep for an entire day. I bet Aunt Morgan has called me by now to let me know that they landed in Japan. She's probably called back several times since I never answered. I bet she's worried.

Paul shook his head to bring himself back to the present. "I... uh..."

"Yes," Luper sighed, "bad joke, I know. When you are isolated like us down here, that is usually the only form of entertainment."

"T-those men... chasing us," Paul stammered. "Who were they? Oh, God! I- I k-killed..."

He leaned over the side of the bed before mercifully finding a waste-bin and heaving into it.

Murderer... killer... The words wormed their way through Paul's mind as he stared at the bottom of the now-soiled waste-bin. The smell made him want to vomit again, but there was nothing in his stomach now. *What have I done? It's like I wasn't me, I didn't know what I was doing! My body just moved on its own. Why did I just lose control like that?*

"By my count," Luper explained, "you haven't killed anyone yet. The body that you destroyed was a Dead Eyes, a zombie if you will, and therefore already dead. In fact, I'd say that you released him from any pain. The second man you fought was only knocked unconscious, although I'm not sure if he will be waking up anytime soon. Bouts of anger, even violence, and a certain haziness of the mind are common during an Amulus awakening. Your decision to fight was likely caused by these side effects rather than your own volition."

"A zombie? How is that possible? *"It's not real. Wake up! I'm still dreaming. Wake up! God, don't let this be real!*

"It's about as real as people being able to weaponise their internal energy," answered Luper, with a hint of sarcasm dripping into his voice. "There are plenty of impossible things that are possible with Amuli. If you stay around here, you'll learn about a lot of those impossible things."

It's just like I thought, my life is over. People go into A.R.C. and A.I.M. and never come out.

"W–What happens to me now?"

Luper replied as he made his way back to the threshold of the room. "That is very much up to you, Paul. Life is full of choices and the one that faces you will be one of your most important. You can join A.R.C. and possibly stay here for the time being, or you can leave right now. Should you choose to leave, I would advise that you wait until the morning. It is quite cold this time of year at night. If you follow the sun rising in the east, you should find a road leading to a nearby town called Fox Hill. Since you are from the area, you may already know it as a stop for deer hunters. The exit is to the left where you'll find a ladder to the surface. If you stay, you will find me in my office two doors down the hall on the right in the morning. Report to me there and we will welcome you into A.R.C."

"I can leave?" Paul asked in a low whisper. "It's that simple?"

Luper shook his head. "It never is. Remember, you just fought against several people. Don't you think that those people have friends and allies that will be after you? Perhaps one of them even caught a glimpse of your face. Maybe they have put it together that you live around here. They could knock down your door tomorrow."

It doesn't seem like much of a choice then.

"Of course, you also held your own out there," Luper continued. "It is possible that you have a great deal of latent fighting ability. You may be able to survive on the run. Others have. Whatever you do, make sure that you keep that with you."

Paul's eyes followed Luper's finger to a slim object on the end table next to his bed.

The sword was still with him. Its green crystal still shined dimly, yet consistently. No matter what he did, the sword seemed to be following him. *It's like a ghost with a haunting green light.*

"Your anima has awakened and there is no closing it again," explained Luper solemnly. "You may think that putting distance between you and your sword will make it hard for other Amuli to detect you. That is not quite true. All Amuli emit a power that can be sensed by others even if they are a thousand miles from their crystal. The further you are from your sword, the weaker you are. You may have begun to sense anima in the form of a feeling, an emotion that seems to irradiate from a person. It would be wise to become adjusted to this new sense. No matter your decision tonight, you will be fighting for your life. Your anima will draw other Amuli to you. You cannot afford weakness. I can provide you with tools to counter that weakness, but it will cost you a lot of your personal freedom. A.R.C. agents typically are not afforded a large degree of autonomy. The organization's restrictions on superhumans make the public feel safer."

The man in the black suit finally made his way out of the doorway, turning into shadow and slipping away down the unlit corridor.

"Just know if you go to the police or any government agency, they will send you back to A.R.C. in all likelihood." Before he disappeared out of the halfway, he added, "One last thing, if you do choose to leave here, do not contact A.I.M. The men and that husk you fought were both A.I.M. operatives. You will find that A.R.C. and A.I.M. don't get along as well as the government or news media would like the world to believe. Unfortunately, I think you may have just made a powerful enemy of them."

Paul stared at the empty doorway for several minutes, listening to his heartbeat pounding away in his ribcage. No matter how many times he tried to catch his breath, the palpitations continued. *Is my heart shaking my entire body or is it all just in my head?*

He lied back down, tossing and turning in the white sheets. The stinging smell of chemical disinfectant crept into his nostrils. Paul had always disliked hospitals. There was something artificial about the white walls, light-colored sheets, and pristine tile floors. *He told me to wait until morning to decide. How will I even know when morning comes? There are no windows or clocks in here.*

More chunks of digested food drifted from his teeth to his tongue, causing him to double over and to spit into the waste-bin again. *I wish I had some water... and a toothbrush.* He then berated himself for not focusing on the more pressing matters. *What am I supposed to do? Go or stay? If I stay, I will be made into a soldier and death is always a possibility for soldiers. If I run, I can't hang around my family or Robby for long. Amuli will come after me like they did for Alice tonight. I will have to fight on behalf of A.R.C. or for myself to stay alive. No matter what I do, things will never go back to the way they were. My normal life is over.* With all of these questions swirling, Paul did not notice the tiredness slowly creeping in. Before he knew it, he felt the effect of his anima depletion once again. This time, however, it came as a slow drift into sleep.

When Paul awoke this time, he realized he hadn't had any dreams. *I wonder how long my anima depletion will continue to affect me. I don't know how much longer I can take losing consciousness like this. I'm worried that I'm going to pass out at any time!*

For the first time since picking up the *katana*, Paul's body felt normal. He was able to climb out of bed and stand steadily on the cold floor in bare feet. It was his mind that was still flustered. The fear and anxiety were inescapable. No matter how much he wanted to accept what had happened and to move on, he could not accept that he might never see home again, or school, or Robby, or his family. It was crushing. *I'm like Atlas, struggling under the weight of the sky.*

He ran his hands over the hospital gown that he found himself in, shivering as he wondered who had changed his clothes for him while he was unconscious. His hands found bandages around both his shoulders and one around his forehead. *Weird. I don't even remember getting a cut there.*

The strangest thing was that he felt no pain in either area, not even the shoulder that had gone through a building wall. Paul traced his fingers over the crusty, dried blood on the bandages with a sour feeling rising in his stomach. A peek under the bandages revealed nothing. No blood, no scars, just pale skin. *I guess Amuli really do have accelerated healing powers as well as extreme strength and durability.* That fact would have enthralled someone like Robby. *He'd probably want to put on a cape and save cats from trees if he were me right now.* Paul, however, thought of the Hunters, the rogue groups of people who despised Amuli. *I am really unnatural? Am I still human?* That latter thought was the most difficult to push from his mind.

Paul found two sets of clothes hanging on a nearby chair. The first set was a simple black T-shirt and a pair of jeans. The second was more familiar, yet ragged. His school uniform was now tattered strips dangling off the end of the chair. To

Paul, they were symbolic of his past life. It was broken and physically gone, but still with him somehow.

I have to say goodbye. The simple thought filled his mind. It was saddening, almost defeating, like he had done something wrong and needed to apologize. *I could go home and wait a couple of days for my aunt and uncle to get home to talk with them. That would mean that I could say goodbye to Robby this weekend, too. After that, I'll call for A.R.C. or whatever government agency to take me in. I just feel like I need the one to do it. That would be better than having some A.R.C. officials notifying them that I can't see them anymore. That would crush them.*

With that, Paul slid into the shirt and jeans on the chair, noticing that he hadn't been given a coat to protect against the chilly November weather. This left him to struggle into the remains of his blazer. *This is an odd clothing combination.*

The last item he noticed was a large backpack, one that would surely take up all the space on his back. A look inside revealed that it was empty, but closer inspection showed a large open pouch on the side. Paul traced his finger inside the pouch, finding a hidden zipper surrounded by Velcro.

It's for the sword, he realized. With the sword inside, he closed up the zipper and Velcro. The pouch and sword magically disappeared into the lining of the backpack. *It makes sense that I wouldn't want to be seen carrying a samurai sword down the street. I wonder how they hide larger swords.*

As he made his way down the barely lit hallway made of bleach-white cedar block walls, he worried that he would see Luper again or someone else who would ask him what he was doing. Mercifully, he saw no one, only closed doors by the time he reached the ladder. The rungs were cold, a reminder of the frigid air waiting above. Paul climbed his way from the warm netherworld he had found himself in and into the cold world above. The "real world" is what Paul told himself. *Where everything still makes sense.*

He found himself emerging from the bunker into a shed. The floor was covered by dirty, browned wood and an assortment of shriveled, autumn leaves. He let the door of the hatch slam shut before it disappeared into the floor.

These people really have a talent for making hidden compartments. The rest of the shed was filled with rusted hand-tools and a rustier pair of lawn chairs. The first rays of the day were creeping through the dirty window, illuminating the dust swirls in the musky air.

The door opened with only a slightly noisy protest from its hinges. The first thing Paul felt was cold air biting at his cheeks. *It has to be close to freezing, and I don't have a hat or a proper coat.* He wanted to keep his head down to brace himself against the wind, but realized that he needed to take a survey of the surrounding woods. *He said to follow the sun.* It was the beginning of a cloudy, gray day, but Paul could see the sun shining beneath the clouds like a flashlight covered by a light blanket. All he could see were trees from all angles. In some places, there were pine trees with great branches that made passing through impossible. Paul could imagine the little green needles digging into his skin as he desperately made his way through them. However, he located an opening through the maze of branches and began his way towards it.

"There is a remnant of a bandage on the back of your head."

The sudden outburst of the chilly voice made Paul jump, quite literally. The girl from the night before was sitting on a third rusted lawn chair just outside of the shed. Gone was the ruined, fancy dress. Instead, she wore a more sensible pair of jeans with a gray jacket. Her white-gold hair curled along the edges of a white, knitted hat. Gone were her injuries in the night before as well, save for some purple bruising around one eye. *Alice. That's what Luper said her name was.*

"Someone may have questioned you about it if they had seen it," she continued robotically. "It would not be advantageous for you to have to make up a lie on the spot to explain the bandage. Or worse, you may have compromised our operation by letting something slip."

"Oh... I... um..." Paul felt the back of his head and found pieces of gauze and cotton stuck to his hair. "I'm sorry. I must have missed it."

"No apology is necessary," she responded coolly, barely looking at him. Instead, her focus was on a small ring of flowers, somehow still alive despite the icy, white frost covering the rest of the ground. Paul noticed that these flowers were actually common weeds. Yellow dandelions mixed with white daisies along with tiny blue flowers whose name he could not remember

"The heat originating from the ventilation system in the bunker rises to this spot," she explained. "The heated air warms the ground enough for grass and plants to continue growing in the late fall. Luper believes that the presence of the flowers here may give away our position to enemies. He has petitioned A.R.C. several times to change the heating and ventilation systems. However, this is a small outpost with limited access to funds, so A.R.C. officials have decided to leave the system as it currently functions."

"I see," Paul responded, slightly confused about why she was explaining all of this to him. "So, you... uh... you like looking at the wee—I mean flowers?"

Paul silently berated himself for his slip in speech. *Can I have one conversation where I don't misspeak and make everything awkward? Why did I have weeds on my mind when she clearly called them flowers?*

"Do you know the difference between weeds and flowers?" Alice questioned flatly with no hint of hurt feelings in her voice.

The question struck Paul oddly. "I'm not really sure. I think that I was always told that weeds take nutrients out of the soil that could be used for other plants like crops and flowers."

"All plants take nutrients from the soil while leaving others," explained Alice. "This was discovered in Europe during the Middle Ages as farmers began using crop rotation to preserve the soil in fields. Your explanation makes the most sense when discussing topics like crop growing, but what of lawns and flower beds? What is the difference between weeds and those plants?"

Paul shook his head. "I don't know. I mean—I remember this time when I was little where I gave some dandelions that I'd found in the yard to my aunt. She accepted them, of course, but she also told me that they attract ants."

Was describing that whole episode really warranted?

"The truth is," Alice continued, "there is no biological difference between flowers and weeds. A weed is simply a plant that the gardener does not want. Certain plants have been classified as weeds because they grow invasively due to their seed dispersal, sprouting up in lawns and flower beds. Others spread and grow too abundantly. As a whole, most people have decided that they simply wish that they were not there. They see no value in them, no matter how colorful they may be."

"Why are you telling me this?" Paul's voice was barely above a whisper. "Oh! Um... look, I'm sorry... I didn't mean... I think that was all very interesting, but..."

"We are weeds, Paul Engel," Alice breathed. "We are the ones that people would prefer did not exist. No matter what you do from this point forward, most people will ignore you if they can't see you, and if they do, they will wish that you were not there. They may even try to dispose of you."

Her chilly tone sent shivers down Paul's spine, even more so than the frosty weather. He gulped hard as he began his way away from the shed and towards his chosen path. His rose-colored cheeks betrayed his embarrassment at leaving this place.

Even though I'm sure that I want to leave... err... that I should leave, I still feel like this Alice girl will be disappointed in me. I can also picture Luper reacting to not seeing me come to his office later this morning. Why do I care so much about what people I barely know think of me?
    "You should stay."

The statement came as a matter of fact.

Paul spun around slowly. "I-I'm sorry. I just have to go. I'm not saying that I won't be back. I just have to talk with some people."

' "It is part of a test," Alice elaborated. "It is one that he often gives to recruits."

"A test?" Paul muttered in confusion.

"Luper gave you a choice that was only an illusion," Alice revealed. "It was meant to test you to confirm or disprove that you can think logically in a stressful situation."

"I don't understand."

"Think logically about the choice he gave you," she ordered calmly, her voice coming out as smoky, warm air in the chilly morning. "With the two options available to you, you could stay in a secured underground facility away from any dangers or you could wander through close to freezing weather in a vague direction. You were not even offered suitable clothing for the cold. Even worse, the Red Mask may still be lurking in these woods."

Paul's mind flashed to images of the man in the red mask the night before. His battle with Alice had been vicious. Paul knew that a fight like that would have torn him to shreds in an instant. He chided himself. *I was really this stupid? With the way she puts it, I feel like an idiot for doing something this stupid.*

"I guess I wasn't thinking clearly."

Alice did not respond, only staring blankly at the weedy flowers.

"But, why did you tell me all this?" Paul asked with his mouth going dry from the cold.

"You and I are allies, Paul Engel," she answered quickly.

"Allies?"

Alice turned her large, hazy blue eyes towards Paul. "You

aided me in my mission to acquire the sword and bring you here to the outpost. You also defended my own person. That is likely why Luper is apt to keep you at this facility."

"Allies," agreed Paul. *I guess we have been through a lot together already.* "Or maybe... frie— I mean acquaintances?"

Alice nodded. "Then we are acquaintances."

She abruptly rose and picked up her rusty folding chair before making her way back into the shed.

Paul swallowed hard. "I-I... just had one question."

Alice paused her walk without turning around.

"After my powers awakened," Paul spoke quickly as the words flew out of his mouth. "when I was unconscious, why did you only take the sword with you? From what Luper said, A.R.C. agents want to take in as many Amuli as possible. Why didn't you try to bring me here, too? I-I'm sorry. I'm not trying to say you did something wrong. I'm just trying to understand."

Alice resumed her stride before disappearing down the secret entrance.

Paul was left standing in the silence. *I obviously offended her, my one "acquaintance" here.* He spent a few more minutes silently chiding himself before following her down the hole.

Chapter 7: A New Life Begins

I slept through a day of school, Paul realized before reaching the door that Luper had directed him towards the night previously. *That's the first day of high school that I've ever missed. I don't suppose that I'll ever be going back. It's not like many people will miss me there. Just Robby and a couple of teachers, maybe.* The thoughts still made Paul yearn for his old, normal, boring life, the one that had been buried in the ground for less than a day. *Why am I thinking about this now? Is this even important?* Somehow, to Paul, it still was.

He now stood dumbfounded in the hallway made up of doors. *He said it was in this direction, but which one is it?* None of the doors were labeled and were surrounded by unforgiving, bleached white walls. The paint reflected the lights overhead. The brightness of the corridor added to the pounding in Paul's temples into a full-blown headache. Taking a deep breath, he chose a door before cautiously and quietly giving it a knock.

Several seconds passed before a bearded face poked out from two doorways away.

"It is this one," murmured Luper before his head left the doorway faster that the mole of a whack-a-mole machine.

Entering Luper's office felt like stepping into that of a college professor that Paul had seen in movies. The walls of the small room were lined with bookshelves, overflowing with yellowed books, and stuffed with seemingly random placed scraps of old paper. Musky, fake-looking leather covered the chairs in the room.

"A.R.C. does not tend to put much money into the décor, especially in small facilities like this one," explained Luper in a half-apology as he noticed Paul surveying the office.

"No, um... I think it's great," Paul mumbled. "I... uh... love books."

Wow. Can I say one thing that doesn't make me sound like a total idiot, especially when I first meet someone?

Luper nodded. "A love of learning is a wonderful virtue to have. It's something that will help you here."

There was a long, awkward silence.

"I take it that you have chosen to stay at this facility?" Luper questioned as a softer, caring look appeared on his face.

Paul nodded solemnly. *If what Alice said was true, then there really wasn't much of a choice.*

"A logical decision," Luper agreed as his face hardened again. "Now, I will not sugarcoat it. You will learn how to kill people with a sword for a living. Are you sure this is something you want to do?"

The words struck Paul like a gust of arctic wind. *Was that a joke? No, from what I've seen here, that type of thing is clearly going on. But... could I do it? Could I really point a sword at someone? Stab them? Slice them? Do I have the right to do that? Why would I have the right to live and have someone else die by my hand? I'm a nobody. No talent for anything. Some book-smarts. That's it. That's all I ever had. Barely any friends or even family. I don't even understand the cause I would be fighting for.*

"So, that's what it's like," he murmured softly. "Um... there isn't anything else that I can do in A.R.C.?"

Luper sighed. "There are many jobs available. A.R.C. operatives, including Amuli, ranging from data analyst to bookkeeper to accounting to archivist and everything you could expect in a private corporation or government agency. However, it would be best for you to be none of these things."

Paul's face betrayed his puzzlement.

Luper pointed his finger at the computer on his desk. "I have already submitted my report for the other night...oh... you were unconscious for about a day by the way. It is highly likely that the higher-ups will see your actions as courageous, if not a little reckless, a key indicator that you will make an excellent combat agent. The top grades on your report cards will be seen as a sign of your intellectual capability as well, even if the comments on them say that you 'could work better with others' and 'could be more vocal in class.'"

Is there anything that he hasn't looked up on me? What computer program allows you to find information about private citizens that quickly? Something from the N.S.A. or F.B.I.? Or are there hackers involved in A.R.C.?

"Yet, what I said before is still true," Luper continued solemnly. "Almost everything in life involves a choice. You will not be forced to be a combat agent. However, it is likely in your best interest. You see, it is not unheard of for our enemies to go after the families of our members. We go through great pains to protect the identities of our operatives, but things sometimes slip through the cracks."

"So, there are...uh... people at A.R.C. that are good enough with computers to hide my identity and my past?" Paul stumbled through the question.

Geez. That was even dumber sounding than the last thing I said.

"Of course," Luper answered patiently, "on the other hand, people may notice the deleting of public records, students mysteriously transferring from school mid-semester, and families disappearing from neighborhoods. Records may be wiped with little trace, but memories often stay."

"And you wear masks for protection, too," Paul added.

Luper nodded. "Yes, however, those are far from full-proof. Occasionally, an enemy agent will catch a glimpse of one of us without a mask, leading to facial recognition. Rumors can lead to inquiries which leads to uncovering evidence."

Paul had stopped breathing midway through Luper's explanation as he had a sudden realization. *I was so concerned with myself that I didn't think of what might happen to my aunt and uncle. They could be in danger right now. If that Red Mask guy were able to find out who I am, he could be tracking them right now. They could be in danger!*

"My family!" he blurted. "I'm sorry... I've got an aunt and uncle. They just took a trip to Japan."

"I've already sent word to agents in Japan to surveil your aunt and uncle," Luper mentioned to Paul's relief. "A.R.C. does put the families in a sort of 'witness protection program' and sometimes even bodyguards. The differentiation between combat agents and everyone else goes in here. Families of combat agents receive the best bodyguards and live in the safest, securest areas. For that reason, I always recommend that operatives who have the capacity to be a combat agent do so."

Paul's opinion of Luper seemed to be forever shifting. *Despite his manipulating of my "choice," he did this huge favor for me. But I can't tell if this talk of me becoming a combat agent is him being honest or just another manipulation.*

"Isn't this whole situation between combat agents and non-combat agents a little-" Paul probed in a half-hearted attempt to test his theory.

"-Similar to blackmail?" Luper finished the sentence bluntly. "Absolutely. The higher-ups would call it 'incentivizing.' It is true that there are only so many agents we can spare for body guarding duties but dissuading non-combat operatives certainly does not promote harmony or morality in our organization. The biggest reason for this is that we have always been led by former combat agents. If it were up to me, I'd try to stretch the manpower to include all families at risk. Alas, it is above my paygrade."

Is he just telling me all of this to make it appear that he is on my side or is he being genuine? The question that came out of was different than the one in his mind. "Will I be able to see them sometime... my aunt and uncle, I mean?"

Luper sighed with his eyes flashing a knowing look at Paul. "It may be some time before you will be allowed to communicate with them. There are several things to consider. Before you are even able to call or text them, agents will have to ensure that the phone lines can't be tapped and the phones themselves will not be hacked. This might take more time that than you would expect. As for meeting them in person, that will take even more time. Usually, the policy is that only trained agents will be able to see friends and family. There is always the possibility that someone would let their guard down if they are relaxing around family. For that reason, agents must be trained to not let that happen. I guess A.R.C. is like a cult in this way... and in some ways, it's worse."

*It's hard to tell when he's joking and being serious. Though...
I can appreciate him breaking down the situation for me and
describing all the elements. It makes me feel as if he is acknowledging my role in all this.* Luper's exact words, however, made
his stomach sink.

"And... who is after me?" Paul questioned, desperate for more
information. "You said that I fought A.I.M. agents last night,
are there others? I've heard about Hunter groups online...
are they real?"

Luper nodded. "Those are the two main threats. Hunter
groups tend to be fragmented. There is no single, unified
group or one ideology. They spend most of their time writing
manifestos and stocking guns rather than actually finding
Amuli. However, they are still a danger. The aura of an
Amulus does function as a shield against projectiles, and
our skin is tougher than a normal human's. However, if
someone were to press the barrel of a gun against your skin
and pull the trigger, it could still cause fatal damage. The
anima barrier will not protect you at close range. No enemy
should be taken lightly. A.I.M. is currently the more pressing
threat. Plus, there's always the chance that the government
or even multiple world governments or the U.N. could turn
against A.R.C."

"But... didn't the U.N. create A.R.C. and A.I.M. to take the
power of Amuli away from governments?" Paul pointed out.
"Couldn't they unmake A.R.C. and A.I.M. if they wanted?"

"Both organizations were created by the U.N., yes, but they

quickly fell out of its control soon after their inceptions," Luper explained. "Both the U.N. and most of the major world governments greatly underestimated the amount of Amuli that would emerge after the Battle of Alaska. The remnants of the Amulus divisions of the American and Soviet armies were one thing, but A.I.M. and A.R.C. put anima weapons in the hands of people from all parts of society. Rather than risking rogue Amuli arising organically, the goal was to regulate the emergence of Amuli and to control them thereafter. This plan gave A.R.C. and A.I.M. more military might than any other entities in the world. Their ranks contained over a hundred thousand super-soldiers, each one invulnerable to most traditional weapons. With that kind of autonomy given to them, the U.N. could not control them. Both A.R.C. and A.I.M. have the capability to wipe out entire countries in a day without the lasting effects of nuclear weapons. They would not even have to do so with a traditional standing army. Amuli agents come in all ages, genders, races, and body types. This means that they can infiltrate any aspect of society."

How am I a part of this? This global conspiracy? It sounds ridiculous. Chills ran up and down Paul's spines like static shocks.

"I-If... they could take over the world... why haven't they done so?"

"It would be chaos," Luper summarized. "A worldwide civil war between superhumans and non-superhumans would lead to an astronomical human death toll. If A.R.C. or A.I.M. forces moved efficiently enough for a total takeover of world governments, such bloodshed could be avoided. However, this would lead to an upset of the status quo as well, likely leading to a world ruled by Amuli over normal humans. Revolts would be likely."

Which would be pretty understandable, Paul considered.

"As of now, A.R.C. and A.I.M. have the rest of the world where they want it. They have the autonomy and secrecy to continue their amassing of forces and experiments for the secret war amongst themselves. "

"If they're at war," pondered Paul, "then why does the government and the media portray them as working together? I mean, many people even use their names interchangeably."

"That's also part of the controlled chaos, a silent agreement between enemies," Luper began. "If the populace knew that two organizations made up of superhumans had gone rogue and were constantly fighting, it would likely not go over very well. Leaders of nations know what is going on, but they hide it. As I have mentioned several times, this, too, is to avert chaos as well as to keep the trust of their constituents."

"If it's a war, then how have they kept it quiet?" wondered Paul.

"A.R.C. and A.I.M. have a sort of mutual understanding," answered Luper. "An all-out, publicized war would lead to panic which would not be contusive to either organization's goals. Instead, battles are kept limited. Many occur in woods, forests, and other remote areas where there are compounds like this one. Typically, remote battles are fought for little pieces of territory or to find enemy records or experimental projects. Battles occurring in large cities have the strictest rules. Typically, combat is one-on-one with teams made of the best agents of both organizations fight until the entire enemy team is incapacitated. Some of these "champion" agents reside at city bases while others rove around the world in order to engage in the most difficult battles. The trick for teams on the offense is to catch an enemy base while it has a weak team since most battles have to occur one day after the initial summons. The trick for defense teams is to have their staff ready to dispose of or run away with any important documents, records, data, and hard drives should their team fall in battle. Of course, it is usually only the more experienced agents that take on those responsibilities. Here, you may have to deal with an occasional skirmish."

"So, I'd be staying here?" Paul asked.

"Oh, yes," Luper confirmed. "You may remain here if you wish. I contacted my superiors already. Small, remote bases like this one are the places where young or inexperienced A.R.C. agents are trained. Despite how quiet this place may often seem, there is always the danger of a skirmish where your life will be on the line. In addition to you, there are currently three other young trainees here. You have met Alice already, but there are two others whom you will meet shortly."

Is it strange that, out of everything, meeting other people my age is also making me nervous now? Will they be as strange as Alice? No, I shouldn't think anything as mean as that. I don't know what she's been through.

"The whole setup between A.R.C. and A.I.M.... these agreements... they sort of remind me of agreements of mafia groups in gangster movies," Paul thought out loud. "Like, how one group may agree to stay away from another's turf. How did it get that way?"

Luper gave a wry smile. "That is a very fitting analogy. As you've now guessed, nothing of what we do here is legal and most is unethical. I tell myself that I am just part of this machine and to break away from the machine is to die. An Amulus on their own is powerful, but faced against A.R.C., A.I.M., Hunters, and governments, it is difficult to last very long, let alone thrive or live a normal life. As for the agreements, we must go back to when the organizations began, and even before that. The first finding of anima weapons did not take place in the nineteen-eighties, as it has been reported. Legends of magical weapons have existed since the beginning of history. Although, no one knows exactly how they were made or where anima crystals came from. Those secrets were lost somewhere during the eighteen hundreds. It seems that differences in how these weapons were to be used have persisted ever since then. Some Amulus have wanted to rule over others while others want to live amongst other humans. The latter idea has mostly come to fruition, or at least the perception of it, thanks to the agreements of A.R.C. and A.I.M. The greater difference in opinion came from how to develop Amuli. What boundaries should be pushed? Is experimenting on humans permissible in order to research their powers or to make them more powerful? When the U.N. founded A.R.C. and A.I.M. during the nineteen eighties, the boundary pushers flocked to where they felt their experiments would be welcome, in the field of medicine. They began Amulus International Medicine. For some researchers, there was no boundary they would not cross, leading to human rights abuses. One of the men you fought, the one whose body you destroyed, was a virtual zombie created by A.I.M. experiments.

"A.R.C. became the anthesis of A.I.M., a force to prevent unethical Amulus experimentation. A force of which you are now a part. Of course, an A.I.M. agent telling you this story would likely have used some different words. As they say, 'there are two sides to every story'. Through fate or by your free will, you will now be affiliated with A.R.C."

I don't get it. At times, he talks about A.R.C. as if he were not a part of it. What's his angle? Is he trying to give me an unbiased account of Amulus history or is that just what he wants me to think? When it comes down to it... I guess I have to decide if he is truly genuine about how he has been treating me. And... I have no idea how to do that. I guess time will tell... or will it?

"It's a lot to process, I know," Luper interrupted Paul's slew of thoughts, "unfortunately, your training will deal with many things that you will have to process quickly if you want to continue as a combat agent. So, any questions so far?

"I just... uh..." Paul shook his head as if to shake loose cobwebs from his mind. "I mean... what is it... this anima... this power? Where does it come from?"

Luper held back a smile. "You're going for the most difficult question. The short answer is no one knows. From what anyone can tell, the Amuli of history operated underground and left no records with information on their powers or the items they left us. People from all professions have speculated on the source of anima. Scientists and doctors say that it could originate from an invisible gland within the body or from the human body's natural electric current. The more religious inclined claim the force comes from the soul or from qi or chakra. In this case, what the rest of the world knows about the nature of Amuli is all that we know."

"So, we don't know the 'why' and 'where' this all comes from," Paul surmised. "What about how it works exactly?"

"There are a few areas that can be explained regarding function," Luper informed him. "The crystals embedded in the anima weapons activate the anima within their user. An anima weapon will only activate for one person and the connection made is for life. Anima crystals do not break until the death of their user. As far as anyone knows, they are completely indestructible. There are two main Amulus classes, warrior, like you, and psychics, like Alice. When the crystal is embedded in a weapon, its user is a warrior who generally has much higher combat capabilities than psychics. Psychics, on the other hand, work with crystals in a purer way. Their combat strength is not as high as an Amulus, but they have the added ability for one-to-one telepathic communication. That is the transferring of internal thoughts between psychic to anyone else, including non-Amuli. For this reason, psychics make for excellent battlefield communicators, although their telepathic range varies from psychic to psychic. Although, as you have seen already with Alice, some skilled psychics can be well-trained in combat and can give warriors a run for their money."

Being a warrior... it's like I'm tied to this weapon now... this violence. Is that who I am now? Or have I always been this way, and that is why the katana chose me?

"I have one more... pressing matter," Luper began slowly. "After this, we can get started and you won't have to suffer through my words for much longer. You may have realized by now that you are quite a curious case."

Curious case? Paul's puzzlement lasted for only for a second as he uncovered the phrase's meaning just before Luper's explanation.

"Having two Amuli in one family is incredibly rare," Luper continued. "The last estimate on the overall numbers of Amulus detailed about a hundred thousand superhumans in both A.R.C.'s and A.I.M.'s ranks along with approximately five hundred unaffiliated or rogue Amuli. That is over two hundred thousand in total. Of this number, I have never heard of anyone but distant family members both being Amuli. We come from all regions, races, cultures, religions, and whatever distinctions that you wish to make, which makes the odds of two people being related to each other out of two hundred thousand out of earth's approximate seven billion people, quite high. Which obviously makes both you and your father special in this fact. This makes me curious. How much did you know about your father or your mother's work in A.R.C.?"

I think this topic didn't even cross my mind at first is because I've always kept it buried or even repressed. It's not that I'm not curious, but it just hurts to think about it. I feel it in my chest.

"Not much," Paul mouthed with the tensions rising in his arms and chest. "My aunt told me very little, and... I never wanted to probe her about it. She lost her brother after all. N-Not that I don't miss them without ever knowing them... it's just complicated."

Paul wiped a bead of sweat off his reddening forehead. *It feels even worse when you can't articulate what you want to say, and you're afraid that you will never be able to.* "All I know is that they were both a part of A.R.C. My dad was an agent, and my mom was an analyst. She was a non-Amulus."

Luper nodded slowly. "I'm afraid that I can't give you much more than that. Information is on a 'need-to-know' basis outside of the council that oversees the whole organization. Often, information is as powerful a weapon as anima weapons and could create harm if an agent were to go rogue. That being said, I did meet Michael once, albeit only briefly."

"You did?"

Luper's words shook Paul out of his melancholy for a few moments before his stutter returned.

"What....How... I mean... he..."

I can't remember of anyone else that I know who even met my father. My aunt always talked about him and my mom but never about his time at A.R.C.

"He was in a separate division from me," Luper explained with a hint of heaviness in his voice. "I first became aware of him years ago when there was talk of a hotshot in the research division. Someone who was smart and a world-class combat agent while still being a psychic. A 'triple-threat,' they said. I believe that he was a reconnaissance specialist, someone who could infiltrate A.I.M. bases and steal information and records and report back to analysts. I spent only a few moments with him during a conference called by the council. He came across as confident, but not arrogant. Someone who was intelligent and knew how to use his brain. The report he read for an audience, with the council included, provided much more pertinent information on the experiments of A.I.M. than most of the A.R.C. agents in the room had ever heard."

So, he was nothing like me. He was much better. No, I should be proud that I can from someone like that.

Despite his best efforts, Paul had to quickly swipe a tear off his cheek. "T-Thank you... for your words... but it's.... it's a little weird... I mean..."

"It is not fair that a stranger like me could have even one conversation with him, while you never could," Luper said as he looked deep into Paul's eyes.

Paul nodded. "Do you have anything records or reports about him? Anything at all? I don't presume to be able to access stuff like that yet. I know that I haven't even started yet, but with what you said before, I just... I want to know more."

"I don't have anything here," Luper sighed, rubbing his beard thoughtfully. "I am sorry. To the best of my knowledge, the closed computer network that we have access to here does not have any of his reports. The information that he worked with... it was sensitive, to say the least. But I think there is one way that you will be able to read his findings... not now, but someday."

Go on! Paul's thoughts screamed during Luper's pause.

"You could become someone who needs to know that infor-mation," Luper summarized bluntly. "You could work your way up the ranks and apply for a post in the research division. Once there, it is likely that you could view any of his extant records. This wouldn't be a simple solution. It could take years, but it is the only way towards this goal that I see."

Another incentive to stay and to do my best in A.R.C. I still can't tell if he is trying to manipulate me or not, or I am just being too cynical about this?

"It's common for A.R.C. agents to find their place in the

organization on their own unless there is a pressing need in some division," elaborated Luper. "You may find that another division suits you better as the years go by. The research division is just one option."

"I see," Paul responded as his brain attempted to soak in all the information. "I... uh... guess I'll think about it."

"Right then," Luper remarked as he stepped out from behind his desk. "I think I have bombarded you enough for now. It is time that we do something different."

Chapter 8: Bruises

Paul found himself outside. He was cold once again. In fact, he was even colder than the other night, now stripped down to his undershirt. His fingers thrummed to a nervous beat on the wooden object in his hands. His eyes were locked onto the similarly dressed man standing in front of him.

Without his suit, Luper's shoulders rippled like that of a pacing tiger, even as he rested his own wooden sword on his shoulder. Paul looked to his own skinny, sticklike arms, feeling something close to shame. *I'm outmatched, to say the least.*

"My anima weapon is actually the staff that you may have seen in my office," explained Luper. "I am a bit of a novice when it comes to sword-fighting. When I was a young trainee, like you, my instructor gave me a crash course in fencing and kendo. While both are sports, they are based on real fighting techniques. They should not, however, form your entire basis on your fighting style. Luckily, A.R.C. provides manuals for possible techniques for Amuli with each type of weapon. You can read those later."

Luper lifted his wooden sword upward, letting the sunlight bend around its smooth, polished edges.

"They call these wooden swords *bokken* or sometimes *bakuto* which are different from the *shinai* used for kendo. These bokken are closer in length to your katana, making them a more natural substitute."

This is what Musashi used to defeat Sasaki Kojiro in their duel, Paul thought as he viewed his own wooden weapon. *Even if it isn't sharp, these can still do a lot of damage. It's funny how it seems like everything you learn in school suddenly appears in real life.*

"Technique and improvisation are both key to warrior combat," Luper elaborated just before he went into a full explanation of kendo stances, blocks, and cuts. "Most of your opponents will have superpowers of their own. Anima amplifies your physical strength, and since all Amuli contain about the same amount of anima, training, and exercise is everything when looking for physical skills."

As the moments passed by, the sheer amount of information flowing from Luper began to overwhelm Paul. *I'll never remember all of this, especially all the Japanese names for stances. I guess I'm lucky that there will be no pop quiz coming next... at least... I don't think there will be.*

"Right then," Luper broke off from his instruction abruptly, "let's see what you can do now."

Luper's body slid into the stance known as Jōdan-no-kamae, his sword raised above his head in an aggressive posture. His weight was balanced perfectly on his two feet with his right foot in front and the left placed diagonally behind. Paul stared apprehensively at the raised bokken.

"W-what?"

"A duel," Luper responded calmly. "Right now. We will not use the rules of kendo, only the stances. Whoever lands a hit first scores a point."

"I-I just started... you know... not ready," Paul stammered before giving in. "I... yeah... okay."

No, not okay. Paul could feel blood rushing to his ears, pulsating. His mouth was dry and suddenly yearning for more air. He wanted to take a breath but was afraid that a protest would emerge. *I don't want to do this. Please, let him go easy on me. Please!*

Paul struggled to move his shaking legs into position. His muscles were tight, ready to spring into a run at any moment. They could barely handle the waiting, the anticipation of the possibility of pain coming his way. His wooden sword suddenly felt heavier as he raised it into position. *If I'm remembering right, he is in an aggressive, offensive position. Does that mean that I should go into a more defensive posture?*

The pose that Paul assumed was called Gedan-no-kamae. He held his bokken low, theoretically ready for a strong parry.

115

But his sword is up high. Could I really reach it in time to stop a downward strike? His arms began to move absentmindedly, raising his bokken slightly. *No. I just have to trust it. I'm so new at this... does it even matter what I do at this point?*

After a slight nod, Luper began slowly circling Paul who responded by mirroring his opponent. *Okay, I think I need to find an angle to protect myself. I...*

Then he was on the ground. For a few seconds, that was all Paul knew. It was like waking up disoriented in the middle of the night. In his daze, no thoughts could form. The pain came moments later, jolting his mind back into action. His cheek stung as if the bone was broken and rattling. He brought a hand up to the wound, feeling a sickening wetness where the skin had been broken.

Paul was on his stomach. The force of the blow had spun his body around so he faced away from Luper. *What is this? What the hell is this? Did he rescue me and bring me here to beat me to death?* He dug his fingers into the ground, crawling since his legs felt unsteady. *If I weren't an Amulus, would that have killed me? Was I knocked out for a second? Do I have a concussion?*

His chest began convulsing on its own. His heavy breath came out in a series of quick whimpers. *I have to get out of here!* Paul's panicked mind could not grasp there was nowhere to run. *His kind words... his refined, intelligent way of speaking. Was it all an act? Is he just a psychopath?*

"Get up," ordered Luper coolly. "We are just beginning."

Paul shook his head. "No... no!"

"Your first lesson is pain," Luper's voice was low but held no anger or malice. "Pain and fear. Fighting is a mental game. Pain and fear undermine all your thoughts and actions. You must learn to control them. They cannot be completely blocked out of mind. Only a fool tries to do that. They must be controlled. Now get up. Simply strike me with the bokken, and we shall move on."

Paul shook his head. A grunting noise came from his mouth.

"I said, get up!" Luper repeated, the tall man's calm and defined manner of speaking had disappeared in favor of a seriousness that bordered on ferociousness.

I shouldn't make him angry. What would he do to me then?

Paul struggled to his feet. His armed swayed around him as he put all his effort into standing back up. He resisted the temptation of pressing his hand to his injured cheek to soothe the pain. The sticky drops of blood on his fingers kept them clinging to the wooden sword.

Luper had already shifted his stance. His sword was lower this time, with his arms locked into his position about his midsection in a pose known as Chūdan-no-kamae. This was the balanced stance of kendo. With the sword in a central position, the combatant could attack as quickly as defend.

Maybe he wants me to be aggressive... to overcome the pain. This time, Paul chose a sloppy version of Jōdan-no-kamae. His lightheadedness and the burning of his cheek made it difficult to focus on moving his feet into a well-balanced position. He felt as though his sword was getting heavier and heavier as he raised it slightly above his head. *I need to attack first... to attack quickly. I think that is what he wants me to do for the purpose of this lesson. At least, that's what I'm hoping.*

Paul gave a half-hearted nod, and the two opponents began circling each other again.

Paul sprung forward clumsily, his messy footwork catching up with him. Anima amplified one's physical ability to a superhuman degree. In Paul's case, his anima was only amplifying a body molded by seventeen years of staying away from athletic activities, save gym class. His eyes focused solely on Luper. *I just need to make contact. I just need to hit... somewhere!*

Paul's bokken touched only air. Luper's head had been in the area only a second before. Paul stood dumbfounded for less than a second. A force slammed into his forearms. He dropped his sword and fell to his knees. He could see the straight red marks on his arms before his brain even registered the pain. He cried out and slumped sideways, his eyes heavy with tears.

This isn't a lesson. It's a beatdown! He's trying to humiliate me!

"Get up," Luper repeated.

Paul gasped, his voice breaking, "I–I can't!"

Luper turned away. "Right then."

"I was wrong," Paul wheezed. "There's no way I can be a combat agent. I'm weak. Get it? I can't even stand."

Luper began walking back to the shed. "The next time you encounter an enemy. You'll likely die. Without your insurance as a combat agent, your family could die. Enemies could interrogate and kill anyone you've ever come across. Everyone you've known or everyone you will ever know could be killed by powerful enemies. All of this because that sword chose you and you chose not to wield it."

"How could you say all of that?" Paul spat out his frustration. "What gives you..."

"I've seen it happen before," Luper remarked sadly, "many times."

He's right. I hate it, but he's right. Paul winced. He thought about his aunt, uncle, and Robby. *I'm not even angry at him for what he's saying. It's this whole situation. Why did this stupid sword choose me? And it's not just about me. Everyone I know is a part of this.*

Unbeknownst to Paul, the frost around his feet began to crackle and melt. Anima began to form around his body like a film made of green smoke. He remembered a quote he had read a few days before.

"The Way of the warrior is resolute acceptance of death."

That's what Musashi said in the 'Book of Five Rings.' I have to accept the danger. This is my life now. It's not a question of wanting to do this or not. I'm doing this because I have to!

Luper turned back around to face him. "Ready for the next round?"

Paul nodded, showing his eyes glowing green rather than their usual brown. He made the first move to circle his opponent this time. His form, this time in the balance of Hassō-no-kamae, was still sloppy, although his feet were tensioned and firm. Luper copied his form. The larger man's arms and wooden sword filled up Paul's entire vision. *I have to be able to see him attack this time. I have to track the bokken.*

Suddenly, Paul felt a burst of air. He saw a flash of brown at the corner of his vision. *I see it! I can..."*

The wooden sword walloped him in the ribs. He choked out an involuntary grunt. All the breath left his body, and he was left swaying. *I need to stay up! Just stay... standing!*

Paul willed his legs into staying planted. Choking and sputtering, he regained his breath.

"Next round," called out Luper.

Unlike Paul, there were no signs of heavy breathing nor sweating dripping from his body. It was as if he had simply swung his wooden sword as gently with little effort expended.

Paul chose a new position, Waki-gamae. This time, he held his *bokken* low and behind his body. Though it required more effort and time to bring a sword into attacking or blocking position, this stance was meant to be difficult to predict since the opponent's view of the sword and its path was slightly obscured. Luper chose the defensive posture of Gedan-no-kamae.

The circling began once again.

"Watch for a forward, upward stab. It is the quickest way to reach you in your stance."

Paul was puzzled for a moment. *Why am I predicting that? No, wait... there was a voice.* He realized that the initial thought had been alien. *"Alice, is that you?"*

There was no response.

Forward stab... forward stab. Paul seared the words into his brain, hoping that his arms and legs would react to the command in time. His eyes drifted repeatedly from Luper's *bokken* and to his eyes. The eyes were those of a corpse. There was no tell in them, only a simmering that indicated an intense focus.

Then there it was. Paul could see the blur of the wooden sword taking the plunge forward. *Move! Arms, move!* He had to will his arms upward. It was the right stance. From his

121

defensive position, all he needed was an upward swing to batter the enemy sword up and away from his body. *Move faster!*

Luper's sword appeared to go supersonic, disappearing from Paul's vision. He could not see the sword anymore, but he felt it. The tip pushed into the region between his stomach and ribcage. Paul doubled over, expecting to feel blood trickling from his wounded abdomen as if he had been stabbed with an actual sword. The pain was sharp, and he could feel the vomit forced into his throat from the force of the blow.

I failed, even with Alice's help. It's like I had the answers to the test and still failed.

"I think that's enough," Luper announced, resuming his usual mellow, almost dull, tone. "Go ahead and take a seat there."

"Y-you said... you said..." Paul wheezed. It still felt as though the *bokken* was lodged in his midsection.

"Yes," responded Luper. "That was a bit of misdirection. It was all part of the first test. You can wait here for a moment."

Luper made his way to the shed and then back to Paul in a matter of seconds. His hand now gripped firmly around a first-aid kit.

"The beatings you just received," Luper began, "although painful, should heal in a matter of hours with our powers.

Doing this outside in the cold weather, although uncomfortable, should numb some of the pain. Oh, and remove the shirt, please."

Paul obeyed. His skinny, pale chest was as white as the frost on the ground. Luper began rubbing cool anesthetic cream on his bruises and cuts. *So, he gave me the wounds, and now he's healing them.*

"What you said about building up confidence in battle," Paul asked. "Was that what this was about?"

"It was the key lesson, yes," Luper answered as he finished his work on Paul. "Humans are strange creatures. For instance, if a pet or almost any animal is taken in for a vaccination, it will struggle against the pain of the needle. Whether by trying to run or even trying to bite the veterinarian, it will try to make the pain go away as fast as possible. A human, on the other hand, understands that the pain from the needle is temporary and the benefits of the vaccination will come later. That is what you must learn. Pain, injury, loss, and whatever you will go through can cause this animal reaction, this fight-or-flight. It is true that there will be times to fight and times to flee, but it is your mind that must make that decision and not your body. You will come across painful situations where you must learn to follow orders or to take charge of the situation. Rash, animal-like reactions will hinder your following of missions give to you or even planned by you."

Paul continued to suck in cold air, still trying to catch his breath. *To fight against everything my body is telling me. It's mind over matter. Is that even possible? Especially for someone as soft as me?*

Luper went on. "This next thing, I will not say lightly. There is a reason why desertion and cowardice have been crimes worthy of execution in armies throughout the centuries. That is the ultimate example of instinct getting in the way of discipline. Not to overly worry, but those two crimes are subject to the jurisdiction of the council of A.R.C. Now that you have chosen to stay, you cannot leave without the word of a superior. Of course, your passing of this test shows that you have the initiative to not commit such crimes in the future. That is why the fear in this test needed to be real."

Paul could feel his heart beating in his stomach. *Words with two meanings: congratulations you passed... and don't ever dessert. I'm in this for life now.*

"As with most training," Luper began again, "there were multiple lessons to be learned. Beyond the mental, there was the physical aspect. Anima boosts cognitive abilities to some extent, as well as its effect on the body. Not only will your body move faster, but your mind will move faster, too. The world will slow down for you. Your eyes will pick up movement faster than those of the normal person, and your brain will process it. With this training, you are learning to move like a superhuman and to tract superhuman movements."

Meanings within meanings. But this is crazy. It's basically tricking someone into thinking you are going to beat them to death. Is there justification for that?

Luper slowly stretched one arm with a sigh. "It's time for a slight respite. You will go meet the others now."

Paul stood up slowly, trying not to aggravate his aching body. He wiped some spittle from his lip and some sweat from his forehead.

It's odd, but meeting more strangers seems almost as nerve-racking as sparing with a man that's trying to kill me with a wooden sword. Almost...

Chapter 9: Common Ground

"Coming in," Luper tapped the nondescript door before swinging it open.

Paul, a few steps behind, followed Luper inside the room. Waiting for him was an almost familiar sight.

A classroom?

The front of the room was filled with desks. The yellow overhead lights reflected off the enabled wood. There was even a dusty blackboard complete with small pieces of chalk scattered along its bottom. The back of the room contained a dozen computers resting on tables. Their fans whined noisily.

And a computer lab?

Paul's body gave a slight shudder when he saw that there were two other people in the room. In one corner, near a row of computers, sat Alice. She was leaning forward in her chair, apparently studying the computer screen, and giving no indication that she noticed the two new arrivals in the room. Another girl sat midway through the series of desks. A wavy, glossy black ponytail cascaded down her back, swinging playfully as she cocked her head to greet Luper and Paul with a polite nod.

She's the girl with the purple mask from the other night... I think.

Luper surveyed the room for a moment. "Where's Jason?"

"I think he said that he had to do some training," the dark-haired girl answered.

Luper sighed. "Jason, when it comes to fulfilling the mission, he will put all the effort that is required and much more. When it comes to anything else..."

The tall, suited man pressed a button next to the chalkboard before speaking flatly into a set of holes in the wall. "Jason, come to the classroom."

Moments later, a boy about Paul's age slid through the door. He wore an off-white shirt speckled with droplets of sweat on the chest. His lean, muscled arms swayed confidently as he made his way to the back of the room, eschewing a chair for a wall to lean against. A long strand of black hair rested above his eyes, which were downcast on the floor.

The guy with the spiral fencing mask. The one who... cut that red-haired man apart. Paul gulped.

"Alright," Luper began, "since we have a new member

staying here, I figured that it was time for some brief intro-ductions. Just state your name, age, where you come from, hobbies, ambition, and whatever else you want to say."

Luper's tone struck Paul as similar to a teacher who had already lost their enthusiasm on the first day of school. The faux educator gave a sideways glance at Paul to indicate that he should speak first.

"I'm Paul... Paul Engel," he coughed. "I'm seventeen. I'm from Palisville, the... um... place near here. Uh... hobbies. Well, I read and play video games. As far as ambitions... I don't think I ever had any. I kind of wanted to be a teacher someday... before all this. My uncle had a software startup. I also sort of thought I'd work for him."

Paul let out an internal sigh. *Am I really as pathetic as the way I just sounded?*

The olive-skinned girl seated at the desk was the next to speak.

"Hi, I'm Camilla Bellano, from Queens. You can call me Cam. I am eighteen and, well, I watch a lot of movies and read a lot of magazines. Someday, I think I want to work in the search and rescue division of A.R.C. I just kind of want to help people."

Despite the pleasantness of Camilla's tone, Paul stiffened. *She seems nice enough, but is there room for niceness in this type of business?*

There was a pause as the final two occupants of the room gave no sign that they wished to speak.

"Very well," Luper exhaled. "Alice, you can go next. You have already encountered Paul after all."

Alice's eyes left the wall to stare straight into Paul's own. "Name: Alice. Age: sixteen Hobbies: none. Ambitions: none. Home: this current location."

If Luper was displeased by Alice's abrupt answers, he gave no sign. In Paul's case, they shook his body with icy shivers. It was as if her stare was made of pure ice. The only reprieve from the snowstorm was a hint of sadness. There, behind the cold, Paul could find a sense of sympathy. Realizing that his vision was still locked on the blonde girl in the corner, he abruptly ended the accidental staring contest. He could feel a warmth welling in his cheeks.

Luper waved a hand to the other far corner of the room. "Lastly, we have Jason."

Begrudgingly, the teenager lifted his head to face Paul and Luper.

"Jason Saito," the young man introduced himself gruffly. "Look, there's only one thing that you need to know about me. I'm going to kill as many A.I.M. operatives and Dead Eyes as possible. I'm going to do that until I've taken down the entire organization or died in the process. Now, you can help me do that or stay out of my way. I really don't care what you do here. Just don't get in the way."

The intense, dark brown eyes switched focus from Paul to Luper.

"Am I free to return to training?" Jason asked almost obediently.

"Sure," Luper nodded.

Paul was left wide-eyed as Jason exited the room without another word.

"He's... um," Camilla started to explain, "he's not really as bad as that sounded. He's just had it pretty rough, or at least, that's what Luper has told us, right?"

"Indeed," Luper responded, running a hand through his beard. "Although, I would ask you to refrain from speaking about the contents of files on other operatives or any information that I have... uh... provided from them for personal reasons."

"Sorry, Luper," Camilla apologized with mock sweetness. "You know I'm always one to follow the rules. I'm sure you've read that in my file."

Luper gave a slight smirk. "Right then, Paul, now that you have met your new... enthusiastic companions. It's time to move to the next step of settling in."

* * *

Now, I'm worried about schoolwork. Paul strummed the side of a cabinet with a nervous, shaking finger. *This is surreal.*

The next step that Luper had mentioned was an oddly familiar one. He spent that last few hours taking baseline tests so that the educational branch of A.R.C. could gauge his intelligence in order to set up a schooling plan for him. According to Luper, a school-age teenager's education did not end just because they had been pulled out of the world and put into a secretive organization. To be a good operative, one had to be well-rounded with knowledge of the world, from mathematics and physics to history, culture, and languages.

School is something that I've always been good at, but with this whole situation, will I still be good at it? What is it even going to be like? Paul pondered as he scoured the kitchen for rations. They were not true rations in the military sense, but Luper said that was their nickname. In truth, they were carefully proportioned, highly nutritious meals said to ensure that A.R.C. operative could remain in peak physical condition. The rumored taste, however, was known to be less than pleasant.

My stomach is still doing backflips. I need something light... something light... His hand stumbled across a can of tomato soup.

"Oh no, you don't want the tomato soup," a voice interjected thoughtfully. Camilla strode into the room with her ponytail whipping side-to-side. "That's unless you like huge tomato chunks. I'd go with the chicken noodle soup. It's much harder for them to mess up."

Paul nodded and pulled a can of chicken noodle from the shelf. "Um uh... thanks for the advice."

"So, was your first drill as painful as it usually is?" Camilla asked as she too selected a container of the same soup.

"Uh, yeah," Paul murmured, unsure if it was wise to say anything negative about A.R.C. or anyone involved in it. "Luper had me fight against him with a wooden sword. It, well, didn't go very well for me."

"The first test is the same for everyone," Camilla explained. "Luper beats you up to see if you can take it. He used a pellet gun on me. It fired slow enough to make it through the anima barrier, but it was fast enough to really hurt. He means well, I think. He's a... warmer guy than he seems at first."

"That's good," Paul mumbled quietly as he looked into the pot of bubbling yellow broth.

"So, your anima weapon is a sword?" Camilla inquired with what seemed to Paul as genuine curiosity.

"Yeah," Paul answered. "It's a *katana*, a samurai sword."

"Sounds interesting, I've seen a few old samurai movies. Not really my thing, but cool, nonetheless. Jason has a sword too, a saber. Luper has a staff, and believe me, he uses that thing like its more than a hunk of wood. Alice has her necklace which has a gold crystal which seems pretty rare. I've never seen another one in that color."

Camilla tapped a holster on her hip. "I got this after going to a wild west expedition on a field trip for school. A Colt .45 made during the last era of anima weapons, apparently. After that, people stopped finding anima crystals. It's ironic. Before this, I had never touched a gun in my life. Now, my life is forever tied to one. I'm a New York City cowgirl, I guess."

Paul could only nod as he scooped some soup into a bowl. No words and no emotions came to him. His mind still felt too cloudy and confused about such things. *She's being nice to me. I should say more, but I don't know what to say. It's like I never do.*

"You're really not one for conversation, are you?" Camilla questioned as if reading his mind.

Paul shook his head. "I'm not so good with that type of thing. I never have been. Plus, with what's happening to me now... it's a little overwhelming."

"Or, a lot overwhelming," agreed Camilla. "Look, if you haven't noticed yet, no one else here likes to talk very much either—except for me. You'll fit right in. It's actually nice to not be the newest one here anymore. I think the others might be the way they are because they've been in this for so long. This kind of stuff sticks to you."

Try to make conversation, try to make conversation.

"How long have you been here... or in A.R.C.?" Paul asked in a raspy voice.

"Those are actually two different questions for me. I've been in A.R.C. for two years and been at this outpost for about one year."

Thinking of time in A.R.C. in terms of years is going to take some getting used to. Membership is for life.

"You... uh... alright there?" Camilla wondered as she tried to get a read on his face. "You look a little pale."

"Yeah," Paul answered as he broke eye contact and scratched the back of his neck. "It's just weird being locked away from everything down here. It definitely feels claustrophobic."

"Like I meant before, that's pretty understandable. You know, we do get to go outside sometimes as long as Luper clears it. That helps a little. Sometimes we do training out there like you just did. Despite what A.R.C. puts us through, they know going days without sunlight isn't good for anyone."

Paul felt the conversation moving toward another awkward pause. That was something that he was used to but never comfortable with.

"You're actually from pretty close to here, right?" Camilla continued curiously. "It's lucky for you that you're in familiar surroundings. I felt so out-of-place when I first came here. So many trees. I mean, the whole area is forest except for a few towns. Nothing like New York. I mean everything looks like a scene from that old movie *Deliverance.*"

Paul gave a slight smirk.

"Oh!" exclaimed Camilla as her tone changed from friendly to cautionary. "I should have mentioned this when we were talking about anima weapons, but Luper usually orders us to have our weapons on us at all times. I don't think he would be angry at you though since it is your first day. That, and I don't think he ever gets truly angry... just annoyed at times. I think he gets more upset at the A.R.C. hierarchy than anyone here. Anyway, where is your sword now?"

"It's um," an electric shock of worry ran along Paul's spine as he tried to remember where he left the *katana,* "it's in the infirmary, I think."

Paul sprang out of his chair. *I can't make anyone mad at me. Not on the first day!* With his arms pumping, he half-ran, half-walked out of the kitchen.

"Paul, what about your soup?" Camilla reminded in vain as Paul's ears had shut out all sound, save for the inner voice of worry.

Chapter 10: Unseen

Everything hurts.

That was first thought Paul had when he woke up in the morning and the last thought he had before he fell asleep at night. The process had repeated itself almost every day for the past three weeks. According to Luper, he needed to build a foundation for his anima powers. Like those of any human, an Amulus's strength and endurance could be increased through exercise.

Why didn't I play any sports? Paul had to swing his legs over his bed with his arms. *I could have at least gone to the gym or ran on the track before all this. Robby would have taken me running with him if I had asked.*

After switching off his buzzing alarm clock, he surveyed his small, sparse room as his eyes adjusted to the overhead light. There was a bed, a chair, a dresser, and doors to the bathroom and hallway. The walls were pure, bleached white. With the light on, they gave off an eerie glow. The room screamed blankness. It was not as if he could go shopping to decorate it. His room at home had its walls covered by colorful comic and video game posters.

No, don't think about home.

Paul stumbled out the door after a short shower and a change of clothes. The gym was always the first thing, followed by an hour of running on the treadmill. The workout equipment found in the bunker shamed the machines found in most gymnasiums throughout the world. It was not the number of noteworthy machines, rather, it was their quality. Treadmills reached speeds that even Olympians would not have dreamed of. The weights would have stumped even the brawniest person. An hour of running on a normal treadmill would have been no problem for Paul after his awakening. However, the treadmills in the bunker gym reached automobile speeds rather than human speeds.

The teenager resisted the temptation of rubbing his tight calves after he pushed his door closed. Head down, he trudged down the hallway.

"Do you wish to switch rooms to me? My room is more spacious than yours. I do not need much space. Perhaps you would enjoy a larger room?"

If Paul had taken another step, he would have run straight into Alice. She had appeared without the sound of even a footstep. *And I wasn't paying attention. Like always.*

"Um, no thanks, Alice," Paul croaked, still trying to find his voice this morning. "It's okay. I really don't mind the small room either."

It's not like I have anything to fill it with.

Alice continued in her usual monotone. "Very well. Luper would like to see you in his office."

The girl left him without another word. She always reminded Paul of an iceberg, cold and icy on the surface with something else lurking below. He had decided to never take offense to her frosty demeanor. In his mind, his own social skills were not much better. The two were "acquittances," after all. *I think that's only the third or fourth time she's spoken to me during my time here.*

Paul's heart became weighed down by dread as he knocked on Luper's door. *The only thing worse than being sore and exhausted is being yelled at. Plus, there's the anticipation of being yelled at. Did I do anything wrong? Am I just an overall disappointment?*

Luper was hunched over a report, a bundle of papers that had come close to bursting its staple. He was always reading reports. Between that and his training, Paul wondered when his mentor slept. *Does anima also increase the ability to go without sleep? Judging by the way I feel, it doesn't. Luper does always look tired. Although you wouldn't know that when you fought him.*

"How are you feeling today, Paul?" a voice called out from behind the mound of papers.

"Fine," Paul muttered.

"Really?" questioned Luper his hid slid some papers to the side. "That would be quite something if you were, in fact, feeling 'fine.' I suppose that would be acceptable in most social situations. People tend to not expect in answer other than 'fine,' 'well,' or 'good.' In this case, I want an honest answer. A leader can only make the best decisions about the personnel under them if they know their exact mindset and physical condition. So, Paul, how are you feeling?"

"Sore and tired."

"I supposed that is a good thing, in a way. It means that the training is affecting you and your muscles are adapting. Just as long as it isn't anything too severe. Is it?"

It feels that way. "No."

"Good. Let me know if it ever becomes unbearable, whether because of the pain in the physical or mental aspect of it all," Luper added. "You may be glad to learn that you will be getting a bit of a reprieve from your usual training schedule today."

Luper dug out a blue-colored cardboard box from underneath his desk. "It may surprise you, but I do have a weakness. I actually have a bit of a sweet-tooth."

Paul's brow ruffled in surprise. *This wasn't what I expected when I walked in here.*

"I have a weakness to a certain brand of snack cakes. You probably know the ones. The small, chocolate-covered cakes with peanut butter inside. Those Kandy Cakes are truly one of the world's great foods. Needless to say, they are not provided to us here in are A.R.C. rations. As such, I need you to go shopping for me."

"Shopping?" Paul blurted. *Is this a prank? Luper admitted to having a bad sense of humor.*

Luper's face retained its usual sleepy expression. "This is not just shopping but a mission. A stealth mission for which I am authorizing you to go out in public in a limited capacity."

This must be why Luper went over stealth tactics with me yesterday. But how is stealth involved in shopping?

"For this special shopping trip," began Luper as he put away the snack cake-decorated box, "you will be visiting a country store several miles from here that is frequented by hunters. Lucky for me, they carry this particular brand of sweets."

"So, that's it?" wondered Paul, trying to keep incredulousness out of his tone. "I just have to buy Kandy Cakes."

"No," replied Luper. "I've decided to make this task a little more complicated. You are to complete this whole transaction without being seen. Simply enter the building, acquire the package of Kandy Cakes, leave the exact cash on the counter, and leave. It is your job to find a way to do this. You needn't worry about anti-theft sensors or R.F.I.D. tags in this store. It is far too small an operation for such things. Food items are not always prepared for anti-theft measures, anyway."

Paul gulped. *So, this is my first training mission. How am I going to get in and out of the building without anyone seeing me?*

Luper continued his instructions. "If you are caught, it is likely that you will be seen as a shoplifter or robber by the clerk and any customers. There are a few things that could happen after that. The first and most drastic would be that the occupants of the store would draw their guns on you. Judging by the location of this place, I am sure that there will be people with guns there. Your anima barrier should dissipate any bullets coming your way as long as the shots do not come from point-blank range. It is also possible that the clerk would call the police or ask for your parents' number. In the instance of the former, A.R.C.'s friends in the government can have you released from jail without issue. Simply call the number that I will provide you. If the clerk or police would wish to speak with your parents, provide them with the same number. It will connect them with me, and I will do my best to pretend to be your disappointed parent. The potential awkwardness of that outcome should be a motivator for you."

Paul gulped. *If things go wrong, I could be shot at or arrested. Before being in A.R.C., I never thought I'd have to go through either of those things.* He could imagine the sound of shots ringing in his ears and bullets whizzing by him. He could feel the cold, metal handcuffs around his wrists.

"Your exercise for the day will be your trek to and from the country store," Luper clarified to Paul's dismay. "There are no roads between here and its location but be sure to use your stealth skills should you come upon anyone in the woods. I will accompany you for a short time to show you the way. Your only supplies will be your custom backpack with your sword hidden inside. You may leave your obi here. Having an openly displayed sword does not suite this mission. However, your katana may only be used as a tool for this mission instead of a weapon. Anyone you may come across at the country store is an innocent bystander in this test. I will not have any innocents harmed under my watch."

Paul undid the traditional *obi* belt that Luper had provided him for strapping the katana to his body. It took a minute longer than it should have as the young man struggled to gain control over his shaking and sweaty hands.

* * *

Paul exhaled hard into his collar to warm up his face. Little streams of mists escaped the soothing cotton. His quick movements slinking through mazes of trees and roots had warmed his sore muscles enough that he no longer resembled a machine in need of oil. A second of immobility caused them to tighten once again. Just running outside with his newfound powers was a new, exhilarating experience. The frosty ground seemed to move faster underneath him. His feet felt lighter, despite any of his leg soreness. If he had attempted a leap, he knew that would have reached halfway up most of the trees. *I feel like Superman!*

The only thing to hinder his joy was the anticipation of the mission, blotting out his confidence. *Luper said that I would be at the store in fifteen minutes as long as I moved in this direction. I must be getting close. I wonder how he calculated that time.*

The rectangular shape of a stained wooden wall slowly emerged at the edge of the curtains of branches. Beyond it was an aged, gray road ringed by gravel. Paul crouched underneath a thick pine tree. *I need to scout this place out.*

From his viewpoint behind the store, he could make out a parking lot, an offshoot of gravel containing four spots, and occupied by one pickup truck. *One truck probably means one person, a clerk or manager. I just have one set of eyes to avoid. It's the middle of a weekday, so I didn't expect this place to be crowded. Oh, wait! What about hunting season? Isn't that around this time of year? That place definitely seems like it would be a stop for hunters.*

He approached the building slowly, looking for windows and being careful to only look at them through a tight angle so as not to be seen on the inside. There were small runs of windows on either side. The young Amulus suspected that there were much larger windows at the storefront. *I need to scope out the entire building, but those large windows would be a risk. It's a slow day, so the store worker may be staring off into the woods.*

Paul chose to take a wide arc around the store and over the road to avoid a direct line of vision from the windows, his torso leaning low over his striding legs. *Luper said to make myself small.* Past the pavement, he slid down a short incline before peaking his head above it. As he had suspected, two large windows and a glass door loomed before him. *It's like someone cut off the front of their log cabin and turned it into a store.* He had a decent view of the inside of the store. The counter was set up towards the right side of the interior. With his enhanced vision, he could make out the figure behind the counter, a middle-aged man in red flannel, and a tan baseball cap who was slightly obscured by a stack of boxes. *I need to find a way in. The windows on the sides look like they open, and I could fit inside. But how could I do that without being seen?*

Paul slinked over to the windows underneath the left side of the building. He hoisted upward on a window as hard as he dared. It didn't budge. *Locked! Of course, why wouldn't it be? It's November! I could push it until the latch would break, but that could be noisy. I need another way.* Flustered, he looked over the building again. This time, he noticed another feature that appeared alien on a building that was otherwise a log cabin. A ventilation system had obviously been added later. It ran along the back and roof of the building like a metal snake. *I might be able to fit in there, too.*

A group of overhanging trees gave him a way onto the roof. The strength of his grip made the climb up the trunk and thick branches easy. He swung onto the wooden roof with a thud, praying that the sound mimicked that of a falling branch to anyone inside. The steep slant of the roof made Paul scurry to its peak on all fours. There, he found a metal grate covering a still fan. *How do I open it? Breaking it would cause too much noise. Plus, it's not fair to the store owner. This is just a test. I don't want to destroy someone's property.* He ran his fingers along the screws holding the grate to the ventilation system before giving one a sharp twist. His fingers slid around it. *I have the power, but not the leverage. The screw hole is large enough...*

Paul opened his backpack and undid the fastening around its secret compartment. *This feels almost sacrilegious, using a katana this way.* Looking at the end of the curved sword tip, he saw that the edge was so sharp that it seemed to fade to nothing at its end. *I apologize to the swordsmith who made this.* He stuck the sword edge into the screw and gave it a twist. *Not too hard. This anima weapon is so strong that it could break anything if I'm not careful.* Mercifully, only the screw gave way after a yank. He did the same to each screw on the grate and then the fan. It was slow work, but he was sure that it was the quietest. After he was almost sure that hours had passed, the fan was ready to be removed. *My boots may make a clanking noise in the metal tube.* He decided to remove them before returning the sword to his backpack along with a handful of screws. *I really hope that those don't slide off the roof.*

He left his socks on to prevent from leaving prints. Warm, black gloves already covered his hands for the same purpose and for protecting them from the biting November cold. Despite his lack of ever having a criminal record and all of his other public records being destroyed upon his enlisting in A.R.C., the lesson of never leaving a trace had been drilled into Paul in the past few weeks. Luper had taught him that anything that could be linked to an agent could be used to track and corner them, their comrades, their family, or the entire organization. Agents could not allow outsiders to know where they had been or what they had been doing. *Luper said that intel can be everything.*

As he had suspected, the ventilation system was a tight fit with the backpack. He had just enough room to shimmy his way through with an army crawl. Following a slight dip into the building, Paul found himself faced with a dirty air filter. He squeezed his nose as hard as possible to prevent a sneeze from escaping. Slowly and blindly, he fumbled through the pack on his pack to find the katana again. Another set of screws was removed, and now Paul found himself pushing the filter before him. There was no room to slide it behind or beside him.

After inching his way along as soundlessly as possible, Paul found another grate and nonmoving fan. Through it, he saw stacks of boxes and bags containing food and ammunition, coat racks smothered by camouflage jackets, and an assortment of fishing poles. *That is an excessive amount of jerky. No, don't focus on stupid things. My mind has to be on the mission only. But if I get caught, there's no way he won't pull a gun on me. With all that ammo, he has to be armed!* Paul forced himself to take a deep breath. It quieted his throbbing heart enough for him to continue.

The young Amulus's eyes darted around each part of the room

that he could see. He located Luper's Kandy Cakes in an aisle close to the counter. *Now, I need to find a way down without being seen. Even if my landing is as quiet as possible, there is no way the clerk won't notice me falling out of the ceiling, even if I'm on the other side of the store from him. I need... a distraction.* No specifics came to his mind. *Luper told me to use what's around me on missions. Use the landscape. Use what's available. But I'm in the ventilation system of a tiny store in the middle of a forest. There's nothing around me but trees, birds, chipmunks, squirrels. Wait. If I drop an intimate object out of this shaft, it will land in place, create noise, and the worker will come over and look up at where it fell from. A rodent, though, may hit the floor without a sound and may scurry around the store before he notices. While he stops to catch it, I have a window to grab the snacks and drop the cash on the counter. That's as long as I'm silent.*

Paul wormed his way back up the ventilation system. *This plan is crazy!* The thought repeated in his head a hundred times over the next few minutes. As he emerged back on the roof, he used his anima-enhanced eyes to scan the area for little furry animals. *Squirrels are bigger than chipmunks and that big bushy tail the clerk should notice one in the store. I just pray that he doesn't see its fall from the ventilation system. It would ruin the plan, but I would be able to hide in the ventilation system without the clerk seeing me. That way, I wouldn't be caught, but I would need a new plan.*

His ears picked up a chattering on a nearby branch. A gray squirrel stared at him with beady, black eyes, and an acorn in his mouth. He recalled that squirrels mostly stayed in their burrows during the coldest months of the year. *I guess I'm lucky that it's not full-blown winter yet.*

Paul leaped onto the branch, grabbing the squirrel in one motion. It was still for a moment in his grasp as if in shock. After a few seconds, Paul could feel its furry hide squirming against his palm and it paws jabbing away at his palm and wrist. He kept its head in place between his thumb and index finger to prevent it from biting him. *I don't blame the poor thing.*

Another jump took Paul back to the roof and the ventilation system. He slid back into the metal rectangle with the squirrel like a snake with its prey. In the tunnel, the squirrel's tail tickled his face as its tiny claws dug into his skin. *I miscalculated how sharp its claws are. If my body weren't superhuman, it would have completely torn up my arm.*

After a short journey, the two came to the opening in the store ceiling. *I really hope that it doesn't get hurt. The clerk isn't going to shoot at a little squirrel inside and risk damaging the store. Although, people do hunt and eat squirrels sometimes. I'm hoping that he just shepherds it out the door.* He let the squirrel fall.

Paul prayed silently. *Please, don't see it fall. Please, don't see it until it starts running around the store.* As he had hoped, there were a few seconds of silence. Then, there was the crash of a stack of boxes.

"What the... aw... how did you get in here?"

The clerk trudged over to the section of fallen boxes. "Where are yah?"

Paul resisted the desire to raise a fist in the air. *Perfect!* He undid the screws around the fan before removing it and swinging his legs over the opening. *Land without a sound. Please, let me land without a sound.* He let himself fall.

The ground came up hard against the balls of his feet. He stayed balance and ducked low behind a line of shelves decorated by bags of beef jerky. The clerk gave no sign that he had seen or heard him as he waded through a pile of overturned boxes.

"Hey, Lou! Lou, you get yer butt out here and bring a broom!"

Paul felt his blood freeze. Time was still and held him in place. *Another worker. I'm so stupid! One truck doesn't have to mean one person!* Suddenly, time began moving too fast. The door at the back of the store and a man in head-to-toe camo trudged out. Paul's legs lifted him through the air and behind a coat rack almost without his volition. He could feel the blood surging through his veins faster than ever before. In a second of clarity, he realized that he was between the two men and the counter. A stack of Kandy Cakes sat just feet in front of the register. *I just need to keep out of sight as I complete the mission.* Through a veil of camouflage jackets, he could see the two men moving around the store.

"Another squirrel," complained the man in flannel. "I told yah to fix up that backdoor. You could drive a truck underneath it."

"Did yah really need to call me out for this?" moaned the larger man in camo. " A lil' squirrel got yah beat? And for your information, the door sits level now. I thought sumpin' important happened. Like with that poltergeist again."

"No such thing as ghosts or polter-whatevers."

"Then, how do yah explain all the weird stuff that always goes on here?"

"My explanation is an idiot brother who never fixes things he's told to fix!"

A glimpse of the squirrel sent the men back into motion. *Turn away! Turn away! Yes!* Paul grabbed a box of Kandy Cakes as he scrounged the money out of his pocket. The entire time, his eyes were trained on the two brothers. The second he had the last coin in his hand, they turned back his way, sending him diving behind the coats again. *I could through the change at the counter, but the coins would clatter. The paper money may not even make it there.*

A glimpse of pure white caught his attention. Just off to his side, Paul saw a stack of envelopes for sale. With his focus still on the two men, Paul stretched his arm out from his position and felt for an envelope. *With a good throw, I can hit the counter as I make my escape. I just need a way out.* He thought of simply backing out through the door, but noticed a bell strapped to the doorframe. *If I can make the jump, I can go out the way I came in.*

As Paul contemplated his retreat, the man in flannel came stepped closer to his coat rack. *He's getting too close! But how do I stop him?* He remembered his recent anima training with Luper. Anima manifested itself differently from each Amuli. For Alice, it came from her body like circular orbs. Paul's own anima tended to pour from him like a stream of fire. Luper had taught him to control its density as he projected it, whether with his sword or body. *I need to knock something over to distract him without completely destroying whatever that something is.* The difficulty of this task was why he had gone a different route in dropping the squirrel into the store as a distraction. Paul eyed another coat rack and outstretched his hand toward. *Push it. Don't burn it.*

A small burst of barely visible green haze surged into the rack, spilling more camouflage coats on the floor. The clerk changed his course away from Paul.

"Did the squirrel knock this big thing over? What the... this one coat looks kinda burnt. What happened here?"

The man in forest camo shook his head. "Don't know. You were the one out here all day. I was just cleanin' the bathroom. Poltergeist again, I bet."

"Yeah, well, you can take yer poltergeist and shove it."

Now, move away from the ventilation. Just keep moving, both of you. After Lou cleared the aisle, Paul moved to position himself underneath the ventilation system shaft. *The envelope will make a sound when it hits the counter. I need to make sure that they won't be able to trace the path after it flies from my hand.* He took a breath. The ceiling in the store was relatively low, maybe about fifteen feet. At this moment, it looked to Paul like a fifty-foot jump. *If I miss the opening, they will definitely catch me making a fool of myself.*

Paul buckled his legs and then sprang. Grabbing the metal frame, he pulled in his legs to reduce his visibility. He let the arm holding the envelope dangle before giving the money a toss. Spurred on by the weight of the coins, the envelope lightly slapped the counter just as Paul finished pulling the rest of his body inside the vent.

"What was that noise?" the man in the flannel pondered.

"Poltergeist," Lou replied. "I keep on tellin' yah there's a poltergeist here, Frank. You've seen the movies!"

Paul caught the end of the conversation as he crawled out of the shaft onto the roof. *I'm done!* For the first time this day, a breeze of confidence rushed through him. The next thing he knew, his body had led him back down a tree. The ground felt oddly cold on his feet. *My boots! Stupid! Stupid! I can't afford to forget anything. I have to cover my tracks.* Cursing his overconfidence, he returned to the roof to retrieve his shoes. He also decided to put the fans, filter, and grates back into place. *I need to be thorough.*

As he fled back into the woods, he thought he saw a glimpse

of a small, furry creature being shooed out of the store's door with an old broom.

Chapter 11: The Red Saber

"Not the most straightforward plan, but it was successful, nonetheless. That is what truly matters in this instance. The holes in the plan tell me that your report, which was well written, by the way, is truthful."

With that, Luper ended his assessment of Paul's first training mission and his subsequent report. Paul had been in frozen suspense as his superior's eyes ran over the stack of his papers. *I can't stand writing about myself. It always feels like I'm being too congratulatory or showing false modesty.*

Luper undid the seal on the package of Kandy Cakes before tossing one to Paul. "For your efforts, you may take a well-earned lunch."

As the teenager approached the door, Luper interrupted. "Perhaps, Jason can show you how to use your sword for more than being a screwdriver. His swordsmanship greatly surpasses my own. He may be a valuable teacher and training partner for you."

Paul made slow progress to the kitchen. His feet were

hindered by doubts. *He wants me to approach Jason. I don't think there is anyone here who wants less to do with me.*

The unsure Amulus stepped into the kitchen with his head down.

"It's a party now."

Paul lifted his head to find the room filled with his young comrades. Camilla, Alice, and Jason were already eating. Only Camilla had looked up from her food to greet him. *This is a first. I don't think we've ever had all our meals together at the same time.* Rather than seeing this as a chance for comradery, the thought of more awkward social interactions chilled him.

"So, you completed Luper's first mission," noticed Camilla, "which means you've met Frank and Lou."

Paul nodded as he reached for a container of what was labeled "sweet and sour" chicken from the fridge. He gave it a sniff and decided that the scent was familiar enough.

"How'd you do it?" asked Camilla.

Paul relayed his story quickly.

"That poor squirrel!" exclaimed Camilla. "You're sure that it got out okay?"

"Yeah, I think I saw it coming out of the store."

"Well, your strategy was... interesting," Camilla complimented. "I did things a little differently. I just blasted tree branches down around the store and on the roof until both guys came running out. I think they thought it was just high winds. With them out, I just dropped the cash and left with the stuff."

Paul fought the need to slap himself. "That was a much better plan than mine." *It should have been that simple. That easy!*

"What did you do again, Jason?" Camilla questioned after swallowing a bite of a chicken wrap.

"I broke into their truck and pushed it in front of the store," he answered bluntly. "A strategy like yours."

He talked about breaking into someone's property like it was nothing. Will I ever have to do something like that?

"What about you, Alice?" Camilla asked, trying to hold the conversation together.

"Luper did not assign me any training missions," the blonde girl replied without looking up from the protein bar on her plate. "He decided that my prior work was enough validation of my preparedness to supersede such exercises."

I thought we were all here to train. If Alice isn't here for that, then why is she here? Is she too young to be a full-fledged agent? Isn't there an age restriction for that?

Camilla finally gave up on any hope of pleasant small talk.

Jason took one last gulp of food before dropping his Styrofoam container in the trash can.

"J-Jason," Paul sputtered quickly before Jason could exit the room. "Um... Luper said that you may be able to teach me about swordsmanship."

"Do you want me to teach you about *katanas* because I'm Japanese?" Jason spoke with his back to Paul."

"Oh, n-no!" Paul stuttered as he launched into an apology. "I'm really sorry. That's not it at all. I mean... Luper just said..."

"Relax, it was a joke," but there was no hint of humor in the stoic Amulus's voice.

"Does that mean you'll help me?" Paul asked hopefully.

Jason's back remained turned as he reached for the door. "Did Luper order it?"

"I don't think it has an order. He kind of just suggested it."

"Then, no," Jason called back as he left the room.

Paul slid back into his seat. *Was it the way I asked him? My tongue always feels twice as long as it should be when I have to speak in a potentially awkward conversation.*

"Are you going to keep after him?" wondered Camilla.

I actually didn't even consider that. Paul shrugged.

"Jason tends to only respond to people he thinks are... strong, I guess," Camilla pointed out. "Maybe that's not the right word. It's like he has to see someone's commitment to A.R.C. It's how he judges people. I don't think he ever even spoke to me until he saw my shooting accuracy get better. If I were you, I'd train in front of him. If you show your swords skills to him, maybe he'll give you some pointers. What do you think, Alice? You've been around Jason longer than I have."

"I agree," Alice stated in-between sips of water. "I believe he often exercises in the training room in the far west training room of the bunker."

"There you go," Camilla slowly nodded at Paul.

Paul suppressed a sigh. *I would rather avoid Jason completely after a rejection like that. But now, Camilla and even Alice are on me about this, too.*

* * *

The western training room was filled with stiff, cold air. As far as Paul knew, Jason was the only one who was ever in here. Everyone else used the other two training rooms. *I wonder if he took what Luper says about the cold numbing the body to pain.* Paul suppressed a shiver when he saw rows of training dummy eyes staring at him. He felt almost guilty as he took a swing at one with a bokken. His feet slid more than he had intended on the smooth floor. *This looks like the combat training room, except that the floor is hard instead of padded. It would hurt to experience one of Luper's ju-jitsu throws here.*

If Jason was surprised to see Paul in his training space, he gave no indication. The teenager with the perpetually sullen face opened a stuffed duffel bag and slid out some of its contents. Out of the corner of his eye, Paul could see Jason take out a fencing saber and give it a few practice swings. The whooshing sword cut through the cold air. Paul noticed that there was no give or wiggle in the dull blade. Unlike an ordinary fencing weapon, it was thick enough to cause injury, at least to an ordinary human.

As he practiced his own cuts, Paul could hear the rushing of air around Jason's blade as it rapped against a dummy again and again. *Right, I have to impress him now. But can I really do that?*

Paul began to focus on varying the angles of his cuts while alternating between stances. He tried to swing harder with every slash, attempting to match Jason's pace. His feet became caught in the wrong position several times. Remembering the exact position of every stance became too much as his speed increased. After a few minutes, he could feel a trickle of sweat running down his chest. He paused to catch his breath.

The dummy stared back at him, unflinchingly. Luper had told him that these dummies, along with all the training equipment, were built with Amuli in mind. Their durability was far beyond what one could find at a normal gym. Still, Paul found it almost disheartening that he hadn't made any dents in the skin-colored material.

"I know what you're trying to do," Jason stated sharply

In the moment of catching his breath, Paul had forgotten his purpose for training here. "Doing what?"

"Look, just get it out of your head that I'm going to train you," Jason warned after he took a sip from a water bottle. "I'm not here for that."

This is embarrassing now. Obviously, he sees that I'm not good at this. I should just leave. Paul's thoughts did a doubletake. *Would it be more embarrassing to admit to everyone else here that Jason knows I'm not worth it?*

"Look, I'm just trying to survive here," Paul spoke before his thoughts could keep with his mouth. His own blunt honesty surprised him. "I want to get through life at A.R.C. by being strong enough to not get killed out in the field. I don't want to die, and I want to give my family as much A.R.C. protection as they can get. I know that I'd die in a real battle in a second. I want to train to survive, but I don't know how."

"I'll stop you there," Jason interjected bluntly. "When you fight someone, you do it to win. You don't just try to survive.

You fight to kill your opponent. If you don't do that, you'll be the one who ends up dead."

"The primary thing when you take a sword in your hands is your intention to cut the enemy, whatever the means... If you think only of hitting, springing, striking or touching the enemy, you will not be able actually to cut him." That's what Musashi said. The intent has to be there. If the mind is there, the body will follow. Still... the killing part...

Jason sighed. "I guess I can't have a team member looking this pathetic all the time though. I just can't see why I have to be the one to train you."

Is he saying that he'll train me? It's hard to tell with the insult.

"We'll do this Luper's way," Jason continued. "If you can hit me in a practice match, then I'll train you, at least a little."

Any relief that Paul had felt a moment before was gone. *Another test. Pass or fail. I think I know how this will go.*

Paul drummed up the courage to ask a question. "How many rounds will we go?"

"We'll go until I think we've wasted too much time," the black-haired boy said flatly. "Now, it's your bokken versus my training saber."

Jason reached into his bag to pull out another saber. Paul noticed with a shiver that the one Jason had been using before was dented. Several slices of the practice dummy that he had been working on were missing as well. Paul gulped as Jason dug through his bag to find another practice saber. There was a hint of red light as Jason's anima saber slipped out of the bag for a moment. Paul's eyes were drawn to the ruby red crystal embedded in the guard of the sheathed sword.

His mind wandered, and he felt spaced out. It was like he was leaving the room.

~ ~ ~

The living room was poorly lit and musky. There was a dusty coach with stuffy blankets piled on the back. Knickknacks and little porcelain animals covered a couple of end tables and populated a glass cabinet. The sword hung on the wall, high above a mantle. The slow curve of the blade was apparent under its sheath, and a thin guard enclosed the handle.

The young boy stared at the antique weapon with large, dark brown eyes.

"Oh, thank you so much for agreeing to watch him, Mrs. Potts," came a woman's voice from another room. "It's just that we're new to the building and haven't had the time to meet anyone else or look at any daycares."

"Don't worry yourself, dear," replied an older woman's voice. "You work so hard. The little one can keep me company. Why, it can be lonely in this teeny, dusty old place."

A woman in scrubs strode into the room, throwing her arms around the boy. He could smell the cherry-scented shampoo she used in her long, black hair.

"I'll be back in a few hours," she whispered, rubbing his shoulders. "You might still be awake then. I packed your toothbrush and pajamas just in case."

"Ok," the boy kept his gaze on the sword to avoid his mother's eyes.

"Look," the woman leaned to the side to interrupt his view of the weapon. "I'm still new at the hospital I work at now. It's just like how you are new at your school. After I work for a while, they'll give me a regular schedule. I won't have to work these crazy hours after that."

Unable to avoid her, he flashed her a disappointed frown.

"Hey," the mother met his grimace with a smile, "remember when we went that that ramen place... the good one? It was so good, and you thought I was so cool because I ordered everything in Japanese. Well, I heard about another ramen place near here that makes the best tonkotsu ramen. Maybe we'll have enough saved up that we can stop there in a few weeks. Your cool mom is makin' bank now!"

The boy's mouth twisted up and down as he tried to hold back a corresponding grin. "You're not that cool."

A sweet, short laugh escaped the woman. "Yes, I am, and I'll teach you some Japanese so you can be cool, too."

She gave him a quick kiss on the cheek. "I have to go. I'll be back in a few hours. I promise."

Mrs. Potts entered the room as the mother exited. "Dear, I thought that we could look through some scrapbooks I made. There are some stories I could tell—"

"Is that a katana?" the boy interrupted with a curious finger extended toward the weapon. "My mom told me about those and the samurai."

"What?" Mrs. Potts murmured in a moment of confusion. "Oh, the sword! I guess I should have known that boys like those types of things. No, that is a cavalry saber. It's been in my family for generations. Why, I had an ancestor who fought alongside Napoleon. My maiden name was Laroche. That is his sword. My ancestor, I mean. Oh, and I believe that I have pictures of his grandson in an old photo book! I'll root around for it. Be right back, dear."

"Woah."

A steady red glow caught the boy's attention. There was a crystal encrusted at the bottom on the hilt where the guard was attached. He cautiously stepped forward for a closer look. With each step, the glow increased. Drawn to the light, the boy reached out his index finger to touch it. The light filled the room now. As the little finger contacted the smooth crystal, the light began swirling around the boy in a tornado of ruby-red.

The storm suddenly stopped, and crystal went back to its light, steady glow. The boy stepped back slowly. His legs wavered, and his eyes drooped.

"I need a nap," he muttered.

He collapsed onto the musky couch.

"I found it," the old woman cheerily strode back into the room with an old book swinging in her arms.

She noticed the dark-haired boy asleep on the sofa. "Oh, dear, you must be tired. You've had a long day."

She tucked him in under a heavy, old blanket.

~ ~ ~

The image of the sleeping boy dissipated to reveal Jason taking practice swings with his fencing saber.

"You ready?"

"Uh... yeah."

Paul barely caught a fencing mask that landed in his hands. He slipped it on. His eyes darted around the room through the fine metal wires of the mask as he tried to make sense of his senses. *What did I just see? It was like the dream I had with my dad in it. It's like I was dreaming, only standing up. Did any time pass? What's wrong with me? Is this another Amulus power that Luper didn't tell me about? I have to talk to him about it. That boy, though... that was Jason! He was younger, but it felt like him somehow. The energy was the same. The feeling from the anima.*

Paul shook his head, trying to shake the images he had just seen away. *Do I bring it up to Jason? No, maybe that I would be weird since it involved him. What would I say? "Hey, I just I had a dream where you were a little kid, but it seemed like a memory?" I guess I will have to ask Luper. Just another awkward conversation. It's like Amulus puberty.*

Jason was getting into position. His left hand gripped the practice sword with the blade slightly angled towards his chest. His left foot was also extended forward with his right making an "L" behind it. *He's left-handed*, Paul realized. *Will that make things different? It is a little unique.*

"The rules are what I said before," Jason advised. "We stop after a hit anywhere. The one fencing rule is that we'll be fighting along a straight line. No circling. We'll go as long as I feel like it."

Paul assumed his own pose. He chose *Chūdan-no-kamae* for its balance. *Maybe I can read the situation better this way. That and my sword is almost level with his, which takes away any quick strikes to the middle torso. I just have to remember how fencers spar... which I can't. I know I saw a match on TV one time, but...*

Jason snapped his spiral-faced mask into place and nodded.

Does that mean "go?" We didn't even put on any kind of protection besides the mask.

Paul heard the hit before he felt it. There was a whoosh and thump before he felt a searing pain in the right part of his chest. He stumbled backward, grabbing at the swollen welt that had already formed beneath his shirt. *I'm getting tired of this. I doubt that my senses will ever be sharp enough to keep track of Amulus movements.*

It took another moment before he had gathered himself to analyze the situation. *He took advantage of his left-handed angle to catch a flaw in my stance. Not only did he hit me faster than I could react, but he did it in the perfect place. It was precise, textbook. He took a step forward, but I didn't notice.*

Jason was already back in his starting stance. His dark eyes glared coldly from behind the mask's wires and red-painted spiral. *That boy from that memory. If it was a memory. How did he become someone like this?*

Paul forced a deep breath to try to calm himself. *Luper says that helps.* He chose the *Gedan-no-kamae* stance this time. *If he is so quick to attack, maybe I need something defensive.*

Jason nodded again.

Paul saw the fencer's left arm ripple as a swing came. Sparks flew as the metal saber bit into the wooden bokken. The impact rumbled through his arms and shoulders. He took a step back to collect himself.

The strikes kept coming. Paul was back to his standard, balanced stance, but each impact took his own sword closer to his chest. He was back-peddling before he knew it. The swordsman in front of him was lost to his vision due to blinding flashes of metal and wood.

Paul felt something brush his back. *The wall. He's forced me back as far as I can go.* A moment later, he cried out when he felt his right big toe being crushed through his sneaker. He instinctively dropped his weapon to crouch down and rub it.

Paul watched Jason's back as he went back to the starting position. *Luper told me that being hit in the foot is the biggest humiliation for a swordsman. It shows a complete lack of defense. I'm assuming that I had a lot of openings after being pushed to the wall like that. He was either trying to humiliate me or make a point.*

Jason let out an impatient sigh as he waited for Paul to gather himself again.

Paul forced himself back into position once again before the pain had faded in his foot. He retook his balanced stance as his eyes still winced from the persistent ache. The nod from Jason came again.

Paul found himself twisting his torso from left-to-right over and over as he tried to put power in his blocks. His enhanced eyes tracked the shimmering enemy blade and as it whizzed about him. He caught glimpses of the furious flicks of Jason's forearm. Each parry caused his wooden sword to vibrate, sending painful shock waves the whole way to his shoulders. He searched for openings in Jason's stance but could not force his way to them during the few times they appeared. All he could do was to keep out of the way of Jason's swipes, whether by parrying or backward dodges.

An awkward step backward made Paul take a slight stumble. Jason's blade rushed upward and caught his mask where the metal wires met the bib. The stroke lifted the mask off of Paul's head, leaving it to clatter on the hard floor.

"Did you need to do that?" Paul felt the words force their way through his throat and explode out of his mouth. He regretted the angry ugliness brewing inside of him, but let the words hang in the air without an apology. For days, he had been hit in training by all the occupants in the bunker. The cuts, bruises, and welts had stacked up faster than his superhuman body could heal them. He was mad at the constant beating, yet furious with himself. *How can I be so weak? How can I be so weak when I have to be strong now to just stay alive?*

Jason took off his masked and scowled. "If this is too much for you, then what is an actual battle going to be like?"

Paul watched Jason's back as he collected his gear. *I've failed at every training exercise, and I failed at getting Jason's help.*

"Wait!" shouted Paul as his lips seemed to move again before he wanted. "Just give me one more round."

Jason paused for a moment and then shrugged exasperatedly. "*One* more round. We'll do it differently. No masks. And if I get to you first, you can't ask for my help training anymore."

Paul nodded after a moment of thought. *If I don't agree to this, then I think there is a good chance that he will never want to train with me again, anyway.*

The two combatants took their places again, but this time with no head protection. Paul devised a new strategy. He mimicked Jason's stance by holding his bokken at an angle with his dominant right hand at the top just below where the faux blade began, instead of at the base as per kendo form. He narrowed the width between his legs and let one fall completely perpendicular to the other.

There was a flicker of annoyance in Jason's eyes. *He thinks I'm mocking him. But I'm doing this because of speed. A more capable swordsman can be quick with a two-handed sword. That's not me. A katana or a bokken isn't so heavy that I can't wield it with one hand. In fact, their lightness is a strength. I just hope every samurai ever isn't looking at me with shame right now.*

Jason's first swipe came as fast as ever. Paul tracked it as swinging from the left. Rather than giving a slight twist with his upper body, he punched sideways the way he had seen Jason pull off his blocks and parries. The enemy sword rebounded. *It only requires a flick of the wrist and forearm. It's fast. Fast enough to reinforce my swordplay as I get better with kenjutsu.*

Paul used the opportunity to step forward, aiming a short, steady slash for Jason's neck. The fencer leaned back so that the wooden sword passed through empty air just below his chin. He was quick to charge back to the attack with two swipes in quick succession towards Paul's head and then his right side. Both attempts thudded off Paul's *bokken.*

Paul could feel a rumbling in the air coming from Jason. He knew that it was anima. The amount was too little to be seen as visible, but Paul could feel it. It was a sense unique to Amuli. The ability to feel the inner energy of other things. Naturally, it was the enemy of stealth, but that was not a problem in the current situation. Paul could feel his ocean of energy rushing inside him like waves breaking under his skin. He was sure that Jason could feel the same from him.

The flashing sword came down again above Paul's head. This time, Paul took a half step backward. *He's overextended himself. That many attacks in a row left him leaning too far forward.* Paul eyed the fencing saber as its blade came close to the floor. *My sword's too low for a quick attack on his body.* He chose the next best thing. With a punching motion downward, Paul pounded Jason's sword into the ground. Jason's compromised grip let the blade slip to the floor.

Paul's senses returned after he felt his wooden sword slam into Jason's sternum. The rush of battle left his ears and he was left gasping and sweating. Despite the furious impact,

Jason gave no winces or even steps backward.

"So, you can get it together sometimes," the slightly older boy remarked in a way that resembled praise. "At least when you stop doing things so stiff and orthodox that is."

"Um, thanks," Paul responded as he kept hidden a prideful smile. "I'm... uh... sorry I followed through with that last hit. It was a little much after I disarmed you. I should have just stopped."

Jason shook his head. "Don't ruin it by apologizing. I deserved it. I was sloppy. I would have walloped you even harder."

"I see," murmured Paul a little unsure.

"You know that you don't always have to use kendo stances," Jason pointed out. "Real fighting isn't that clean."

"I don't know," responded Paul. "It's kind of what I'm the most comfortable with."

Jason adjusted the tightness of the guard of his practice sword via a nob on the pommel. "You aren't going to confuse someone with something they've seen before. At least until you're so good at it that they can't stop you. There are more techniques and stances out there. There are even battle manuals for some that describe some that have been specialized for Amuli. That's not always enough though. Everyone's body is a little different. Sometimes it pays off to make your own style if you know what you're doing and if you're adaptable with it. People don't always fight like they do in training manuals."

"I guess I'll get reading and testing stuff out then," Paul agreed.

Jason whirled his fencing saber about in a circle. "That's all I've got the say today. If you bug me enough again, maybe I'll tell you some other things."

"Yeah... um... thanks," Paul stammered as he gathered his things and hastily retreated from the training room. *I don't think he likes me at all, but it at least seems like he will help me out. Mission accomplished mostly.*

Chapter 12: The Game

Paul trudged down the hallway, rubbing his shoulders. *Jason is even tougher at training than Luper.* He felt his wet shirt clinging to his chest. *I feel like I need a hot shower and an ice bath at the same time.*

A spark shot up Paul's back when he noticed a pale figure sneak in front of him. *She has a habit of doing that. Although, I guess I should be more alert to my surroundings if I'm going to be a fighter.*

"Luper has called us to the shed entrance," informed Alice in a voice just above a whisper. "Leave your sword in the Bunker."

Paul watched the quiet girl walk purposefully towards the bunker ladder at the end of the hallway. *Looks like we're going outside. Normally, I like to stretch my legs and get out from the underground, but it feels like I'm going to fall over. That's not going to garner sympathy from anyone, though. That shower will have to wait.*

Mercifully, Paul's room was on the way to the ladder which

gave him time to step in and slip on a new shirt which he covered with a light but warm jacket. After a climb, Paul, Alice, Camilla, and Jason squeezed out of the cramped shed. Brisk air filled their noses with the almost smoky smell of fallen leaves. They were greeted in the cold night by a figure in a black wool coat gracefully landing on the ground after springing out of a tree.

"After all the hard work you all have been doing," began Luper playfully. "I decided that it was time for a game."

Paul tried to conceal the obvious puzzlement on his face

"Of course," Luper continued philosophically, "games are often how animals and humans learn about the world. They can teach physics, strategy, risk-and-reward, game theory, and dexterity among other things. The game that you four will be enjoying is a mainstay of overnight sleepovers. You are going to play flashlight tag mixed with capture the flag. Capture the flag by flashlight, if you will."

Camilla and Paul gave each other look that said, "He's going to make this much more complicated than normal flashlight tag."

"There are many variances in this game," Luper explained. "I have come up with my own rules. I have just tied four different ribbons to four different trees with each being located an equal distance away from the shed in different directions. There is a gold ribbon, a red ribbon, a purple ribbon, and a green ribbon. When I say so, you zoom off towards your designated ribbon. The goal is to steal the ribbons of your opponents while retaining your own. The person who returns to the shed first with all four ribbons will be the champion. Their prize will be a break from watch duty for a week. That is a lot of extra sleep. You will use no weapons in this game. All methods of obtaining the ribbons are allowed, save for those that may result in permanent injury or fatalities. Since you four can create light through the luminescence of your anima, you will be your own flashlight. Use it with care. Any questions or are you all ready to play?"

I played flashlight tag with Robby and his other friends at a sleepover once. The rules were a lot different and there was no combat involved.

There was only silence in answer to Luper's question.

Luper nodded slyly. "The four of you will begin once I give you the directions of each person's ribbon. Just follow in the direction I give you, and you will find it by running in a straight trajectory. The ribbons will be hard to miss, but you may need to light your way to find them."

Luper looked at each participant in the eye. "Paul, your green ribbon is to the east. Camilla, your purple ribbon is towards the north. Alice's gold ribbon is in the west. And Jason's red ribbon is in the south."

After Luper had given him the direction of his ribbon, Paul tensed up. He leaned partially forward on his toes with his feet at should width. His eyes focused on the dark web of trees as he plotted a path.

Luper raised an arm. "Well, if everyone is ready," the arm dropped, "go!"

A green blur, a gold blur, a purple blur, and a red blur took off in different directions.

The air whipped through Paul's ears as he dodged tree branches as they emerged from the night. His right arm lit the way with a burning green light. With his enhanced speed and strength, he could easily bound up and down hills no matter how choked they were with thorny bushes.

He forced his emotions down into his stomach, trying to prevent them from boiling back up. Feelings controlled anima. The more anima an Amulus secreted, the easier it was to sense them. It was like a sixth sense that Paul was still becoming accustomed to. He knew that Luper had meant for the dark to block out their distance vision. The trainees would have to rely on their ability to sense anima to find each other. *I'll need to extinguish my light when I reach the ribbon, I still need to think of a plan. Do I hide and wait to sense someone? But when will I get to the ribbon? Luper said that we wouldn't be able to miss the ribbons. I wonder if they are incredibly large or maybe it even lights up.*

Paul was lost in his thoughts until he sensed a rush of movement directly ahead of him. In the small amount of light that he was conjuring, he could only make out a boot and the trailing of a green material. He froze.

177

Someone got to my ribbon before me. Was it Luper? Is this a part of the game? Did he give us misinformation to through us off? Paul scoured his thoughts for Luper's exact instructions, trying to find a hint in the wording. *He never throws us off without a bit of foreshadowing, but I can't think of anything he said to indicate that. Did someone break the rules? No, they each value the training too much. Jason would want to win fair and square to show how good he is. Alice never goes against orders. Cam is too nice.*

Paul suddenly exhaled in frustration. *Someone did take my ribbon! They didn't break the rules, though. Luper never said that we had to tie on our own ribbons. And I was the easy target. I'm the least experienced one as well as the slowest. Whoever took my ribbon can now easily pick up their own and gain an advantage over the others. I guess I'm out.*

He felt an odd sense of relief, knowing that his drill was over. The sense was dulled, however, by the embarrassment of losing only minutes into the contest.

Wait! Luper also said that it was only the goal of the game to retain your ribbon and steal the others. He never said that losing a ribbon disqualified you. Then I'm losing, but not out. Why was I so slow in thinking up all of this? I have to be smarter than that.

Paul took a deep breath. *I just need to sense the anima of the others when they have a fight. It should be easy to sense them. I'm in last place, but I'm not out.*

He closed his eyes, waiting to feel energy prickling his skin like static electricity. It was several moments before he felt a swirl of anima coming towards him like buffets of wind. *There!*

Paul took off in that direction. The feeling of energy in the air was fading, but it was just enough for him to track. This time, he was sure to look out for any clusters of leaves or low branches. Any sound could give away his approach.

It was a different kind of sound that stopped his approach.

"He got you, too?" came a young woman's exasperated voice.

Cam? Is she trying to trick me or...

A lean figure leaned out from behind an oak tree. Dark hair flowed behind the girl like a shadow. A pillar of purple light lit up Camilla's face as well as Paul's own.

"I'm glad Jason's on our side and all," sighed Camilla, "but half the stuff he pulls in training just ticks me off. It's like he's always flaunting how good he is. Anyway, you okay?"

Paul nodded. "I lost the ribbon without him ever touching me."

"Lucky you," moaned Camilla. "He flung me into a tree and took the ribbon at the same time. I guess he exploited the rules and went for each ribbon aside from his own."

Why is she having a conversation with me when the game is still

179

going on? We're combatants, after all.

"There is a silver lining to this, you know," explained Camilla. "We can work together to steal our ribbons back from that jerk. Plus, we can try for his as well."

Paul nodded. "A truce then." *This could give us the advantage.*

Camilla smiled. "A truce until we take out Jason. Then it's on. What's our plan?"

"I guess it's all about sensing the anima," Paul pondered. "That's how I found this spot. I'm assuming that Jason is putting an enormous amount of anima in his legs to move so fast. We may be able to track him from just that. If he gets into a fight with Alice, there is going to be a lot of anima flying between those two. Also, remember that he has three destinations in mind, his own ribbon in the south, Alice's ribbon in the west, and possibly the shed in the center if he has all the ribbons. That's the triangle we can search in. Above all, we know that he is moving south from here."

"Right," responded Camilla with a hint of admiration in her voice. "Then let's go south and open up our sixth sense."

Interesting. I think he went after me first because I'm the weakest. Cam isn't weak, but only Alice can compete with Jason. He chose the easiest one and then the second easiest one. However, that second choice took him the farthest from his own ribbon, which may have been an easy pickup if Alice doesn't reach it. He's gambling, but he's gambling on his own speed and skill. Cam and I will have to make him pay for that risk.

The two temporary allies cautiously waded through bushes and leaves as they tried to pick up a signal. It took several minutes for Paul to feel a buzzing in the night. He and Camilla nodded to each other before embarking on a faster pace. *We still can't let him hear us. He's fast enough to get away and strong enough to take us both down. We need the element of surprise.* Both Paul and Camilla kept their anima depletion to a minimum. Jason was as likely to sense them as they were to sense him.

A bur of movement that was too large to be a bat shook a couple of nearby branches as it bounced from tree to tree.

Camilla and Paul split in two directions on opposite sides of the blur. Following Luper's training, they knew less movement a single direction was harder to spot. In addition, if one of them were to take up all the attention of the target, the other would be in the target's blind spot. The constant drilling of tactics had caused the moments of the two allies to be done in sync. Paul took the right as Camilla veered to the left.

Paul swerved suddenly as a bundle of heavy branches slammed down in front of him. A crashing sound to the left told him that Camilla had been required to the same action. *He's cutting down branches with anima to slow our pursuit or take us out. We need to use our anima to speed up and catch him. I know that Cam will think the same.*

Paul channeled the ocean of energy within himself, letting some of it drift into his legs. A steady, green light emerged from under his pant legs. *If I know Cam, she'll try a long-distance attack first.*

As Paul had predicted, a shimmering purple bolt streaked towards Jason just as Paul was gaining ground. Jason dodged and turned to greet his attacker to the left. *Now!*

Paul let the anima explode out of the bottom of his feet. He turned his head sideways while airborne, while spreading his arms forward.

Jason moved to sidestep his second attacker. The juke was not enough to escape the hurtling Paul. Instead, Paul's outstretched arm caught him in the leg, grabbing on for a second. The two went tumbling.

Paul was aware of only his head and shoulders bouncing along the ground. Everything else was black. A certain numbness told him that those areas of his body would be hurting in a few seconds. The rolling finally stopped.

Jason appeared on Paul's chest, his knees pushing in deep. The slightly older boy's face was twisted in an annoyed grimace. Paul became cognizant just in time to dodge a punch aimed for his face by straining his neck to the side. Another shot of purple light flew by, barely grazing Jason's shoulder. The injured teenager rolled towards his injured side. Paul was again given a license to breathe and reach his feet.

A spiral of red hummed toward the section of bushes where Camilla hid. A cloud of dust and sticks clouded the area. Paul used the opportunity to leap at Jason from behind. He primed a kick at the taller boy's calf, aiming to make his legs crumble, but Jason was ready. A rotating kick of his own took Paul in the thigh. Paul fell to a knee for a moment before bouncing back to his stance. He was just in time to see another purple blast catch Jason in the lower leg. His own weight sent him to ground chest-first. Paul dove on his back, wrapping an arm around Jason's neck. He felt the stronger boy struggling in the crook of his elbow. Paul spread his legs wide, letting the full surface area of his body take the brunt of Jason's efforts to free himself. *A judo technique. Judo is a martial art where leverage is everything. It can conquer the strength that Jason has over me as long as I'm disciplined.*

Paul's eyes caught hints of several colors around Jason's waist. "Camilla, grab the ribbons! I need both arms to hold him!"

Camilla emerged from remained dust cloud to snatch purple, red, and greed ribbons from Jason's midsection. Dutifully, she tied the green one around Paul's leg after securing her purple ribbon along with Jason's red one to her own waist.

Cam kept her word, Paul realized. *I guess she's just that nice. Either that or she doesn't care much about winning. She is definitely not as competitive as Jason.*

"It was a fruitful partnership, Paul," Camilla announced sweetly. "I'll leave you two to it."

Paul could only stare as the girl raced off towards a line of trees. *It's not a team exercise afterall. We did accomplish what we agreed to.*

"I'm not done," Jason breathed from beneath Paul just before blindly sending an elbow into his stomach.

The wind exploded from Paul's lungs as his grip and pressure on Jason slipped. He tumbled off of Jason's back as the dark-haired teen rose.

Paul was on his hands and knees when a saw a red spiral strike Camilla in the back. *It's a free-for-all now.*

He did not have time to reflect as an anima-clad fist came rushing towards his face. He dashed sideways.

The punches and kicks came in a flurry. Each created a blinding rush of air. Paul found himself reeling and ducking. He searched for openings in Jason's stance, but none appeared. He was aware that they were approaching a group of trees. In the dark, Paul could envision himself backing into one or tripping over a root. *I have to stop this!*

Paul let out a growl. A bubble of energy rose inside him. For an instant, a blinding green fire enveloped him. Its spray made Jason slide back and shield himself. Another flash of purple stung Jason in the shoulder, spinning him to the ground. In the distance, Paul could just see Camilla by the light of the still fading anima in her hand. She was on her knees. Her clothes were partially torn from the back, exposing some olive-colored skin beneath.

Thanks, Cam.

Jason was rising back to his feet. Paul could hear his joints cracking. *He's like some undead monster. He just won't go down.*

The last burst of anima had drained Paul. *I'm still getting a grip on how much I can use. Luper said that everyone has the same amount. It just takes getting used to using it.* Despite feeling like a spent battery, he dove towards Jason, attempting another pin.

This time, a fist caught him in the solar plexus. Paul wheezed to the ground with his eyes rolling back into his head. He was left frozen, crumpled in a heap. Grabbing at the painful new bruise above his stomach, he felt a nudging on his arm and a slight relief of pressure. *I lose. I can't get back up right now.*

However, through a wince, Paul could see Jason still on the ground. His arm was still outstretched from when he had punched Paul. *Then who? Cam can't move either.*

Jason muttered a string of curses with, "... outsmarted us... took advantage."

Alice! It's so stupid of me. I forgot all about her. She waited for all of us to make a move. She saw how intense the battle was and waited to take out the weakened winner. Even better for her, there were no winners. We all took each other out.

185

"Did you have to shoot me so hard, Jason?" complained Camilla from her resting place. "I liked this coat... and shirt."

"I could say the same to you," Jason croaked.

"Fair enough."

"C-can we catch up to her?" Paul asked as he finally took his hands off his aching stomach area.

"Nah," Jason replied shaking his head, "she's too fast for any of us. Plus, none of us are running any time soon. Limping maybe."

* * *

"Nice to see that all of you made it back safely," Luper quipped while looking at the tattered crew in front of him. A chorus of groans greeted him.

Undeterred, Luper motioned toward a waiting Alice. "It's Alice who gets the prize of a week's reprieve of guard duty. Great job."

Alice simply nodded her thanks.

"You had a lot more sense than the rest of us," Camilla praised after clapping her on the shoulder. "Staying out of conflict unless you had to. Minimizing risk while maximizing possible reward. You could have beaten all of us in a straight-up fight, but you chose the even easier way."

Alice only nodded again.

Paul began dragging his tired body back to the shed. *And I was tired before all of this. Still... how did Alice get such a sense of strategy and combat? She's more skilled than all of us. I wouldn't be surprised if she could fight on par with Luper. Camilla said that Jason is strong because he's been at this longer than us. How long has Alice been doing this?*

Chapter 13: Identity

The buzzing of the video monitors was giving Paul a headache. He rubbed his eyes again. *I wonder how Alice is always able to take the last watch so early in the mornings.* There was some movement on one monitor but none of it was it was human. A cardinal shook the branch of one camera while taking off. A couple of deer nibbled on frosty grass surrounding a nearly bare oak tree.

Paul took a swig of green tea and felt its steam gently fill his mouth and throat. *I have to keep myself cognizant. This job is important but boring.* He moaned internally about his lack of sleep. He had found it much harder to come by ever since the day he learned that he would be putting his life on the line to protect his loved ones and himself. The four hours he had just gotten had come from a better night than most. His next few moments were filled with yawns between sips of tea.

The camera on the shed entrance was fixed on a similar figure. *She really does like sunrises. She's up this early, even when she won a break from guard duty.* An early morning ray of sunlight touched her golden hair as Alice leaned on the windowsill. Even in the absence of any other observers, Paul's face still went red. *Stop staring at her, you creep! She has that view covered.*

It was another solitary figure on a different monitor that shifted Paul's attention. Lumbering through the forest was a man clad in a heavy coat patterned in camouflage. A similarly colored backpack swung about his shoulders. He waved a rifle back-and-forth as his feet crunched along.

Paul scratched an imaginary beard on his smooth chin. *I think it is around hunting season. My aunt, uncle, and I were never big on hunting, but I always got a day off of school when deer season started. It's all everyone talks about around here during this time of the year. Still, it can't hurt to run his face through the database. He could be someone who's just using the hunter outfit as a disguise.*

Paul zoomed in on the man's face. His view became full of a grizzled face with a frizzy, gray beard that could have been the bottom of an old broom. *Probably just a hunter with a lowercase "h," but I'll run his face through the database just to make sure.*

A blinking rectangle now surrounding the leathery face on the screen. Another monitor scanned through pictures of known Hunters and A.I.M. operatives. Paul suddenly found himself drawn to the set of moving lips. *Is he talking or singing to himself? Whistling?* On closer inspection, the mouth was twisted and grim. A rising redness could be seen down to the man's throat. *He's angry. He's yelling something. If only I could read lips.*

The fast-churning monitor was now frozen on a picture similar to the live feed.

"Donald Baines," Paul read aloud.

Paul continued down the page with fast-racing eyes to match his heart. Each line of information was a new twist in his stomach. The man was known to frequent Hunter websites, ones that advocated for the imprisonment or murder of Amuli as dangerously powerful members of society. He was divorced with a criminal record, mostly misdemeanor assaults, and disorderly conduct. *Why is he here? Does he know where the Bunker is? How? We're so remote. Even hunters usually don't come around here. Everyone here rarely goes out during the day. We mostly go out for a few minutes to stretch our legs. I have to get Luper.*

Paul slammed the alarm. Before freezing in his chair. *Alice! She can't hear the alarm up there!*

He launched his way out of the room, nearly colliding with a sprinting Luper. The tall man appeared calm, as usual, despite the ringing in the air.

"What's happening?"

"H-hunter in the farther sector!" Paul stammered. "One of them. Alice, she's in the shed! I..."

"I will get her," advised Luper before confidently striding off.

He arrived back with the solemn girl less than a minute later. By then, Camilla and Jason had joined Paul in staring intently at the monitors.

Luper silently looked over each of the monitors. It was a pulsating few moments for the trainees before he broke the silence.

"Seems to be a lone wolf," he announced, "no indication of any others. The only trouble will be if he makes it to the shed. Then, we will have reason to believe that he has a lock on our location. Rumors spring up about secret Amulus centers in remote areas from time to time. Most people do not know how true those rumors often are. The occasional flash of anima can bring observers as well. I have never heard of that being a problem here, however."

He tapped on the mouse, closing the screen in on the man's backpack. "Ammunition. You can see the outlines in the fabric Unfortunately for him, those rounds will never hurt and Amulus. He is looking for a fight. Let us see if he finds one."

The man did not move like an experienced woodsman, stumbling up and down gentle hills.

"Possibly inebriated," noted Luper. "That sometimes makes people want to take on someone obviously stronger than them."

The man continued on his staggering, uneven journey. His

path looked anything but purposeful, yet each zigzagging step took him a little closer to the shed.

Paul was glued to the monitor. *What do we do if he gets close?*

The answer came an agonizing few minutes later. The old Hunter was within a mile of the shed.

Luper sighed. "I believe that it is time to do something about this. Alice, Paul, follow me. Jason, Camilla, stay on the monitors. I will return in a moment."

Paul noticed that he had said "I will return" and not "we will return."

Luper walked Paul and Alice to a storage room. Opening the door unleashed wafts of stinging lemon scent from cleaning supplies. Luper slid a supply cart out of the way to unveil a back wall covered in an assortment of masks. Several were similar to Camilla's minimal style of a mask in varying shades. Other masks matched Alice's masquerade fashion. Another section contained masks that covered the whole face. An entire row of faces twisted into smiles sent spiders under Paul's skin. They joined the bunches that had already nested there from the fears of what he was about to do outside.

"It is time for a bit of a rite of passage," explained Luper. "All A.R.C. operatives were masks to hide their identity at times, particularly in secluded places. Of course, wearing a mask in a well-populated place causes one to stick out more than blend in. Many use a mask as a calling card, a symbol for who they are as an operative. Paul, I do advise you to choose quickly, however, as you will need to prevent our visitor from finding us. There is some chance that the camouflage of the shed will do its work, but we cannot afford to be lax in this business."

Paul surveyed the faces before him. His attention was fixed on the mission at hand, however, sending his heart rate soaring. He had already made up his mind to grab the first mask before him without giving thought to its meaning, but a pair of masks in the corner caught his attention. Both were a dull, mottled gray but had contrasting expressions. The painted mouth of one had a slight smirk to one side underneath a pair of eyeholes covered in black while the other was identical, but its mouth ended in a faint frown. *A take on the "sock and buskin," the masks of comedy and tragedy. The smiling one represents Thalia, the muse of comedy. The frowning one depicts Melpomene, the muse of tragedy.*

Paul felt his hand drawing towards the frowning mask. *If one mask fits my mood since I arrived here, it's this one.* He slipped the straps on the back of the mask onto the back of his head.

Luper briefed Paul and Alice as they ascended to the shed. "Paul, you will apprehend the intruder. You may use any means aside from killing him. The higher-ups will want to know if he had information on this base or if he simply wandered here. Alice, you will stay out of sight, unless backup is needed. Your chief duty is to provide Paul with information and advice through your mental link. Any questions?"

In a moment of clarity between the hammering beats of his heart, Paul asked. "What happens to him after he's questioned?"

"He will probably be imprisoned," stated Luper bluntly. "Particularly if he does have information on the base."

"Without a trial or anything," Paul murmured under his breath.

Picking up on the comment, Luper relented. "It is not our call after we apprehend him. He will disappear off the face of the earth like the rest of us. That is the way of the higher-ups."

Paul's timid hands grasped the final wring of the ladder.

"One last thing," Luper called upward. "You will likely already know this, but the bullets from his gun will dissipate in your anima unless the barrel of the gun is right against your skin. You will be fine as long as it doesn't come to that. Unless he is right up against you, he cannot harm you."

Paul pulled the hood of his sweatshirt over his head as he exited the shed into the cool air. Chilly mist encircled the trees like those in a rainforest. He tapped the end of his sword with a nervous finger.

"How far out is he?" questioned Paul.

"*All communication from this point onward should be through telepathy,* came Alice's voice in his mind. "*He is one half a mile to the north."*

"Right, sorry."

The two raced off into the trees, their footsteps leaving no sound behind.

Chapter 14: In the Blood

They heard the target before they saw him. Between strings of slurred curses, Paul and Alice could make out unflattering statements about Amuli. The most often repeated phrase was, "They're damn unnatural. Born evil. It's in their blood."

Paul forced his thoughts to flow coherently. *"Alice, advice on how to pursue him?"*

"I have assessed two options. You may attempt to wait on one of the tree branches suitable for your weight until he passes beneath you. This may risk exposure if he looks upward as it may be difficult for you to conceal yourself on branches that are now mostly bare. His inebriated state may cloud his observational skills. Another option would be to sneak behind the rows of coniferous bushes to our right. This would offer more advantageous cover but will take more time."

The talk of strategy brought Paul back to the present. *It's just another game*, he told only himself.

To Alice, he thought, *"The second option seems safer. Slow and steady. The tortoise and the hare."*

"I fear that you sent an incomplete thought with that last sentence," Alice stated. *"Please repeat."*

"The tortoise and the hare?"

"Yes, what is that?" Alice questioned. *"A code for a formation pattern? I do not know of it."*

"No, it's... um... a children's story. One of Aesop's fables, actually. Sorry, maybe it was silly to bring it up in this serious situation."

"No, it is simply a gap in my own knowledge. Continue with the plan as you see fit. Luper instructed that I shall assist you physically should you endure an injury. If that situation does not occur, I shall continue relaying my observations to you."

"Right. I'll get started," Paul confirmed.

What kid grows up without hearing about 'The Tortoise and the Hare?' he pondered to himself.

With his legs pumping and his body crouched as low as possible, Paul made a wide arc around the thick bushes. *A quick blow to the right part of the head may knock him out, but it's risky. It's difficult to discern how much force to use to knock someone out, according to Luper. You have to use something else, just to be safe.*

He reeled the man in closer and closer until he was just about at the man's back. The Hunter's babbling and cursing rang through the air. Paul crept out from the bushes. The man

197

turned as if prompted by some superhuman sense.

Paul's mind went on autopilot with his fears wired into the controls. Influenced by muscle-memory, his arm swung his *katana* out of the sheath tied around his waist. As the blade arced, a crackling shock wave of green anima sliced through the air, splintering a dead tree. The old man pointed his rifle at Paul. The wrinkles around the Hunter's eyes tightened as he locked in on his dangerous prey. Paul froze in the gaze of the dilated eyes, the pupils cold and black. A series of booming snapping broke both of their attention and crashing noises.

The damaged tree plunged down towards them. Paul and the Hunter threw themselves separate ways as the tree intersected them. Paul found himself coughing and spitting in a cloud of dirt and sticks.

"Paul!" Alice cried out.

"I'm ok."

"The Hunter is regaining his composure. He seems to have suffered only minor cuts and bruises." Alice's cool, matter-of-fact thoughts faded away into warmer ones. *"Remember, Paul, this is a simple mission. It is well within your capabilities to complete it. That is my assessment based on your training to this point."*

"Right," Paul gathered himself before leaping over the fallen tree trunk with his sword. He came face-to-face with a gun

barrel.

The anima-infused blade cleaved right through the metal and finished-wood barrel. Still on his back, the grizzled Hunter tossed away his ruined weapon in surprise.

Paul threw himself on top of the man with his back slamming into the man's chest. He felt a pained heave escape the man. The young Amulus threw his arm around the man's neck and planted his legs wide with his calves against the ground. It the first judo hold Luper had taught him, *kesa gatame* or the scarf hold. Paul added his own variation, with the arm that was meant to grasp one of the opponent's arms, he tucked the enemy's arm into his armpit but let his sword rest in between where the man's armpit met his body.

The green aura around the *katana* blade made the man's dirty, camouflage jacket sizzle. Based on Luper's words and his own observations, Paul did not believe that the man had a secondary weapon. Just in case, this variant hold made a threat clear, "Fight back and you will watch this blade tear through you."

Paul gripped the man tighter and tighter. Each breath from the man sent Paul's morning tea further up his throat. Then it was over. It had been faster than what Paul had expected. The man's still-thumping chest meant that he was definitely alive. His rolled-back eyes showed that his conciseness had momentarily left him.

Paul was left sitting next to the man, panting, and still

holding the tea down. *I can't believe I just did that.*

Alice appeared from behind a mass of trees. "Do you require my assistance to carry him back to the bunker?"

Paul found it refreshing to hear a voice that was not in his head. "No, I think I've got him."

He's so light, Paul noticed as he slung the skin-and-bones man over his shoulder. In his forced sleep, he simply appeared as a wrinkled, old man.

* * *

Paul gently plopped the Hunter on the cot in the holding cell. He stepped out as Luper slammed and locked the heavy metal door.

"Your first mission is accomplished. Not cleanly done, as we saw on the cameras, but an important first step. Congratulations."

Paul nodded. "Thanks."

He's going away. Even though he didn't really do anything until I provoked him. Is this really right? Is this something that I want to be a part of? No, I don't want to be a part of it. I am a part of it because I have to be. There is no alternative that I can see.

"Yeah!" exclaimed Camilla as she extended her arm out for a fist bump that Paul unenthusiastically returned. "Nice job, Paul."

"Thanks, Cam."

She nudged Jason with a pointy elbow. "Wouldn't you like to congratulate *your* student?"

Jason distanced himself. "Congratulate him for what? Panicking while fighting an old man and nearly crashing a tree into himself? I'll congratulate him when he's killed an army of A.I.M. operatives."

"You always have to be the killjoy, huh?" Camilla complained. "You probably wouldn't even pat him on the back even if he did that."

Jason let a tiny smirk show.

"You know," mentioned Paul, "Alice is the one who helped me out in the field. Talking me down. She always has a cool head. Where is she?"

Camilla looked around. "Probably back to her room as usual."

"Should I thank her?" Paul wondered.

"Probably," Camilla replied. "Of course, she'll probably say something like, 'I was only adhering to the mission.' You know what? I'll go with you. I've never been in her room before."

Camilla grabbed Paul by the sleeve and led him along. *She reminds me of Robby a lot sometimes, and also Aunt Morgan a little.*

Camilla wrapped on the door. "Alice?"

"Yes, I am here."

"Paul has something to say to you."

"Uh," Paul swallowed hard with his face simmering. "When you say it like that..."

"Does he wish to comment on the mission?" came the robotic voice behind the door. "Am I required to assist in compiling the report?"

"Well... kind of the former," answered Camilla.

Paul sighed. *I hate it when people talk for me, but with my habit of clamming up, people seem to feel like they need to.*

The door cracked open and Alice slid out.

"Alice," Paul began, "I wanted to thank you for your calming me down during the mission. It helped me to complete it."

"As you say," Alice began, "I did what was required to complete the mission. That was all that I did. The rest was accomplished by you. Do you require me to assist you in completing the report?"

Paul shook his head. "No, Luper has me doing it all. That was... it."

Camilla peeked an eye through the gap in the door. "Are those lamps for growing plants? Are you growing weed down here?"

"No," Alice responded with no hint of acknowledging the humor. "I required the lamps for my studies of botany."

"You like studying plants?" questioned Camilla curiously as she continued to look for a better view of the room.

"I have nearly completed a bachelor's degree in botany through an online program," Alice answered.

"Oh, I didn't know that," said Camilla, finally giving up on getting a better view of the room. "Congratulations."

"Yes," was Alice's only response as she slipped back through the doorway.

Camilla sighed. "You know, I really do like all of you, even if none of you are good at small talk."

Chapter 15: Through the Cracks

Paul closed his aching eyes for a moment in an attempt to soothe them. He absentmindedly rearranged the wad of papers in his hands against Luper's desk. *Luper warned me that there would be a lot of paperwork. I didn't think that it would be enough to keep me up all night, though.*

Luper crashed into his office while stuffing protein bars and water bottles into a backpack. "Oh, good morning, Paul, or good night. I will relieve you of guard duty for today. I suspect that the paperwork was about as torturous as the mission and far more time-consuming."

"You're going somewhere?" realized Paul. *I don't remember any of us leaving for an extended period of time since I've been here. Having Luper leave is... discomforting.*

"Yes," confirmed Luper. "Quite perceptive and quick-witted as always, Paul. While the cameras have shown no suspicious activity, I feel that a wider sweep of the area is needed."

Paul felt his tongue roll into his throat but still rasped. "You think... he wasn't a-alone?"

"Do I think he was alone?" restated Luper. "Yes. Do I know that he was alone? No. When it comes to this business, which deals in lives, it is better to be sure."

"How long will you be gone?" asked Paul, sounding like a whimpering child in his own mind.

"Hours likely," answered Luper as he zipped his bag. "I will be scouting the surrounding wooded area, scouring the roads, and heading to local town squares to listen to any gossip about suspicious men or vans. I shouldn't be gone for more than a day. You would be surprised at the ground a grizzled Amulus can cover, if I may boast."

Paul stared down at his papers dejectedly.

"I am afraid that I will have to wait to read your report," mentioned Luper. "Although, I'm sure that it will be well written as your work usually is. Your online tutor has remarked that your streak of straight A's has continued. You will probably be able to take college courses as soon as Alice has done."

"I'll take the compliment," responded Paul.

"Right then," Luper continued, "I was actually just about to tell the others. Alice has seniority, so she will be in charge during my absence."

He then gave a half-chuckle. "Jason will undoubtedly be pleased to hear that. As for you, my last order before departing is to get some rest."

* * *

Paul heard a chorus of banging on his door. *I'm pretty sure I just got to sleep. It's weird how even being dead tired doesn't help me sleep any better. I'm pretty sure that I just had a dream where I was in bed at home but couldn't sleep. It's like I'm too tired to even sleep. Everything I experience here weighs too heavily on me. Everything sticks to me.*

A deep, teenage boy's voice interrupted. "Why are you knocking? Just barge in."

Paul was already sitting up when Jason, Camilla, and Alice emerged from the lighted doorway into the dark room.

"Paul, you need to get up," Camilla stated in the harshest voice that Paul had heard her make, "now!"

That sentence alone was enough to send Paul to his feet. "What's happening?"

"It would be better to show you," Jason responded gravely.

* * *

They reminded Paul of a nest of ants when someone kicks over a rock, thick in numbers but also orderly.

With his mind wheeling, Paul's body stood frozen.

"We've pressed the alarm," recounted Camilla. "The caravan to pick up that old Hunter was on its way today anyway. They are still about an hour out. They would have been here sooner, but they were flying in their best interrogators for the prisoner. I hate to say it, but we're on our own to deal until then."

In almost any other situation, an hour doesn't seem so long. Right now, that's the amount of time we just have to survive.

"There are three groups of them," Alice explained. "We have been watching their approach for three minutes. It is likely that they split from one group coming from the same direction as the lone Hunter we previously encountered. Each enemy appears to have received military-style training and is armed with an assault rifle, a sidearm, and a knife. None of the groups are heading straight for our position, meaning that they do not know our precise location. It is likely that the earlier Hunter was a scout. One scenario suggests that when he failed to report after a reconnaissance, his allies were alerted to our presence."

"These ones are a lot different from that old guy from earlier," surmised Jason. "There's no way he was trained like these Hunters. He was probably some local supporter they hired out. He was sent first because he was disposable."

"What about Luper?" croaked Paul.

"No word," answered Alice. "He has not answered his communicator. It is likely that he is in the midst of battle and is unable to reach us."

"Luper is the strongest fighter I've seen," Jason said. "There's no way he would be taken down by Hunters. I'm guessing that he's fighting another group somewhere further off. But that still means we're on our own."

"So, what the hell are we doing?" asked Camilla. "What kind of plan do we want to make?"

Paul kept his lips locked. Fear would have made it too difficult for him to speak anyway. He let the more experienced Amuli handle the planning. His scared brain did not seem to want to devote one cell to solving the situation.

"There are two likely reasons for Hunters to appear here," Alice rationalized with no hint of tension in her voice. "The first is that they are here on an information-finding mission that is not strictly reconnaissance. Rather, they may wish to steal our records from this base to make them public. That will no doubt put both A.R.C. ad A.I.M. under scrutiny from both the general population and governmental entities. In such a case, killing us is would be a secondary objective. The alternative scenario would be that they are entirely fanatical and only desire to see Amuli dead. In that example, their concern would be our deaths and the destruction of our base."

"Makes sense," responded Camilla, "what about a plan?"

Alice wasted no time. "I propose that I remain here, viewing the monitors. My telepathic link will aid each of you as you encounter the enemy. There are three groups. We have three Amuli ready to enter the field."

"You're the strongest one of us," said Camilla. "Wouldn't it be better if you went out into the field."

"No," Jason disagreed. "The plan is sound. We need to constantly know what we are facing out there. Who knows? Maybe they have more troops coming or more weapons. Whether they want to destroy this bunker or steal its info, she will be a powerful last line of defense."

"Can they get in?" croaked Paul, causing everyone else in the room to stare uncomfortably at him. "After the hatch is sealed?"

"Enough explosives will blow open any entrance," Jason related. "It may take time, but there's always a weak point. We can't take chances."

Paul gulped and nodded.

"Masks on," ordered Jason as he exited the monitor room. "Kill them all. As long as they live, they'll want you dead."

Chapter 16: Monster

Paul could feel beads of sweat well before he should have, given the temperature outside and the nature of his super-human body. *I'm taking on the smallest group. Remember, the smallest group. What did Alice say? This is well within my capabilities.*

This time Paul selected a line of well-covered evergreen branches to stakeout in. He did not even notice the thorny needles rubbing his mask and scalp.

"Paul, I see that you are in an advantageous position," came Alice's voice. *"You are at the end of my telepathic range. Should you advance any farther, I will not be able to stay in contact with you."*

There were five of them approaching, each wearing forest camouflage in shades of gray and brown to reflect the time of year. Shaded, full-faced visors sloping down from black helmets covered their faces.

Don't focus on your heartbeat this time! Paul screamed at himself. *Get out of your own head!*

Paul raised a hand as steady as he could make it. *I will always have the advantage from a distance. I just have to trust my anima barrier.*

He focused on the man standing to the center of the formation. *I need to create chaos.* A fiery green bolt leaped from his hand.

The stream of light impacted the man in the center, sending him skidding across the ground. More light exploded outward, pushing each Hunter away from each other.

Paul did not let himself become consumed with any level of confidence. *I need to pick them off.*

A second blast caught another Hunter on the shoulder and sent him spiraling across the ground. The remaining three regained their senses quickly.

Paul felt a buzzing and sizzling sensation right in front of his body. *Bullets!* In spite of himself, he retreated to another sturdy branch behind the trunk of the tree. *I'm so stupid! They can't hurt me.*

"*Paul!*" He realized that another voice in his head had been screaming there for several seconds. "*They-*"

A dark object filled his vision to the right of his head, toppling end-over-end. *Grenade!*

Paul half-leaped and half-fell from the tree in time to watch the flash above him. Shrapnel fizzled in his anima barriers, dispersing into streaks of green light.

We missed those on the monitors! The way that one was thrown... it would have been inside my anima barriers when it exploded!

"*Close combat is now the most advantageous approach,*" Alice instructed from far away.

The *katana* seemed to unsheathe itself as if yearning for air. *Now, I have to get in close... use the advantage of my speed. I don't know how many grenades they have.*

Another two projectiles appeared to pass Paul in slow-motion as he raced around the tree. *Good. Waste them.*

The first of the remaining Hunters appeared. Paul aimed a sideways cut at the man's chest but caught only a jacket and a bullet-resistant vest, slicing them clean. Paul diagnosed the sidestep as it happened. One of his legs hooked the moving leg of the Hunter, bending it backward and then upwards behind his back. As the Hunter fell forward, his helmet crashed into Paul's knee. The young Amulus could feel the splitting of the helmet and the sickening crunch of the man's nose being broken.

A second Hunter had rushed to Paul's other side to aid his friend. Paul's free fist found the softer-visor portion of the helmet. This time, a cheekbone cracked.

A kick sent the final rushing Hunter down for a moment. In a second, it was clear that Paul had done less damage than he had intended. The Hunter that Paul winged in the shoulder got to his feet, then sprung into Paul, tackling him. Both went sprawling onto the ground. In the scramble, the katana flew wide.

The man was on top of him. In his heart-stopping panic, Paul clawed at the man's waist for his sidearm. The Hunter's assault rifle was well out of reach after the kick. Feeling the shape of the weapon, Paul gave it a yank, tearing the holster clean off the Hunter's belt before tossing it. He felt a burning on the back of his head after his mask was jerked off.

A fist hammered down. To Paul, the blows blacked out everything. There was the fist and then black, the fist and the black, over and over. Each hit dazed the Amulus far beyond what Paul would have thought a superhuman would have felt. A rocky set of thighs choked his chest.

A piece of metal flashed Paul's throbbing eyes like a mirror. He threw his head to the side before a knife impaled the ground beside him. An uncomfortable warmness ran down Paul's cheek. The Hunter freed the thin blade from the ground.

A sudden streak of purple flashed and fizzled through the air.

Then, a blackened hole burned its way through the man's chest. Paul felt the man sag limply to the side without a sound. He lay frozen with the dead body on top of him.

"Paul! Paul!"

Paul moved to push the Hunter off of himself. The second his hands touched the slackened shoulders, he was racked by retching as bile filled his throat. It felt so horrible to touch a body without life in it. *It's like a sack of warm pudding!*

Someone else pushed the body away from him. Paul saw Camilla kneeling beside him. Her jacket was in tatters, but the rest of her appeared unharmed.

"Let me see your face."

Paul could feel welling of blood and the swelling tightening around his eye sockets.

"The cut's not deep," came Camilla's voice from seemingly far away. "I'm guessing that the anima slowed the knife down. Head wounds tend to bleed a lot, though. Those eyes are really going to hurt. That guy really went for the head, huh?"

Camilla easily ripped a piece off of her tattered jacket. "Hold this on it for now. Paul?"

He finally looked her in the eyes with his breath coming in rapid, short bursts. He pressed the fabric to his wounded cheek.

"These guys are all dead?" Camilla questioned.

"I–I dunno," Paul squeezed out in-between gulps of air.

Camilla surveyed the scene. "Unconscious, except for the one I took down. But if they were hit hard enough to shatter their bullet-proof visors, I don't think they will be getting up soon, and when they get up, life may not be so fun for them from now on."

I did that, Paul was seized by a short shivering fit. The entire world had gone cold.

"Jason and I got finished with our groups early," Camilla explained. "We met up then decided to look for you or any other Hunters coming in. He's probably still hunting some down."

Paul was barely listening. He fiddled with sheathing his sword over and over. It would not go back in.

"Paul, look at me."

He shifted his attention back to Camilla. Her look was one of concern underneath her mask.

"Listen to me. You had to do this. They wanted you dead. They wanted all of us dead. You feel this way because you are better than them. You're not a murderer. You're a defender."

Paul finally slid his *katana* back into place at his waist. He recovered his mask and slipped it on.

"Is Alice in your head right now?" Camilla asked softly. "Is she trying to talk you down too?"

Paul's mind snapped in realization. "I haven't heard from her in a while."

Camilla's expression went from worried to panicked. "Me neither. Jason said that he hadn't heard from her either back when we met up. We're just stumbling into each other. We have to go check on her."

They both dashed off the way they came.

* * *

The shed was in splinters.

"They got through," whispered Camilla from behind a nest of fallen branches. "We must've missed a group on the monitors."

"Or, they staggered their approach," hypothesized Paul. *Luper said that the shed protected the hatch from the elements so that we couldn't be buried alive. But it led them right to us.*

The two of them eyed the surrounding area. It was clear.

Camilla took on the duty for casting a glance down the open hole where the hatch door had been. She motioned Paul over.

"What did this? Explosives? Why didn't we hear them?"

"I'd say the shed was torn down," murmured Paul, "and these marks, it's like they did the opposite of welding somehow to undo the hatch."

"We have to go down there," asserted Camilla.

They descended. *She has to be alive. She's the strongest one of us. Why do I feel like she isn't okay? She was busy taking everyone down. That's why she isn't using the link. Right?*

Paul and Camilla felt it before they saw anything. There was a pressure in the air. A thickness like solid fog. *Anima. I've never felt it like this.*

Up until now, Paul had only experienced the slightest hint of emotion in anima. Luper had told him that this was a look into what the Amulus was feeling. Amuli could also feel a pressure like a sixth sense when anima was activated. This, however, felt different entirely.

A few steps off the ladder and the pair found it hard to walk. Paul perceived what seemed to be a golden haze in the air. Each step further added weight to his entire being.

"Gas?" choked Camilla in fear.

"No," Paul summoned his voice, "it's anima, but it's different..."

It became too much to say anything else.

The golden fog was contrasted with the red on the floor. Paul did not notice it until he felt a stickiness at the bottom of his boots. The drumming in the air made it difficult to concentrate on anything, even the grotesque floor.

"I-I can't keep going," Camilla panted after a few more paces.

Paul understood, the air was just so heavy, it was draining him, sucking out his will. Undoubtedly it was doing the same to Camilla. The feelings emitted from the anima in the air were putrid, stomach-churning.

Paul did not answer her. He kept plodding. Somewhere in his silent, stricken mind, curiosity was peaked. He wanted the knowledge of what was at the end of the hallway. Adding to that feeling was that he sensed Alice at the end.

The bodies began far past where Camilla was catching her breath. The first was faced down in the middle of the hallway. The blood was its darkest crimson around him. The rest were riddled against the walls. Paul truly smelled blood for the first time. Tinny and metallic-like its taste. The pounding on his body was numbing and made it easier to mentally separate himself from the scene.

The heaviness in the air reached its peak. Paul was forced to crawl. His sweatshirt became soaked from the floor and his own sweat. Drops ran off of his mask. The black paint around the eyes and mouth was dripping off.

Two people were floating as if hanging from wires. Paul had enough awareness left to see that one was flailing his arms and legs like the fins of a caught fish on a line. Somewhere far away, he could hear a man's scream. The other figure turned its head towards him with its eyes glowing a cold, metallic gold.

"A-Alice."

The name launched itself off Paul's lips.

"Alice, put him down," Paul called softly. "This is enough."

"*Not Alice.*"

The phrase scraped against Paul's mind. He lent a hand to his temples to stop the ringing. The thoughts were not Alice's. She had always slipped her own into his mind steadily and carefully.

"*Then who?*" Paul questioned.

"*The one who is necessary.*"

It took all of Paul's might not to run away from the pair of dead eyes that glowed at him. "*Where's Alice?*"

"*Not here. Not necessary.*"

"What are you talking about?" Paul screamed. "Of course, she's necessary!"

"You are only afraid."

The word began rattling over and over again inside. *Afraid. Afraid. Afraid. Afraid. Afraid. Afraid. Afraid. Afraid.*

The room melted away. There was a garden with only a blanket of whiteness in the distance. Sunflowers dotted the perimeter. Inside of those were rows of tulips, daffodils, and chrysanthemums, all gleaming yellow and gold. Wild daisies and dandelions mingled with ground-covering green plants in the center. A blonde-hair girl surveyed the plants while crouching, every so often running a hand over a flower petal.

"Alice?"

She did not turn to him.

"Alice."

Her blue eyes dripped with tears. "I am sorry. I am so very sorry, Paul."

"Where is this?" Paul asked in wonder.

"In my mind," Alice answered meekly. "Some Psychics can assemble thoughts in a way that can trick the brain into believing it somewhere else. It is an illusion, a non-existing plane made up only of senses."

"These are your thoughts," surmised Paul. "You're sharing them with me. Why is this happening?"

Alice turned away again. "I do not believe that it will hurt you, that is, if you are seemingly unconscious in the actual world."

"What is happening out there?"

Alice closed her eyes and the tears streaming faster. "It is my fault. I was alone. I am always alone. When I was a baby. When I was a toddler. When I was young. When I was a teenager. I am dangerous. Dangerous to everyone. They thought me less so when they let me out. I thought the same. No, it was there for a long time. It is still here, the Monster."

"What is it?" mouthed Paul as gently as he could.

"I was not strong enough to deal with it. I was not human. I was too lonely. I was too strong for myself to handle. I needed something else. Something else to share my burden. She came to do that. It is because I am weak. I am weak from being too strong."

Paul went to crouch beside her. "I can't imagine what any of that was like. There have always been people who have cared about me. Oh, but I'm not trying to brag. That was stupid to say it that way. It was always a small group and most days they were all I needed. Sometimes, though, I felt like I was in the background. I was in the background in everyone else's lives. I was just scenery in their story. I blamed myself. I don't know how much of it is my fault or if it is everyone else's. I was sure that most of it was on me. I think I still do believe that sometimes."

Paul paused for a moment before saying, "I said something really stupid to you once."

Alice was back to her usual self for a moment. "I do not recall anything you have that I might classify as stupid."

"When I first came to the bunker, you talked about regarding each other as allies. I said something about that being too formal. I told you that we should be acquaintances. That was too cold, too. That was me sabotaging myself with my inability to open up to anyone. I always put this lock on myself and don't know why. I think it's just who I am. I don't think I'm good enough to be associated with anyone. Why would I not want to be friends with someone who just saved my life? I should have said that we were friends."

Alice shook her head. "You must not take blame for that. I cannot interact with other people efficiently..."

Paul shook his head back at her. "I will take the blame. Because we are friends. You, Cam, Luper, Jason, and I all depend on each other with our lives. We train together and eat together. What else could we all be but friends?"

"I have never had a friend," mentioned Alice.

"I think that we both have more friends than we realized," responded Paul. "Friends share each other's burdens. I grew up with this friend named Robby. He was too loud, and I was too quiet. We balanced each other out. He would do something stupid and I would have to get him out of it. Then,

I would be too smart for my own good and he would have to get me out of the situation. You're my friend, Alice. I'll help to take on what you're carrying."

Paul was back sitting on the wet floor. The pulsing denseness in the air was gone.

Alice lay unmoving. Paul crawled over to her. She was breathing peacefully.

Chapter 17: Ending the Beginning

Paul heard a fast-paced rustling in the distance as he checked Alice's pulse. A door to a storage room hissed and clicked shut.

"Cam?" Paul called out.

He crept towards the door when there was no response. He pushed the door open slowly.

"Not another step!" a voice growled.

Paul froze on the threshold. His heartbeat faster again after it had been allowed to rest for a moment.

A Hunter stood unmasked at the center of the storage room. His dirty blonde hair was greased back. The man's thin face was tightened into a scowl. Each of his gloved hands gripped black cylinders topped with singular, circular buttons.

"You and I will play a game," the man spoke through a course, Eastern European accent. "Much more exciting that Russian Roulette."

Paul noticed something strange on the room's right edge, halfway between himself and the Hunter. A smartphone had been placed on a makeshift tripod.

"I wanted to play with that other creature," the Hunter snorted. "I would have been dead by the time the camera was on. You will be better."

"What game?" Paul questioned. "What is this? This is serious-"

"No words," the Hunter warned. "No more from you. This is what the Soviet army did not understand. The power to play to people. To give a show. The world needed to see what happened in Alaska. No one believes without video. People are skeptical. They always need proof."

Paul breathed through his teeth. *He must be a Soviet veteran from the Battle of Alaska. When everything got wiped out by Amuli fighting. Much of the western islands are gone. I can't imagine what seeing that does to you, how it would twist you.*

"You creatures are clever," the Hunter ranted. "You do not slip up. People do not see what you do. I have to make them see, even if I just force it."

Who is this guy? Doesn't he just want us dead?

The Hunter continued. "The death in the air that creature was making gave me a distraction. Enough time to plant bombs. One of these sets them off. The other, nothing."

He held up the detonators. They looked deceptively ordinary and crude. At this moment, they were more dangerous and threatening than Paul's superpowered sword. They loomed large in the teenager's eyes.

The Russian continued his explanation. "Bunkers are safe from bombs above but not from bombs inside. I've seen you creatures move. You may take out one arm but not both in time it takes me to push fingers down. You probably want me alive for questioning. That won't happen. You can't sever both arms in time. Too hard to tell how much black magic would knock me out. You will have to kill me to stop bombs, but you may not want to."

The Russian gestured toward the camera phone. "The feed is going to a private computer. From there, it can go everywhere on the internet. In the view of the camera, I put my arms up and no detonators visible."

He raised both arms. "I am innocent to the camera. There's no sound. I have no weapons. From this angle, it sees you, a thing in a blank mask. You could kill an innocent man in the eyes of the world. Imagine, many comrades joining us to rid the world of you. How many of your kind will you kill? Let me press the detonator and only you creatures here will die. I win no matter what. You creatures rig the world against us, so I rig this game against you."

Paul's heart was pounding so hard he feared it would come loose. His head hurt the more he taxed his brain. *I just have to think! THINK! THINK! THINK! It's so impossible! Could this really become the moment that leads to the Hunters rising up in numbers and massacring Amuli? Could I really sacrifice myself? Could I really sacrifice Cam and Alice?*

"No thinking. Decide now!"

Both of the Russian's thumbs twitched.

Just before he was going to hit the buttons, the Hunter saw the guard and then the hilt of Paul's katana between his eyes. The blade of the sword emerged from the other side of his head, a perfect throw by Paul. That was it. He was gone instantaneously. He lifelessly sank to the ground in front of Paul's outstretched arm.

Paul dove for the detonators as the man's grip went slack. It was all reflex as he closed in towards the fast-falling cylinders. He felt his hands brush them in midair. When his body slid to a stop, he was cradling both of them.

With the detonators in hand, the realization began to hit home for Paul. Where there had been a man standing a moment before, there was now a body quickly leaking blood. He could not bring himself to look at it.

It's happened. Someone is dead by hands. I know A.R.C. agents kill people, that's part of the job. I just thought that, somehow, I could avoid it. But he's dead. A life, someone with thoughts and dreams and ambitions. He was someone's son. He could have been someone's brother, or husband, or father. What right did I have…. no… Why did I have to do this? Why!

The fluids he had been holding down for so long all came up. He threw up until it hurt his throat and then threw up more. In the end, he was gagging on saliva. Between his retching, he was screaming, beginning with words before they broke apart and failed him.

A few weeks ago, thinking that I would have to kill someone would be the most ludicrous thing! How did this happen?

A large hand softly hung on one of his shoulders.

"Get it all out," a man's voice advised.

Paul shook his head. "It won't all come out. It will never come out."

"The bombs are all disarmed," related Luper. "The clean-up crew is here. We should be leaving. Listen to me. This is not your responsibility. It is mine. You did everything as well as you could and went well beyond what you have learned here. Any teacher would be proud."

Chapter 18: Refuge

The interior of the van was large enough to hold a table. Paul thrummed his fingers over his seat. He shivered behind a full cup of tea.

"He had things his way the entire time," Luper explained gravely. "Either detonator would have set off the bombs. They were on a timer as well. No matter what happened, he wanted the bombs to go off."

"I did nothing then," Paul grumbled. "The bombs would have killed me if you hadn't gotten there."

"Do not sell yourself short in this," warned Luper. "You prevented the bombs from being immediately detonated. You provided Camilla and I the time to disarm the bombs. Not only that, but you had also been fighting for hours. You were fighting the Hunters and yourself. The Hunters that you knocked unconscious, along with the one you captured hours earlier, will provide insight about the formulation of this attack and why they chose to pursue this remote location. Most importantly, A.R.C. may learn how they found us. The fault is entirely mine. There were feints within feints with their plan. They sent the seemingly unaffiliated Hunter first. I took the bait and looked around. They sent me on a wild-goose chase and then moved in. It was an international group. One of the most organized that I have seen coming from Hunters."

"What about the video?" Paul asked sheepishly.

"Time will tell its effectiveness," Luper analyzed, "My prediction is that it will make less of an impact than they were expecting. A.R.C. can put out the word that the video is clearly doctored. They can put words in the mouths of politicians and businesses. That is how far the reach goes. For them, the video came as a cost. The cell phone left at the scene will yield more evidence. With the phone, it may be possible to track all the locations it has been to, along with fingerprints of people who have held it. In addition, intelligence operatives will attempt to decipher where the feed was being sent."

Paul kept his head down.

Luper leaned over the table. "There were no good options. However you chose the best of the bad options. It was the decision that I would have made. Alice, Camilla, Jason, and I are alive because of you. Focus on immediacy and not what comes next. You feel the way you do as of this moment because you are human. Contrary to what the Hunters believe, you have proven yourself to be much more human than they are."

"I'll take the compliment," Paul responded hollowly.

"See that you do that," Luper quipped. "Now, that brings us to Alice."

"How is she?" Paul blurted.

"Asleep," Luper answered in a low voice. "She is resting soundly in another van. The medics on hand have found no issues with her. My question to you is, what issues from her did you see?"

Paul related his episode with Alice in the gory bunker.

Luper clasped his bearded chin when Paul had finished. "Paul, I am going to have to do, perhaps, the most difficult thing that I will ever ask of you. Tell no one what you saw from her."

Paul's fingernails dug deep enough into his seat to tear the fabric. "What?"

Luper leaned toward each window of the van, scanning the area outside. This was the second time he had done so.

"I have already checked this van for bugs, so I will be able to speak to you freely about this. It is not only me that needs this favor, but Alice as well. I wanted to keep it hidden from... well, the world. I am profoundly sorry for what you experienced and what I am asking you to do now. I need you to promise me."

Luper is frightened. I've never seen him scared. Still, he's never given me a reason not to trust him. Even when he is deceptive, he always seems to have my best interest at heart.

Paul winced. "Right. If it's for Alice."

"Paul, that is the best answer that I could have hoped for," Luper relented. "That is exactly why this must be a secret. It is for her sake. To know Alice's past is the know who she is. Tell me, Paul, what do you about the anima supply within each person?"

"Everyone has the same amount," answered Paul. "You can even feel that amount in non-Amuli. I'm beginning to understand that now. Anima feels like someone's life, their vitality. They don't exude it, but you can pick up the feeling when you're close enough to them. It's the true essence of someone. You taught me that it is what you do with our anima supply that matters."

"What if someone had more than that amount?" Luper questioned.

Catching on, Paul answered with a half-formed question. "But you said before-"

Luper shot him a confessionary look. "What I taught you before is what I am required to teach. I told you about the general knowledge about Amuli as far as most A.R.C. operatives know. Only the highest levels of A.R.C. know the truth, in addition to those who have seen the proof with their own eyes. There are Amuli beyond other Amuli. Amuli who have more power than anyone else on the planet. The term among those who know is Alpha Amulus. That is who Alice is."

Paul let Luper's words sink in for a moment before asking, "How many are there?"

Luper leaned back in his seat. "They are exceedingly rare. Perhaps one or two are identified in every generation. As of this moment, Alice is the only Alpha Amulus that A.R.C. knows about. She is, in essence, the most powerful being on the planet."

Things were beginning to click in Paul's mind. "She said that she was always alone."

Luper nodded. "That is the crux of this conversation. Alice's powers manifested when she was at an absurdly young age. From the moment she entered A.R.C., it was clear to the high-level researches who she was. She was only an orphaned baby, but marked as the most dangerous person on the planet. For that reason, she was kept isolated for years. She was constantly locked behind doors in cells, hospital wings, and even science labs while being kept far from her crystal necklace. Yes, there are hypocrites in A.R.C. that do not see what separates us from A.I.M."

How will I know to watch out for them? Paul swallowed.

Luper continued. "Most of her contact with other humans came through a video screen. Tutors taught her about a world she had never seen. She learned social mannerisms and conversational skills from books. You have witnessed the effect that method has had on her. Between the hollow lessons, she was molded into a weapon. It was the intention of a few to turn her into the greatest weapon in A.R.C.'s arsenal. In the minds of those people, it was okay to use some of A.I.M.'s methods if it meant crushing them forever."

Paul thought of Alice's aloofness and the coldness he had always felt from her very being. *No, she is more than what A.R.C. turned her into. I've seen her comradery with Cam and Jason. I made the decision to consider her a friend because that is what she is to me.*

"What changed?"

"Some changes at the top," Luper responded, looking through a window and into the distant woods. "As more new people came in, the less even the higher brass could stomach what was being done to a young girl. There was that... and that I finally kept an unspoken promise I made a long time ago. When the decision was made to let Alice train as any A.R.C. recruit and to join her peers, albeit except for a few missions sent from the Council itself, they wanted someone they could trust. It also helped that I was on the outs with the old regime. In the beginning, it was the two of us at one of A.R.C.'s most secluded bunkers. Once in a while, an important mission would come down that they wanted Alice to handle. They said it was to hasten her progression. The truth is that they wanted to see her in action. The last of those missions came just before you joined us. She was meant to attend a party in Tokyo in order to acquire a certain sword which was unknowingly infused with an anima crystal. For whatever reason, plans changed, and the sword was sent in the mail. Either way, Alice was sent to procure it. She even had electronic-crippling E.M.P. devices in hand as a precaution. The change of plans was so sudden that she did not even have time to change out of her party dress. She was to wear it on the private plane there so that she could step right into the event. I find it somewhat ironic that we in A.R.C. take so many precautions but sometimes forget the smaller details, like giving an agent a change of clothes."

Paul stared wide-eyed at the sword at his side. *That's the reason she broke into my house that night and why the phones didn't work. I thought she had just been patrolling in the area. It also explains the dress. Something else—I guess she chose to be found after I became an Amulus. She wanted to draw the A.I.M. agents away from me. She did all that while terribly wounded... for me. Those definitely weren't the actions of a lab rat.*

Luper did not stop relating the story. "During one of our first missions together before Jason and then Camilla joined us, we were called in as backup after a match for the city of Pittsburgh. The challenging side, whether A.I.M. or A.R.C., tends to send spies into the city and the surrounding area to scope things out should they emerge victoriously and take it over. It is a gray area in our gray world. This particular time, A.I.M. wanted to draw blood. Alice and I were well outside the city and suburbs in a forest like this one when we became separated. When I found her, she was ripping an A.I.M. operative apart limb from limb. Her personality and mannerisms had completely changed. She was a being of pure rage and hatred. I was foolish enough to try to intervene."

Luper pulled down his collar to reveal an indented scar running the length of his collarbone, which Paul had glimpsed during their first training together.

"She only stopped after she exhausted herself," Luper explained solemnly. "After that episode, I must confess that I was resolved to explain the episode to the council, knowing full well what it would mean for her. When she awoke as her usual self, I could not go through with it. There she was, a young girl innocent of what her body had just done and innocent of what the world had done to her. I realized that this other personality of hers, the "Monster" as she named it, was the culmination of all the loneliness, suffering, and rage she felt at the world. Humans are meant to be social creatures, and she was deprived of her very nature. She bottled it all up inside, leaving herself an empty husk void of feeling. However, she is human. All that emotion needs to come out sometime. She is like any other child. She needs to learn how to express her feelings and how to interact with others. The pity is that this has not been permitted to happen until late in her teenage years. That is why you are so key to this situation."

Paul pointed to himself in confusion. "Me? I'm not a psychologist or-"

"No," Luper interjected. "You help to solve her problem by

just being you. It is not just you but Camilla and Jason as well. You may not be able to see it, but it is undoubtable to me that she has been her most open and happy with you three. Before you three came, Alice remained in her room at all times. She ate there, trained there, and studied there. It felt as though I was living alone in the bunker aside from the time spent on missions. Now, she eats and trains with the rest of you. She is finding a real way to interact with three peers who have vastly different personalities and to feel emotions fully. The Monster may then disappear on its own."

"What about today?" Paul questioned.

"The Monster emerged to defend the three of you," formulated Luper. "I am sure of it. Her fear emerged to protect the only companions she has ever known. The Monster did not rampage. It aimed itself. Not only is that progress, but I had never felt it even come close to surfacing before today. You may not believe me, however, I am sure that she a progressing towards a more normal life. I was positive of this hypothesis days after you came here."

"I don't know what you see in me," Paul complained. "I mean, I can barely talk to other people."

"This is not about the usual social norms of the outside world, Paul," Luper dismissed. "The night you encountered Alice for the first time was symbolic. I read over Alice's report over and over again. That night, you saved her, and she saved you. Alice never had a reciprocal relationship like that with another person. You depended on her and she depended on

237

you."

"I almost-" Paul began before he was cut off again.

"Friendly agents incoming," Luper relayed as he gestured to the window. "They seem to be in a bit of a rush."

"Is she in here?" a man in a skull mask demanded as he barged into the van.

"Who?" asked Luper quickly.

"The blonde one."

Luper nearly bowled the man over as he leaped out of the van. "Who was guarding the van? How many guards did you have?"

"Uh... there was just one," the flustered man stuttered. "His name's Stevens."

"One guard?" barked Luper. "What if this attack is not over? What if there are still Hunters lurking around and looking to carry a young Amulus off? Or perhaps she awoke but was dazed by a concussion and wandered off confused into the woods? How can I trust you with my charges?"

Paul realized that he had never seen Luper truly enraged before. He could feel the burning anima radiating the surrounding air.

"What's this?" asked a lean man wearing a white mask emblazoned with a golden scale hanging evenly.

The skull mask explained hoarsely. "We can't find one of the young ones. The blonde girl."

"Ayers," the white and gold mask stated, sounding more disappointed than angry, "I said at least three guards by the vans. Always expect more from the enemy, and you will not be disappointed even if you are wrong."

"Stevens and I thought... well... they're Amuli themselves..." Ayers rambled.

"Amuli-in-training," corrected the scales. "Our greatest resource for the future. You cannot take lightly the lives in your hands."

Ayers shrunk back and nodded.

The man in the white and gold mask tilted his disguise upward. Behind it was a clean-shaven, fresh face with warm brown eyes.

Paul's brow furrowed in surprise. *Adam Avery. I must have read over his file a million times. He was a prodigy as a teenager, working his way up to an experienced operative by the time he turned twenty. No one has ever done missions as efficiently or effectively as him for A.R.C. His fighting level is unmatched. Recently, he became part of A.R.C.'s ruling Council while only in his mid-twenties. He is the youngest Council member ever by more than a decade. Why is he here? Wait, he's the operative in charge of all of North America!*

Avery seemed to instinctively rattle his purple crystal-encrusted rapier at his side. "Luper, all other words are useless at this point. Are you and your trainee willing to come off your moment of R and R to help search for her? You two know her best if she's left any trail. I've already sent out the word through my Psychic."

"Of course," Luper affirmed. "We'll scour opposite directions, Paul. You know these woods."

Paul was shaken out of his moment of star-struck. "Right."

Despite his aching body, he dashed off.

* * *

The branches and bushes grew thicker the more time Paul spent passing through the forest. He pushed through the scratching thorns that choked the sky. Rain had turned the ground into sucking muck. Despite the short break, Paul felt that the anima inside of him had faded to little more than an inner shadow. *I'll be in trouble if a fight comes, even against a normal human.*

Paul broke through to a small clearing. The grass was overgrown with tiny blue flowers interspersed in the dark green. *Flowers and green grass in November?*

He saw her then. She was on her knees with her torso bent slightly backward. She looked unflinchingly upward while the raindrops mixed into her blue eyes.

Paul made a strange observation. *She's not looking at the flowers, just on the gray sky.*

"The flowers and grass grow can grow here into autumn because this is where some of the heat from the bunker escapes," Alice whispered. "The heat softens the ground and prevents frost. It is just as it is around the shed."

Paul saw through the explanation. *Is that how the Hunters knew where we were? Maybe local hunters and hikers talked about strange patches of green growth, and the Hunters learned about the rumors.*

"Leave," she murmured, though it was not a warning.

"Alice, what about what I said before?"

"That is the reason," Alice explained breathlessly. "If you are my friend, then you will be close by me. If you are close to me, then I will hurt you. I do not wish to see a friend hurt."

Paul felt words welling up, but none let themselves out.

There was a rush from the bushes, leading Paul to put a hand on his sword. Luper came striding out. It was then that Paul realized that Alice was no longer conscious. Her eyes were closed and her breath came out in slow wisps of white steam.

Without a word, Luper leaned down to gently cradle her in his arms with all the kindness of a caring father. He slowly paced back into the woods with Paul following behind.

Chapter 19: Inquisition

Paul's mouth was dry for a different reason than it usually was lately. Still, the uncomfortable experience of being scrutinized by a room of strangers felt familiar. However, he felt no solace in the familiarity.

"We have read the reports of each member present during the ordeal."

That was Noor Ahmad of Jordan, the current Speaker of the Council and overseer of Asia. Even in middle-age, her mass of hair was perfectly black.

She continued in her deep, authoritative voice. "What we seek now is your personal observations and comments on the event. Please know that your words here will be kept only among the Council for our deliberation."

Beyond the files he had read, Luper characterized her as tough yet fair. As the Speaker of the Council, she had the highest position in the shadowy, true version of A.R.C. The leaders that the general public knew were simply figureheads. It was Ahmad's job to set agendas for the Council and plan meetings. When it came to voting, she had two votes while the rest of the Council had one each.

A green crystal gleamed from a golden ring as she sorted through papers.

"I first have to ask you," she continued, "did each of your fellow trainees perform to the best of their abilities from what they have demonstrated in training?"

"Ye-yes," Paul stammered when he realized a "yes" would better fit the formal occasion than a "yeah." "We all took up tasks and completed them. Cam... um... Camilla, Jason, and... Alice each contributed to the defense of the bunker and its intel."

"According to all reports and comments, you performed admirably as well, despite only joining us several weeks ago."

That was Adam Avery, who was the most amiable face out of the group, in addition to being the youngest by some twenty years.

"Wouldn't know it by the look of you, but you're apparently a fighter," complimented and insulted a leathery faced, yet handsome, man with a rhythmic voice. "You each have my praise for your actions. A success is a success at times, right?"

Kai Parata, from New Zealand, Paul recognized. *Luper called him the most independent member of the Council. On the other hand. I hear he inspires loyalty. A true Maori chief who represents*

Australia, New Zealand, and the Pacific island nations.

"Was there anything out of the ordinary with any of your team members?" asked Sofia Vidal of Argentina. "Any strange behaviors?"

Paul remembered Luper's notes on Vidal. *"Another cool-headed but no-nonsense member of the Council. She may seem similar to Speaker Ahmed, even down to the luscious black hair. However, she has a way of reading people that is quite uncommon... even among shadowy agents."*

The South American overseer was known for her previous work in A.R.C.'s intelligence branch. A purple crystal stayed perfectly still on her necklace as she spoke calmly.

This is it, Paul realized. *The loaded question. They all want to know if anything went wrong with Alice. I can't even give away the fact that I know she is an Alpha Amulus.*

"No," remarked Paul with mock poise. "Nothing that I was aware of. I mean... we were all very scared by the life-or-death situation, especially in my case. That was the only way in which I saw any difference in the way that my team members act regularly."

Hidden behind his lips, Paul gritted his teeth. *It always seems easier to sprinkle in some bits of truth when you have to lie.*

"Understandable," affirmed Sena Abara, overseer of Africa. "You believe that this was the only reason?"

Paul's eyes drifted to the large iron knife the Ghanaian had in front of her. A lime-green crystal danced in its crossed middle.

Luper characterized her as, *"Purely stone-faced, impossible to read, and difficult to sway in any direction. I have not met many people more resolute than her."*

"Yes," Paul replied quickly.

The final council member to his turn to speak. "Right. I don't believe in tip-toeing around things."

Paul's body went cold. *He's going to ask directly about Alice! Luper didn't prepare me for this.*

"How do you characterize the actions of your superior, Gregory Luper?" interrogated the Englishman, Gareth Jackson, with his purple-crystal longbow leaning against his chair.

"His actions?" Paul asked as he tried to rewire his brain towards this new thread in the conversation.

"Yes," said Jackson. "From all reports, it does not appear that he provided an adequate defense of his bunker neither before the attack nor after it. Rather, he left it to trainees as he allowed himself to be tricked by Hunters."

Paul had caught a sense of creeping dislike in Luper's tone when he had spoken of Jackson. *"He is a man who will do anything if he believes that it will serve A.R.C.'s interests. That attitude inspires loyalty, among other things. That is why he has been elected as Speaker more times than anyone else. Beyond that, he is a military man through and through. He was S.A.S. before he became an Amulus. He was there when A.R.C. was first founded."*

"Luper–" Paul's words broke.

"I will phrase it as a question. What were your impressions of what he did during the incursion?"

Paul scrambled. "Well... I think that... he may have made in error in judgment, but it was one that I probably would have made as well. He did leave the bunker to trainees, but Alice and Jason are extremely experienced and Cam... Camilla is very capable."

"An error in judgment that you may have made," Jackson repeated, "and yet, you are a trainee who can afford to make mistakes in his training. Your superior is not in the same position."

"How many experienced operatives would have done the same thing?" commented Adam Avery.

"That is far beside the point," argued Jackson as a vein bulged amongst his close-cropped gray hair. "If a mistake has been made, it does not matter how many others would have made it."

"In the short time I've known Luper," Paul interjected,

surprising himself, "I think he has done everything he could for all the trainees under him, including me."

"We appreciate your candor," said Speaker Ahmed. "I believe that is all the questions we have for you at this time. We will now deliberate and call you and your fellow trainees back in when we decide what will be done for you after this point."

Chapter 20: Mirror

Paul found two of his teammates in a sitting area that seemed stylish but had cushions that seemed about as comfortable as thin planks of wood. Camilla, clad in a white button-down shirt and black skirt, watched him slide onto a chair to fiddle with his tie. *This feels so bulky. It's worse than my school uniform. I don't know why Luper always wears one. Whoever first decided suits were fashionable, anyway? What makes them different from other clothes?*

The office building was built around the Chesapeake, giving it a curve and full view of the water from this side. A few tiny pedal boats slowly paced the placid blue amid shimmers of reflected rays. *Luper says that Baltimore is a prized city to have since it's so close to D.C. The occupying organization can keep an eye on the politicians in its pockets to make sure they are really doing what they want. Holding meetings here is meant to be a testament to pride in the organization and the Council's power.*

Alice stared off into the distance of the sparkling, dark blue bay.

She still feels guilty. Paul tried to stomp down on the images of the Monster, which ripped men apart. The sad girl in the simple green dress resting her head on a hand seemed so different from the person or thing he had seen in the bunker that day. *I want to tell her something to make her feel better. I don't know what. I tried at the time. I never know what to say to anyone.*

"That bad, huh?" Camilla asked after observing him.

"It could have been worse." *It could still be.*

"Have you seen Jason?"

"No," Paul answered with other worries still consuming his mind.

Camilla looked around. "I lost track of him a while ago. I know Luper just went in so-"

"I'll find him," Paul interjected as he rose back up. *Just the monotony of walking would feel good right now. Sitting or standing still feels uncomfortable.*

"Paul-"

He was already down the hallway. A few minutes of wandering around the office building left him forgetting what he was doing. *Do they know what happened with Alice? Is Luper in trouble?* The questions circulating in his mind took over the rest of his senses.

"P-Paul? Paul Engel?"

A small man with glasses came scurrying towards him. "My God, you look so much like him." A soft mahogany hand extended his way. "Oof, I'm sorry, do you know me or... who I am?"

Paul looked into the kindly, tiny eyes which studied him before extending his own hand. "Um... I don't. Look, I'm really sorry. I don't mean..."

"Oh, no, it's fine. I guess that I shouldn't expect you to," the man said through a wide smile. "I'm Dr. Hamilton Barnes."

"Paul Engel, but I guess you already said that."

Dr. Barnes took a step back and continued to look Paul over. Paul's eyes shifted down to the floor.

"Oh! I'm sorry that I'm staring," the skinny man apologized. "It's like seeing him again... and her again. Seeing you I... I'm making a mess of things. I was very good friends with your parents, Paul. In fact, I really think they were the only friends I had at the time."

"Oh," Paul murmured in his surprise while lost in his own mind. *This is what I've been waiting for. This is what I wanted to learn here.*

"You know what?" Dr. Barnes bellowed enthusiastically. "If you have time, we could talk a little in here. I was just on this way to set up a briefing, but that's not for a while."

Paul nodded, forgetting his purpose for roaming the hallway. "I can do that. I mean... I really would like to do that."

Dr. Barnes led him to a conference room with an arm around his shoulders. Once inside, he dumped an armful of portfolios and began flipping through them.

"You know, you've got your dad's shape," Dr. Barnes began. "I mean the head, mouth, jawline, and everything. You even have the messy hair that's just a little bit wavy, which is something that always made him a little frustrated. But your nose and those brown eyes that don't let anyone what you're thinking, other than that you're deep in thought, those are definitely your mom's... along with that expression."

Paul suddenly became aware of the intense look of curiosity on his face, wide-open eyes and a slightly ajar mouth marked it. Strangely embarrassed by the attention, he tightened his lips together and relaxed his eyes.

"How did you know them?" Paul asked quizzically.

"Oh, right," Dr. Barnes said. "Forgive me. I'm analyzing you. That's an analyst's job, after all. You probably knew all of what I've just said from pictures you've already seen of them. We all worked together in the intelligence division. Those were great times."

Paul glanced about Dr. Barnes, looking for a colored, glassy flicker of light.

"Oh no," realized Dr. Barnes. "You won't find any anima crystals on me. None ever clung on to me."

"I'm sorry.... I just... I," Paul rambled, red-faced and mortified.

Dr. Barnes waved a hand and smiled. "No need. It is probably surprising to learn, after what you've just been through, that there are non-Amuli out there who are willing to help out Amuli. Your mother was one of us, too."

"Right, I knew that," stammered Paul. "I should have... remembered. Will you tell me about them? I mean... I know things about them away from all this. No one could ever tell me what they did here. I mean, if you have time, Dr. Barnes."

Dr. Barnes beamed. "It's Hamilton for you or Ham. That's what your dad called me. I actually have a nervous habit of showing up to places way too early. I've got plenty of time."

"I don't know where to start," Paul murmured uneasily.

"Then I'll start for you, Paul," Hamilton insisted softly. "In the early nineties, I was a linguistics major about to graduate early, who was afraid to even leave his dorm room except for class. It was a few years after Alaska and A.R.C. had just started up. Out of nowhere, they approached me in a school cafeteria, promising a lot of money for a lot of work. At the time, I thought I was going to be something like a C.I.A. analyst like Jack Ryan. I jumped at the offer."

Hamilton gave Paul a knowing smile. "Sorry, I needed to get that out so I could get to the part where I met your parents. After landing a job, I was quite literally shoved into a closet that had a couple of computers. I stress that these were the very early days. Working beside me in the closet was a dark-haired woman who always made me feel stupid, even though she never wanted to."

Paul returned a small smirk.

Hamilton went on. "During my entire life before that, I felt like I was the smartest guy in the room. I was not the smartest person in that closet. Sam was something. She could triangulate a position and give you exact directions there long before everyone started using a G.P.S. I thought her keyboard would break or catch on fire every time she was ironing out an equation or flipping through research notes. She was kind and not the fake niceness you put on just to work with someone. She really cared and always asked me how I was doing. When I was tired or struggling, she knew and gently pushed me through."

Paul could tell that Hamilton's starry eyes were not in the present.

"One day, they told us that an Amulus would be joining our tiny division. Sam and I didn't know what to expect. I mean, would some superhuman be bossing us around because they were physically stronger than us? Then, one day we see this guy using all of his strength to carry bags upon bags of takeout Chinese food come to our door. He awkwardly said something like, 'all they told me was that I'd be joining a division, so I wanted to bring everyone lunch on the first day. I didn't know the exact number of people so... here ya go.'"

This made Paul laugh a little.

"We were eating chicken and broccoli for two weeks before it got moldy!" Hamilton cracked. "He thought that Sam and I always took things too seriously. He was always pulling pranks like sticking a picture of a horror movie monster in a stack of papers to get a jump-scare later on. He enjoyed brightening things up, if only for a moment. I get the sense that he was trying to lighten the load of his own past as well. I always figured that something bad or tragic had once happened to him, but he never told me what it was. He was an open book in every other way. I'm sure he told Sam. They told each other everything, but you probably guessed that. Oh! You should have seen when-"

~ ~ ~

The room changed into something darker. There was a misty blackness everywhere. Water dropped as if from a loud, leaky faucet. There was sniffling and the dull whine of a child who had been crying for hours. A small pair of hands pushed jarringly against a set of bars that were too strong to even rattle.

The bars slid open for a moment, but none of the occupants struggled for an exit. What seemed like a skinny sack was shoved inside.

"Who?" asked a young voice cautiously from behind the dark.

"It's Johnny!" exclaimed another young voice, frail in desperation. "He's bad! He's real bad, Mikey! Just... just try getting into his head like you do."

"I... I just don't know if it will help," sobbed Mikey. "It doesn't always-"

"Try! Just try!"

A little figure put a hand on the collapsed child at the entrance of the cell.

~ ~ ~

Paul came back gasping. His eyes darted across the conference room. A deep urge to shiver arose in his core. *It was so dark! The anima in the air... it was sad and scared... so impossibly scared. Even in the dark, even though it was younger, I will always recognize that one face from the pictures I grew up with. Mikey. Michael Engel. Dad.*

Hamilton was pointing a pen in his direction while reading his face like an interesting report. "Wait a minute, I've seen this! I've seen this! Well, not exactly like this, but I need to write down."

"D-Did you see it, too?" Paul choked.

"No," Hamilton replied in-between pen-strokes, "but I

do know that you saw something. That fast movement of the eyes. The tensing of the body towards a non-existent situation. Everything within the span of only a few seconds. Tell me, what did you see?"

"It hard to see but... everything was so... awful," Paul moaned while still seeing the cell in his mind like flipping through a moving-picture book. "Why did I see it? What is wrong with me?"

"On no, Paul, nothing's wrong with you, per se," said Hamilton over his notebook. "It's that you have something different. Something that makes you stand out, even among Amuli. It is rare enough that it doesn't even have a name, but I can explain it to you."

"It's like having a dream," Paul explained. "Except everything feels real and makes sense. I'm not in any of them."

"That's because it is real," Hamilton clarified, "or, at least, we think so. The theory is that anima leaves a residue that Amuli can sense. It is similar to feeling emotion in live anima in the air, which I'm sure that you have experienced. I don't need to tell you that emotions can invoke a memory and vice versa. Since we know that Amuli constantly emit anima and believe that even non-Amuli do as well, this anima residue may float around in the air or cling to objects and people."

"If they're someone else's memories, then why don't I see things through their eyes?" questioned Paul. *Everything sticks. Everything sticks to me.*

"A good observation," Hamilton pointed out. "It leads to another theory. You will probably see those memories from the viewpoint of a construct of yourself. It would be difficult to see and feel all stimuli in exactly the same way someone else does. We are all wired differently in our brains. Think about how difficult it is for an Amulus Psychic to even send a mental image. That is a process that we haven't figured out either, by the way. It just may be easier for your brain to make sense of things through a construct of yourself, even if you were not at the event. Now, I have questions for you, if you'll allow me. What did you see this time? Also, how many times has this happened before this moment?"

"Two when I've been awake... I think," Paul answered unsteadily. "That is including just now. There was also one time when I was asleep."

"All three times after you got your powers?" Hamilton questioned.

Paul nodded.

Hamilton sighed. "Now, here's the awkward part. I know that we just met. I doubt that the fact that I knew your parents matters in this. This is all personal for you. Would you be willing to tell me what you saw?"

The foreign memories played out once again in Paul's mind. There was his father's confrontation with the couple at the house. There was a young Jason finding his anima sword. Then, there were the children in the dark cell that had made him shiver like his bones were freezing from the inside. *Think back. Did I see anything that could hurt someone? Dr. Bar-Hamilton seems nice, and he definitely was friends with my parents. Why did I never hear about him? I never know who I can trust anymore. I did trust Luper... and I think that has worked out. Is the fact that he is asking me and not forcing me a kindness or a manipulation in the guise of kindness? Why do I have to think about these times of things now?*

"C... Can I ask you two questions first?" Paul demanded with mock poise.

"Absolutely," Hamilton agreed emphatically. "I'm a stranger to you no matter what I say. If you don't want to-"

Paul's turned a soft pink in shame for his being forceful. "First, you were good friends with my parents, so why don't I know you? Second, did my dad have this ability? I mean... the seeing other people's memories."

"I should have probably told you those things before you even asked," Hamilton replied. "Paul, I never got to know you because your Aunt Morgan and I agreed on that. I would have loved to be there for the child of my two best friends, but we didn't think it was in your best interest. There is no getting around it. This is a shady business. It is worldwide deception mixed with superhumans murdering each other. We didn't want you to be a part of this violent world. We especially didn't want you to be an Amulus. The odds were astronomically high for having two Amuli in the same family when there are only a few hundred thousand in the whole world. The second reason was that I was lost after Sam and Michael died. The only two people who had ever been there for me were gone. I grew up with more pressure than you can imagine from my folks to do well for myself. We were never close. Growing up like that didn't let me get close to anyone or even learn how to let myself do that. Sam and Michael just came into my life so easily that I didn't even realize it until after it happened. With them gone, I threw myself into work and even went back to school at the same time. I went the whole way through to my doctorate. All my family ever taught me to do was work and work hard, so that is what I did."

Paul nodded, trying to understand.

"Your second question," Hamilton continued, "it would be a 'no.' Your dad didn't have it. It is usually limited to Psychics though. The thought is that they are already adept at working at things on the mental plane. I think there is only one other mention of a warrior, like you, having this ability. Mind you, Amulus studies are still a new field of study, but you're definitely quite rare. It is rare enough not to have an official name due to a shear lack of scientific observation. I've just taken to calling it 'Dreaming.' That's just me."

"What happens to me now?" Paul questioned, dreading the words falling from his mouth.

"So, a third question that I have an answer to. Now, you go on with what you have been doing," insisted Hamilton in an upbeat voice. "This condition is not debilitating, but as you've felt, it can be unpleasant. The memories seem to unfold like a dream in all the cases I've seen or heard about. We may not think it, however, dreams typically unfold in our minds in a matter of seconds and sometimes less than that. It doesn't matter how long the dream feels to us. With such a short duration and lack of consistency, it should not affect your life or work in A.R.C. The problem probably is that it won't help you much either. No one seems to be able to control this power in order to see important things that may be beneficial to a mission. If it is a condition built on emotion, then it makes sense that the experiences come randomly but are attached to a specific instance. That is, being somewhere or seeing something may trigger a memory, but you have no control over what the memory will be or even if it will occur at all. You may see something useful, but you may not. That doesn't really make for a great tool or strength."

Paul nodded. *I'm a freak among freaks.* He then swallowed. "I'll tell you what I've seen."

Paul let the words fly off of his tongue without thinking hard about them. It helped to separate himself from the uncertainty and despair he felt from memory to memory.

Hamilton processed the three stories without writing them down.

He spoke after tapping on his smooth chin. "You've seen your father's memories twice, and your friend's memory once. It makes sense that their anima would be swirling about you. How long it stays, I can't say. The memories seem to give you more personal insight instead of useful intelligence. Interesting."

"Do you think I should tell anyone else about the memories?" Paul queried.

"Have you told anyone else?"

"Not until now."

"From what you've told me," Hamilton began, "I think that is up to you. I would say to tell someone if the information you glean from the visions could help or hurt someone. In these instances, your father is, unfortunately, not around to explain his memories. If I were you, I would probably tell your overseeing operative. Telling other people that you've seen their memories is up to you. Memories are usually delicate, personal things."

Jason would hate the fact that I've seen one of his memories. Especially one that showed him when he wasn't the tough guy he is now.

"I just remembered, I have something to give you," Hamilton announced. "Or rather, I decided that I'm going to give something to you."

The analyst unfurled a well-bent piece of photo paper from his wallet. "I always keep it around when I need to remind myself of better times. I think it belongs more to you than to me."

The image contained three well-dressed people, two women, and two men. The woman at the center had a warm, full-faced smile, while the man next to her had a goofy grin underneath a pair of sparkling blue eyes. Aunt Morgan beamed as she held a bouquet on the one side, while Hamilton had the face of someone failing to stifle a laugh.

Paul had seen his parent's official wedding photos before, but this picture was different. It was real, flowing, and not a carefully choreographed piece from a photographer's mind. He wished this was a memory that he could leap into.

"It was just the four of us and the priest in a little chapel," Hamilton described nostalgically. "Your dad was cracking a joke that if he was a Warrior, then he would have something cooler to cut the cake with later."

Paul could see his own features reflected on his father. The older Engel was only missing the tired, muddy eyes, acne, acne scars from nervous picking, and the tightly drawn lips over clenched teeth. The image was a mirror that made him look handsome and carefree. He saw that his mother was more radiant than her simple, white dress as well. *How did two good-looking people end up with a kid that looks like me?*

"A-are there ever any openings in the intelligence division?" Paul asked timidly. "That might be a stupid question. I'm sorry."

Hamilton waved his hand excitedly. "Oh, not all. Things do tend to open up from time to time, as with any job. Why do you ask?"

"Luper... my uh... trainer," Paul started, "he said that I may have access to my dad's reports if I join in. I'd like to know what he was up to, if that makes any sense."

Hamilton nodded emphatically. "Of course, it does, Paul. I couldn't think of anything more natural than that. I'd love to have you on when you're done with training. I may have sneaked a peek at your files... more than a few times. You may just be as smart as Sam. I even know that you're here today because you fought off a whole invasion! Keep going on like that, and I'll sweep you up!"

Paul's eyes turned downcast. "The whole thing at the bunker... we didn't make it out of there because of me. It was all my teammates. I would be dead a few times over without them."

Hamilton smiled. "Take it from my experience, sometimes aquatinting yourself with good teammates is all it takes. Oh, and by the way, I think I may have heard a young woman calling your name down a nearby hallway, but I also may have been greedy with you by pretending not to hear her."

Paul eyed the door before deciding to linger for a moment.

"I have one last thing to ask you. You may not have talked to her for a long time, and I understand why. But... if you have the chance, could you say something to Aunt Morgan? With my training and everything, I know that I'm not supposed to contact her or my uncle Nick until I can protect them in person. I was just thinking that your situation is different. Could you just tell her that I'm okay? I'm sure that people in A.R.C. have contacted them and moved them somewhere safe from A.I.M. and the Hunters. She doesn't have to worry about me. She's been through enough with my dad and mom."

Dr. Barnes nodded profusely. "Absolutely! They keep the contact information and the location for A.R.C. family members under tight wraps. It's information you don't want to get out, obviously. But, yes, I'll see what I can do. I'm sure, even if they can't hear from you, it will make them feel better to know how you're doing."

"Thanks," said Paul. "Meeting you and everything you've told me, it's all really helped. I feel a little better about things now."

"You're very welcome. If there is anything you ever need, just let me know. You're a good kid. Sam and Michael would be proud."

He scribbled down his A.R.C. secured line number and email on a piece of paper.

Paul swept up the slip and the photograph from the table as he left. *Now, I know that I have something to work towards.*

Chapter 21: Concrete

Paul did not know if he wanted the clock to move slower or faster. Slow would mean that he might be able to finally find sleep during the quickly fading night. Fast would mean that it would soon be morning and that he could have a respite from lying uncomfortably in the dark in a strange room. He was too tired to sleep.

No matter how hazy his mind became, he could shake the images or, mostly, the feelings. Alice bleeding in his house in the middle of the night. Being chased through the woods. Men with helmets coming only to kill him. His sword embedded in the Hunter's forehead. Everything he felt at those times reverberated in his head and pounded against his chest and stomach.

It was almost six o'clock when he opened the door, his sleepless eyes blinking uncontrollably in the hall lights. Finding sleep in a new place had never been easy for him. Now, it was harder with everything stuck to his mind. *Everything sticks.*

The Council had made it sound like Paul and his teammates were getting a promotion, while Luper was getting a demotion. Other than a shift in location, things were still very much the same. The team was still under Luper, but Luper no longer held his own compound. He had been put under the command of the Pittsburgh leader, and Paul, Alice, Camilla, and Jason had moved with him. To Paul, it was more work in a bigger place. There were also more people to have awkward, first-time interactions with. Here, there was a medical staff along with new trainees and agents coming and going. Since Pittsburgh was a newly won city for A.R.C., its core group of agents was still being built up.

Paul rubbed his eyes as he began treading on the thin carpet. The wide-open hallways and windows were reminders that he was in an office building and not a residence. Every room door on this floor looked like they would lead to conference rooms rather than accommodations. It was supposed to look that way. The facade that A.R.C. put on with its Pittsburgh headquarters being an office building for data actually doubled as an actual base for its actual purposes. Both A.R.C. and A.I.M. liked that approach. They could fight over the headquarters, while the public did not think twice when the buildings changed hands. It was all contained warfare.

This is the first time in a long while where I can look out of my window and not see trees or hills in the distance. You can still do that in most places in Pittsburgh, but not here. The cluster of buildings is too thick from the view on this floor. But, geez, the view had been the same for me since we got back from the beach a couple of summers ago.

Thinking about spending time with aunt and uncle always stopped the rest of his thoughts with cold longing. The good times with them felt so long ago. *I hope they'll feel better when Hamilton talks to them. I feel terrible for making them feel what they must be feeling right now. It's not my fault, but I feel like it is. What happened to my body is the cause of all of it.*

Alice silently came up behind him like she always did. *Why is she– oh right, the sunrise. She always watches the sunrise.*

"You are unable to sleep?" she asked softly.

"I guess it's that obvious," murmured Paul groggily.

"Come," Alice ordered. "Lie back down. Sleep is essential to clear brain function."

"Yeah, I tried all night, and it wasn't happening," explained Paul.

She pointed to his bed, which was little more than a cot. Paul sat down slowly, his face slowly turning from pink to full-blown red. Alice grabbed his forehead with a steady hand.

The bleak, sparse room fell away to a garden. His head lay on a bank of soft grass with yellow primroses within reach. He could even smell their sweetness on cool air. In the distance, he could hear the gentle trickle of a stream.

* * *

Paul was sluggish climbing out of bed. *Still, some sleep is always better than no sleep. I should thank Alice.*

He drifted towards the sound and smell of crackling grease in a pan. *Grady really does wonders with A.R.C. rations.*

Paul crept into a chair in the nearly empty kitchen.

"You're the first one here today," Grady mentioned while easing a pan from the stove. "Usually, it's Alice, except she doesn't stay long."

"Do you need me to help with anything?" Paul offered.

"No, but thanks, Paul," Grady refused politely. "I've got a system here. They used to call me 'Greasy Grady' or 'Gravy' in the army, and no one was allowed to touch my kitchen."

"You were an officer and a cook?" questioned Paul curiously.

"Yeah," affirmed Grady. "A good officer knows to keep his men fed. That way, they're happy or, at least, not complaining as much. It's the same thing here. A city base leader needs to keep his people fed."

"'An army marches on its stomach,'" quoted Paul.

"Exactly," agreed Grady.

Inside the openings of his tank top, the large man's bulging muscles looked like kneaded caramel.

Luper came strolling into the room with a stack of papers.

"These just came in."

"I think you're over-qualified to be a secretary," quipped Grady.

"It is an underrated occupation," noted Luper.

"I guess I'll get reading," sighed Grady as he wiped his hands. "Paul, it is make-your-own-egg-white-wrap morning. Make sure everyone gets some when they come in. You should dig in, too."

"If there is one thing you need, Paul, it's protein," Luper stated dryly.

Paul pinched his bicep as the two men walked away. *There's more here than there used to be.*

He then passed Camilla and Jason their cooked ingredients as they entered the cafeteria. Camilla went on the sweet side with tomatoes and caramelized onions, while Jason packed his with hot peppers. Inspired by them, Paul put all of the above into his own. When Alice came in, she kept her eggs plain. They had barely taken a bite when Grady poked his head back in the doorway.

"A mission's come in," he announced. "You can take your food with you. I can't have you guys feeling faint out there."

* * *

Camilla chowed down on her wrap while she stood in a line with Paul, Alice, and Jason.

"I could eat like six more of these," she declared in-between bites.

"Alright, today's mission," Grady began while tapping a manila folder against his desk. "I'm giving Luper the lead. We both decided that this mission could be an opportunity for several of you to grow in the field. Since it's Luper's team, it's Luper's rules."

"We will be joining a tragic but common story today," Luper illuminated. "The situation is this: two days ago, seven-year-old Devin Rutts was playing with his mother's bracelet. He awoke his anima powers from the purple crystal embedded in the jewelry. Of course, there's almost no way of telling a crystal apart from a gemstone until its activated by its Amulus. His family did not appear to notice at first. Later, while playing with his brother, he accidentally broke the boy's arm simply by gripping it. This and intermittent bursts of anima apparently frightened his parents, who took the brother and ran. They have not returned to the house. Police received word from a neighbor. They then surrounded the house without setting foot inside before contacting us."

Paul could already feel his nerves jangling. *How could a parent abandon their child? I can't even comprehend it. Family is family.*

As a curious and morbid child, Paul remembered asking his aunt if she would always love him, no matter what he did or what happened to him. *Always. She said that there was nothing that would stop her from loving me. That is where I come from, not something like this. How can I understand this kid? It's almost insulting to him for me to even try.*

Luper continued with the senselessness of the situation working its way even into his calm voice. "Camilla and Paul will take the lead on this one. You both are to talk to this child, assess the situation, deescalate any threats to the child or anyone else, and to place the child into A.R.C. custody."

"Aren't there child psychiatrists or therapists that should be handling something like this?" questioned Camilla abruptly.

Luper nodded slowly. "Yes. However, there are not many who are either of those things and an Amuli. That child is currently a danger to himself and others, especially non-Amuli. Simply take him out of the house, and he will then be taken to a secure location. The psychiatrists and therapists will follow. This must be a process."

"Am I dismissed now?" appealed Jason impatiently.

Luper shook his head, seemingly unperturbed. "You will be with Alice and me. We will assist if necessary. Camilla and Paul will simply speak to the child and attempt to coax him outside where he will be gently secured. Only a small amount of force may be wielded. This may go without saying, but do not perform any action that may injure the child. Bring him out of the house safely. Be wary of any manifestations of his uncontrolled anima."

Chapter 22: Gone

Paul trailed behind Camilla. *I don't know what to say to him. What can I say to him? How can I even understand the beyond-horrible thing that has happened to him?*

The house was in the hilly Pittsburgh suburb of Moon Township. It stood apart from the others of the neighborhood. It was hard to tell if the house was rundown or simply needed a coat of paint. The white on the siding was browning and crumbling. Paul turned back for a second before locking eyes with a stone-faced police officer and spinning back around.

A few doors down, a couple of boys played with the muddy dusting of snow on the ground, rolling half-formed snowballs. They giggled as they tossed the balls and stained each other's' coats. *That's where this kid should be. That's what I was like a few years ago.*

Camilla pushed the doorbell next to a dented screen door. Her finger went right into the doorframe without a noise from the bell.

"Devin!" Camilla called cheerily as she rapped the door. "We know you're scared. We want to help you. We'll take you somewhere safe. We're kids just like you."

The doorway remained empty on the inside.

Camilla frowned. "He must be so frightened. God knows I would be."

She gave the door handle a slight pull, and it came open.

"The police were probably even too scared to touch the door, let alone lock it," she noticed.

They came into a dim living room. Grungy, gray shag carpeting seemed to absorb all the light in the room. A box TV flickered but with no sound or clear picture. Foam could be seen spilling out of a section of a brown coach behind a couple of overturned armchairs.

If appearances are anything, it doesn't seem like he's had the best home life to begin with.

"Deehhhh-viiiin," Camilla continued calling in a singsong voice.

She and Paul picked up on a gentle scraping coming from the next room.

The kitchen floor was an off-white linoleum that was spotted with several stains. One of the walls was indented with pieces from wooden chairs. They could see a bedroom through some of the punched-out holes in the drywall. The flakes from the chairs and the wall had dusted the bed.

A thick, black-haired boy sat on a stool, the last piece of intact furniture in the room, behind the bar. He sloshed through a bowl of cereal that had degraded into a mealy grime in its milk. His dark brown eyes viewed the sludge on his spoon with disdain.

"There you are, Devin!" exclaimed Camilla with patronizing enthusiasm that Paul knew was for the sake of the young kid. "We're friends, and we're here with the police. You don't have to-"

"I want my mom," the child interrupted angrily.

"I WANT MY MOM! I WANT MY MOM! I WANT MY MOM!"

Camilla and Paul grabbed their foreheads in unison. It was not the same unforgiving aura that Alice had given off during the invasion, but it was enough to give a blinding headache.

"It was Benny's fault!" Devin cried as his thoughts chanted. "He started it! He broke my racetrack! I only wanted to hurt him a little!"

"COME BACK, MOM! COME BACK, MOM! COME BACK, MOM!"

"I-I need you to stop, D-Devin," braved Camilla in the pounding temporal waves. "You don't know what you're doing."

"Go away!" the child screamed. "Nobody wants me! You won't want me either!"

"GO AWAY! GO AWAY! GO AWAY! GO AWAY!"

"W... We can take you to... we can t-t—" Camilla sputtered as she held onto the wall of the spinning room.

"Cam!" shouted Paul. *She looks like she's going to faint! He's affecting her more than me somehow.*

The surroundings slipped out of his vision. *Not again!*

~ ~ ~

The room was darkened aside from a tear-shaped nightlight. A small girl lay on her back with her dark hair splayed about the covers of her bed. There was a commotion outside. A pair of loud voices streamed into the room quickly. The girl leaned out of the bed, pulling up a single pink sneaker. She eyed the sneaker and then the door, pondering.

"¡Ay!" a woman shouted. "You know what your daughter did in school today?"

"Oh," a man grumbled. "So, when she gets in trouble, then she's just my daughter? You're always saying it like that!"

"Maybe because you need to be reminded," the woman argued. "The teacher said she was pushing boys down and kissing them on the playground. She has detention!"

"Alright, alright!" the man relented. "So, just talk to her about it. Ya know, sometimes kids just do dumb stuff like that. It's what they do."

"Maybe if you were here to talk to her when she's awake, then she wouldn't be getting detention every other week!" the woman pleaded. "She needs discipline."

"So discipline her yourself!" the man proposed loudly. "You act like I'm away during the day getting messed up. I'm working. I'm bringing in money!"

"It's the father's job to discipline," the woman insisted.

"Look!" the man bellowed. "I don't care about what things were like back where you came from. In America, things like that don't matter. It doesn't matter if you do it."

"¡Ay!" she exclaimed again. "¡Este hombre cobarde!"

"I told you," the man called back, "I hate it when you talk like that! Why do you have to speak Spanish so fast! I don't get a word out of it, but I know you're making fun of me."

"Forgive me for trying to let off steam!" the woman spat with a clump of sarcasm. "Same thing every day. Absent husband. Troublemaker daughter."

"How many times have I said it?" griped the man rhetorically. "If you're tired, let my mom watch her. She's basically retired from the stores. Plus, she loves Cami. She's always raving about her."

"Hide behind your mama like always," the woman sneered. "No, she needs her father."
    "I think what she needs is clothes on her back, food in her belly, and a bed to sleep in!" the father pushed back.

The woman stomped away emphatically, shaking the girl's bed frame from the other side of the door. "¡Imposible!"

~ ~ ~

The little girl's face slipped away to be replaced by Camilla's pale face as her back slid down a wall.

"Cam!"

Paul steadied himself with a hand on the table. He slowly let reality slip back into his view. *The best way to help her is to get him to stop or at least calm down.*

"Y-you know," Paul began with mock calmness, "you have to come out of the house sometime."

"No, I don't!" Devin insisted, pouting.

Logic. Kids understand simple logic.

"What about food?" Paul questioned as if talking to a peer about a more complex subject. "You will run out eventually."

"I'll go get some myself when that happens!" the boy declared confidently.

"What if someone strong tries to get you when you're out?" Paul probed. "It could be someone else with powers like yours."

"No way! I'm strong," boasted Devin, pointing. "I'm stopping you and her without doing much."

"What if there's someone stronger?"

"There's not!"

So much for logic. Paul's brow furrowed in a mix of frustration and amusement. *I need a new tactic.*

"I know you're scared," Paul sympathized. "It's pretty lonely in here, isn't it?"

Devin shook his head fiercely. "No! I'm strong!"

"Just because you're strong doesn't mean you're not scared," Paul cautioned. "I know some strong people. They're afraid of many things. Everyone's afraid of something. Being strong is just like saying, 'I'm scared, but that's okay.'"

Devin fussed about in his chair, looking puzzled.

Finally, he murmured, "I do want to see my mom, or my dad, or Benny. Where are they?"

Paul felt like the air from his lungs to his mouth was thinning. *The parents are no family to him. How could they do this?*

"I won't lie to you," Paul vowed with a deep stare into the boy's beady, angry eyes. "I don't know where they are. I only know that they are not in here."

"Why should I go with you?" Devin demanded.

This time it was, "*WHY? Why? Why?*" that internally struck Paul and Camilla like blows over and over.

"I just told you that I was being honest," Paul reminded him. "Honestly, there is a lot that I don't know about family. I never had a big one. It was just my aunt, my uncle, and myself. I do know one thing, though. Sometimes, when you're around people enough, they feel like family. You care about them. You even fight with them but really know that you'll make up later. And you know they'll be there because they chose to be around you. If you come with us, then maybe you can find people like that."

"Not true," the sullen boy disagreed. "Nobody wants me!"

"*Nobody! Nobody! Nobody!*"

Paul felt his body physically shaking. The words throbbed in his mind. A half-formed flickering of images surged through his mind. He could only make out a woman's face, twisted in surprise and fear. Her eyes were wide as if about to pop. *A mother looked at her own son like that? He's doing this*

281

accidentally but is still showing signs of transmitting images. Hamilton said that ability is rare even among well-trained Psychics... apparently!

Paul yelled above the current. "In my opinion, just being a person is enough! There's something about everyone... some value inside. It's like our anima, some people are just too stupid to realize that! The trick is finding people who can really see that!"

The boy leaped up from his chair. His small face was tightly drawn in determination. Paul noticed that the telepathic waves had slowed.

Please don't fight me. Please! Paul's mind never wandered to the sword hidden in the compartment of his bag.

Devin picked up speed. A purple glow appeared around one hand.

Paul caught the boy by the wrist. A spark of anima left a singe on his shirt.

"Ow! Ow!" Devin yelped.

Paul loosened his grip. *He's lucky. I almost broke his arm on instinct. Is that the machine I have become?*

"Okay! Okay!" the boy relented, dancing off the pain in Paul's grasp. "I'll go. I just wanted to see if you were really strong."

Devin's eyelids suddenly drooped. His legs buckled until he was only supported by Paul's hand around his wrist.

Using the anima is still too much for him. Paul realized as he beheld the sleeping boy. *He seems much less creepy now.*

"Cam!" Paul shouted, spinning around.

"Fine," she breathed while feeling her way up the wall and back to her feet. "I don't think that's the way you're supposed to carry a kid."

"Oh."

Paul noticed that the sleeping boy still dangling in his grip. He gently slung him over his shoulder. He took a step towards Camilla.

"Do you need any help?"

"Nope," Camilla mouthed. "I'm fine."

She doesn't sound like it. I've never known her to give a three-word answer before.

Paul found that his ears were still ringing as they exited the house.

"You're good at that," Camilla complemented. "That's the second time you've done it. I know... with the first time... Alice wasn't trying to hurt us. She didn't know that we were

283

coming into the bunker. It still felt like this. No, it was even worse."

"Thanks," Paul responded graciously. "I don't think I did anything during either time. I just talked."

"What about all the stuff that was going into your head?" questioned Camilla.

Paul answered after thinking for a moment. "I think I just ended up letting them in. Both times, I tried to feel like they were feeling because that's what they wanted me to do. I don't know. It's all based on what I feel. It still hurts, but it is easier to see things from someone else's perspective when can hear their thoughts. I guess that's obvious."

"Every time," Camilla began slowly. "It makes me think of... stuff. I feel like they're just trapping me inside my own head."

They continued to the police line in silence, aside from Devin's deep, restful breathing.

The stuff she mentioned, it must have been memories like the one I saw. She never talks about her past. None of them do besides Grady. It's weird. I've known him the shortest and probably know the most about him. I know about Alice's past, but that's only because there is apparently not much of it. I feel like... even before this... life was hard for all of them already. I didn't even know about Cam's life before until now. I came in soft by comparison.

Chapter 23: The Volunteer

"This whole thing doesn't feel right," Tyson Grady thought aloud, standing in front of the video screen.

Luper advised. "When I am knowingly walking into a trap but do not know when it will occur, I usually take comfort in the fact that I, at least, know that it is there. Sometimes, it is best to probe the trap and then step back to see what emerges."

Logical, Paul noted, *but not comforting at all.*

"Wise words," Grady complimented.

He tapped his iklwa spear embedded with a green crystal as he thought for a moment before speaking again.

Paul found himself spacing out. *The mid-range spear of the Zulu and said to have been created by Shaka Zulu himself. He used to make his warriors run barefoot over thorns to toughen their feet. That sounds like a Luper idea.*

"Here's the final rundown," Grady began, "and some of you

will have a say in what we do. Beyond that, A.I.M. is sending a bunch of nobodies for the match. We have no intel on them. No reputation. No names. Plus, we've never even seen their masks before. That probably means one of two things. Either they're sending some talented newcomers, or they aren't taking this match too seriously."

Paul noticed Jason flinch from an anger that could not be contained within.

Grady went on. "It would be typical to send out your new blood with your old blood. That way, you've got youth and some sure things. They are approaching these matches in an odd way which means that they are likely up to something."

"But, why?" questioned Camilla whose one eyebrow twitched. "Sure, Pittsburgh isn't the biggest city in the country, but it's a city. It's the only one around for miles of territory. Plus, you can control all the politicians of this side of the state and probably most of West Virginia. Are they busy with other matches? Or do they know that this base is still a work in-progress?"

Grady shook his head. "Not with the intel we've been getting. No, there's some other excuse. Show them, Luper."

Luper manipulated the screen with a finger. Two profiles popped up.

"If I had not seen photos of these two in the area recently," Luper started, "I may have thought this whole match was

some sort of inner power struggle with A.I.M. That is, someone would be trying to make someone else look bad. Now, I
don't believe that hypothesis is true. The one on the right is
Carson Colter. The other one... well... no one in A.R.C. is aware
of his name. The codename that we use for him is, The Rat."

The image of Colter showed a man with a shaved head and an
amused look on his face. It was as if he were about to smirk.
The bulging muscles in his neck hinted at the chiseled body
outside the contents of the portrait.

Grady continued. "Colter is kind of an open book, especially
compared to The Rat. Before he became an Amulus, he was
an MMA fighter in a small-time league in Texas. He had a
spotty criminal record made of mostly misdemeanor assaults.
Needless to say, he likes a fight. When he picked up a Scottish
claymore with a blue crystal, that desire only grew. He loves
one-on-one fights and sometimes even toys with our agents
before ending them. From what we can gather, he doesn't
seem to get along with authority well. The authority, in this
case, is The Rat."

The profile beside Colter's face showed a man with a thick
salt-and-pepper beard and a worn, nondescript black hat
obscuring most of his features.

"Like I said, we don't have anything on this one's identity.
All we know is his record and habits. He's popped up just
about everywhere in the world. Fights with him and his
blue-crystal Bowie knife have been rare, though. He seems
to be a scout through-and-through. He's an intel gatherer

who blends in by usually looking like a homeless man, hence the unflattering nickname. The strange thing about him is that he doesn't just run recon. He may be a leader on some level. From our own intel, we've seen him with some other powerful loose cannons from A.I.M. That includes Yu Li, the former Wushu champion in weapon forms, and Emerson Whaley, a genius-level intellect. I'll give you all a packet on both of those two later."

"If I have this right," Paul spoke with his eyes unfocused in thought, "the problem here is that we should be fighting those two in the matches, but we're not. Is that right?"

"Exactly," affirmed Grady. "A.I.M. is up to something. They're sending two powerful agents as scouts and not as combatants in the matches. Scouting during a match is common. We do it, too. It's how you gauge the city that you may be taking over should you win the matches. You can also find routes to take out the enemy if they have to retreat out of the city. The most important thing is that scouts are able to rush inside and take intel before it is destroyed or moved by the retreating side. It's a gray area in this cold war. It might be proactive, but strike at the wrong time, and risk World War Three."

Luper addressed them next. "The countermeasure is to send scouts of your own. After all, your faction has control over the city. You are within your rights to spy on them or even apprehend them. Scouting during matches is a dangerous mission to be given. Typically, you select either your most talented covert agents or those who you want out of the way."

Paul choked down a painful swallow. *That's a job that I never want to be given. Am I on A.R.C.'s bad side for being around Luper? The Council doesn't like him so...*

"We're at a crossroads," assessed Grady solemnly. "With the limited personnel we have, we'll have to divide up. As the defenders, we called the style of matches. They're one-on-one with three combatants. As soon as either side's three Amuli are incapacitated, they're out, and the other side gets this city. That means that three of us will be taking part in the matches. The other three will spy on Colter and The Rat, engaging when only necessary. Luper and I have discussed and argued. We both think that the matches are too important. Our two most experienced agents will be fighting for sure. That would be Luper and myself. Cam and Paul will be on the scouting team for sure. I know you two work as hard as anyone, but neither of you two are ready for matches yet. That's just how it is. Luper's thoughts on what Jason and Alice will be doing are different from mine."

Luper nodded. "My proposal is to utilize Alice for the matches. It is rare for a Psychic to be powerful enough to compete in matches. That may create some confusion or even overconfidence in our opponents, which is an advantageous position to be in during the start of a battle."

"I can see the wisdom in that," explained Grady. "On the other hand, a Psychic is valuable for relaying intel out in the field. But it's my policy to only give orders to agents who are ready for them. So, I will leave it up to you two. Who wants to fight in the matches and who wants to do some recon?"

"I'll do the recon," announced Jason breathlessly without hesitation.

His fingernails dug into his palms hard enough that Paul was sure that they were about to draw blood.

"Really?" questioned Grady quickly. "I would have thought that you of all people would be itching to fight."

The black-haired boy's neck bulged slightly.

"Luper is right," Jason hissed through gritted teeth. "Alice is a good bet. She will throw them off."

"If you're sure," confirmed a doubting Grady. "Alice, what do you think?"

"I will do whatever is asked of me," Alice answered blankly.

"I guess it's settled then," remarked Grady, "and, Jason, I think it is mature of you to put the team first. I'm sure that it means a lot to everyone here. Don't worry, you will get your fights soon enough at your level."

Jason half-nodded. His eyes stared intensely forward at nothing.

Paul cast a glance in his direction. *Something's clearly going on with him. Does anyone else see this? The problem with Jason is that you can ask, but he will never tell you.*

"All right," said Grady with a clap, "let's get Camilla, Paul, and Jason geared up so they can start their patrol."

"I would like a word with Paul beforehand," mentioned Luper casually. "Some last-second advice to from another close-combat specialist."

"Sure," agreed Grady. "We just need to get him out quickly."

Four of the agents took their leave, making the room feel sparse and airy.

"So, advice?" Paul asked, doing little to dampen the appearance of pre-mission nerves.

"A lie," whispered Luper gravely. "I hope that it is a white one at that. My plan was to keep Alice out of the field. It came to fruition, albeit in a roundabout way. It is never wise to assume what an enemy does and does not know. The strange actions of A.I.M. in this instance may come from the fact that they wish to capture Alice. Perhaps they know what you and I know."

"You think so?" Paul breathed back hoarsely.

"What have I taught you, Paul?" scolded Luper softly. "It does not matter what any of us 'think.' We must plan for the worst possibilities. It is not out of the question, and so it is a possibility that must be considered."

"D-did you tell, Jason?" Paul stammered out the question.

"Is that why he is acting... differently?"

Luper shook his head. "No. I still believe that the fewer people who know of Alice's condition the better. My words to Grady, through no fault of his own, may have been hollow had it not been for Jason unwittingly playing his part. Somehow, it worked out... to the surprise of each of us. On the other hand, it is heartening to know that you noticed a change in Jason's behavior as well. No, I do not know the cause of it. Clearly, something has him in distress. I ask you to be mindful of him on your mission. As always, what we do is a matter of life and death. As comrades, we hold each other's lives in our hands. When something is the matter with one of us, it can jeopardize us all."

Chapter 24: Backstage

Paul weaved his way past a crowd of students sipping steaming drinks from a mom and pop coffee shop. A dog on a leash gave him a quick inspection before continuing on its plodding way. The air was cold but not to the point of reddening noses and cracking dry lips.

He breathed white air into his collar, allowing the warmness to fill the upright hood of his olive drab jacket.

"No sign of them," he murmured into the supposed cell phone at his ear. "I just crossed over towards Oakland."

Having a walkie-talkie disguised as a cell phone is too simple... yet too smart. I've never understood why people have hidden-ear walkie-talkies in spy movies. Talking to no one draws attention. Talking into a cell phone doesn't.

"I'm clear, too," responded Camilla. "It's quite warm inside this waiting room if you guys are wondering."

"No jokes," warned Jason sternly, "this is a mission."

Camilla sighed. "You're just jealous that I got to stay inside, looking out of a skyscraper window. Luper and Grady said it was because of my sharp eyes that come from my long-distance combat experience. I can do well with an eagle-eyed view."

"It's annoying," Jason growled.

"Y-you know," squeaked Paul, "we are supposed to check-in with our locations."

"Don't be a stickler," Jason chided. "Any of us will just check-in if we see something. Anyway... Polish Hill. I'll cross the bridge soon."

"Which bridge?" asked Camilla. "There are like... a million of them."

"It doesn't matter?" Jason shot back. "You know my route."

"Still in Mellon Square, by the way," Camilla reminded them haughtily.

The three let the next few minutes pass in silence. Paul found that he had crossed from one university campus to another. Another group of students poured out of a building with their bobbing backpacks and jacket hoods. There was a flurry of both exultations and jeers over test results which fluttered up-and-down in each hand. Once again, Paul found himself striding against the waves of young people.

They probably think I'm a student, too. I even have a backpack... but it has something different than books inside. I wonder if I will be allowed to go to college. Maybe online classes or something. A few months ago, I was getting ready for the S.A.T.'s. That seemed daunting enough at the time. What would I major in? I used to think about education or computer science, but I don't know what would help me now.

For a moment, Paul thought he had glanced a short teenager with a buzz cut.

Robby?

Paul swore that the young man's coat had looked familiar and that his walk had a childlike bounce to it. His eyes darted back to the spot where he thought he had seen the slightly built, male figure. Whoever it had been, he was now lost in the crowd. That is if the person had been there at all.

Paul shook his head. *I'm seeing things that I wish were here right now. Robby is miles away, probably pranking a teacher behind their back or getting rejected by a girl.*

"This is my routine check," radioed Camilla. "All clear. All boring. Are all stakeouts this way? 'Cause, right now, I just feel like I'm just waiting for the dentist."

"Still clear here, too," answered Paul. "I'm near South Oakland now."

They both waited for Jason's voice. There was only the

crackling of static.

"Jason," called an annoyed Camilla. "I know you think checking-in is pointless, but the point is that you will freak us out if you don't do it."

Nothing.

Paul could feel his own pulse as if it were ticking in his head.

"Jason!" Paul shouted nervously.

A couple of surprised college students with angled eyebrows spun around at the sudden outburst. Paul was jogging before he even felt embarrassed.

"I just checked," Camilla indicated quickly, "his G.P.S. is off. I'm going to look up his last location."

Paul felt his senses buzzing during every silence.

"I sent you the location," informed Camilla. "I'll head there, too."

Paul shook his head at the person who was not there.

"I'm closer, and I don't need to use an elevator," Paul insisted.

"Wait for me!" Camilla warned. "If he is in trouble, he may need both of us."

Paul was now in a dead sprint, ignoring the bystanders who he was cutting off at each street corner.

"Every second matters. I think what is important is that we find him first."

"Okay, okay," said Camilla, trying to inject some calmness into the both of them. "Don't do anything rash. Who knows? Maybe he just spotted them and needs silence, because he doesn't want to blow his cover.'

"With his G.P.S. off?" Paul questioned rhetorically.

We're all each other has for support. I have to get there. Have to get there!

Paul forced his twitching legs to slow as he got closer to Jason's last known position.

Cam's right. I can't blow anything.

He swiveled his head around, checking every face on the street from his view beside a deli that spelled of hot spices.

Neither of them would want to be found. That means getting lost in a crowd or in the backstreets.

His gaze went back-and-forth between alleys and groups of people. A black jacket caught his attention. It flashed in his vision for a second, disappearing down a narrow alleyway.

Jason!

Paul slunk along the sides of the alley, one hand creeping along the old, brown brick. Another person occupied the small strip of the street. A man in a ratty, brown coat loomed just in front of Jason.

The Rat! From this distance, they should have both noticed each other. What are they doing?

Paul could just make out a flicker of red on Jason's fingertips, singeing the already-ruined coat of the man in front of him.

He's taking him as a hostage by threatening him from behind! This is only supposed to be an information-gathering mission! Why is he going this far?

Paul continued creeping at a distance. In this seemingly abandoned stretch of city, he put on his frowning mask.

If Jason gets surprised by seeing me, that could give The Rat a window to run. Still, I need to keep them in view in case Jason gets in trouble. I just need to be far enough away that they won't hear me explaining this whole situation to Cam on the communicator.

The pair were now exiting the alley, walking towards a boarded-up building. Paul put the walkie-talkie to his ear.

"Boo," breathed a chilly voice from behind him.

Chapter 25: Centre Stage, Part I

The underground arena had been adapted from a parking garage. Buzzing, nearly yellow lights illuminated the cold pavement in all but the area's darkest corners. Swiveling cameras hung from the high ceiling, informing the waiting combatants of the current state of their teammates and enemies.

"They chose to put forth the archer first," reminded Luper from the open elevator. "Alice would likely have been the better matchup as someone who can compensate for distance."

"Nah," disagreed Grady. "They are trying to throw us off. We will just have to throw them off."

"Sound enough," responded Luper. "Alice and I shall be waiting for your return. Good luck. You are a fine city leader, and it is tough to find those. Do try to return to us."

"I will," Grady said confidently. "If I didn't go into every fight thinking I could win, I wouldn't be standing here."

Luper disappeared behind the sliding doors.

Grady's opponent emerged at the same moment. She was a woman with broad shoulders in a sleeveless top. Her short, brown hair was drawn back tightly. A handful of purple lightning bolts marked her mask.

"So, the city leader's going first to rally the troops?" she quipped in a husky voice.

"Something like that," Grady replied. "You know, my parents taught me to never fight a woman, not that there aren't many who could give me a run. They had a thing for old-time chivalry."

"A gentleman, huh?" the woman snorted. "Good. Don't fight me. Just stand still."

"You've got the wrong idea," Grady growled in a low voice. "This isn't going to be a fight. It's just going to be a kill."

"Enough!" the woman snarled.

"Any time you're ready."

She quickly drew back her small, recurve bow. A purple arrow of energy between her fingers on the stiff bowstring. Tyson Grady lurched forward and then sideways as the arrow sped off towards him.

The anima split the ground beside the large man. Concrete

splinters littered the air like heavy dust. Grady closed the gap between himself and the archers as he saw another anima arrow readied. He lifted his spear upward in his running stance.

The woman's fingers let go once again. Grady grunted loudly. His green-shrouded spear flew to meet the arrow. The A.I.M. agent's eyes grew wide as the two objects collided like comets crashing into the other. A shower of green and purple sparks rained down, blocking the views of both combatants.

The A.I.M. agent had no time to react when the iklwa spear came bursting forth through the flashing explosion. The force from its emerald-green shining tip roughly pried the bow from her hands. A sideways foot came next.

It struck her at the base of her ribs, sending her sprawling backward. Her shoes screeched along the ground. Only semi-aware, her body launched a ball of purple light forward. It hammered her now-emerged opponent in the shoulder, shearing apart a sleeve.

The female agent doubled over. Somewhere in her pain-stricken mind, she realized that her bottom ribs were no longer firmly in place. She gasped out splotches of red. A sharp elbow to the back of her head ended her moaning.

Tyson Grady ripped the rest of his shirt away and used it as a makeshift bandage on his glistening shoulder.

"Sloppy," he muttered.

Grady peered down at the unconscious agent.

"I said it was going to be a kill, but I'm too soft."

Chapter 26: Stage Left

"Inside," hissed Jason, prodding his quarry in the back.

The Rat entered the abandoned building without a word.

The two came to a large open area streaked with rust. Machines lay in disrepair in heaps on the concrete floor. Many were now too decrepit to discern their original purpose. Only an orange, metallic machine in one corner held the dusty remnants of newspapers. Even the boldest headlines were too worn to be read easily. Red paint on the brick walls now peeled in most areas while the rest littered the floor like ashes.

With his free hand, Jason allowed red heat from his palm to burn through his backpack until he grasped his sheathed saber. The blade now rested half a centimeter from the beard of The Rat.

"You're going to die here," Jason threatened almost excitedly. "I will tell you why, but you have to answer some questions for me first. Firstly, do you remember me?"

A sudden pressure to his cheek sent Jason skidding on his shoes. The kick was so abrupt that he had not even seen the leg move or The Rat's body turning despite the man's heavy, matted coat. Still, he would not allow himself to be knocked off of his feet by this opponent.

Images of a knife flashed before Jason, making it seem like the deadly blade was in multiple places at once. Even off-balance and out of stance, Jason parried each thrust. The Rat's eyes gave no show of emotion, appearing nearly downcast and uncaring. That made Jason boil even more.

Finally settling into a stance despite the flurry of constant attacks, Jason finally found the resounding parry that he had been looking for. His sword blade pushed the knife blade wide, sending swirls of red anima spinning through the air. The Rat was quick to fall back, rapidly closing the opening that Jason had just created.

Jason's saber found The Rat's still-outstretched knife arm. Disappointingly, the bite he landed was only a nibble.

One sleeve of The Rat's musky coat flopped to the floor, revealing a less dingy black, long-sleeve shirt underneath which was stained with a spot of crimson.

Sensing the injury, Jason shot across the floor. His grip on his saber went from one hand to two. He aimed his slice downward on the man with the slackened arm. Just below his shoulders, muscles of both arms squeezed tightly from the effort. Veins rose to the surface of his hands.

His sword caught only air.

The Rat's fist caught him in the stomach like a thrown brick. Jason splayed painfully in the air. His momentum slung his arms and legs wide along with his weapon. The sword escaped his loosened grip. With Jason still hanging in the air, the same fist swung upwards, smacking a booming uppercut into his chin.

Jason landed on wobbly feet. The muscles around his jaw were too painful and stiffened to close his mouth. The best he could do was to raise both arms to form a sloppy guard.

The fist of The Rat's good arm blew right past Jason's upraised arms. The punches came with the same fervor and form as the knife thrusts. Even with his head tucked, the fist still found his forehead. Blood on his face, flowing like slow syrup, now made it hard for him to see the strikes coming. He barely felt his back scrape against a wall.

The Rat put a forearm to Jason's collarbone and left it there. For the first time, Jason could make out the muscles in the man's neck and chest, which had been obscured by the ratty coat. A wiry beard scraped against Jason's chin like steel wool. The feeling made him too sick for words. He wanted to roar into the man's face but could only let out blood and saliva from a bit tongue.

"No," The Rat rasped. "I don't remember you."

Jason could only glare in spite. He had just taken harder

shots than he ever had in his life. Each punch had felt like a rocket, threatening to end his consciousness if he had allowed himself to go down. His arms and legs would only twitch for him.

"Pathetic," stated the bearded man matter-of-factly. "If you had started in A.I.M., you would have been made into a Dead Eyes."

The Rat let Jason drop to the floor. From his chest, Jason's glassy eyes could only watch his opponent walk away.

"Killing you would be too good for A.R.C.," informed The Rat with his back to Jason. "If you die, they might replace you with someone stronger. No, it's better to keep their ranks weak. You're as good as a blank space."

Jason silently begged the tunnel not to close on his vision. Even his eyelids were too numb to move.

The tunnel closed.

Chapter 27: Centre Stage, Part II

Tyson Grady watched the elevator open as he continued to put pressure on his shoulder.

"Deftly done," complimented Luper as he emerged from the opening doors.

"Not as well as I hoped," Grady remarked humbly. "You know, I can keep going."

"You are the leader, and it is your decision," spoke Luper bluntly. "If I may offer my advice, why not let each of us trade-off at each opponent? Why allow fatigue to set into any one of us?"

Grady nodded. "You're right, as usual. I'll never know why I'm the first-in-command here."

"That is quite enough of that," Luper warned. "You are a leader. I just try my best to be a teacher. We both play two different roles. Who is to say which is more important? Now, I would say it is time for Erica to give that shoulder some attention. I have taken the liberty of calling her to the control room."

Grady tapped the older man on the shoulder before stepping into the elevator.

"Go get 'em."

"Certainly."

The next A.I.M. agent strode his way out of the other elevator. Slicked-back blonde hair greased the young man's head. A pair of cruel, narrowed green eyes scrutinized the large man in front of him. They came from underneath a mask with a golden crown painted at the forehead.

"Unbelievable," the agent commented. "At A.I.M., there's a saying, 'Death wears a black suit.' Is that supposed to be you? You're the legendary 'Death in the Black Suit,' the A.R.C. ringer who's killed hundreds of A.I.M. agents? I doubt it. You're probably just a washed-up old man. I'll just say that I killed 'Death' and get a reputation. I'll even bring the suit back to prove it."

Luper let his jacket and shirt slip to the floor before stretching his massive shoulder muscles.

"Where's your weapon?" asked the young agent rhetorically. "A stick? Now, I know you're an imposter! The person who made that anima weapon must have had a sense of humor. What does it say about you that you're bonded to a stick?"

The blonde man readied his own weapon, a curiously de-signed dagger. The grip was placed in the middle of an "H" shape so that the wearer's fist was perpendicular to the blade. The blade itself was straight, signifying that it was an Indian Katar. At the base of the blade, a blue crystal shone a light that enveloped the weapon and the agent's hand. He cocked his arm back, readying a thrust.

The young agent no more than stepped an inch when he saw a whirling shape that created a blue outline in the air. He was struck by a cracking pain in one foot and then the other. Shooting agony left his legs weak, and he found himself landing on his backside. A staff jutted just in front of his nose.

He grabbed both shoes and swore loudly into his chest.

"Okay, okay!" the A.I.M. operative relented, dropping his dagger beside him. "You win! You win! I-I just give up. You shattered both my feet. J-just take me prisoner and get on with it!"

Luper let his staff rest by his side with its blue light extin-guished.

"Idiot!"

The young man used his dark blue anima to spring off of his aching feet. His hand wrapped itself around his Katar once again.

One side of Luper's staff rapped the elbow of his opponent's extended arm before the other side knocked his knee. He then reversed the pattern with the other elbow and the other knee.

The A.I.M. agent collapsed on his back, howling.

Luper spoke to him coolly for the first time. "I am not opposed to trash talking. It has its uses for distracting, intimating, and gaining confidence in oneself. I, on the other hand, have not found it very useful in my own battles. Perhaps you will now think the same."

Luper retrieved his clothes while his fallen opponent squirmed using only his torso.

"I would lie still if I were you," advised Luper smugly. "You really should have surrendered at the first chance. Regardless of the nicknames I have received over the years, I do not kill when it is not necessary. It is a pity. Broken feet are one thing to recover from, shattered elbows and kneecaps are another. You are quite lucky to be an Amulus."

Suited once again, Luper hefted the tearful agent over his shoulder before taking a slow stroll to the elevator.

Chapter 28: Stage Right

Each rusty rung of metal took Paul uncomfortably closer to the ground.

"I don't think anyone will bother us down here," came a voice from above him. "If they do, one of my guys or one of your guys will buy them off. That's how it always works. Stuff like that is for other people to concentrate on. Ya know, frowny face?"

Paul's plan had come together hastily in his head. *Run when you reach the bottom. Maybe there will be another set of rungs or a crossroads where I can lose him.*

"This place is different from the ones that carry around waste," the booming voice informed. "This one's more for water drainage and whatever. Still stinks, though. Guess it's the rotting leaves and stuff."

Paul's foot stepped away from metal and on to slippery concrete. He sped off in the dark, sloshing through grimy puddles. Water was whipped up into his socks. There looked to be an area ahead where the roads above intersected.

Just get there...

A blue blast caught his lower back, wiping out his legs. Paul's chest landed hard in a patch of sludge.

"I really wish you hadn't done that. Running away probably means that you won't be any fun."

Paul found his feet in time to meet the hulking figure looming over him. The anima in the air was intense, nearly constricting his chest.

Carson Colter had let his hair grow out after the picture in A.R.C.'s files of him had been taken. Black hair with a smattering of gray rose like spikes from his wild head. Its color matched a short beard. The chiseled man let his jacket fall away to reveal a sleeveless shirt. He reached his hands into the banked walls and pulled out a massive sword. The silvery claymore gleamed dark metal in the half-light.

"Good, good," he chanted excitedly. "Stand and face me. Out with the weapon."

Why is he waiting for me to prepare myself? It would be so easy to charge me. The intel on him does say that he likes to toy with opponents. Maybe I can use that to my advantage... just to keep myself alive. Now's not the time for delicacy.

Paul quickly ripped open his backpack to reveal his katana.

Colter roared his approval. "A samurai sword. Nice! I used

to collect them."

Since Colter had not yet taken his stance, Paul remained fluid, looping through various stances of his own. *Keep him guessing. Let him give away his moves.*

"I let you in on a secret," began Colter nonchalantly. "I'm in a good mood. I became a dad today. It's the ex-wife's though. Chances are she won't let me see him. I only know 'cause it's the whole 'her mom called my mom' thing."

Paul could not keep his eyebrows from furrowing in puzzlement.

Colter laughed. "Your face! You wanna know why I'm not all serious? Oh, I am. I just get happy knowing I'm about to fight someone. That's why I do this. Sure, A.I.M. watches out for me, which is good since I can keep on battling. Drugs and booze have nothing on adrenaline. It's the power you feel when you realize that you're just better than someone else. It's even better when they're strong. Fighting's an art. The body moves prettier than in any painting or statue. Anyway, I hope you'll give me a good fight. I mean, you look like a string bean, but my mom always told me that looks aren't everything."

Paul continued to tread lightly on his feet, keeping his muscles and joints ready. Colter only stood with a hand on his sword's pommel, with the tip of its blade on the ground.

"So, I start every fight this way," Colter explained. "I like to give myself a handicap to keep things fair. You take the first swing at me."

Paul stayed where he was with his katana at the ready. *He just wants me to make the first move so that he can parry or counter.*

"What's wrong?" asked Colter, dropping his claymore even lower. "I swear that it's no trick. I don't swing back on the first one. If you can kill me with the first go, then that's on me. Go on, or don't. I'll stand here all day if you don't attack me. Just know that I won't stand for any running away."

It's still a trap, Paul assessed silently. *How, though? I have the advantage of the lightness and speed of my sword. You would think that his strategy would be to use his much larger sword to beat me down.*

Paul formulated his plan of attack. He held his sword aloft, and he charged, his heart beating faster with each step. Anticipating a counterattack, block, or dodge, he feigned a powerful downstroke from his katana's place above his own head, and in one movement, used the momentum of his arms to sweep the sword to the side for a swipe at the side of the larger man's ribs. Paul's eyes caught no sign of movement that would worry him into quickly falling back.

The katana stopped inches from Colter's body as if held there by a powerful, invisible hand. The sudden stop caused a jarring so strong in Paul's arms that he nearly dropped his sword. Paul sprang backward, studying his opponent with wild eyes.

Colter only chuckled before finally taking up his sword again. "I even gave you a free attack! Now, I'll tell you my secret. That'll keep things fair and keep things going as long as you battle smart and have a little grit. You know how us Amuli have a constant barrier around us? Usually, you can't even see it. That's why bullets usually don't affect us. I just make mine stronger with my focus. Not even anima weapons get through unless you're beyond strong or crafty. On that count, you fail that test, kid."

Paul grimaced. *How can I fight him if I can't even touch him? It makes everything hopeless! No! If I think like that, like I always do, I'm dead. There has to be a way to hit him! I just have to find it. No one is invincible. Right?*

It was Colter's turn to come rushing. Paul sliced the air, on purpose this time. The horizontal outline of the anima from his blade surged forward. Due to the miraculous properties of anima, it was solid, burning, and sharp all at once. It lit up Colter's protective barrier. Green and blue energy spiraled together.

Colter kept running. Paul threw his right foot and shoulder to side to dodge the great sword. Another swing coming upwards at a diagonal, creating the need for Paul to hop backward. The attacks kept coming. Two-handed strokes continued down and then up, giving Paul no time to even think of a counter. Only his slim body and light sword gave him the mobility to dodge.

After the slightest moment of thought, Paul resolved his next move. As another downward slash came, he escaped with a last-second tilt of the shoulders. Colter's sword careened towards the ground, and Paul helped it along. A half parry from Paul, so that his smaller sword would not bear the brunt of the claymore, sent Colter slightly out of balance while coming forward. Paul took a step and a swing at once. He aimed his katana at the small of Colter's open back.

The blade met too much resistance once again. Paul instinctively retreated several paces.

"Yes, yes!" cried Colter. "That's what I want, a fight! Your body language makes it look like you're constantly about to wet yourself, but you're not so bad. You're not powerful, but you are smart. I can have fun with that! But I have to say, I'm sorry, kid. I don't have any weaknesses in my armor. I may seem dumb, but not in fights. I'm prepared for sneaks like you."

Paul caught what he could of his breath. *Going on like this, he's just going to wear me out until I make a mistake. Unless... he has to be burning through a lot of anima to be shielding so strongly. Everyone has the same amount. Plus, it's like blood. You make more of it but losing too much of it at once isn't good. My only chance is to keep him bleeding.*

Colter was on him again. Paul found himself at the mercy of sidestepping more crushing strokes. Last-second escapes had reduced his jacket to tatters. He tried to guide some blows away from himself with nudges from his katana. Nothing kept the claymore off of him for long. Impatient, Colter followed one sword strike with a quick kick to Paul's stomach.

Paul skated backward until he found himself resting unsteadily against a wall. Ignoring the new pain that he now felt with each breath, he brought his katana up so that it was perpendicular to his left shoulder. He charged it with a green beam of light.

"You already something like that," pointed out Colter. "Come on, don't get boring or desperate on me!"

Paul ignored him and let his energy loose. This time, the anima was fully in the shape of the sword blade. One spear-like blast was followed by another.

Colter tossed his head to one side and then to the other. One bolt went whizzing to the right and the other to the left.

"Whoa!" Colter called out. "You got me to move on reflex there! Now, you're just trying to make me look silly. You're the silly one. That would have just hit my barrier if I hadn't moved."

Paul stayed focused in the same position.

Colter suddenly cried out in surprise and pain. He gingerly cocked his head towards his back. Two blades of anima dissipated after they have impaled his back.

Paul rushed forward. *I've wanted to do that since I saw Alice control her anima far away from her body on the night when she fought the Red Mask. It takes a lot of concentration, but I finally got the hang of it.*

He was met with a backhand before he could make the finishing strike. Paul spun to the ground. In his shock, his sword left his grasp on the way down. He crawled to put distance between himself and his assailant. The pain in his cheek was making the ground sway as if it were sustaining an earthquake.

Colter boomed laughter. "Yes! It's been so long since someone has gotten me like that. You're a legend! I think I'm shaking. This is battle! This is what it means to be alive! You knew that I would be depleting my shield and that I would let my back be the first thing to go. Wow! If you're this way now, I would have loved to see you full grown. You would have been something. But this is what I hate. I love to fight, but I've made it my job. I gotta follow orders, which means you gotta die now. I'm sorry about that, but just know that you've made me really happy today."

The ringing in Paul's ears made it difficult for him to hear Colter's eulogizing. His entire face had gone numb. Something there felt wrong and distorted. Something rumbled in his stomach, and he felt like he was going to be sick. He rose but had to continue switching from standing to going onto all-fours.

"That's right," approved Colter as he strode forward slowly. "Die on your feet like a man. I'll remember you. I swear it."

Paul noticed something like a soda can rattling across the ground. His vision filled with smoke, blocking all else. It took him a moment to realize that his eyes were burning as if someone were pouring hot water directly onto them. He hid his face in his sleeve and did his best to waddle in one direction, hoping to find an opening in the cloud of anguish. Shots rang out.

The police?

Paul finally stumbled into a low batch of clear air. He could make out a metal-gleaming humanoid shape. The robotic figure held a handgun towards the side of Colter's ribcage. Paul's superhuman eyes could make out the discharge and the aftermath. The bullet had dissipated in Colter's failing energy barrier, but its force had pushed him backward. Colter disappeared into the smoke.

The large Amulus's voice still rang out, "Hunter! You're ruining everything! Don't you kill him! Kid, find a way to stay alive! I know you will. We'll fight again someday, and it will be glorious!"

A Hunter!

Paul desperately muddled his way through the dirty water to find an exit while the smoke still seemed to be hindering the Hunter's view of him.

In clear air once again, Paul nearly ran into the figure standing before him. Now, in front of him, he still guessed that it might be a robot. Interlocked metal armor covered most places on its torso and legs. Only glimpses of a skintight bodysuit told him that this was a human before him. This person was short. Paul half-assumed that it may be a woman, but the proportions did not line up. The Hunter holstered his gun.

"Dang!" exclaimed an oddly familiar voice from behind a full-faced, darkened visor. "I don't see you for a couple of weeks, and you go and get superpowers on me."

The Hunter lifted the helmet off of his head.

Paul's brain didn't comprehend what his eyes were telling it. *I'm hallucinating and not thinking straight. It's the fight and then the tear gas. This is too ridiculous.*

A pair of warm eyes and a bright, mischievous smile greeted him. The Hunter smoothed his hair despite the fact it had been buzzed short.

"Robby?"

"Hey, Paul," said Robby Swanson, "it looks like you're finally ready to be my sidekick."

"H-How?" Paul questioned in a voice that was thin and harsh from the tear gas.

"Oh, that's right! This might look it's bad for you," Robby apologized. "I'm not like... technically a Hunter. I'll explain everything when we get out of he-"

A purple blast sent Robby flying down the tunnel.

"Don't move, Hunter!" warned a sprinting Camilla as she reached Paul. "That was a warning, the next one will kill. Just stay down!"

Camilla cradled Paul and whispered, "I'm sorry. I got here as fast as I could. Thank goodness your tracker stayed on. Are you ok? Do you know where Jason is?"

Paul pointed towards the dumbstruck Robby with an exhausted arm.

"N-No... he's ok. N-Not not a Hunt..."

Paul felt the darkness silently and quickly squeeze in.

Chapter 29: Centre Stage, Part III

Luper and Alice made for a somber-looking pair, riding the elevator downward.

"The rules for this outing were set that fighters are eligible to fight so long as they are able," Luper reminded her. "I would certainly be willing to enter this next round. I am unscathed, and Grady has received only a flesh wound. Either one of us would fit the criteria. You need not put yourself in danger this time."

"Do you order me to stand down from this match?" Alice asked blankly.

"No," insisted Luper. "I am merely weighing the options. What are your thoughts on this?"

"I believe that using a new fighter each round is one advantage that we may play," analyzed Alice flatly. "Also, the enemy may not be accustomed to fighting Psychics who are typically viewed as weaker than warriors. My entrance into the round would provide us with two advantages."

"Yes, but what do you feel?" questioned Luper. "Is this something you want to undertake?"

"I do not understand those questions," the blonde girl explained flatly.

"What do you mean?"

"I do not see why what I am meant to be feeling or how a feeling may affect our contender in this match. If you chose to relegate me from this match, I will obey. If you wish me to continue, I will obey."

The slightest sliver of a tear appeared in Luper's eye. It disappeared as he advised, "I pray that you will learn to understand such things."

The elevator reached its destination.

The next enemy fighter had already made a hasty exit from the opposite set of sliding doors. He looked to be barely a man with a schoolboy haircut and darting eyes behind a blank mask with only eyeholes. Like his predecessor, he held an Indian weapon. This one was a blade overtop of a strange guard that encircled his entire hand, wrist, and part of his forearm with armor like that of a knight. It was a pata, the gauntlet-sword. The A.I.M. agent was hunched over slightly, as if unsure it was time to ready his stance.

Alice exited the elevator, thinking, *I have received no word from Luper or Grady about my withdrawal from the match. As I understand, I will be the combatant.*

She studied her opponent. *His weapon is defensive. Difficult to maneuver yet performs well for guarding.*

"Alice," Luper called gently as he held back the elevator door. "I dislike this matchup. I shall take it."

Alice shook her head. "You asked me how I felt about this. I am trying to understand that. I believe that I simply want to be of use. That is my wish."

Reluctantly, Luper let the door shut.

"Very well."

Alice let her confused thoughts wind down to focus on the enemy before her.

"I-I know that I'm the last one left," said the swordsman, unsurely. "I'm just going to do... what I have to."

Strange words to speak to an adversary, Alice noted. *Almost all of the words that I have been hearing for the past month have been strange. I do not understand the purpose of many of the things people say. Literal words and figurative words. What purpose do the figurative words serve? The words spoken with only feeling instead of logic. There are words with more meaning than I can understand.*

The final A.I.M. agent was in his stance now, firmly rigid with feet firm on the ground. He searched Alice with his eyes for a weapon but found none.

Alice allowed the golden crystal of her necklace to glow steadily. Perfectly round orbs of light formed at her hands.

The first two shots were a test. One was sent straight forward while the other veered in a circle. Both headed in the same direction.

The young man's parries were sloppy, but his reaction time made them effective. At the last moment, he realized that the girl had used her shots as cover and was now using her short statue to leverage a strike to his stomach. He turned, only to feel a fist jam into his side. He dropped to a knee.

Alice next went for the head. The other agent was facing her with his sword arm on the opposite side. He was only able to raise an empty arm to guard. A golden-clad fist made the arm crunch in two punches.

Desperately, the A.I.M. agent swung a sword arm around from the other side. A strong kick sent the gauntlet-sword flying off of his wrist. He used the last of his strength to attempt to push himself backward with his feet. A sweeping leg sent him crashing into the floor, crushing his hip on the hard pavement.

Alice stood over the boy. Her arms still appeared dipped in gold.

"*Eliminate the threat.*"

Alice raised an anima-emblazed hand once again. The boy on the floor quivered in pain and fear. Alice lowered the arm to her side, but the light remained.

No. He is no longer a threat.

The other voice was strong. "*Eliminate the threat.*"

No. Luper, Paul, Grady, and Camilla would not do such a thing.

"*Eliminate the threat.*"

It... it would scare him... like before. I don't want to see that. It... hurts. It hurts my chest and my head to see that.

"*Eliminate the threat.*"

"No," Alice whispered aloud.

"W-what?" the injured boy on the floor asked defeatedly.

"*Eliminate.*"

No. His face. The mask fell off. The way he moves. He reminds me of... of...

"*Eliminate.*"

Alice moved one hand to tightly squeeze the still glowing one.

The shaking started in that arm and rattled her whole body.

"Please!" the wounded young man sobbed on the floor. "I want you to do it! If I'm taken prisoner, who knows what they'll do to my family. Please, I have a little sister and brother! When I die, they'll finally be left alone. Get them out of it!"

Alice spun around abruptly and began pacing rigidly away. A gasp of pain stopped her.

She turned back around to see the sword, which she had thought was out of his reach... impaled. The blood was beginning to seep out onto the concrete. Alice looked away. Her eyes were drawn wide with the eyelids twitching inter-mittently.

Moments later, the elevator opened once again. Luper watched Alice closely as she came inside to join him. He was unable to hide the deep lines of worry on his face. Neither of them said a word.

Chapter 30: Human

~ ~ ~

The black-haired boy raced around with a piece of paper in his hand. He had made it that day in computer class. The assignment was to create a holiday card for your parents. He had thought the Santa Claus and Christmas tree had come together so well that he had not bothered to put it into his backpack. No, he had to show it to his mom as soon as she opened the apartment door.

The elevator ride was agonizing slow for him. He bounced up and down in place.

The doors opened, and he soared towards his home with outstretched arms.

He used one hand to ring the doorbell and the other to knock. It took several rounds for him to surmise that no one was coming. The doorknob would not budge either. Begrudgingly, he stepped towards the door on the right. His mother had always instructed him to Mrs. Potts's apartment should she get called into work.

A slight knock sent the slightly ajar door wide open.

"Mrs. Potts?" the boy called out meekly.

For some reason, every step seemed to take so long for his foot to hit the ground. His skin prickled. The air was chilly as if a window had been left open. In a haze, the boy found his foot contacting another shoe on the floor.

He stood still for a moment, seeing but not registering.

"Mrs. Potts?" asked the boy softly as he lightly tapped the back of the woman on the floor.

Her back was hard and cold.

"Did you fall? My mom's a nurse. She can help. Maybe I should call..."

His young brain struggled to connect the dots as he followed more dark red splotches on the musty carpet. Next, he came upon a woman whose dark hair was splayed about on the floor.

"Mom!"

The boy came closer but noticed a man standing over her. He had a short but unkempt beard and a ragged coat. The man's hands enclosed tightly the sword the boy had seen on Mrs. Potts's wall. Unlike the carpet, the sword was unstained.

The boy stared back and forth between the grim man and his fallen mother. The tears rolled in and the world seemed to crash around him. His body went numb except for a frenzied shaking.

Suddenly, the mysterious man cried out in surprise and pain. The saber in his firm grasp blazed a ferocious red. Spirals of red shot out from the sword and the boy. Their heat and intensity peeled the old wallpaper off the walls.

The boy screamed loud and then louder. He kept screaming until the spirals died down and the man had disappeared, leaving the flaming sword.

~ ~ ~

Paul could still hear the screaming when he awoke in a fog. He could feel the young Jason's anima, crying out in despair and hate. It rattled him to the bones.

"You good, Paul?" a sympathetic voice questioned him. "Easy now. You're all good."

Paul suddenly felt the need to itch his face. His fingers brushed up against gauze and only brought throbbing instead of relief.

"Oh, don't touch that!" warned the same voice.

Paul saw that he was lying on very white sheets and a very white pillow. A head with hanging glasses and dreadlocks gazed back at him.

"Dr. Burrows," he hoarsely greeted the A.R.C. medic.

"I told you last time, calling me Erica is fine."

Paul sat up.

Erica shook her head. "Really, you Amuli never stop surprising me. From what I can see, it looks like you got hit with something with the force of a truck!"

From his position, Paul could only see scratches and scrapes on the rest of his body. The feeling in his face said that there was something more. He resisted the urge to touch the bandage this time.

"It was a hand... that did that."

"Heck of a backhand," Erica noted. "Anyway, you're looking at a broken orbital bone, burst blood vessels in that eye, and a concussion. If you weren't an Amulus, I'd say that we would be looking at a shattered skull in addition to the face. In your case, you're only looking at a week's worth of rest. If we could all be so lucky..."

"This isn't the med bay at the base," noticed Paul.

"I know!" Erica answered enthusiastically. "It's much better equipped, right? Listen, I think someone else should explain what is going on here. It's a bit... complicated."

Paul made a bumbling move to get out of bed.

"Oh, no!" warned Erica as she pushed a wheelchair his way. "If you have to move, I can't have you passing out and slamming your concussed head back on the floor."

Paul swallowed his pride without a word and climbed on.

"Wait!" Paul remembered as electricity jolted his spine. "Where's Jason?"

Erica sighed loudly. "He was worse off than you... originally. Lacerations, broken ribs, bone bruises, etc. The thing is that he's been at this longer than you, so he bounced up first. Only, he wasn't smart enough to use the wheelchair."

"What about the man he was chasing, The Rat?" Paul wondered.

Erica sighed again. "Don't know. Jason started a report but won't talk about what happened outside that. Me, I don't get to read the reports. I just have to patch you all up. I guess I graduated from Harvard Medical School at age twenty-five just to take care of a bunch of people always looking for trouble."

"Sorry," Paul apologized, unsure if he had to. "I... We appreciate you."

"Nothing to apologize for," said Erica. "I wanted to study and take care of Amuli after all. Nothing like being Superman's doctor. Everything you each do every day is... awesome to see. I just worry."

"Sorry."

"Do you say sorry to the people you fight, too?"

"Sor-" Paul caught himself that time.

Paul wheeled himself out from behind a white partition. *That concussion even had me hallucinating that Robby was there. Ridiculous.*

He froze to stare at several lines of people going through exercises. They were doing pushups and judging from the beads of sweat dripping to the floor, they had been at it for a while.

More Amuli? Wait...

Paul realized that he was in something like a hangar with a hard pavement floor and rows of armored trucks far off to the side. Several familiar-looking suits were lined up along the other end on metal stands. These gleamed with dark gray steel, lacking the finish he had seen on Not-Robby's outfit.

Hunters? That doesn't make sense.

"Yo!" called a warm, familiar voice.

If Paul had been frozen in thought before, he was now an

iceberg.

A short boy with a smile that took up most of his face came trotting towards Paul. He was joined by another familiar face, a girl with wavy, black hair.

"Robby?"

It really is him.

"Did you have a nice nap?" joked Robby.

"But, really, are you ok?" asked Camilla more seriously. "I'm sorry that I didn't get to you sooner. The coms were all over the place with you and Jason. It's no excuse."

"I'm fine," answered Paul with skin-deep calmness. "It was just a bad situation."

Jason was out for revenge. I understand that, but... he left us.

"What is this place?" queried Paul as he finally nailed down one of the questions floating in his mind.

"I present you with A.R.C.: Human," replied Robby, who outstretched an arm. "Or A.R.C.: Project Human, I guess. You know the problem with Amuli? You get bonded with crystals at random. There's no controlling who becomes an Amuli. Here, we decided to use my family's money to supe up normies so that they stand a chance against Amuli. We may not have powers, but we do have the technology that helps us keep up with them. We are with A.R.C. though."

"They're basically Hunters with better gear that are authorized by the government," summed up Camilla.

"Yes, but we don't like to use that term here."

A woman in military-like fatigues came striding in to fall in line beside them. A pair of green eyes were lit with intelligence and wit as she spoke in an authoritative voice.

Jessica?

Paul recognized the bright red, wavy hair first. *Robby's cousin? I've seen her a few times at his house. She's a about ten years older than him, I think.*

"Hello, Paul," Jessica Swanson greeted him. "You were always my favorite out of Robby's friends, and I don't just say things like that."

"Thanks, I guess," Paul murmured.

"We don't focus on what the Swanson family did in the past," Jessica explained. "However, we do try to make up for it. Instead of supplying Hunters, we now fight alongside the Amuli who reside on the right side. You can thank your teacher for convincing us to be a part of this."

"Teacher?" pondered Paul. "Luper?"

"Absolutely," confirmed Jessica.

"Cool guy," agreed Robby. "He's got a sense of style. Actually, your eye looks cool right now, too. That dark red where the white should be. It's very anime-like."

Was that the reason why he was sent here? It wasn't a demotion?

"Because of what Luper set in motion, we found you," Jessica explained, ignoring Robby. "When there are explosions detected in a drainage sewer, there are only a few things that it could be. Fighting Carson Colter and surviving? That's a heck of a job."

"Thanks," Paul replied modestly. "It was really Robby that saved me. I was about to..."

The fearful word sunk into his brain rather than escaping his lips. *Die.*

"My idiot cousin does seem to come through in jams," said Jessica.

"An insult and a compliment," pointed out Robby. "It's usually just the first one."

"Where's the blonde-haired girl?" question Jessica abruptly. "She rarely left your bedside."

"Alice?" asked Paul, dumbfounded. "Really?"

"She even missed a sunrise," related Camilla.

Both Jessica and Robby gave her a puzzled look.

"It's an Amuli thing."

"I'll leave you to catch up," Jessica spoke as she walked towards a woman, reading an opened file. "Robby, you've got fifteen, and then it's back to drills. Remember, you said that you would take all this seriously... for once."

"Aye, aye," Robby saluted.

"I should see where everyone is," Camilla discerned. "You two probably have things to talk about. Oh, we still have the city by the way, if it wasn't obvious. Alice, Luper, and Grady came through. No casualties on our end."

Robby watched the dark-haired girl stride away.

"So," he began, "if the blonde girl is your girlfriend, would it be okay if I asked out the brunette?"

"She's... and she..." Paul stammered, blushing deep red. "I don't even know where to start with that. I guess that would be where your mind would go to. First, Alice is not my girlfriend. Everything about her is... complicated. Second, I actually don't know the A.R.C. rules for that stuff. It seems kind of... unprofessional."

"Only if it interferes with work," Robby rationalized. "Do

you think she likes me?"

"I'm not really good with that type of thing, but I would say the look on her face when you were talking said, 'no.'"

"Dang."

Paul looked at his pure-eyed friend for a moment. *Robby. Breaking the ice in some awkward way like always.*

"It was my guess," started Robby in a more serious tone, "about what happened to you. You didn't come to school, and everyone said that your family moved. I know that you would have talked about that beforehand. I also know that you didn't want this. I knew from the way you always talked about Amuli. I'm sorry."

"I guess there's nothing I can do about it now," surmised Paul, trying to believe himself. "How long have you been doing ... all this?"

"Well," Robby began, "you know how I wasn't really talking to my parents a couple of months ago? I kind of found out what Swanson Chemical was doing with Hunters... at least a while ago. My parents weren't really involved, but still, it's not a good family secret to have. Jess heard that I was ticked and let me in on her secret. I started here around the time you left school. Speaking of school, I'm one of those homeschooled kids now... well, I mean my parents got me a fancy tutor. That was the exchange for letting me work here."

"This is a lot to get used to," murmured Paul. "I am glad you're here though."

"Oh, believe me, I am too! Wait 'til I show around. I've got my own room complete with every console you can think of, along with the old, reliable, powerhouse PC that I built last summer. It's nepotism at its finest around here. You know what? I'm blowing off drills. You gotta see the setup!"

Chapter 31: Deep Scarlet

It was the beginning of the second week of combined drills. Grady's team of Amuli trainees and the new agency of A.R.C. Human trained together, side-by-side.

At one end of the warehouse, non-powered agents weaved through simulated debris, dodging Camilla's soft shots as they bent towards them. Off to the side, non-Amuli practiced sending their thoughts to Alice for the first time. Each seemed to be overcome with an odd sense of wonder. More than a few smiles sprung up before fading to cool professionalism.

Then there was Paul. He stood on a set of mats with a group of stern-looking men and women peering uncomfortably into his face. *A lot of them are veterans. How am I supposed to teach people who chose to put their lives on the line? They should be teaching me if anything!*

He noticed an awkward pause in the air. *Right. Close combat training. I have to show them how to deal with an Amuli in close combat. That's my "specialty."*

"Um..." he started, but no actual words followed.

"Sir," a woman with buzzed hair called out to him, "our information logs have always said that a gun or knife directly held to the skin will due the most damage to an Amuli because of the anima layer. What should we do if we're disarmed?"

Oh please, don't call me "sir." I don't deserve it.

A few others nodded in affirmation of the on-point question.

Paul's mind drifted to the Hunter who had briefly gotten the better of him. He could still feel the stinging blows to his face. *I was barely trained. In retrospect, I could have thrown him off of me easily. I was just frozen in fear at the time. What he did have was leverage.*

"Well," Paul thought aloud, since the nervousness seemed to be slowing the gears of his mind, "there is a big difference in strength. Hmm... not a big difference in weight though... I mean it would be the same as anyone else. A throw might work. Judo or ju-jitsu, maybe. Then, you might disengage before the pin since they can just push you out of it. That could give you time to find your weapon."

"Right," the woman nodded. "Should we try it out?"

"Yeah, sure."

Paul recognized the Koshi Guruma as he was on his way to the ground. The woman had already thrown an arm over his shoulder and sent him spinning off of her hip. He hit the mat.

Judo means "gentle way." And ju-jitsu means "gentle art." Why doesn't it feel that way? It was a good choice for a throw. It's even easy to do on someone not wearing a gi which makes sense since there's little chance for that.

"G-Good," Paul croaked from the mat, noticing that the woman was now pressing him with the wooden prop gun. "Next person, I guess."

After ten throws, even the young superhuman had a sore back and was forcing air back into his lungs.

An upside-down Luper strode over and abruptly said, "I shall take over from here, Paul. I believe that we are missing another close combat specialist. See if you can find him."

Paul rolled over, so that everything was now right-side-up.

I don't really understand why he is asking me to "find" Jason. Everyone knows where he is.

Sweat flew off the black-haired boy's bangs like liquid stones from a slingshot. With nothing more than a fencing saber, he chipped away at the wooden post. There were red and purples knots between his fingers from where his own grip had broken blood vessels on the inside. He was about to slip on his mask as the wooden flakes in the air became more numerous.

"Um, Luper wants you."

Jason only cocked his head in Paul's direction for a moment before going back to work on the post.

"I think it's an order," Paul insisted more seriously.

Jason either pretended not to hear him or had actually not done so.

He's going to get me in trouble, too. Short of Luper or Grady dragging him, I don't think there's any way he's going to leave.

Paul stood silently, watching for a minute. Something unusual sprang into his body.

I feel bad for him. I really do. But he doesn't have to make it so hard.

"Fine, stay on your own," Paul fumed quietly. "Again."

"What was that?"

Paul had not noticed the sound of snapping of metal on wood suddenly stopped.

"What did you say?" Jason asked, his face unreadable from behind his mask.

"I said that you can stay on your own," Paul said again, only slightly louder.

343

"Do you have a problem?"

"It's beneath you to pick a fight," Paul snickered.

A prideful part of himself was self-congratulatory about spouting out the perfect insult, but another part of him fought against it. "You don't know me."

"I don't. I thought I did before you left Cam and me on our own."

Almost unknowingly, the two boys were taking slow steps toward the other.

"You should have figured this out by now," Jason spat. "You need to take care of yourself. That's obvious."

"Okay, good," Paul shot back sarcastically. "Tell us that next time. We'll have each other's backs while you run off on some self-destructive vendetta."

Paul cursed himself out. *I said too much... in more ways than one.*

Jason had him by the collar before he took another breath.

"Who told you?" he demanded, his dark eyes seething through the mesh of his mask. "You just said 'vendetta.' What do you know or, rather, what do you think you know about me?"

"I see things," Paul stated flatly without backing down

from the eye contact. "I have visions and dreams that come from anima. Sometimes, it holds memories, especially powerful ones that people can't let go."

"So, what did you see?"

Paul stayed silent.

Jason shoved him backward. Paul stumbled only for a moment before continuing his stare-down.

"What gives you the right?" Jason cried with seeping malice. "Do you think you're special? Do you think you have me figured out because you saw something in my past? No, you didn't live it. You weren't forced out into a world that didn't make sense. You had a life. So, don't think you can know me. Don't think that you can really know anyone."

"Fine," breathed Paul. "I just ask that the next time you pull something, you don't get anyone else hurt. I don't care if it's just me, but if its Alice, Cam, Luper, Grady, or anyone, I'll have you written up."

Paul felt the metal mesh of the mask slam into his jaw, sending his head buzzing and making it hard to close his mouth. Jason's arm was still extended from the throw.

"Wow! How noble of you! You're a lost cause, you know that? I saw it from day one. You don't get it, you just don't get it! This whole thing! Your dumbass honor or chivalry or whatever! You don't get to keep that! You don't get to be good. You're here to kill. This world doesn't make sense. Good people die and bad people live. You have to kill the bad people to make everything make sense. That is the only job! Everyone you mentioned has blood on their hands. They aren't here to be your friends. There is only the job and nothing else! Get strong and kill as many as you can until they get you. Stop diluting yourself before you bring me down with you!"

Jason let the storm of words sink in before adding, "I can see it in your eyes. That stupid naivety. You'll die on the next mission. You won't even be around to hear me say, 'I told you so.'"

He had to raise a hand to block Paul's fist. His reddened vision left him unable to see the second fist. Paul had put both fists to work in a Yama Tsuki double punch. It was a cheap, illegal move in competitive karate. The victim would block the punch to the face, while the other struck lower.

Paul could feel the wind being pulled from Jason's lungs the further his fist sunk in.

"Don't act like you know me either. You don't know why I do this. You want your teammates to die? I can't imagine anything lower."

Both boys were then tumbling off of Jason's ensuing tackle. Each boy lost track of the number of punches, elbows, forearms, and knees thrown. There was only the trained desire to strike each opening.

Paul only became aware of a pull on his shirt after seeing Jason being slid away.

"The way I settle things like this is to let a few shots go in," Tyson Grady grumbled with a boy's shirt hanging from both hands. "You blow off some steam that way and may even come to respect the strength of the other. When it goes farther, that is when I draw a line. No one gets injured over something stupid on my watch."

Paul could still feel the black gunk in his core. It still sat there, but now felt ugly and shameful. He tried to close his mouth after catching his breath, but a swollen, bloody lip frustrated him.

"You don't have to like each other," Grady explained bluntly. "You do have to respect each other. You have to know that you'll have each other's backs. This is life or death stuff!"

Even Jason's eyes turned a depressed downcast.

"Now, you two are going to work together right now. You're going to get mops and buckets and clean your blood, snot, and whatever else off of the floor. At least respect this place and what we're doing here."

The odd pair now walked in unison to the supply closet under Grady's watchful gaze.

"I'll remember what you said," Jason whispered. "I'll only dig two graves. I won't dig any more than that. You don't

347

have to worry."

Hearing Jason almost imply an apology flushed the rest of the gunk out of Paul's system. He felt so silly now. *I'm supposed to be the shy one. I'm comfortable in that role.*

Chapter 32: Small Glories

"So, why are you here again?" asked an exasperated Camilla to the boy sprawled out comfortably on a lobby couch.

"Dropping off video games for Paul and anyone else who wants to play them," reported Robby serenely.

"Jessica is letting you off to do that?" questioned Camilla quizzically.

"Oh, you want the 'official' reason that I'm here and not the honest one," surmised Robby as he sat up. "Well, I'm here for more training against Amuli, of course. Jess trusts Paul. If he tells her that's what happened, then that's what happened."

"Do you usually get your friends to lie for you?"

"Only when it's the right thing to do. He gets video games, and I get a break. Plus, he agreed to it."

"It's fine," related Paul as he walked in while fingering one of the ever-present bags underneath his eyes.

"I didn't think you were one to take time off to play video games, Paul," pointed out Camilla with some concern. "I guess it's a good thing though. You have a work ethic, but sometimes it makes you a little..."

"Thanks for the honesty," yawned Paul, cynically happy that the sleepless hours he had tossed around in bed were over.

Robby smiled. "See, this is for his health. I mean, you guys worked through Christmas. Except, I think you two went to church, so you only did the boring stuff."

"Which was spiritually refreshing," Camilla added. "I guess I sound more like my grandma, but you have to find some way to bury all the Catholic guilt. Especially in our line of work."

I used to go with my aunt and uncle a few times a year, Paul remembered. *This time, it was almost hard. Does a violent person belong in a sacred place?*

"So, what are we doing for New Year's?" pondered Robby. "There will be fireworks and stuff."

"Training," Camilla sighed, "and working. You know, doing the stuff to keep the world together! You might not be used to it, but we're important whether we like it or not."

"Nah," Grady disagreed as he waded into the room, "I'm with Robby on this one. What are you guys doing for New Year's?"

"You're giving us New Year's?" questioned an incredulous

Camilla.

"Well, New Year's Eve at least," clarified Grady.

"So, today?" ventured Camilla.

"Affirmative. Luper actually said that you guys should have a day off soon. For as much as he beats you up in training, physically and emotionally, he sure likes putting you back together again."

"What did I say?" asked Robby without expecting an answer. "A cool guy in a cool suit."

"Why don't I call Alice and Jason in, too?" hastened Grady.

Then the five trainees were assembled.

"Alright," addressed Grady, "today's mission is the most important one yet. It's to get your heads right for whatever comes up next. Take some R-and-R. Go out and get some air. Nobody is allowed back until... well... it's next year. That's an order. It's a holiday, after all."

"If I may," Jason began to complain, "I think that my time will be better-served training or reviewing strategies. I'll just take it easy doing those things if you suggest."

"Jason," groaned Grady, "I'm aware that your 'taking it easy' usually involves going through a carload of dummies or wooden posts rather than a truckload. The answer is 'no.'

351

I've already told you your orders."

Jason shrugged and skulked to the side.

"So, we're getting air," Camilla pointed out. "Cold air."

"Twice as refreshing," assured Robby.

"At least I can take Alice shopping," thought Camilla aloud. "Are there any stores open on New Year's Eve? It's been so long that I can't remember."

"I believe that my current clothes supplied by A.R.C. are adequate," interjected Alice.

"Exactly! They're just adequate."

"I do not understand."

"You will."

* * *

Paul watched coat-and-scarf-clad crowds scuttle past the window of the coffee shop which was, for some reason, open for the holiday, apparently to the dismay of a bored, young woman at the counter. She was the lone worker at the tiny, nearly empty café for the moment, pulling cashier and barista duties for a crowd that had not shown up. Paul let the steam from his ginseng-infused tea gently bathe his face.

I almost feel normal. I don't remember feeling that way in a while.

"You still don't like coffee?" noticed Robby curiously. "Is that why you always look tired?"

"Yeah, that's got to be the reason," Paul quipped sarcastically.

"Do you want to go find Jason?" queried Robby.

"If Jason doesn't want to be found, he won't be found."

"Right. 'I'll see you tonight,'" parodied Robby, mimicking Jason's gruff tones.

Paul grinned before sipping from his hot cup.

"I'm glad you're here," Paul spoke as the sappy words popped into his mind

"Me too," replied Robby. "I always said that I was going to be a superhero! Well, either that or a Transformer."

"No really," Paul insisted. "It's like I've been inside my head for so long just trying to figure everything out. With a familiar face, it's like I'm free again... at least a little."

"Aw, well put," cooed Robby. "With words like that, you'll

353

be stealing hearts soon. Speak of the devils."

Camilla plopped a couple of bags on the floor, while Alice continued clutching hers.

"We hit every place that was open, and it's still isn't dark yet," Camilla explained.

"I still do not understand," declared Alice. "Do the aesthetics of clothing so far outweigh their functionality? I do not see the mission-readiness of these."

"I-I guess it depends," stammered Paul.

"Yes," replied Camilla assuredly.

"Yes," agreed Robby.

Camilla sat down while Alice remained standing.

"What's in your bags?" Camilla questioned the boys.

"Books," Paul answered.

"Comic books, manga, video games," listed Robby.

"Well, a mixture," assured Paul.

"You don't have to explain yourself to me," insisted Camilla. "Paul doesn't. Robby on the other hand-"

"Has impeccable and tasteful taste," completed Robby confidently.

Camilla sighed. "Well, I'm hungry. Anyone else want to go somewhere to get food?"

"I believe that we are currently in an establishment that serves food," realized Alice.

"I mean like real food, an actual meal," clarified Camilla.

The cashier gave the group another bored, yet dirty, look.

"Oooh, I've got it covered," offered Robby without clarifying.

* * *

The ground was little more than a brown mush. A few gray strands remained to signify there was once grass. In January, seeing the ground at all was something of a miracle, but the uncovered site was not quite a payoff. A few icy sprinkles fell on the three teenagers huddled in their coats on a park bench as they waited for their friend.

"Remind me. Why are we outside again?" asked Camilla, not quite rhetorically.

"Robby wants to see the fireworks," explained Paul with misty breath.

"Why aren't we sitting in a restaurant?"

"Robby said it would ruin the surprise for whatever he's bringing us."

"Do you always do what he wants?" questioned Camilla, her tone shifting towards serious.

"No, but I've realized my life is a lot more interesting when I do."

"We could ditch him. That would be interesting, too."

Alice interjected. "I would also like to see the fireworks."

Camilla sighed. "I guess we're not ditching him then."

Alice wants something. That seems... normal... and good. Luper said that she would get better with people by just being around us. I've never been good with it myself, though. Paul smiled on the inside if not on the outside. *Maybe, Robby is expediting the process for both of us.*

Robby returned later with arms full of greasy, soggy bags.

"I hope you're ready to throw all your training and diets out the window!"

Paul sniffed the air in slight dismay. "We're in the Strip District. It's famous for having just about every type of food imaginable, and you're bringing back burgers?"

Robby mockingly put his full arms on hips.

"Come on! These are from one of those retro nineteen-fifties-ish diners with the malted milkshakes and everything. It just opened. They're gourmet burgers. This is coming from someone whose favorite food is chicken and broccoli from Chinese restaurants. And I'll add, Americanized Chinese restaurants."

"I like the sauce," explained Paul, conceding.

"That sauce is good," agreed Camilla.

"Don't agree with him!" exclaimed an exaggerating Robby. "It has broccoli in it. You're a teenager. You don't get to like broccoli. Act your age!"

"I have never eaten a hamburger or cheeseburger," interrupted Alice.

The other three young people froze as if surrounded by a picture frame.
    "Explain," demanded Robby.

Alice shrugged. "That food has never been offered in A.R.C. rations due to a high fat and cholesterol content."

"A health food nut," assumed Robby cluelessly. "That ends today."

Alice surprising and silently resigned herself to that statement. They settled into chatting in-between bites of burgers and fries.

"So, what was Paul like growing up?" Camilla asked Robby. "Try not to exaggerate and blow things out of proportion."

"He was born a forty-year-old man," claimed Robby through a mouthful of crispy fries. "I swear."

"Better than never growing up," murmured Camilla.

"Who says?"

"What was Robby like?"

"The same," explained Paul. "Just smaller."

"That's hard to imagined," commented Camilla. "Being any smaller than he is now."

Robby snorted, but his mouth was too full to respond. Finally, he gulped and questioned back, "What were you like as a kid?"

Camilla smoothed her hands on her jeans. "You know, kidish."

"Were you like the girl in this photo?" asked Robby holding up a faded sheet of film paper.

The girl in the picture was frowning hard as if on purpose.

Globs of runny black covered the area above her eyes. A short woman with weathered skin and a forced smile stood by her, almost leaning on her.

"Robby!" warned Paul.

"That's mine!" shouted Camilla as she snatched the photograph with her superhuman speed. "You stalker!"

"Hey, hey, hey," interjected Robby calmly. "I think it fell out of your pocket earlier. I just found it on the ground a second ago. I was just glad that it wasn't of your boyfriend. I never would have pegged you for the emo-type, though."

"At least the music holds up," sighed a frustrated Camilla as she tucked the picture back into her jeans. "It's better than the vapid pop stuff I here during your workouts."

The next silence weighed uncomfortably on Paul. *Robby, you always take things a step too far with your fun. I'm usually the one who tells you not to.*

"No," Camilla started hoarsely. "When I was a kid, I had to make sense of the fact that my parents didn't want me. That messes you up."

Paul felt the heaviness she spoke with. Each word seemed tied down by shackles.

"You know how it's supposed to be?" Camilla continued. "Two people fall in love. They get married. They have kids.

They fight sometimes, but everything works out at the end of the day. Yeah, that wasn't my family. My grandma told me that my parents loved each other at one time. I don't remember a time like that. All I can remember is my parents screaming at each other whenever they were together. I used to try really hard to fall asleep before my dad got home at night so that they wouldn't keep me up. You know how it is, though. The more you think about sleep, the harder it is to do it. I never got it and still don't. If they loved each other, how could they hate each other even more? Both of them looked at me like I was the other parent's child. I was just another problem in the relationship.

"I thought that since I was that bad already and everyone wanted to ignore me, that there were no consequences. So, I acted out. I crammed on all this makeup when I was too young. I did stupid pranks in school. I even made up a game called 'kiss tag' to humiliate shy boys during recess. One day, that was it. My parents split up. They had new boyfriends and girlfriends and then a new husband and a new wife and different kids. I was invisible again, but things were quieter. I didn't know what to do in the quiet. It was too weird and uncomfortable. So, I just did more of the same."

Camilla continued after looking off in the distance for a moment. "My parents had enough then. They made me stay at my grandma's, the one on my dad's side. I've never met anyone on my mom's side. She left Bogota to get away from the cartels and everything. The only times I heard them were when I could hear them coming through the phone because they were screaming at my mom for marrying too young and not finishing school like she was supposed to. On the other hand, my grandma wanted me. I was her first grandkid. She was this tough-talking, chain-smoking, Italian widow who had taken over her husband's string of grocery stores and bodegas. She didn't take any of my crap but said, 'I love you,' every time she or I left the room. She put me in a Catholic school. There weren't nuns and rulers, but there was this sense that you had to be better at the school. It wasn't the public school that had to take you. If you didn't have the grades or acted up, they could just drop you. It was strangely comforting to have a place to stand up to you and tell you to take charge over yourself. You weren't just a kid. You were someone, and things were expected from you."

Camilla wiped an old raindrop from her eyebrow and muttered, "Damn. I didn't mean to say all that. What did you guys do to me?"

The rhetorical question was greeted only by silence. Robby broke it.

"I would have killed to be one of those boys on the playground," he commented.

"You wish, Swanson," Camilla, surprisingly giggled.

Did Robby really get her to open up? Paul questioned himself. *He wasn't just hitting on her and bombing? Is he a mad scientist when it comes to people or just mad?*

"C'mon," said Robby, "we still have hours until the fireworks.

What else are we supposed to do besides bare our souls to each other? I mean we're practically family now. Cam and I are the parents. Paul and Alice are the kids. Jason is the weird brother-in-law and the not-fun uncle."

"I'll stop you there before this turns into a game of house," interrupted Camilla.

"I need another burger," announced Robby. "It's not a want. It's a need. A need to stuff my face before I have to go back to rations."

"What would you have done if one of us had said that they were a vegan when you brought all of this back?" Camilla questioned before finishing her own cheeseburger.

"Unfriended them," joked Robby while fishing inside a paper bag. "I don't know. I would have jumped off that bridge when I got to it. Hey, where are the rest of the burgers? I had like pounds of them."

He looked to Paul first who had only one empty wrapper near him. Off to the left, there were stacks of ketchup and mustard squirted wrappers in front of Alice.

"That famous Amulus appetite, huh?"

"You know what?" Camilla began with a smile. "You go, girl."

"That's my good deed for the day," stated Robby. "I turned

someone into a real American."

"I apologize," Alice said with downcast eyes. "I did not think that the rest of you were going to make use of the bag."

"Don't apologize," warned Paul. "You're just helping Robby find a way out of his addiction to grease."

"Burn!" laughed Camilla.

They were still talking by the time the fireworks started. Paul contributed now and again but felt comfortable just listening to the more-talkative Camilla and Robby. It felt good to fade into the background, lost in the warm stream of friendly conversation.

Paul watched the fading glows of reds and blues and whole rainbows on his friends' faces. Alice's face had a hope of wonder to it. She was like a child wondering if it was okay to smile in this situation. He noticed something different about her eyes under the knit cap her golden hair curled around. There was more than a hollow bleakness there tonight. The blue eyes were still unreadable, but now because they looked as if they were stared at a pleasant dream that Alice was keeping to herself. A thunderous, energetic volley of light tore Paul away from the dreamy eyes. He felt the pounding of the explosions in rhythm with his heartbeat.

The fireworks ended with silence. The few other people in the shadowy park clapped, even though the event organizers would never hear them. Paul realized how chilly it was when his friends stood to get up. He flipped up his cozy hood and scrounged around for the hand-warmers in his pockets.

"What's next?" pondered Robby. "Should we get coffee or soup to warm up?"

"Ugh," moaned Camilla. "You know that Luper will have us up training by seven tomorrow. We'll have to make up for the time we lost today."

"Ok, mom!" muttered Robby noisily. "Besides, coffee doesn't affect me."

"Who says?" Camilla shot back. "It seems like it stunted your growth and turned your blood in caffeine."

Paul chuckled lightly behind them.

"Paul," called Alice from his side.

"Yeah?" answered Paul, for some reason, hesitant to meet her gaze at this moment.

"I know that gifts are standard for this time of year," Alice pointed out almost cautiously. "We did not exchange presents as friends this year."

"You don't have to worry about that," said Paul with flat honestly. "We all live a crazy life."

Alice rustled one of her paper shopping bags with more noise than she was intending. She brought out a long piece of knitted fabric.

"I noticed that you do not have a scarf like the rest of us," she explained. "They are quite useful for protecting against frostbite, hypothermia, and unpleasant feelings of cold on the mouth, neck, and head."

Paul slowly took the soft clothing. He noticed its dark green shade.

"T-Thanks, Alice," Paul stammered. "It even matches my anima. I guess that's a weird thing to say."

Paul felt the scarf being warmed by his own body heat and breath as he slung it around himself.

"I didn't get you anything," he apologized. "No wait—I have an idea. I mean you're a botany... or um... you're getting a botany degree, right? Maybe, if we ever get another day off, we all could go to the Phipps Conservatory. It could be a day like today. There are lots of... plants. It's a nice place!"

Why am I getting nervous? Paul berated himself internally.

Alice nodded with something close to a smile starting at the corners of her mouth. "Yes."

The rest of the walk consisted of Robby yapping, Camilla countering his yapping, and Paul barely containing his laughter at the friendly insults being thrown about.

"Now, I've walked you home like a true gentleman," declared Robby as the hidden, parking garage entrance to the A.R.C. city headquarters loomed before them.

Camilla was about to fling something back. She was only able to give another exasperated breath.

Everything appeared to Paul as a flashing white as if a firework was occurring in front of him. It was then red. Then black and still. He could hear nothing. There were slipping fears as he realized that he felt nothing.

Chapter 33: Under

~ ~ ~

Camilla sat on the side of the room by the window. A slip of sun set her glossy hair shining. Her face was tightly drawn, resting on a fist. She almost jumped when she heard a stirring from the bed but only slumped forward slightly instead.

"Jeez, girl, don't you have a life?" the old woman asked while being propped up by a stack of pillows.

"A livelier one than yours," Camilla replied, intending a joke but, instead, voicing something much meeker.

"As it should be, as it should be," the old woman wheezed. "The young should be young."

The cap on the woman's head was askew, betraying the smoothness underneath. As weak as she looked, there was still power in her sharp mouth.

"You know why I started smoking?" she asked.

"Yeah, but I'm sure you'll explain it again."

"Back then, everyone did it. The movie stars, the kids at school. It was weird if you didn't do it. Isn't that a thing?"

Camilla said. "Nonna, I told you, I quit months ago. Back when-"

"Hush now," interrupted the grandmother. "I'm talking about something different. You know, everyone doing something because everyone was doing it. We were hurting ourselves, when we didn't know it, just to be like everyone else. Makes you think. Is anyone doing the same thing right now?"

"Nonna, why are you getting into this? You need to rest!"

"You won't hush me," said the woman without anger. "I've only got a little time, so I'm going to say what I have to say. And I'm saying, it can be bad to be like everyone else. It's actually... boring. You only pay attention to the ones who stand out."

"You don't need to make me feel better! I should be making you feel better."

The woman shook her head. "I'm only thinking about the person with the longer road ahead. That power you just got, I don't get anything about it. I do know this, if you're different, that's just fine. That just might be you, and that's healthy. Hey, at least you'll be interesting."

~ ~ ~

Paul had thick tears in his eyes. He could not see anything but felt them. He was unsure if they were coming from the memory he had just witnessed or from the uncertainty that was beginning to grip his stomach. He had no idea of anything. Memories and thoughts fluttered, unable to be pinned down. It did not occur to him that he needed to remember where he was or what he was doing. Even the new, foreign memory was faded and tossed aside. Everything was just haze. When his eyes slowly opened, they did not comprehend anything around him.

There was a beeping sound. It was steady, blinking in and out every few seconds. Paul could not think for a moment as to what it signified.

The room was barely lit. Coupled with Paul's weakened, compromised vision, he could barely make out anything. Shadows stretched menacingly from all directions. In the corner of his eye, he thought he saw a video screen. A zigzagging line moved about it. His neck was so stiff that he could not even move his head to study it. Every so often, his eyes would drift over some set of wires or tubes. As to what they were exactly, his mind could not connect the dots.

His limbs were no better than his eyes. They were like soggy noodles. Just trying to move them was too much. He quickly grew tired—absurdly tired.

* * *

He thrashed this time.

All he knew was the uncertainty. There was the anxiety of the dark unknown. His movements were animalistic instinct.

He thought that he had struggled with some power. When he stopped, he still felt wedged onto whatever he was lying on.

Paul was only dimly aware of two other people in the room. His consciousness felt lighter than a flicker of flame.

"You are experiencing several injuries," said a calm voice without concern. "A shockwave to your head has caused your brain to impact your skull in what is commonly known as a concussion. Your inner ears have been damaged, causing a shift in your sense of balance. Debris penetrated your chest, initiating hemorrhaging. I have taken steps to placate these problems. I will need them to dissipate before I move on with the experiment. I look forward to seeing the results."

Paul only felt the gist of the words drifting into him. He was far too hard to cling to any one of them. There was the haze. There was the anxiety. Those two feelings were all-encompassing.

* * *

Paul was sure that he was dreaming. He had never seen this place. There was gunk in the gears of his mind. The walls were rough cinderblock, unpainted. There was a mess of wires and open outlets. Some he traced to his insides. This disgusted him, but his whole body felt asleep. He could not fight the wires and tubes. He could move his head to find the source of light but saw its lime hue. His bed looked only just big enough for his tired body. A loose blanket covered an old, grayed hospital gown.

It took him several moments to move his head any more than an inch. The rest of the room was sparse. A metal table sat off to the side and was covered by instruments that Paul could not make out from his position. He heard meticulous tapping and clicking coming from beyond an open doorway. The instinct to move was great. The slight turn he could make sent the bed lightly creaking. Someone moved outside of the room. Cold blood rushed his veins.

"I believe that your name is Paul Michael Engel," stated an emotionless voice. "Is that correct?"

Paul only wheezed. It did not matter if he wanted to confirm the man's words or not.

"Too soon for you to vocalize," realized the man.

Paul could just make out the man's figure. A long, white lab coat covered his lanky frame. His face was middle-aged and nondescript. He was not handsome nor ugly. His face was one to be forgotten after moments of passing him on the street. His only memorable feature was a large set of glasses that glared strongly in the light.

"Forgive me for being longwinded," apologized the man. "However, you and I have the time. Humans are unique animals. The most intelligent and therefore the only with higher reasoning capabilities. At some point in time, it became popular for humans to hypothesize a reason for their existence. I used to think this was hogwash. After all, we exist. We know how we came into being. Do we need a reason or a calling? Then, I found mine. I decided to pursue the most logical thing in the logical world. Some may say that science is simply a study of phenomena. It describes what is rather than what is not. It is the great advancer of humanity as well. Scientific inventions and theories are the driving forces for positive change. Is there no greater thing than the pursuit of science, then? No. I study what is and advance it. Science is the study of the logical, and the only logical thing to do is to expand it. Nothing else is of importance. That was my epiphany and that is my calling. I tell you this because you have a purpose as well. It will be subservient to mine and will be learned in time."

Paul sensed a hidden danger in the straightforward words. As each cryptic sentence sunk in, more bumps grew on his skin.

It was only after more resting that Paul was able to speak. He first did so involuntarily as his painful squirming in bed led him to groan. His hand felt around his bed for the first time. As it ran down the rough sheets, it glanced against the cold metal. Paul peered underneath his covers.

Oh no...

There were chains around his midsection, forcefully restraining him to the bed. The fear now weighed down his body like a bitterly cold block of ice. His pathetic shoves did not even slide the chains an inch. His heart was beating out of control. The fear was not just in his mind, but now animalistic instinct had seized his body. There was no telling it to calm down.

The scientist appeared at his bedside again. A glare still shone off his glasses.

"I hear that you can now vocalize. This is positive. The next stage of the experiment can begin. That is data collection, if you are unacquainted with the scientific method. I have already completed the previous stages. Your purpose is reaching its realization. It will come progressively, as science does. Are you curious as to what that purpose is?"

Paul tried to glare at him but blinked. His eyes strained in fear and contempt.

The scientist sighed and scowled. "Please, tell me that you at least understand the scientific method or the progress of science. So few do. Humanity has the capability to reason yet rarely uses it. What can be done, must be done. It must be seen. It must be observed and studied. All else is nonsense. There is no progress in anything else. I will tell you not in anger but in the studious poise that I desire to achieve. You will be a subject in the study of the effect of pain on Amuli. You see, Amuli are such a recent development that many of even their biological differences from humans have not been studied. Instead, A.R.C. and A.I.M. focus on pointless saber-rattling. Although, some in A.I.M. do agree with me which is why I stand before you."

The scientist stared at him for several moments. All expression was hidden behind his glowing lenses.

"Nothing to say? Disappointing. I would have enthusiastically agreed to be the test subject if I had the opportunity. Alas, I cannot experiment on myself and be an impartial observer. There are no other scientists experimenting in this way, much to my chagrin. If nothing else can be gained from this one-sided conversation, I will take my leave. The experiment will commence in the coming days. Please, perform naturally so that I may obtain unblemished data. I have heard it said that science is not science unless it is repeatable. How true. You will be the first of many test subjects."

The scientist began his exit with his back straightened in perfect posture.

"I advise you to resign yourself towards your new duty to science. The plan that brought you here was well-thought-out, in theory. Explosive ordinances are not typical parts of A.I.M.'s arsenal. Also, it goes against custom to strike in a city won by the enemy. There is the old stalemate due to the risk of exposure for both organizations. A.R.C. intelligence will come to the conclusion that the explosion that led to your abduction was the work of Hunters. They will not expect you to be in A.I.M.'s hands. That is to say, no one is coming for you."

Paul waited for the footsteps to trail away into silence.

Then, his hands flew to the chains, jerking them wildly. They only stuck tightly to his midsection.

Come on! Come on! Metal chains should be easy to break! I'm an Amulus!

He continued jostling as loud as he dared. His fingertips became indented with the marks of the chains.

The I.V. drip. I'm being drugged. With the injury... that's why I'm so weak. But, still...

His body still shuddered in anxiety-ridden jolts. He felt his muscles stretching impossibly tight with every spasm. Everything on his mind, every terrifying fear was manifesting itself physically. His fingers dug and dug at the chains. He tried burning everything with anima at the same time. Green flames only flickered like a candle and when out. He could not conjure the willpower in himself to produce the plasma-like energy.

COME ON! COME ON!

His fingers now squished blood with every desperate squeeze

around the chains. Before long, he felt grains of dried blood mix in with the fresh. He was sure that the scientist could hear him now, wherever he was in whatever this place was.

He stopped for only a moment in his soiled bed of blood and sweat.

The bed. If I can't break the chains, I'll break the whole bed!

Paul took a breath, knowing that this next move would blow whatever cover he had. He hammered his elbow into the bed.

The metal bedframe rung but stayed perfectly solid.

He struck again. He struck again and then kept going.

He stopped only when his armed felt too weighed down by exhaustion. The mattress was dented. His elbow was black with bruises. The bed was still together.

The scientist had not yet come, in spite of the commotion.

The drugs! Even my katana must be far away! I can't stop! If I stop, I'm dead!

He squirmed, wildly throwing his body toward every angle. The chains were too tight-frustratingly, unbearably tight! They restricted him and constricted around his core. It cut off his movement and bit him hard.

If I stop, I'm dead! If I stop, I'm dead!

He was barely aware of his legs kicking. All fortitude had left his brain for his exhausted body.

If I stop, I'm dead!

His movements were slowing now. His kicks were more akin to a toddler throwing a tantrum. In his exhaustion, the mantra in his had shortened.

I'm dead... I'm dead...

Chapter 34: Breaking

~ ~ ~

Tables of frogs looked pitifully up at the class. Their arms and legs were pinned so that they spread their farthest degree outward. Slimy formaldehyde dripped off of a few.

The class was in a commotion. Some talked about TV shows from the night before. Others blabbed about the new shopping mall. More than a few moaned at seeing the dead amphibians before them. One pale-faced boy sat at his desk and away from the lab tables. He was eyeing the trash can, ready to make a run if the contents of his stomach moved up any further.

There was a boy with thick glasses peering over the worksheet for the assignment. His partner was a girl with hair in the shape of a curling iron.

"I saw this TV show where they had C.S.I.'s," she said excitedly over the frog. "They're people who work at crime scenes. It's cool because they solve mysteries and stuff! I love that kind of stuff. I think that's what I want to be."

As she spoke, she jabbed the frog with the knife, causing groups of incisions.

"Ooh," she exclaimed, poking frog guts. "Look at all this stuff!"

The boy spoke up meekly. "Uh, the worksheet says... the worksheet says..."

The girl did not hear him.

"Ooh! That's pretty neat. Oh look, that parts squirts!"

The boy slid the other knife into his hand.

"We have to..." he stammered.

The girl only kept prodding the frog.

The boy sighed and made up his mind to do the work himself. He moved to make the correct incision into the arm. The knife came down, jamming into the finger of the absent-minded girl. It cut into her as well as it did the frog.

"Ouch! Hey, what's your problem?"

The boy had her attention now. The eyes of the whole class centered on him and the girl with the finger running red. It was dead quiet now. There was no more blathering.

The injured girl rushed off for a band-aid.

Even in the silence, no one heard the boy murmuring, "It's not so different. It's not so different."

~ ~ ~

Paul did not remember falling asleep. He did not even know how he had done so. There was no merciful moment when his sleepy mind forgot where he was. No, he was painfully alert from the first moment. His body jolted and screamed, catching itself on more chains. There were some around his arms this time, too. He noticed a gentle brushing on his fingers. Small beads of wetness filled in the scabs.

He opened his eyes to a mass of red-orange hair, splayed about like an unfurled ball of yarn. There was a young woman underneath it. She softly scrubbed his damaged hands with soap and water from a basin.

"For what it's worth, I'm sorry," she whispered, realizing that he was awake. "If you were able to get out of those chains and kill me, I'd call it justice. No one ever escapes though."

Paul stayed silent. The fear and panicking had drained him, and the rest had done little to recharge him. His mouth felt like it had been scoured with sand. There was an I.V. that he assumed was giving him just enough fluid and nutrients to keep him alive, but there was nothing to wet his desert of a mouth.

"I'm May," she continued softly. "I don't want to be here either. See, I have a little brother. He became and an Amulus over a year ago, and that's when A.I.M. took him in. At first, I thought he would be getting what he needed. Then, they came knocking on my door, too. I found out that A.I.M. does messed-up things. Some people in A.I.M. do such messed up things that not even the other members want to be around them. That's the guy we have here. He needed an assistant for human experiments, and I was a pre-med student that they had leverage on. I'm only here for my brother. As long as I'm here, he won't be sent to the frontlines and won't be turned into a Dead Eyes."

Paul did not say a word. He did not feel like it.

"You can hate me," assured May. "I deserve it. He's crazy. I know you know that. He's brilliant and has this drive, but he takes everything about science and medicine and distorts it."

Paul let the silence hang. There were no thoughts except for the fear. There was only the prickling anticipation of more suffering.

The scientist came without a word again. He simply materialized in the doorway. If he had heard May's complaints and confessions, he gave no sign.

"Leave us."

Paul felt the air chill. The anima coming from this man was cold. It was like sterilized dental implements being shoved into his mouth and giving him a shiver in his gums.

381

He realized that the deranged man had never given his name. Paul guessed that he had discarded it when he had put complete devotion into his cause. It was clearly of no importance to him now.

He's just his own twisted version of a scientist. I've been calling him "the Scientist" in my head, but that seems too good for him.

"You know, I actually hated Amuli when they were first revealed," he spoke in the same calm voice. "People said that they were magic. They claimed they had special souls or chi or chakra that oozed out of them. Even the unique energy was named, "Anima" which is Latin for soul. Amulus came from the same root. It was unthinkable to me. The laws of science rule over all. Why should some beings be exempt from it? That is the very definition of impossible. Then, I decided to set aside the nonsense that the masses prattled about. I became sure that anima and Amuli could be studied. If it exists, then it should follow scientific principles. It should have laws that are unbreakable. My research says that it does. That is my life's mission. To elaborate on this new field."

Paul found that anger could now share a portion of his mind now. There was the fear and something fermenting beneath.

"I must ask you to refrain from injuring yourself again," the man advised coolly. "This experiment seeks to measure pain and might be clouded if you have other sources of pain than the ones that I produce."

382

"Shut up," Paul croaked it at first. "Shut up!" It was louder as the sound cleared phlegm from his aching throat.

"Now, see here-" the Scientist tried to interject with some surprise.

"No! Shut up!"

The Scientist moved his lips to speak again.

Paul drowned him out. "No! You shut up! You're insane! You get nothing! You understand nothing! No one would ever consider you sane! No one would ever consider you a scientist!"

The Scientist's mouth slowly twisted. He brought a gloved hand over Paul's still yelling mouth. Paul tried to bite at it, but the fingers squeezed both his cheeks painfully.

"You do not understand yet. You will. You will see the inevitability of science and progress. Humans evolve through knowledge. What we are doing is a part of that. Now, you must be silent! I need to relay information to you. It is important. You will understand in time."

The Scientist held his grip.

"In this business, one must be flexible. I have had to make do with I what I am given. There are many experiments I wish I could have done. You are an example of what I have had to make do with. I was supposed to experiment on the

Atlantean. The rarest of subjects! I was given you instead, a captured A.R.C. agent too weak to be considered for a Dead Eyes. Oh, I forgot you never had that information."

The Atlantean? What kind of nonsense if that? Is it a codeword or some raving?

The Scientist slithered a tablet computer from his pocket.

"Read," he instructed his subject as he enlarged the text on the page.

Terrorist Bombing at A.R.C. Headquarters, Paul read the head-line and then continued as his heart pounded in his throat. *Seven are feared dead. Unfortunately, none of the slain have been able to be identified...*

It all broke in Paul's mind. It crashed like glass being hammered. *All A.R.C. agents have their identities erased. That's why they wouldn't... No. Not like this! How can it be? I was just with them. That's what it feels like. No! It can't be like this! They can't be gone in a flash!*

His eyes trembled as they moved down the page. They did not want to see. If he did not see the words and pictures, he thought it still may not be true. His heartbeat reached a crescendo when he got to the picture. There was the charred building and scattered glass. Chunks of building had smashed cars on the street.

"I think you see it now. I wanted the girl. I would have thought

384

that the Atlantean would have more chance to survive over a normal Amulus. That was part of the plan and why the particular payload was used. No, she apparently took the brunt of it. She was standing closer to the denotation point. Her body lessened the shockwave that struck you as well as absorbing most of the shrapnel."

Alice? Is he talking about her? She died and I lived! What kind of cruel joke is that? She was so much stronger than me! I'm nothing compared to what she was! So why...

The Scientist continued after finally taking his hand from Paul's face, "I will leave you to your recovery. As I said, we cannot start the process until you are free of other pain."

Paul did not even notice him leaving. His chest and stomach felt impossibly heavy. He felt as if they would both fall through him to the bed. Tears poured messily, like blood from a fatal wound. The faces. He could not turn away from the faces in his mind. Each one made him feel so sick.

Robby. He was too good. The only friend I really ever made. The only one to like to such a weird and awkward kid like me. He never made fun of me for that. We spent so much time at each other's' houses that he felt like family. He was family. He was my brother.

The image of him as a young kid with that stupid grin made Paul the sickest. He could not push it away. That would have felt wrong.

Cam. Whenever she spoke, I couldn't believe that she was eighteen. She seemed so worldly and wise. In all the chaos and anxiety that my world had become, she was the first to try to make me feel better. She must have had such a hard time with her family. She was just now opening up about it.

Alice. Nothing about her life was fair. Nothing in the slightest. She was born a science experiment, just like I am now. In the end, she was trying so hard to be human. I think she just wanted someone to tell her that she was normal and that she was just a girl. Normal enough. I should have at least told her that. I thought she was cold and empty at first, but she wasn't deep down. She just wanted to be my friend. Why did the world have to do all that to her?

Luper. If anything, I thought he was insane at first. I swore that his training was going to kill me. It turned out that it was just what I needed to keep myself alive for as long as I did. I think I would have been dead long ago if someone else had taught me. He cared, too. You had to look for it, but his students were his life. He tried to do so much for Alice. He lied and lied to protect her. He deceived one of the two most powerful organizations in the world with a straight face. It was for a young girl that he thought was worth it. She was.

Grady. He served his country like a hero and gets killed by a coward. That's not right. He was someone who could lead men and women into battle. Underneath that, he was so friendly. What kind of world is this that someone like Tyson Grady gets killed and someone like me lives?

Jason. I'm really sorry that the last thing I did was fight him. That wasn't like me. Why did I even do that? It was so stupid. I knew that at the time and didn't even stop myself because of some phony sense of pride. He had everything taken from him. He wasn't even able to live since he was little. He just wanted the world to make more sense. I guess that's just too much to ask.

Every time one face passed another would take its place. It was cyclical. The guilt and grief left him physically retching. He realized that he was choking on mucus and tears. With his hands chained, he could not even wipe his face.

Robby's got a family. Parents shouldn't have to bury their kids. Cam had family, too, even if they were estranged. I don't know about the others. They must be someone else crying for each of them with me.

Paul looked up and through the ceiling.

If you're up there or out there, I'm so sorry. It should have been me. If it were just me, then it would have been okay. I really cared about all of you. I will until I die, and that could be soon. Will that make it better? Will things be fairer then? I'm sorry! I'm so sorry!

He did not find sleep after that. How could he? Why should he? There was an end to the tears only when they ran out. His tear ducts were left dry and sore. He stared at the wall for hours but never saw it. He told himself that he would be even more guilty if he let the memories stop circulating. He had to keep them alive in his head. It was the least and only thing he could do.

Chapter 35: Gone

Paul was still awake when May came in to treat him and wash him down again. He knew time was passing. At some moments, it felt like eons. It felt like no time at all at others. The lack of sleep was making it hard to keep his thoughts straight. His vision seemed to flash in and out. Darkness always rimmed the edges.

May took some time to clean off the mess on his face. She did not say anything this time. She probably knew what Paul knew and that there was no apologizing for that. Paul did not even look in her direction. The world was only the cinderblock wall he saw from his side. Even the cleansing water felt colder this time.

The Scientist was upon him again in the shivering silence.

"It appears that you are still healing," he noted without expression. "We still have time before the experiment starts. Science takes patience after all."

Paul could only manage to knock over the I.V. stand in protest this time. "Then why are you here?" he grumbled hoarsely.

"For observation," answered the Scientist. "For the sake of transparency as well. Science needs to be transparent. How else can we build upon the work of others unless we view it ourselves? I wish to be transparent with you. Call it a habit."

The nondescript man meticulously tapped the screen of a tablet.

"I believe that you will even find me more than transparent than your former allies at A.R.C.," he voiced slowly.

He brought the tablet down to Paul's face which had long since turned away from him. Paul held his eyes tightly closed until the horrible curiosity begrudgingly opened them.

A gaunt man and woman appeared in grainy footage on the small screen. The angle was tilted like that of a security camera. They seemed to be speaking, but there was no sound. The woman held a worried hand on the man's knee. Her face, which was nearly always bright and cheerful, appeared exhausted and weary.

Paul's eyes shot as far open as they could. *God, no!*

"This is what happens when your identity becomes the enemy's knowledge," explained the Scientist coolly. "Even if your fate is sealed, they tend to do this to send a message. There is no doubt that this video will end up in the hands of A.R.C. which will serve to terrify their agents. The curious thing is that this video is from days ago. Your aunt and uncle may no longer be alive. It is as with Schrodinger's Cat, alive or dead until proof is seen."

Paul felt tremendously sick. He felt acid bubbling in his throat. His sore eyes let flow the tears he had thought were tried up.

"As I said, this is for transparency. My work is honest."

He disappeared without another word.

The whine that came from the bottom of Paul's being started low. Then, it became a powerful, loud wail. He let out sounds until it exhausted him to the point of feeling faint. He welcomed that feeling in sick regret. His eyes saw only more memories. Every family dinner that Aunt Morgan was so intent on having. Every holiday with just the three of them. The everyday pieces of advice. They had been a family of three and that had always been enough. Now, it was gone.

Jason was right. This world doesn't make any sense. The good die just for being good, and the sick and twisted live on. It's too much. It's just too much. There's nothing now. Nothing in the world. The world is crushing me more every second. I wish that it would just finish me. Finish me now! Is that a sin? Is it wrong to want this to be over now? Every moment is too much. Why? What did it have to happen to them? Why did it have to happen to all of them?

The crushing sorrow was pushing down on his insides. Even his limbs felt numb. In the agony, there was a split second of clarity.

391

That's right. In both situations and in all this loss, there is a common factor. Me. If I hadn't been captured, then they wouldn't have found my aunt and uncle. If I had been more observant and kept my guard up like I was taught, I might have sensed something was amiss before the bomb went off. If I had been in front of Alice, at least she would have lived. A.I.M. wouldn't have captured her either. She was too strong for that. At least she would have made it.

Oh, God, why did you put a pathetic person like me in all of their lives? I was cowardly and hesitant to everything. Even before I had the pressure of being an Amulus, I could barely carry on a conversation or make friends. I even had a stupid, smart mouth when I had the courage to talk. It's like I was unfit for human society. I became a superhuman and was still pathetic. I was so pathetic that I got good people killed. I didn't deserve them. I didn't deserve anyone. I really can't think of anyone who was better off for meeting me.

Maybe, it will end here. Maybe that's what I deserve. Yeah, that's some recompense for how I ruined everyone. I hope they feel better, somewhere, for that. No, I don't even have the right to think that.

The same thoughts repeated over and over. Paul's exhausted mind could think of nothing new.

At some point, he thought that he had fallen asleep and had a dream. He could not remember what the dream was and if he had slept at all. Being awake and asleep felt the same here. It was all a nightmare.

He thought the Scientist had come and gone again. If he had, he had muttered something about experimenting with his father in the early days when Amuli had been revealed to the world.

That would explain my vision of him as a kid. You know what? My parents had me and then died. I was bad luck from the start. I'm not sure why I was born at all. Was there a purpose? Was I supposed to choose one out of my own free will? I guess I chose horribly wrong. Then, all of this is on me after all.

Chapter 36: Out

Paul really had fallen asleep at some point. It did not make him feel any better. He felt just as exhausted as he had before, only he was more confused now.

He seemed to be hovering above the ground. A slight jolt would rock his numbed body every few seconds. It was completely dark. There was no dim light and no basement.

I'm dreaming about when Alice rescued me. Alice, you should have left me for A.I.M. then.

He thought he would wake about then but did not. The night air felt cool and real. His leg was dragging on the ground. His head was resting against something soft, a mess of hair that covered a sniffling face.

Paul tried to speak, but no words formed in his confused mind. He only let out a groan.

"You're awake," whispered May faintly. "I'm glad."

"Wha?" murmured Paul meekly.

"He's dead," sobbed May. "My brother. I found the records. He's been dead for months. He was an experiment, too. They had me working for them, the people who murdered my brother!"

She continued pattering while clutching him against her shoulder.

"I'm not their puppet anymore, I'm going do to something about this! I'll blow the whistle, even if it brings the whole world down! That's why I had to get you out. I wanted to do something good for once. Your chains were loose. I think he was distracted by another experiment and got sloppy. He'll pay."

The air was freezing Paul's nose and dry, cracked face. His arms waddled with every bump. May had put a blanket around his body to shield the cold. He felt his feet being dragged through wet snow and brittle sticks. Dark trees consumed the edges of his vision. *The woods again.*

"Hey, can you walk?" asked May cautiously. "Your arms and legs must be close to atrophy. I know it's hard. Can you try?"

Paul's limbs felt asleep. He could not even find the muscles to shake them into feeling. Those muscles must have been asleep, too. Besides, he did not want to move.

"Leave me," he croaked softly.

"What's that?" asked May as she pushed her face closer to

his.

"Leave me."

That's it. That's the one good thing I could do. I could stop being a burden to May or anyone. I stay here, and May gets away while the mad scientist retrieves me. The cold hurts, but it's numbing me even more. It wouldn't be so bad.

"Of course not!" shouted May in a horrified voice. "I couldn't save my brother, but I'm going to save you."

She trudged on for only a few more steps.

"I just need to readjust my grip," she said, catching her breath.

She leaned him down to the snow softly.

"Or we could take a short break. We're going to be hard to find in the dark, right? We've been going for a while. We're sure to find a road or town soon. It's not too far off if I remember."

She took a step forward and was about to speak, but only a cough and blood came out.

Paul thought there were tentacles bursting out of her chest. They were black, shooting quickly outward as if propelled by missiles. He screamed, scrambling backward in the snow.

What... What is this? Is this... real? Is this in my head? No, no I don't think so. May...

What he had thought of as tentacles were chains and a pale blue hue gleamed off them hauntingly. The chains hit the ground with a rattle, followed by May. The Scientist strode into the dim light. The mass of chains floated just above the ground. In their center was a blue crystal.

"One of the results of my experiments," he remarked slowly as he marveled at the glowing chains. "Embedding crystals into objects is a lost form of science. I am still seeking to rectify that. However, I have adapted my own, jewelry-embedded, Psychic crystal into a new object. I have gone from Psychic to Warrior. What I have lost in mental abilities, I know have in raw strength. I chose a suitable weapon, chains. It greatly aids in restricting the movements of my subjects. A.I.M. researchers dig far deeper than the close-minded incompetents in A.R.C. My colleagues and I have pieced the secrets together from scant, partial records which we have discovered only recently. The knowledgebase of Amuli from the distant past is quite astounding. From those, I have come up with my own formulas to test and expand the science of anima."

The chains churned towards Paul who could only gasp as he struggled on the ground. Finally, they coiled around him and hoisted him upward. The Scientist let his chains carry his prey as he moved back towards his compound. Paul could only watch May's body from an opening in the metal snakes. *Again. I got someone killed again. Why should I even exist? I am nothing but death.*

"And here, our first experiment comes to an end," the Scientist proclaimed when he lay Paul back on his bed. "It may be a surprise for you to hear that."

Paul did not respond in words. For some reason, his body seemed beyond his control. It contorted at some moments and froze still at others. It was as if all the anguish and exhaustion had caused his brain to relinquish his body.

"I have told you that your experiment was to determine pain tolerance in an Amulus," the Scientist explained to his immobile subject. "I was honest about that. The only half-lie I have been telling is that the process has yet to begin. No, it has been well underway. I am testing the threshold for mental and emotional pain in Amuli. We already know that the bodies of Amuli have pain receptors that are dulled so that they may accomplish feats of strength beyond the ordinary human. I hypothesized that the Amulus brain is more resistant to feelings of emotional or mental pain. In this instance, I would say that this notion was not supported. Observing you, I would say that you are closed to catatonic or an acute depressive episode at the least. Of course, I do not simply judge by observation but by heart rate and hormonal transmitters that you ingested while unconscious. However, as they say, 'it is not science unless it is repeatable.'

"You will only be the first of many in this experiment. I do hope that the process will be as simple with the other subjects as it was with you. In your case, all I had to do was tell you the truth about your family and loved ones to cause you emotional pain. I knew allowing Miss Hart to stumble on

398

information about her brother would likely cause an escape attempt on her part. Her empathetic personality was an indicator that she would take you as well. Her death brought a final means of pain. Not only did her loss lead to your anguish, but the failed escape attempt was hope snatched away. It was a fresh, different kind of pain for you."

Paul did not respond. His mind was as locked by chains as his body.

"It is not often that one finds a new purpose in life after the original is fulfilled," the Scientist continued. "I am happy that has just occurred in your example. I have just been allocated money from the highest levels of A.I.M. for a new research endeavor. You should prove a great help to me once again. One day, when the world comes to its senses, our names shall both be written in textbooks and the finest scientific publications."

Chapter 37: Honor

"I understand your haste," began the Scientist, milling around the visitors to his underground lab, "however, this is science! Tests need to be repeated and studied."

Red Mask waved the paranoid man off. "I've just given you the resources you need for further research beyond your wildest dreams. Would you like to bite the hand that feeds you?"

The Scientist shook his head frantically. "Not at all! Not at all! I am just saying there are procedures!"

A pair of intense eyes flashed from behind the mask.

"We have made some brash moves. If we don't move to cement the new status quo, our entire operation could be jeopardized. Your resources could just disappear. Do you want that?"

"T–There has to be some kind of...compromise. I'm sure..."

"Shut up," interjected Carson Colter. "Red pays for your fun just like he pays for mine. Scratch my back and all that, right? You don't need to be so snooty about everything. Now, you're promising something I want to see. Are you gonna show me on your own or am I going to have to make you?"

"I... I..." stammered the Scientist. "I have not even started the process."

"Enough of the arguing," warned Yu Li in a clear, low voice. "We know why we're here. Let's just get it done."

"I am in agreement with that," mentioned Emerson Whaley measuredly. "We are here to do some learning and to improve ourselves. Let us pass, and we will be out of your way soon."

The Scientist reluctantly relented before leading them down the barely lit hall. In the last room of the dank corridor, there was a sweat-drenched bed, an I.V. stand, and a despondent boy, staring vacantly at the opposing wall.

"So," rattled Colter. "I'm not the smartest. Remind me what we're doing here again and how it'll help us. No offense, I trust Rat, who brought us here, but I barely know Red and the doc."

"O-Of course, Mr. Colter," agreed the startled Scientist. "I am sure are aware of the fact that anima crystals synchronize with the body's own anima. I have long theorized, with plenty of supporting evidence, that this synchronization may be improved. Regretfully, I have never studied an Atlantean personally, but I have scoured the notes. I believe that, in some yet undiscovered way, that is anima-crystal-substance has worked its way into the various genes of Atlanteans which has led Amulus power to be spread hereditarily. Could, then, this be made possible in Amulus who are less synchronized with anima? Could injected crystal particles into the body cause enhanced synchronization?"

"Impossible," scoffed Yu Li. "Anima crystals are unbreakable. They only break when the owner dies and then dissipate into nothingness. Even the public knows that."

"Yes!" the Scientist reacted enthusiastically. "In almost all cases. However, what if someone did find a method for breaking down a crystal? What if someone created an anima weapon stronger than the average one that was capable of such a feat?"

"Cut to the chase," ordered an unamused Red Mask. "That's what you did, correct?"

"Yes, my apologies. I can crush anima crystals. Well, that is an over-simplification to describe it for your benefit. The process also involves a special acid which I have imbued with my anima That wears the crystal down enough that my chains can cause it to burst. The side-effect, however, is that it results in the death of an Amulus. When an Amulus expires, the crystal breaks and the opposite is also true. In my experiments, I have had success recovering the crystal material and injecting it into another Amulus. The result is increased synchronization and increased abilities several fold! The only thing I have yet to test is to determine that if the donor crystal residue may be injected into the dying Amulus in order to stabilize the subject. It stands to reason that the synchronization factor will be at its highest then. Now, I wanted to test both methods many times before your arrival to cement this theory, but if you really insist..."

Colter approached the bed and observed the boy who was somewhere between consciousness and unconsciousness. The large man swore loudly, causing the Scientist to jump.

"I know this kid! I fought him!"

"Are you going to brag again?" asked Li rhetorically.

"For God's sake, no!"

Colter moved closer to Paul. He craned his neck down to stare into the teenager's listless eyes.

"Damn! What did they do to ya?"

Paul did not even blink.

"I believe the expression is, 'what's done is done,'" quoted Whaley. "I believe that we should really be moving on with the Scientist's work. We did come a long way."

"Hold on!" shouted Colter abruptly. "I fought with this kid. He's not the strongest, but he's crafty. He's a fighter, and you're going to experiment on him as he's probably dying? He's not a lab monkey! Find someone else. I say give him a good meal and his sword back and let me finish him off if you want him dead. That's the way he should go out!"

Red Mask chuckled with the sound reverberating inside the sturdy material on his face. "You're pitying him. I have to admit that I'm taken aback. The most blood-hungry Amulus on earth and you're finding common cause with an enemy? How hilarious."

"I'm afraid that he is quite serious about this," warned Whaley. "He has a stubborn code of honor. He will not let this go easily."

"Don't talk about me like I'm not here!" snapped Colter.

"Sad," remarked Li. "Your head is always on flights of fancy and not the mission. You need some Ritalin?"

"Forget you guys," mouthed Colter slowly. "Yu Li, Whaley, I've been around you guys for a long time, but we have no common ground. The truth is I don't like either of you. You've got your justifications and try to act all professional about things. No, we're all killers. That's all we are. This life is simple, and you all just make it complicated for no reason. Do you know why I tag along? I trust Rat. He lets me do what I do. I'm not sure why he had us come here. Maybe it was Red's orders. You know what? I don't think he can stomach this stuff either. That's why he volunteered to guard outside. I listen to Rat and myself, and that's it. I barely know Red or this other psycho. From what I do know, I think you make me sick. Damn hypocrites."

"Funny," reacted Red Mask who had stopped laughing. "It's still so funny."

Colter pushed his way towards Paul.

Whaley blocked his way.

"Think this over, Carson," he advised calmly. "Do you want to throw this all away for a child who once tried to kill you? Would you make an enemy out of everyone standing here? You are a true warrior, but could you handle all of us?"

"I dare you," sneered Li with a hand resting on the pommel of her *Jian*.

Colter grumbled. "I'm out. I won't take the kid, but if you're doing stuff like this to the real warriors, then I'm gone."

Li drew her sword. Red Mask put a hand over it.

"I'll let you pass," he declared. "We didn't come here for a bloodbath. However, the moment you step outside, you become fair game. I'm not worried about you going over to A.R.C. They want you dead even worse than we do."

"Carson," Whaley whispered.

"Shut it," griped Colter as he turned his back. "I've never been surer that I'm doing the right thing. After all, challengers from both sides? I'll be sure to get some good fights now."

He locked eyes on Paul as he walked away towards a tunnel leading to the base's hill-hidden, back entrance. "Sorry, kid. I'll see you in Valhalla. I've always liked that legend."

"Disappointing," bemoaned Whaley after Colter was gone.

"It's of no consequence," said Red Mask coolly. "We'll continue now."

The Scientist rushed over a cart full of wobbling jars. "I've taken the liberty to prepare the solution beforehand."

"Much appreciated," Red Mask acknowledged, "now start."

The Scientist brought up Paul's katana from the bottom layer of the cart. Even seeing his weapon of power brought no spark to Paul's glassy eyes. Only his rising and falling chest betrayed the fact that he was still alive. In his consciousness, locked away deep, life and death now seemed very much the same.

The chains twisted their way off of Paul who made no moves to escape. They levitated again in the eerie, blue light. They coiled like tendrils, wrapping around Paul's sword. When they came to the part of the hilt with the crystal, they tightened. The chains put more and more pressure on the indestructible, glasslike stone. They creaked as the Scientist began to perspire from the effort of using his anima.

There was a pop. There was only a hole in the hilt now, filled with dust.

The effect was not immediate on Paul. For several moments, there was only anticipation as the small crowd watched the catatonic boy.

Paul's body suddenly jolted his mind back into thought. It convulsed and rattled all of his bones. Then, there was the pain. The physical pain he had been dreading had come in this form. It was the worst pain of his life. He was being squeezed so powerfully that he felt like an ant being stepped on. He was sure that blood or guts would come out of his mouth. It was as if all his insides were being scraped away.

There was weakness, too. It was so heavy. Everything was being drained: energy, emotion, thoughts, and all feeling except for the pain.

Anima was flooding out of the teenager in the form of a green mist. It came from every part of him. He was a bottle turned upside down, and the only cork for him had just been destroyed. There was no getting the anima back, there was no stopping it from bleeding out of him.

The Scientist had not wasted a second. He had scooped the crystal powder from the sword hilt before stirring it into the solution. That solution went into another solution and then several more times. Finally, he loaded a syringe.

"The moment of truth," whispered Whaley auspiciously.

The Scientist primed the syringe for the screaming, howling boy on the bed. He stuck it into the I.V. bag without a word.

The cries were slightly softer now. The solution was now visible in Paul's blood vessels. It raced through him, turning veins and arteries green. His skin sparked and flared green flame. For a moment, he lay sweating and still. The observers stepped closer, peering over him intently.

The agony started again, slowly. It was a dull ache this time. Paul could feel his consciousness slipping with the green smoke now lifting off of him.

Whaley adjusted his glasses and smoothed his blonde hair.

"Not what we wanted to see, obviously."

"It is a process!" insisted the Scientist loudly. "I will need to create more data on this phenomenon. In this case, it seems the injecting of one's own crystal only serves to slow down the 'bleeding.' It is likely that he has hours now, instead of minutes, as with the other cases."

"You're right," chimed Red Mask. "It's a result, and now we know. Time is still of the essence. Inject these two with crystal powder from dead Amuli."

The Scientist was taken aback.

"E-even that needs more testing! To try it out on the most valuable troops is-"

"It's what we need," finished the man behind the bloody skull mask. "We just pulled a bold move on A.R.C. with that bombing. If they find out it was us, they will respond in kind. They may be war, and we will seize the moment. Momentum us ours. We cannot afford to stop making bold moves now."

"Very well," relented the Scientist, nearly choked up. "Follow me. I do not want to miss any observations of the current test subject, but if you say that I must..."

The group followed the Scientist to an adjacent room filled with more glass beakers and tubes filled liquids and powders. He prepared two more syringes.

"What about you, sir?"

"Not me," explained Red Mask. "I need a clear head moving forward."

Li reluctantly offered her arm.

"I still don't like the idea of this. I earned the strength I have so far. But if this is what I'm ordered to do..."

"It does lack a certain kind of elegance," agreed Whaley as he did likewise.

The notions seemed lost on the puzzled scientist.

"Call it what you want," snorted Red Mask, "you'll need it in time."

The Scientist took Li's arm first, slipping in a needle glowing purple.

Her look remained one of assured confidence. The next moment, she stumbled to a knee and grunted. The purple glow raced through her, turning her body almost translucent. Purple waves of energy washed over her, gradually changing in hue. The purple became lighter until it matched her own crystal of red. Her body slowly regained its normal color.

She let a glow of red escape her hand. The veins of her arm matched the color. She smiled, delighted.

"I like the feeling."

"There are some side effects," the Scientist warned. "Feelings of increased anger and confusion during anima release, mostly. You should be accustomed to them in time."

Emerson Whaley's turn was next. A mint-green solution raced down his veins and bubbled on his skin. He was racked by a sudden strain before quickly regaining his composure. The color then shifted to sky blue before dissipating.

"It is a strange feeling," he remarked ponderously. "I felt as if I heard an echo of some kind when it was first injected."

The Scientist nodded. "Auditory and visual hallucinations often occur in the first few minutes. I suspect that this is due to a strain on the brain. Any that may emerge will dissipate quickly. That is what the evidence has shown."

"And how many have you done this to?" questioned Li. "Are we special?"

"There has been only one other subject," answered the Scientist, ignoring the second question that slightly perturbed him.

"Very special indeed," Li declared as she lit her veins red again.

Each A.I.M. operative turned when they heard a painful gasping coming from the other room.

"Sad to hear," reflected Whaley. "Though I do suppose that it was necessary. Is there anything to put him out of his misery at this point."

"Certainly not!" shouted the Scientist. "His last few moments will need chronicling and analyzing. I must see how long he will last before the strain on his body and mind becomes too great. I have already started a timer to keep track. If you will excuse me, I will get back to the data-gathering."

"We will take our leave out the back entrance," announced Red Mask. "I left The Rat to guard the front in case our scientist friend here has need of him. Let us not be wasteful. Let's put your new powers to the test."

Chapter 38: Rise

Paul could feel it now. Beyond the pain, there was the darkness on the edges of his vision. Strange and cold yet welcoming. The anima was only dripping from him now. He was just tired. So tired.

"Paul!"

There was his name. It was called by a shaking, breaking voice. It was familiar and kind. He wanted to tell this person not to fear whatever they were so afraid of. Someone should not have to suffer like that. *Why are you hurting? Who are you? It's okay.*

"Paul! Paul! Paul!"

He opened his stiff eyelids. He could make out some gold hair and dark blue orbs, shining beautifully.

Is it an angel? Coming for me? I guess I am dying. Why me? I don't deserve an angel.

His vision cleared slightly. There was Alice. He had never

suspected that such emotion could be displayed on her usually stoic face. Fear and worry were making it scrunch, and her eyes dripped.

Alice's spirit is coming for me. I don't deserve that either. I'm the reason she died.

He tried to wave her away but could not move his arm or anything else. There was a deeper voice in the room as well.

"I will leave it to you," Luper's voice said. "I'm sorry. I am so very sorry to both of you."

Don't be sorry. It's all my fault.

The dark shape that was Luper moved and disappeared. Suddenly, something approaching strength and clarity from the pain came to Paul. His vision became fuller.

Alice. It really seemed like she was there. She held something aloft. Paul realized it was his sword. One of her fingers stretched the gaping hole in the hilt. Others grasped her anima necklace which shined brilliantly. She pushed her crystal closer and closer to the gap. The golden light was now blinding.

"I am so sorry, Paul!" she cried. "You are too good for a life like this. You are my precious friend."

Green light from the katana reached out toward the golden aura. They combined together but did not mix. They spun

413

together and twisted in the air as if dancing. The closer the lights became, the more they became like a swirling tempest, engulfing the room.

To Paul, it seemed as if there were two Alices in the room, one with the usual blue eyes and one with intense gold. They were speaking quickly in frantic voices.

"*We made need this for our survival later.*"

"No! He needs it now!"

"*It will only be a burden on him. He will hate you for it!*"

"His life is my priority!"

"*How far have we fallen? We do not even prioritize our own life.*"

"I have found another way to live!"

"*I may leave you because of this. What will you do without me?*"

"I am sorry. In a way, I am grateful to you. You kept me alive. You helped me with the burden of my own existence. I am sorry. I do not need you anymore. I have found people who are selfless and will help me shoulder that burden!"

The Alice with the cold, gold eyes departed.

Finally, Alice's loose crystal was fit into the hole in the sword hilt. Green encircled and penetrated the gold crystal until it was stained permanently green.

The anima raised Paul's body from the bed which had been absent of chains since his crystal had been crushed. His head was slunk backward, while his eyes rolled back and quivered. The crystal residue in his blood turned it green. This was not the usual, medium green his crystal had released before. Its edges were tinged with black, turning the swirling green darker.

Paul's body lifted off the table, pushing past an exhausted Alice before it took him through the halls of the compound. Green lightning struck the walls as the heat from the flames turned the place into an oven. Paul's mind was missing once again. The power welling in him was too powerful for his tired brain to comprehend. There were, however, still feelings. Rage was the strongest among them.

Chapter 39: Reckoning

Jason breathed hard and deep. Luper had taught him that early on. Anger and fear only tainted the mind. Clarity was key. It was a lesson that he had never taken seriously enough. It was now time to try.

It was beyond difficult though. The man before him had taken so much from him. He had taken his blood. He had taken a sweet, old babysitter. He had taken his mother. He had given him only hate, and that was now his reason for being. Now, he just had to be a target and only that.

The events of the past few days flashed by him quickly as he continued analyzing the man in front of him.

They had all blamed themselves when Paul was taken. Alice had taken it the hardest.

Jason had been inside the parking garage elevator when the bomb went off. He had spent his awkward and unappreciated night off at an M.M.A. training dojo. He was only there to watch since stepping into the cage would have meant the end for any non-Amuli opponents and exposure of his cover.

Nevertheless, if he had been barred from training for the day, then he would study techniques from others.

The hidden entrance and even the elevator had been designed to stop even the strongest Amulus. The bomb had fallen short of that extreme. Still, it was dangerous and disorienting to anyone, even Amuli, at close range. Alice was confused and dust-covered when she had stumbled in without the others. Seeing him had snapped her back to her senses, and she had flown back to search for the others. Only Paul was gone. Even Swanson, with some otherworldly luck, had been standing far enough away on his walk back to A.R.C. Angel that he walked away with only scrapes and bruises.

They did not stop after that. They mined camera feeds and called every agent in the area to look for Paul. All the anger that Jason had felt towards the naïve Paul began to feel silly and almost sick. No matter how infuriatingly soft he was, he did what he was told and tried to do it well. He was an ally in Jason's war, and he had been let down.

He swept parameter after parameter. He often went with Alice, since Luper and Grady were concerned that she would run off to find Paul on her own if she went alone. Jason marveled at the paradigm shift in her behavior. Before, she seemed to have no desire in the world beyond serving A.R.C. While saving an agent was a help to A.R.C., Alice did not seem to care about that specifically. She blamed herself for not being prepared and losing him.

Until hours ago, they had assumed that it had been the work

417

of Hunters. A.I.M. would not dare cross into enemy territory. That could have meant the end of the world or at least life as the world knew it. A.I.M. would have sent Amuli anyway. That is what everyone at A.R.C. had thought.

A scouting agent had reported a spike in anima in some middle-of-nowhere woods near the West Virginia border. They had traced it and found this abandoned mine shaft that must have doubled as a Cold War bunker at some point. With their vicinity to the incident, the Pittsburgh team had been asked to respond. Luper had brought his most experienced trainees, Alice and Jason with him to investigate. When they arrived, a familiar aura had permeated the place. It was the innocent feel of Paul's anima, there was no mistaking it. This is where he was or had been. They had not stopped looking for him, and Alice's search had grown obsessive. Luper's heart had broken for her. In a moment, she had lost the first friend she had ever made. Feeling Paul there, Alice was clearly emotionally compromised.

The three of them had been greeted with the most unpleasant sight at the entrance they found. There, in the dark, was the shaggy-haired, bearded man who did not seem to care for fresh clothes or any other amenity. The Rat had stared them down with his anima knife raised. They were going to fight Amuli and that changed things.

"I have this," Jason had barked. "Go! I have this, this time."

Luper gave him a worried, knowing look as he passed him for the entrance. He would do his best to return. Secretly, Jason hoped that it would be over by then.

The Rat appeared unperturbed at letting two of the A.R.C. operatives inside. Maybe, there were more guards in there.

Jason waved his sword about, keeping his wrist loose. He would not make a stupid first attack this time. There was too much riding on this to go in with only his rage and hate.

"Well, well," came a voice from behind them. "I'm glad that we decided to turn back when we felt the anima."

Jason felt cold arms wrapped around his neck. He slid up an arm to prevent the stranglehold and bucked the person behind him with his back before retreated and assessing the new enemies.

There were Yu Li and Emerson Whaley, two of The Rat's operatives. He remembered their faces from the files Luper had given the team.

"You won't even fight me on your own?" spat Jason, trying to bait his opponent into a rage of his own. "Coward. You're just a butcher and a coward."

"You!" shouted Li in warning with a sword raised.

"Go!" barked The Rat.

"Why?" questioned Li incredulously. "The three of us can take him in a second."

"There are two others who have slipped by!" informed The Rat. "Now, Go!"

"It would..." began Li before she decided to follow Whaley into the shaft.

Jason let his sword leap around in his grasp. He would not let the confusion pass without taking advantage. This time, he was patient. He probed The Rat, looking for openings. The Rat more than aptly parried each blow, but Jason used the reach of his sword to prevent a counterattack.

Seeing no advance in this, The Rat changed tactics. He sent a twirling blast of spear-like energy towards Jason. It was too late to dodge, so Jason sent a spiraling beam of red energy to match the blue. The two attacks canceled each other out amid a cascade of sparks and flashes.

The Rat kept on him with anima bursts. Jason was quick to block each one with his own anima. Red and blue explosions lit the woods like fireworks. Jason clenched his teeth together so tight that his gums hurt. He let his determination take over his body, letting him go beyond defending to attack with his seething anima.

Both fighters were out of breath when they realized the explosions had pushed them yards back from where they started. Neither dared risk depleted more anima in straight blasts. It was back to blades.

The knife and the sword danced. One Amulus would attack

and then the other would parry the same direction before launching a follow-up attack. The burning blades glanced up from the combatants' knees to their heads in flashes. Where they crossed, the blue and red mixed to spots of purple hanging in the air. They screeched and hissed like fighting cats.

Jason's breath began to run fast and hard, and he saw that The Rat was doing the same. They both retreated slightly for a breath but never failed to take their eyes away from each other. Jason's own boots sloshed mud and slush onto his damp pant legs. He could feel warm blood from half a dozen small cuts along his arms. At least, they felt small to Jason. He could deal with them later... if later would come for him. The anima burns to his shoulders and neck were causing greater pain.

Both enemies rushed each other again. Their movements were slower this time, although each strike was still bone-rattling. Jason pushed the ache away throughout his whole body, tapping into some numbing, survival instinct. His mind moved his tired body as if it were a worthless toy. He decided it was time for risks. He had enough of this man's raggedy face and the hate he felt when he looked at it. For the sake of his mother and himself, it was time for this man to be gone from this world. Jason drove his knee into that of his opponent.

The Rat's guard broke amid the jarring, cracking pain. It had been a foolhardy but effective move. It was one that could cause catastrophic injury to the attacker as much as the victim. In this case, it injured both. Jason did not care if his knee was intact or in pieces.

Jason wound his arms up before powering downward for an overhead, turning feint. The Rat bit on it, raising his large knife to block. Jason used the momentum from the feint to twist his body the entire way around, doing a one-hundred-and-eighty-degree spin. The Rat only realized the deception at the last moment, jabbing his knife through the back of the teenager's shoulder. Jason, facing away from the Rat, reversed his grip and stabbed backwards. Blind to his own attack, Jason only felt the saber go through something soft.

The Rat slipped off Jason's blade and waddled backward toward the shaft entrance, propping his head up on the side. Dark blood seeped through the side of his tattered coat. Jason cackled a giddy laugh without realizing it. After all the years, the time had come. It was at an end. He could die minutes from now and feel fulfilled.

He dragged his own, hobbled body towards the man he had hated for so long. The anima knife had long since been dropped from the man's grasp. Jason plopped down in front of his nemesis before pressing his sword to the Rat's bearded throat. It shook in place, causing blood to well into the matted hair.

"I made a mistake the first time," he acknowledged, unaware that the corners of his mouth twisted into a smile. "I asked the questions beforehand and only distracted myself. Now, it's the end. I'm not a doctor, but I think I hit your liver. Only the best hospital could patch that up before you bleed out, and we're miles from that. You're about to die. I can make it slow. I can take fingers and toes and you'll die screaming. Or I can end it right now. Just tell me what I want to know! Do you remember Hanahime Saito?"

The Rat smiled as blood ran down his lips.

"Of course, I do, my little prince. I loved her."

Chapter 40: Penance

There was at least a mile of dried blood in the bunker complex by Luper's reckoning. A wry thought in his mind remarked on the lack of sterilization in this place manned by A.I.M.'s supposed scientists. He would have never had rushed into such a place on so little information if it had been any other situation. Paul had been taken into his care. A young life that was kind-hearted and eager to do right was in danger of being cut short. It happened all too often in this business of death. Now Alice, too, was in this haunting place. She had broken from his grip and warning of caution to pursue her dear friend.

He felt so close to losing both of them. They were both in this place because of him. No, he amended the notion. Alice was going in no matter what, and he just tagged along. Paul had done a real number on her. That launched some unexpected, nostalgic memories for the wire-haired man.

Yet, they had found each other again. Alice would use her miraculous powers as the world's only known Alpha Amulus to heal Paul as best as she could. That was all uncharted territory now. Luper felt that sweeping the interior for dangers was the best he could do to guard the two young people who had grown so close to him.

Places like these were never empty at a time like this. No matter how many corners and rooms were bare, it was all to lull the enemy into thinking that. Any operative foolish enough to open a door without expecting someone behind it was as good as dead.

Surprisingly, he felt the anima behind him first. It felt colder and more sinister than any he had felt in his years of experience. There were multiple sources. He felt his disadvantage then. This underground compound was a maze of tunnels

Luper stayed where he was. Sneaking into a room to hide would only compromise his mobility. This was not a reconnaissance mission but one to buy time.

"It seems like we've found something interesting," muttered Yu Li.

"Oh," exhaled Emerson Whaley, captivated, "this is an honor. It's Death in the Black Suit, as the legend goes. I have looked forward to this day. I'm glad Red Mask ordered us to double-back when we felt those Amuli presences, otherwise we would have missed you completely."

"I'm sorry that this will be quick then," Li goaded.

Luper felt the ominous energy coming in buffeting waves.

Dark veins appeared to pop out of the skin of the two A.I.M. agents before him. Anima visibly whirled about them.

Luper dropped his jacket and readied his staff. He had felt something similar to this presence of ugly, mutated anima before during his years combating A.I.M. and the organization's inhumane experiments. Something evil had been done to boost this power. Any other Amulus would have passed out releasing that much anima at once. They were just wasting it away in a show of intimidation. If it bothered Luper, he did not let it show.

Li lunged forward first, flying at a speed that meant Luper could only rely on battle-hardened instinct to stop her sword. She hammered at him in a flurry that sent him jogging back through the tunnel.

Li kept her attacks to one side. Whaley had his weapon drawn. It was an English longbow aimed at Luper's other side. He let fly a blistering anima arrow to the left of his partner. Luper struggled to knock it to the side with the other side of his staff.

The A.I.M. operatives fought in unison. Li sought to drive Luper into Whaley's arrows which, in turn, aimed to break Luper's guard to leave an opening for Li. Luper's staff deflected deftly against his stronger opponents. His mind calculated angles and leverage innately. The years of experience had given him reflexes beyond even most Amuli.

He used the narrow hallway to his advantage. Whaley dared

not hit his ally and was only able to fire sparingly at obvious openings. Luper could feel Li's frustration in her rhythm. He knew that she was questioning why her newfound strength was not speeding up the killing process against a regular Amulus. From that, Luper knew that she was inexperienced with this new power.

Another shot from Whaley came. Luper went to block with one end of his staff as he had been doing. This time, he torqued his body with the follow-through, snapping the staff into the side of Li's head.

Li seemed to be in more surprise than pain. She kicked out, catching Luper in the ribcage. Luper flew backward, bouncing off both sides of the tunnel. He held his chest when he stopped on his knees. In all his years, this was close to the worst pain he had felt. He could not find breath. His hand told him that his chest was no longer its usual shape. White flashes sparked when he blinked.

Li did not stop. She came to finish her downed opponent.

Her inexperience with her new power had given her sloppy form which was a far cry from her Wushu champion days. Her legs, while in a run, got in the way of her footwork. Her left leg trotted too far inside. It was a cardinal sin for a swordsman or swordswoman.

Luper scooped her leg forward with his foot as she made a downward strike towards him. The woman's own leg blocked her sword's reach of Luper. It cut deep into her thigh, nearly to the bone. She fell forward to the ground, screaming.

Even in his own agony, Luper did not wait. He went on top of her, lodging his staff under her neck.

Whaley rushed to aid his comrade. The largest arrow that he had yet produced soared towards the man on his partner's back.

It was all to Luper's predictions. He spun with Li in his grasp, pushing her over him. The arrow shredded both Luper and Li.

Whaley sunk to the side of the wall, staring in disbelief at the bodies in front of him.

"How? Why? You used me to..."

A tap on his shoulder sent him shivering. A man in a hideous, red mask admired Whaley's disaster beside him. "It is fortunate that I decided to follow you two back. Do not grieve Li. She couldn't handle my gift to her. The old man even used it against her. You're leaving now. You've done enough here, and we've been made."

"Colter was right," Whaley shuddered. "Things were better when it was only Rat calling the shots."

"That's a pity then."

Chapter 41: Beyond

For several minutes, Paul did not remember what he had been doing in the previous moment. Whatever it had been, it still seemed very important. The thoughts were stuck in some crevice of his brain but would not shake loose. It was beyond anxiety-invoking.

He was standing still in the school library. The few stacks of books loomed before him. The older volumes gave off a musky scent which Paul actually enjoyed. It gave the place character as if it were providing relaxing energy for the space. The more regularly used computer stations, as well as the tables and chairs, sat strangely quiet.

The only thing that Paul knew was that it was weird for him to be here. This was not where he had been previously.

With a startle, Paul realized that he was not alone amongst the shelves. A short male who could have been aged anywhere from fifteen to twenty-five pulled off several dictionaries and set them on a table. Paul could not help but stare at the youth with almond eyes and curly, black hair.

"Absolutely marvelous!" he declared while looking up from his pile of books. "You don't disappoint me. It's quite the opposite actually. My own mental space is actually quite similar. On the other hand, the books do look a bit different. I should take you there sometime. If I'm not being presumptuous, I think you would enjoy it."

"I-I'm sorry... you are?" Paul stammered out his question.

This person seemed to know him, but Paul did not remember the face.

"Ugh," the mystery person shrugged, "it's time for the long, drawn-out explanation. I never like this part. It has gotten... repetitive. First of all, I know that you are Paul Michael Engel. I've been watching you. Not in a creepy, all-the-time way, but here and there. I have been there for the important parts at least. Just call me, the Observer."

"I'm sorry. I don't think I remember you."

"You wouldn't. We've never really met."

Paul sensed something strange from this person wearing his school uniform. There was no visible aura of anima, but there was an eeriness about him.

"I-I'm sorry are you like a..."

The mysterious person barely stifled a laugh. "No. Not an angel nor anything holy. I'm closer to someone like yourself."

He lifted a pant leg to reveal a metal anklet with a shimmering blue crystal embedded.

"See?"

Paul continued searching the room in a haze. "I'm not sure why I'm here. I feel like I was doing something important before this. Oh, I'm sorry if that's rude. I don't mind talking to you, but I really think there is something I should get back to."

"That you do," replied the Amulus. "You will return to it soon. Unfortunately, it won't be comfortable or pleasant when you do return. I felt like you needed the time to re-center yourself while your mind, at least, was free."

"I don't understand."

"Well, what's the last thing you remember before coming here?"

The words jogged Paul's mind. He flew towards the doors of the library and found them locked impossibly tight.

Paul shouted. "Please! Let me go! I think I was dying and then I was with Alice who I thought was dead. She helped me live somehow, or did she? Anyway, please, let me go. It's a matter of life and death!"

"You're confused," the Observer said in a calm voice. "That is beyond understandable, believe me. However, if you don't work out some of that confusion, things will be much worse when you return."

Paul pounded on the door again before sliding down it in defeat.

"I'll explain," the Observer offered. "Your anima crystal was shattered. In almost all situations, that means certain death. After all, only one crystal can be truly bonded to an Amulus. The only method for survival is the transplant of an unbonded crystal which is beyond rare."

"Unbonded crystal? Alice used hers and not one that had not yet awakened an Amulus."

"That's the deception you've been under," the Observer explained. "I assure you, however, that it was the whitest of lies. No, it was not Alice's bonded crystal. She has none. She does not require one."

Paul shook his head. Heaps of frustration layered on him. "But she's an Amulus, she has to have a crystal."

The Observer shook his head. "Not true. In most cases, an Amulus is awakened by a crystal. What if I told that there was a way around that? You have now seen anima crystals transferred into the body by blood correct? What if that process was repeated over and over in one family for generations? Well, I can tell you that it will actually affect the genetic material of the family members. In time, children will be born with enough crystal residue in their bodies that they are born awakened."

"An Alpha Amulus," realized Paul. "What about the crystal?"

"Many of today's people are mistaken when it comes to the bonding of crystals," asserted the youth. "Nearly every crystal you come into contact with is bonded to a human. They may not have awakened its Amulus and may never do so. They are bonded, nevertheless. It takes lost rituals to unbond a crystal, at which time it turns yellow or gold. Anima may be poured into it by any number of people. That way, the user of the crystal has access to not only his or her own anima but the anima from donors."

"That's why Alice has been so strong," realized Paul.

"There is a cost, however. Despite its strengthening characteristics, anima use is taxing to the brain. Anima is a source that is typically untapped in the body. The brain becomes confused at its loss and shift of equilibrium. For most Amulus, the effect is negligible. Most of the strain comes at awakening and later the brain is adaptable enough to become accustomed to the new normal. An unbonded crystal, on the other hand, represents anima that is alien to the body being put into the body. The strain is far greater and can result in many side effects with psychosis common among them."

"Like Alice's monster," whispered Paul as the revelation

stirred in his stomach.

"Precisely."

"How did you..."

The Observer waved him off. "While it may trouble you, I do know a great many things. I watch the world with my own anima powers. I connect to people like a Psychic but on a much grander scale. The place that you see before you is nothing more than your own brain attempting to make sense of a stream of sensations that I have put into your brain. I told you that I watch people. I only watch people who are important since there are a lot of people in the world. Alice has been chief among them... as have you."

Paul's mind wrapped around the slippery and uncomfortable information.

"Wait a minute. The visions and memories..."

The Observer smiled brightly.

"This is why you are one of my favorite people to watch! You have such a strength for thinking. Yes, I have been sending you real memories to guide you. As people, we typically struggle to see things from another's perspective. And so, I have let you do that. You see the moments that make up the people around you. The more information, the better."

Or a lack of privacy, Paul thought, forgetting where he was.

The thought rang out embarrassingly in this mental plane.

The Observer sighed. "Unfortunately, yes, However, if it were not necessary, I would not do so."

"I still need to get back," Paul breathed impatiently.

"Of course," the young man relented. "Time passes here as well. I would not want to deprive you of something as precious as time. I brought you here only to inform you of your new station. Alpha Amulus is the term I think you know it by. What you've seen in Alice is only the beginning of it. You are becoming as different from Amuli as Amuli are from normal humans. It will be frightening and difficult, but you will work wonders with powers you've never dreamed of. As I said, I am just giving you more information. What you do with it is your choice. That being said, if you are the person I have observed, I cannot wait to see the choices you make."

A lock twisted open on one of the doors.

The Amulus motioned Paul to it.

"One last and regrettable thing. This new path that life has given you will not be easy. The moment in which you will emerge could be one of the most difficult ones that I can foresee. I hate to see a boy like you caught up in it. You have a kind aura about you, even without the anima. I'm sure that is what Alice sensed that night she tried, in vain, to take the sword from you. I truly am sorry. Just know that I am somewhere rooting for you."

Chapter 42: Release

Jason stumbled backward.

The voice of his mother rang through his mind. "My name is Hanahime. Do you know what that means? "Hana" means flower. "Hime," means princess. Do you know what the son of a princess is called? A prince!"

He regained himself before pressing his sword towards the neck of the bleeding man even harder.

"Don't screw with me!" he hissed.

The dying man smiled with blood in his teeth. "I want you to look at me."

"What?"

The Rat motioned a wobbly hand to his face. "You're so lucky that you got your mom's looks," he complimented in a pleasant, even voice. "Look here, the jawline, the nose, and the forehead. You get those from me."

Jason shook with rage. "You shut up!"

In fear, he took the man on his words without meaning to. The forehead and the way it creased. The strong jawline and tight chin. The slight bend in the nose. They were all the same.

"The beard and the hats were supposed to help hide the resemblance."

Jason threw his head from side to side. "I don't get it! I don't get it! What are you saying?"

The Rat coughed before saying, "Nice to meet you. I'm Mark Ratowski. You're smart. I think you can guess who I am."

Jason dropped the sword and grabbed the man by his collar. "I don't believe you!"

The Rat gazed away nostalgically into the starry night sky.

"I met you once before your mother died. I don't think you would remember. Hana wanted me in your life somehow. The problem is that I was in such a dangerous line of work at the time. Amuli were in a free-for-fall before A.R.C. and A.I.M. and even a little afterward. We both decided to leave me off of your birth certificate. That's why you're Jason Saito and not Jason Ratowski. I'm glad for that. She took you to a park when you were five and introduced you to an old friend of hers named Mark who pushed you on the swings. I didn't get to drop in much after that."

437

"It doesn't make any sense!" cried Jason. "Why did you kill her?"

"I didn't."

"Of course you did! I saw you!"

The Rat shook his head sadly.

"Remember back. You saw me with her. You didn't see me do it. I would never have…"

Jason racked his brain. He waited to conjure some imagine that proved this man wrong. He could not.

"Who? Then, who?" he demanded.

"I've been piecing it together for years," The Rat relayed through tears. "Look up Howe and McGreevy. They were part of Jackson's crew who worked Chicago at the time. They either knew Hana's link to me or she fought back when she figured out they were A.R.C. since she knew I was A.I.M. They may have been scared off when they heard me coming. I think the three of us felt your awakening the day before. A.R.C. and A.I.M. resources weren't what they are now, so it took some time to track anyone down."

Jason let his sword sink into the chilled mud. "I always knew it was because of me that they tracked her down. I've been working for A.R.C. all this time! They're the ones! Why didn't you tell me? Why didn't you ever find me?"

The Rat sighed as his blood pattered on the ground. "Everything I did was for you. You don't have to like it. When you were on the streets, I kept A.I.M. and A.R.C. off your tail. I paid off people to give you places to sleep. You never saw me, but I was always there. When A.R.C. and A.I.M. got so powerful, I knew that one was going to have to take you in. I'm in A.I.M., but I don't care about the cause. It's all about surviving in this screwed up world. In A.I.M. when you're not strong enough, you get written off as a Dead Eyes or some other experiment. A.R.C. was safer. You could grow stronger there."

"Why fight me then?" choked Jason.

"I told you that this world is screwed up. If you have a mission or a purpose, sometimes that drives you to get through it. If wanting to kill me would get you through, then I was glad to finally be of use to you. I just had to make sure that you were strong enough to kill me with no punches pulled. That way, I know that you can make it."

"What the hell am I supposed to do now?" screamed Jason into his father's face.

"You... know," the bearded man murmured weakly. "I do feel faint. There'll be no waking up... afterward. You decide. I just gave you the skills."

That Rat's skin went to a pale white. There was no breathing without a painful struggle in his chest.

"Ya... Y-You, d-don't have to forgive me. Don't... worry. I-I'm not going where you're... mother... went."

He closed his eyes. His face seemed less ragged than before. It was peaceful and littered with gentle tears.

Jason slouched down in the mud beside the dead man.

Chapter 43: Behind

Alice grunted loudly as she zapped the fallen man again. She had barely groaned when she had cauterized her own wound months ago. This time, somehow, it hurt more. Luper was sweating. His eyes were open, but he was unconscious. A haunting moan pushed its way out of his throat. She was making progress on the wound. The gap near the neck was sealed. In the half-dark, some blackness still welled out of the collarbone area.

She cried and berated herself. The process would be so much quicker if she could keep her hands steady. It was a simple mission. She had been created to only follow orders. Why were her hands letting her down now?

There was a wail, echoing down the tunnel. She realized, in shock, that it was coming from her own mouth.

"Why?"

In the locked rooms where she had been raised, there had been no emotions there. There had been no feeling. Now, in these past few days, there were so many. They hurt like a real injury. Sometimes, she had to look at her own chest to see that there was not a gaping wound there. She realized that to live on the outside was to be hurt. There were other, wonderful feelings, but still, all this hurt. She wished that she was the programed shell that she had been created to be. Then, Luper would be fine. Maybe, Paul would not have been captured. She let them down. Her mentor. Her first friend who had led her to more friends.

"C-conserve," croaked Luper, now more lucid. "Save it... for yourself."

"I will stop the bleeding," she asserted unsurely.

"I-I know my body," he whispered. "I'm hemorrhaging... internally. D-Don't waste it... on a dead man."

"No!" Alice pleaded as she shook tears from her eyes.

Luper looked at her with warm eyes. "A-Alice. I-I'm s-so... sorry."

"No! You should not speak!"

"Alice, I did... so much wrong by you."

"You did not!"

"I-I hate myself for it," he choked. "A-All the years... nothing I did worse. W-When you were born, I-I told myself you were just Aiden's child. Y-You would be like... him. I would not...

let myself believe... you were Abby's daughter. Y-you are... so much more so..."

"Do not hate yourself for me!" Alice insisted. "Please!"

"I-I loved her... you know," Luper whispered. "B-But, A.R.C. s-said... the last two Atlanteans had to..."

Alice nodded emphatically. "I know. Somehow, I dreamt of the memories."

"I see," murmured Luper. "Y-You that... ability. You... really are... so wonderful."

An agonizing coughing fit rattled his body. He fought it to keep speaking the words he had to voice in the end.

"I-I m-must confess... another sin," he implored while heaving. "Training you... I began to see... you as what... our daughter would have been together. I-I had... no right."

"You are!" Alice yelled with a shaking hand to her chest. "You are my father in here! You brought me to the world. I am the daughter of Abigail... and Greg Luper!"

"G-Go!" Luper wheezed meekly. "W-Why spend time on... the dead. S-Someone needs you. H-Help him."

"B-But..." stammered Alice.

"L-Leave me, m-my w-wonderful... daughter."

He closed his eyes amid a weak smile. He had always wondered what dreams would come.

~ ~ ~

Luper strode through the warehouse. His only company was shipping crates and large cardboard boxes. With his acute senses, the scent of glue and adhesive were almost to make him lightheaded. There were those smells and whatever it was being hidden in the packages. He suspected that the contents were less than legal substances.

I am the first one here, I suppose.

In privacy, he checked his reflection in one of the windows.

I wonder if the beard is really making me look older... more experienced.

He continued to an offshoot of the warehouse where there where a number of old couches and chairs, likely a place where workers would take breaks.

He noticed a young woman sitting nonchalantly on one of the couches.

Human cargo? I do a lot of bad things in this line of work, but I do not like where this one could be heading. I may have to talk to Rousseaux. I did not know that he dealt in this kind of thing.

"Oh, hello!" called the young woman eagerly.

She had a long, bronze hair draped over her shoulder. Her eyes were a warm blue like the ocean being warmed by the sun. Her smile was light and airy.

"Hi?" responded Luper, confused, and with a slight blush.

"I believe that I will be working with you today!" she mentioned pleasantly. "It's nice to meet you. I'm Abigail."

"N-Nice to me you, too?" Luper replied. "My name is Greg. I apologize. Working together?"

"We're guarding the shipments, right?" she explained.

"You are the other guard?"

The woman sighed. "Come on. You don't seem like someone who hasn't seen a tough woman."

Luper shook his head profusely. "N-No, no! That is not it at all. I just don't meet many other people who do this type of thing who are so... friendly."

"Well, why not, right?"

"I suppose so."

The woman tapped a gold crystal on her necklace. "I'm guessing that you have something like this in that guitar case? Or are you going to serenade me?"

"The former," answered Luper as the situation was becoming clearer.

"Two superhumans, huh?" Abigail pointed out. "This must be an expensive trip. If you don't mind me saying this, you have an interesting way of talking. It's quite nice exactly. A little formal."

Luper nodded. "I came from some money actually. I had to leave that all behind being... someone like us. My father would not have stood for any slang or even contractions at times."

"You wear the suit well, too," she complimented.

"Really?" he asked, tugging on a sleeve. "I think it is too unwieldy for bodyguard work. You likely know how Rousseaux is when it comes to finer things. It was his idea."

"You should keep it. You were born to wear black."

~ ~ ~

Chapter 44: Loss

"Wonderful! Wonderful," the Scientist exclaimed with arms waving.

The pillar of lightning and flame walked closer to him. A pair of emerald eyes shined through the anima.

"Not two but three!" he boomed. "Three displays of the scientific possibilities of Amuli! You continue to find purposes that advance science!"

There was no reply from the walking storm. Only rage poured from the flames.

"Y-Yes, yes," stammered the Scientist, finally feeling some of the seriousness of his predicament. "Come this way! There is a back entrance in the tunnels! I'm sure that, once outside, we will be detected by A.I.M. agents, and then we will be taken in."

Paul's body surged forward. It was his body alone, filled with only animalistic anger towards the one who had hurt him. His mind had not yet returned.

The Scientist brought up his chains and hurled them towards Paul. They bounced away as if they had run into a wall.

"I-I see, I see," pondered the Scientist. "Anima of an intensity that I have not yet seen!"

He felt cold air as he backpedaled, finally reaching the mouth of the back exit.

"Yes! Come to me! This way!"

Paul's anima-infused body lit the night sky like a green sun. Nearby, fallen leaves shriveled from the intense heat. Anima in the form of electricity crackled across rocks. Deep inside the storm, Paul's veins glowed a sickly green.

"Any minute now," the Scientist insisted.

The powerful figure only crept closer. One arm outstretched the fiery katana. The Scientist put up his network of chains like successive walls. The sword batted them all away with pure power.

"Stop!" screamed the Scientist.

He recoiled his chains, putting them between himself and the monster before him again. The sword crashed through them. This time, the anima chains bent. They bowed as they were hammered again and again. Then, the katana was eating away at them. Links of the chain flew off, one by one.

"No!" cried the Scientist. "My process was correct. I implanted the crystal correctly to make an anima weapon! It cannot be!"

The chains grew shorter and shorter as the sword razed through them.

The Scientist shouted again in fearful delirium. "No! No! There is so much more to study! There is so much more to advance! I can help the human race even more! It cannot end here, I have so much more to do!"

The chains ran out, and the sword bit into him as well.

* * *

Paul did not know how long he had been standing there. He did not remember ever leaving the room that Alice had found him in. He had just been conversing with the mysterious Amulus. The one who was watching him and who knew how many others. The Observer, as he called himself.

He noticed his katana in his hand. Anima flames were just dying down from it and the rest of his body. Somehow, he felt stronger than he had ever been. He felt as if he could sprint for miles. Maybe, he could jump over all those trees in front of him.

It's almost too much.

Finally, he looked down before falling to his knees. The man who had owned the dead body laying before him had caused him only pain. Now, he could only see another human dead by his hand.

Paul tossed his sword in disgust. With his new strength, it went further than he had expected, but he did not care. He cried and the sobbing hurt his parched throat.

"I didn't want to do it!" he screamed at the body. "I didn't want to!"

This was no reply.

"It's too much for me! It's too much for anyone! I didn't want to be a monster!"

He pounded the muddy, sloppy ground.

Abruptly, he felt a soothing warmth wrap around his back. He recognized warm breath and hot tears.

Alice was weeping, too.

"I'm sorry. I'm so sorry! It was the only way. I had to keep you alive! I did not want this!"

Paul's tears stopped amid his guilt.

"Alice, thank you."

* * *

Luper was still breathing when the dreams ended hours later. Each breath was heavy, but he was able to manage them. The empty bunker seemed foggy. He could just make out blackened scorch-marks on the sides. He could not move an inch from where he rested in the mud. In his delirium, pieces of his last conversation with Alice repeated over and over.

He did not hear the muffled sound of treading until a figure looked down at him.

Adam Avery looked down at him somberly.

"A-Av..." wheezed Luper.

"You're amazing, Luper," the younger man commented. "That's really an understatement. You fought two advanced Amuli and even killed one. And you know what? I think an Amulus could survive these injuries. A recovery team is on its way to recover all of the enemy data. They will get to you soon."

"G-Good," struggled Luper. "I'll be able to see her..."

Avery's sheathed rapier smashed through Luper's ribs, forcing only a last breath out.

"I'm sorry," he told the glassy-eyed corpse. "It may not seem like it, but I really am. It's just... the way things are now.

You would only get in the way if you survived, no matter how noble your intentions. You're a good man, Gregory Luper. I'll create a world where people like you can live."

Avery reached into his heavy coat and pulled out a red mask before slipping it on.

Chapter 45: Purpose

"It's really incredible," remarked Erica, even though her tone was less enthusiastic.

Paul said nothing in reply. He simply slipped his shirt back on over his new muscles as he sat up.

"You have evidence of past injuries," Erica summarized. "That's for sure. It's beyond what Alice's body even does. It's like her crystal boasted your abilities even above hers since it compounded your energy with its own. Everything associated with Amuli is just bigger and better within you."

"I see," responded Paul bluntly.

"I see?" shot back Erica. "You may be the strongest person on the planet! Doesn't that mean something?"

"It could," Paul replied hollowly. "I'm just trying to focus on what's next."

"Which should be rest," Erica noted.

"You just said that I'm the strongest person on the planet."

Erica shook her head.

"It's not your body that worries me. It's your mind that I'm worried about. I read your report and nearly threw up. You were kidnapped. They tortured you and used you for experiments. They even made you think everyone you cared about was dead. You lost your mentor in the rescue mission. I can't imagine what that does to a person! I am definitely prescribing rest. Screw the council and whatever they want to do with you next. You should talk to someone, too. It doesn't have to be a therapist. It could be me or anyone who cares."

"I will," Paul lied as he left the examination room quickly. "Thanks, Erica."

He walked purposefully down the office hall. *It seems like, in A.R.C., the more important you are, the bigger the city they station you.* It almost struck a nerve in the small-town kid.

This was New York. It was a crowning achievement for A.R.C. to hold it. The other jewel currently in the crown was Washington D.C. Many of the world's most influential politicians and businesses were located in these two cities, and A.R.C. had exclusive access to them both. *It's no wonder A.I.M. is taking risks when A.R.C. has the upper hand.*

A gray-haired man rounded the corner, coming directly in Paul's path.

This will save time.

"A word," insisted Gareth Jackson, "if you will, Engel."

"Of course," breathed Paul, stopping.

"I have to offer my apologies on the death of your mentor," the Brit began solemnly. "Luper and I did not often see eye-to-eye. However, he was an able agent. He was always driven towards his goals."

Paul nodded.

"I have an offer for you," Jackson explained. "You have no desire to be still. I would not in your position. No, you need the mobility to find your missing family members. I can give it to you. You see, I am forming a team. As the newly elected Speaker, I am responding to the concerns of my fellow council members and operatives. A.I.M. is moving quickly. Their experiments have progressed. We may hold many of the world's most powerful cities, but that may change with the dawn of enhanced Amuli and the continued use of Dead Eyes. A wounded animal is dangerous. I have decided to form a team just as bold as A.I.M. While still being secret from the larger world, we will take the fight to them. We will storm their hidden compounds and challenge from their cities. The strike-force will not be held back by the deliberations of the Council. It will have its own autonomy to make quick decisions and will consist of the young, brightest, and strongest A.R.C. operatives. Agents like yourself, if you will agree to it. Rescuing hostages will no doubt be high on the list of priorities, and rightly so."

"If I agree," Paul answered quickly. "I will need some assurances."

"Listen here," gawked Jackson in surprise.

"I apologize," said Paul coolly. "I don't want to disrespect the man who has been named Speaker more times than anyone else, but I have my own priorities. Forgive me if Luper has rubbed off on me. He was my mentor, after all. I agree that you hold the authority and many of the cards. I may be being pushy, but I have some cards, too. I don't like it, but I am the strongest Amuli. Ask any evaluator or doctor. I can be A.R.C.'s most important operative. That's only if you let me."

"Name your price, Engel," grumbled Jackson, mortified.

"First," started Paul, "there's Robert Swanson. He's an A.R.C. Human operative. Give him an important job to keep him occupied. Make him an instructor or tech designer or something like that. You won't find anyone better. Just keep him off the front lines."

"Done," responded Jackson almost before Paul had finished speaking.

"Camilla Bellano," Paul went on. "She's an Amulus operative. She has always wanted to be moved to disaster relief. Put her there or find another place where she can help people without fighting."

"Done," replied Jackson again.

Now, time for the hard one.

"Last," Paul continued. "Put Alice on long term R-and-R."

"Absurd!" interjected Jackson. "Be reasonable. Besides you, she is our greeted asset! Surely you understand. She is an Alpa Amulus."

"An Atlantean," Paul corrected. "I've been going over the data taken from that madman's lab. I know all about that sick breeding program and her lineage. I'm assuming that the A.R.C. scientists thought that term was too fantastical and replaced it with Alpha Amulus. You've even taken her heritage from her, and I don't plan on letting you take anything else from her. So you either get me or her. You won't get both. That girl's entire life has been devoted to A.R.C., literally. Do you think she has ever had time to even come up with an identity for herself? She deserves a break more than anyone. Take me instead. I have some of her strengths compounded with my own. You will get enough from me."

"I'd better," warned Jackson as he left him. "We will put all of this in writing later."

"Of course," murmured Paul.

Paul continued striding through the building with purpose. He was soon joined by a boy with long bangs.

457

"I was listening to all that," informed Jason, almost giddily. "It surprised me. You have really changed."

"I've had to," agreed Paul.

Jason nodded. "I just have to know, why didn't you try to keep me away from the fighting, too? You did it for rest of the old team."

"I knew that there was no getting you away from the fight," answered Paul.

Jason smirked. "True. You might have also guessed that I was named to Jackson's project as well."

Paul nodded. "We will have work to do then."

"Before then," Jason interrupted, "there is something you should see."

He led Paul to a nearby waiting room. A group of people that Paul did not recognize were intently watching a mounted TV.

"Our top story continues to be the unprecedented seismic activity across the Atlantic Ocean," the news anchor relayed from the desk. "Coastal areas from eastern North and South America to western Europe and Africa are being advised. In some areas, authorities are contemplating evacuation efforts due to the possibility of tidal waves. Obviously, this puts billions of people in the crosshairs. The world's top scientists are baffled. Many of the episodes have occurred away from known fault lines. What is known is the epicenter of the current activity. It seems that the first reported activity originated from off the coasts of the Iberian Peninsula and North Africa. We will-"

The picture suddenly flickered. The TV buzzed and fizzled for a moment before the picture became clear again.

A collective gasp echoed in the room. It was followed by an intense silence.

The entire screen was now filled by a red mask.

"I come to you at great, personal risk," announced the familiar, distorted voice. "This signal is being broadcast on every outlet that I can make use of."

Paul and Jason looked at each other in shock, then back at the screen.

"Dear humanity," he began a manifesto, "every one of you is now either a liar or a victim. To the victims, you have been lied to. The liars have kept the true world from you. You may think that today's power rests in nations, groups of nations, or religions. That is not the case. No, in this world, power is power. The Amuli have it. I am not vilifying the Amuli for existing. I am an Amulus myself. There is nothing that can be done about this burden and privilege put upon us. The ordinary Amulus is in the same boat as the rest of humanity. They are the victims. It is the Amuli leaders that are the liars. You may think that the Amulus Regional Containment and

Amulus International Medicine organizations, founded at the behest of world governments, keep us safe from rogue Amuli. After all, without nuclear weapons, only an Amulus can truly contain an Amulus. The truth is, it is the entire two organizations that are rogue. They are at war with each other. They fight over lands in secluded locations in order to set up secret labs for experimentation. Urban territories are decided in brutal fight clubs. This is to prevent noticeable conflicts. That is why you will never see A.I.M. and A.R.C. headquarters together in the same city. From there, it is a shakedown. The politicians and businesspeople fear them. That fear keeps those cowards held in sway. Resources are, then, infinite.

"Yes, the world is not in your own hands but theirs. They take young people and children and turn them into killing machines for their own profit. However, the day when our oppressors falter is at hand. You see, this seismic activity is their fault. They have drilled for crystals on the seafloor. In doing so, they triggered the earth's wrath. Do I expect you to believe me without proof? I don't. Computer files, video recordings, and organizational records are being leaked to the internet as I speak. It is time now to peel back all masks."

The screen flickered black.

Chapter 46: A Memory

~ ~ ~

He marched his way down the off-white corridor. Every metal door along the way was heavily bolted with only the slightest of window slits. His heart was beating fast. It seemed to tap on the inside of his ribcage. It had been a long time since he had felt like this outside of a battle. Every step felt deceptively slow.

Jackson suddenly charged down the hall behind him.

"Luper! Luper!"

Luper only stopped without turning.

"Greg!"

"You have come to stop me, I see," Luper noticed. "My mind is made up."

Jackson shook his head. "You are the best we have, as I am sure you are aware."

"I'm getting older, Gareth. Soon, my skills won't be as sharp."

"You know that a less-than-sharp Greg Luper is a more capable fighter than ninety percent of all the Amuli in the world! You are the one who helps in holding back the chaos of A.I.M. and the Hunters. Why abandon your post?"

"If I'm half as good as you say that I am, you should look forward to me teaching the next generation."

Jackson's tone turned cold and bitter. "I was a fool to think you a soldier who knew his duty and priorities. We both know that you have never fancied teaching. Your preoccupation with ghosts of your past is the only thing drawing you in. What duty do you have to ghosts when the living are before you?"

"That is why A.I.M. calls me 'Death,'" jibed Luper. "It is my line of work."

Luper let the words sting before informing, "It is in writing now. Read it."

"Papers can be lost."

"Gareth Jackson skirting the rules?" chided Luper. "Heap whatever scorn you want on me. Assign me the smallest, most poorly funded outpost. That may actually help the situation. Frankly, I no longer care."

Jackson ceased his trailing of the large man.

"She'll be the death of you. The danger within her is inherent. You've seen it with your own eyes."

"If she stays in here," Luper declared as he disappeared from Jackson's eye line around a corner, "she will be the death of us all."

With Jackson gone, Luper paused were the corridors ended. A single, metal door loomed before him. He was glad no one was around to see his knees shiver. It struck him that he was unsure of what to do next. Should he knock? That would be polite. Was that common here?

He gave the door a half-hearted knock.

No answer.

Luper sighed as he collected himself and opened the door quietly.

He stood transfixed in the doorway. She looked just like her. There was the way that the hair was naturally between wavy and straight. Her eyebrows wrested gently. The dark blue, almost indigo, eyes seemed to sparkle like rain drizzling on the ocean.

Abby. He nearly whispered it.

Her hair was shorter than he had ever seen her mother's. It

came just down her neck and was somehow more golden. The expression was far different. It was so blank that it was haunting. He could tell that not a thing in the world mattered to this girl. She had been made into a tool. She was not to think for herself and never even taught how to do so. She was a living robot.

Luper fought to keep tears away. Somehow, they did not come. His eyes had been dry for years, anyway. *Abby's child. It is true. I am as terrible as death. She is not her father. She did not ask to be born. Was she ever truly wanted by anyone... as a person? Is it not enough just to exist? How could anyone deserve this? I'm sorry, Abby. I am always failing you.*

"Alice," Luper said as bluntly and professionally as he could. "You have been called to field service. I am to be your mentor in this. My name is Gregory Luper."

The girl simply got up off her bed.

"Do you have any questions?"

"No," she answered quickly.

"Nothing?"

"No. It is as you say," she acknowledged.

"Very well," Luper replied with the sadness still brimming within him. "I look forward to working with you."

I will do this, Abby. I will do what I can to make her whole. I only pray that I will not be alone in helping her.

As the two walked outside the facility, they were greeted by a glorious, golden sunrise.

~ ~ ~

The End

Leave a comment?

Preview of The Mask of Tragedy

Chapter 2:

This area of Tokyo's Koto Ward bustled during the day. Unlike the warehouse districts of other cities, this place was not too far off from the foot-traffic of museums, gardens, and corporate centers. The outer facades of the buildings were remarkably clean with well-kept trunks parked beside them or in garages. The majority of people had long gone home after a long workday. The machines that had hummed during all daylight hours now were quiet. A few could listen to the hidden barbarity going on in one warehouse.

There, metal brutally scraped metal, making clashes of a sound not unlike fingernails on a chalkboard. Sparks leaped furiously off two gleaming weapons as they met again and again. One was a blue, shimmering kusarigama. It was a wicked-looking, samurai weapon consisting of ball, chain, and sickle. The ball circled its opponents, probing despite blocks coming from a wakizashi short sword. The man with the sword batted the metal ball aside repeatedly with the side of his wave-striped blade. His arms worked furiously as they bulged through his partially unbuttoned dress shirt. The younger man with the kusarigama worked the chain with his anima, spinning it far faster than he could with his wrists. In the fight from distance, this man in urban camo had a hard-pressing advantage. Any hints of confidence were hiding behind bandana the same colors of his outfit.

Still, the simplicity of the short blade with its red sparks let the older man be more fluid. He gained ground slowly, working his way towards a path of his own advantage. A number of men watched from behind shipping containers and wooden crates. None said a word of encouragement or discouragement. One said matched their champion's mottled gray. The others looked as if they had just stepped out of a board meeting.

As he zoned in, the swordsman made a barely visible flick of his fingers. One of the men on his side of the warehouse tossed him a slender shape. With his free hand, the man flicked off the scabbard of another wakizashi. This one showed a lazy purple.

The young man was surprised, and it showed. Two anima weapons? It was impossible! An Amulus had one crystal and a crystal had one master.

In the shadows of the roof beams above, a new figure emerged. Without warning, it landed just to the side of the Japanese swordsman. The shrouded male figure landed on his feet like a cat—without breaking his stride.

"Where?" it whispered to itself in a husky voice.

A chorus of shouting came from the swordsman's side as

well as himself. They pointed angrily at this figure in a dark blue coat and gray mask. Rows of men lit up their anima crystals. It was like the Aurora Borealis emerging from both sides of the building. Metal blades and wooden yumi bows aimed threateningly at the newcomer. Based on the figure's body language, he felt no pressure from the waves of anima building up around him. His mask did not reveal his own eyes, giving him only a blank stare made of black felt circles. Painted partway down the face was an upturned, grimacing mouth.

Despite the commotion, no one directly approached the sleek intruder. However, the match had screeched to a halt as both combatants focused on the man in the frowning mask. The man with the two swords threatened to be the first to move. His fingers twitched along his wakizashi. Only some sort of nervous apprehension prevented him of apprehending the source of the disruption.

Ignoring everyone else, the newcomer's scabbard swung about as he strode purposefully towards a wooden crate. He gave it an ear-shattering kick. A man spilled out before skidding on the ground. He came to a rest in a heap of arms and legs only after putting a dent in a shipping container. Echoes of a purple glow faded from the unconscious man and one of the swords the one fighter held.

The swordsman's side ceased their outcry. It was now louder on the other side as the men came close to entering the battlefield. The man with the chain weapon held them back with a wave. He then used the opportunity to ensnare the swordsman with the chain. The swordsman tried to fight back but was pulled in. With his arms pinned, he made weak swings toward the other man who blocked with his sickle.

The younger fighter used his angle to his advantage as he flicked the sickle blade deep into the wrist of the arm holding the red crystal sword. At the same time, he kicked the other, faded wakizashi aside with ease. The swordsman sunk to his knees with an agonizing cry. With the blade inside him, he dared not move. It was even difficult for an Amulus to survive a severed artery. Without a word, his men filed out of the building. No one followed them.

The swordsman's eyes were not fixed on the man who held him in checkmate but on the shadowy figure who had come down from the ceiling.

"Why the mask?" he asked defiantly in perfect English. "Most of us know who you are."

Checking on the injured man draped on the shipping container, the masked man did not answer.

"It's funny," the swordsman continued, giving no indication of the pain he was enduring. "This American savior of A.R.C. coming to Japan with a nihonto. It reminds me of something. When my father first went to America to get investors for his company, he dressed like a cowboy. He had a bolo tie and hat. After all, America was the Old West in movies. People laughed at him then. I should be laughing at you now."

The gray mask slid out his sword and rested it on the businessman's shoulder.

Disregarding the man's jibes, he questioned in a monotone voice. "Where are the other hostage locations in Japan?"

He received only a stubborn glare.

"I need to know," it was less of a demand and more of a statement of fact. "Where are the other hostage locations?"

"You don't scare me," the businessman growled.

The man with the katana let a green flame burn down his captive's shirt.

"I did the research," he relayed. "I checked your books. The real ones on those hard drives from the last place we hit. How will the public react when they learn where your father got the seed money for the company?"

The remainder of the man's shirt dipped to reveal a red, dragonskin tattoo encircling his entire torso. From the chest, the willowy, Asian dragon looked up with burning eyes and an open mouth.

The gray mask continued. "You said that you lost part of your pinkie during a skiing accident when you were young. I'm guessing that is a lie."

"There are yakuza groups older than your home country!" declared the businessman.

"You are forgetting that we represent A.R.C.," asserted the camo mask. "Now, tell us. At least your company's name will survive. Your children will have futures. That is more than we can say about some of the children you took from our agents."

Takahashi Hideo, C.E.O. of Taka Corp Electronics, relented. "You've hit them all. All the ones in Japan. I know what you seek, and you will not find them here, young man."

"Then, where?" barked the gray mask, finally letting his feelings boil.

"I do not know. That is the truth."

The gray mask held his sword back, readying a cut on the unarmed enemy. His upper arm shook with tension. He paused, studied Takashi's eyes, and backed down.

By then, a cavalcade of agents in jet-black vans and S.U.V.s had surrounded the building. A procession of masked people surrounded the group. The agent holding the blade impaled in Takahashi's wrist let the sickle slide out. The business-man's arm fell slack to the ground. The group of agents pulled him away as one readied a bandage for the bleeding arm. A stretch hurriedly made its way to the man denting the metal shipping container.

"We will find them," assured the camo fighter with his mask billowing forward as he spoke. "We have my word."

"I'm sorry, Kishi," the gray mask apologized to the chain fighter. "I think you had it covered. I just had not make sure."

Kishi shook his head. "Better to make sure. I appreciate your concern for me. Our job was done. Takahashi and A.I.M. were humiliated for cheating. More reparations will be demanded and received. We could not have asked for a more successful mission. And, I could not have asked for a better subordinate."

"I'll be going then," notified the gray mask as if he had not heard the compliment.

"Where are you off to?" asked Kishi. "The mission was mine. The report is mine."

"I'm heading back to the U.S., anyway," clarified the young man with the katana. "We still have our source."

As he made to leave, Kishi clung to his shoulder for a moment.

"Afterwards, rest. That is an order."

"Right."

* * *

The hooded and masked young man made his way towards

the plane. In ordinary circumstances, no one would have gotten near an airplane with their identity hidden. However, this was one of A.R.C.'s private jets, marked for special use and kept in a special section of the airport. Special taskforces had their privileges.

A black-haired youth stood next to the airstairs.

"You won't like this," he announced through a smirk. "There is a stowaway problem, and she's angry."

The gray mask stopped for a moment, confused. He regained his stride quickly.

I had a feeling this day was coming.

He dragged himself up the stairs to meet a girl with a wavy, dark ponytail. She said nothing at first, only staring at him intently and disapprovingly. She swung out a hand. The masked young man had to struggle against his superhuman instincts to not react. In one motion, she yanked off the frowning, unhappy mask on his face.

"Paul Engel," Camilla scolded as her large brown eyes narrowed.

The yank was followed up by a heavy, resounding slap from her opposite hand.

Chapter 3: Unmasked

Paul stood there blankly. His head remained in the same position as it had before the slap.

"At least make it look like it hurt!" complained Camilla. "I don't care what you have in your veins."

"Hi, Cam," Paul greeted her quickly in a low voice.

"Six months!" she shouted. "You cut everyone that cares about you out of your life for six months, and you just say: 'Hi?'"

Paul averted his gaze.

"I'm sorry."

Cam shook her head. "Paul, what isn't getting through to you? Six months ago, I thought you might be dead. Then, I heard you survived, but you were horrifically tortured. Next, I get transferred, and they tell me that I'm not allowed to contact you. Here's the last straw. You're not the only one who's detail-oriented enough to constantly run through reports. I found one saying you were behind the transfers. Not just mine but Robby's and Alice's."

"I thought that you always wanted to be in disaster relief," Paul pointed out curiously.

"I did... eventually!" Camilla shot back. "I was going to earn the promotion myself. Plus, I definitely wasn't going to leave when my team was a crisis. Luper died, Alice went off the rails, and you got screwed up!"

"How did you get here?" asked Paul, uncomfortably trying to change the subject.

"Apparently," Camilla responded. "When people know that you're friends with the Mask of Tragedy, they give you some clout. I said that I wanted to get a private plane to assess possible seismic activity in Japan, they said: 'perfect, there's a jet about to head out.'"

"The plane needs to take off soon," Paul informed, trying again. "We should get inside."

"Great!" exclaimed Camilla with upfront sarcasm. "I can yell at you in there."

The interior of the aircraft was outfitted with hardwood paneling and a velvety carpet. There were a couple of sets of comfortable recliners and even baskets filled with reading material. Most of the space was dwarfed by a massive TV. Paul caught his own beleaguered expression in the dark reflection.

This is unnecessary for me. A cargo plane with some seats would be fine.

"You know how I know something's wrong?" Camilla asked before answering herself. "Because I got in touch with Robby. Apparently, you won't see him either, and he's worried.

Robby Swanson, the guy who never worries about anything, is worried! How could you cut us all out?"

"I had to," Paul responded quietly.

"That's not an answer."

"Because you died. You all died."

Camilla, taken aback, sunk into her seat.

"You all died from my perspective," Paul explained, tension leaping into his haggard voice. "I know you didn't, but when I was told that, it seemed real. He didn't just convince me then. He made the scenario so realistic. It really could have happened. It could still happen, especially now that I'm a target."

"It wasn't your fault," related Camilla in a softer tone. "It never would be."

Paul shook his head. "I've learned that the only thing I can control is myself. That means that I have to do all I can to do good. I have to do things myself."

"You blame yourself," Camilla realized. "Paul, when some-one pulls the trigger, it's their fault. It's not the fault of the person who couldn't dive in front of the bullet in time."

"What matters is what happens in the end," Paul argued.

"Even it ends with you destroying yourself physically and mentally?" prodded Camilla.

Paul did not respond but the affirmation was there.

Camilla looked over to Jason in the corner.

"Did you just stand by while he got like this?"

"This isn't a game," Jason put it coolly. "We can't always afford to think about everything happening outside. What matters is what comes next."

Giving up on Jason, Camilla cried out. "Look, Paul! Whatever happened, it wasn't your call to cut us out. We put our lives on the line ourselves. It isn't fair to torture us or yourself with this. You know what? Just tell me that you'll at least call Robby and Alice. You know that I won't be leaving you alone."

"I'll think about it," murmured Paul.

Camilla swore at the air. "Paul, you've changed, and I hate it. What did this screwed up world do to you?"

Paul let the conversation hang like rotting fruit in front of his nose.

I can't afford to even think like that.

"So, when's the last time you slept?" Camilla finally questioned. "You look terrible, even if you're stronger than before."

"I was planning on sleeping on the plane ride back," replied Paul. "It is a long flight."

"That's not what I asked."

Camilla let it slide.

"Fine. I'll make sure you do."

Self-conscious, Paul put as mask down as he climbed onto a leaned-back recliner at the other end of the cabin. He felt very tired. Only the shapeless dread outweighed it. There were anxious feelings that Paul feared would form into full thoughts now that he was alone in his own head.

I've learned to hate this part.

The thoughts took hold. There were the usual ones.

You can't rest, not until Aunt Morgan and Uncle Nick are found! Think about all they've done for you! They raised you as their own child as the most loving parents! You probably don't need to sleep like a normal person; you're an Alpha Amulus.

No! I need to sleep! I need to sleep now! I have to rest and be fresh for whatever comes next! Should I even be out doing things like this? If A.I.M. has it figured out who I am behind the mask, what will they do to Aunt Morgan and Uncle Nick if I keep messing with them?

There were new doubts, too.

Cam's right! I've hurt the people closest to me!

No! I did it to protect them! I can unequivocally say that their lives are better without me, especially now with what's happening to me. They would be better off if they never met me! So, just forget me already!

Oh, God! That man inside the crate... a little more force, and he would be another in my body count. I even held back! Is he crippled now? Even as an Amulus, is he crippled for life? I'm losing it. Each day, I'm losing it a little more.

He was distracted by his own heart beating. It was banging in his chest so hard; the skin around his ribcage was rubbing against the inside of his shirt.

I wonder if it looks like I'm asleep to Cam.

Somehow, impossibly, he was able to stop thinking.

Other Books By Private Dragon

Former FBI Agent battles secret societies in a dystopian future

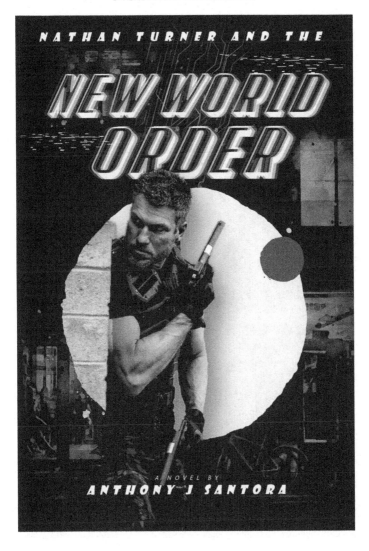

A young man goes on an unexpected journey and learns magic!

THE ENCHATNER'S QUEST:
THE VOID OF SOULS

JL ESQUIRE

About the Author

LaTrobe Barnitz is the author of the Soul Crystals series. He lives in rural Western Pennsylvania, U.S.A.

You can connect with me on:

🌐 https://latrobebarnitz.com

🐦 https://twitter.com/BarnitzLatrobe

📘 https://www.facebook.com/LaTrobe-Barnitz-Author-106624177837806

Made in the USA
Monee, IL
11 November 2020

47252199R00272